MYTH AND STORM

GUILDS OF ILBREA BOOK TWO

MEGAN O'RUSSELL

Ink Worlds Press

Visit our website at www.MeganORussell.com

Myth and Storm

Cover Art by Sleepy Fox Studio (https://www.sleepyfoxstudio.net/)

Editing by Christopher Russell

Interior Design by Christopher Russell

Printed in the United States of America

To the ones trapped in the storm.
The shore will be worth the waves.

WHITE MOUNTAINS
Royal Palace
BARRENS
Ilara
Arion Sea
Barrens Bay
Frason
Harane
Ian Lioche
ILBREA
Ian Mithe
Ruthir Mountain
Mountain Road
Ian Ayres
Southern Citadel
Pamerane

N
Spice Trail
Spice Trail
EASTERN MOUNTAINS
Mountain Road
WYRAIN
Spios
Golden Sea
NGLESS
RITORIES
Acalia
The Horn

MYTH AND STORM

1

ENA

I had always loved being surrounded by the scent of flowers.

Not for the beauty of the blooms. Pretty things can be damaged, ravaged by disaster and cruelty. Fragile beauty is too weak for a world that's caught fire.

I loved the petals for what they could do. The right bloom could make an ink so vibrant it seemed born of magic or be ground into a balm that could save a life. A skilled hand could turn a few petals into a poison that could change the fate of a kingdom.

To a girl who could wield that weapon, the scent of flowers offered a promise of power.

But as I spent days sitting in the window in the library, looking out over Ilara, I grew to hate the floral perfume the Guilds had fabricated.

The healers and sorcerers that passed through the head scribe's sitting room never glanced toward the common rotta girl perched on the windowsill. They bustled in and out all day, always speaking in hushed voices. Always hurrying as though one lost moment might change the scribe's fate.

I tried not to watch them, not to draw the attention of the

paun. I didn't know if they chose not to notice me, or if the gods had somehow made me invisible.

I wished I had turned into a shadow no one could see. I had no faith the gods could ever be so kind.

It seemed the whims of gods and men had bathed the whole world in blood and cruelty as I spent my days staring out over the ruined capital of Ilbrea.

The flames had gone out after the first night. Then word came they'd killed Cade and his demons. The paun announced it so proudly, as though killing a few dozen men would somehow stamp out the hatred the common folk carried for the Guilds.

By the end of the second night, the smoke had stopped drifting into the sky.

That's when the stink had begun. The putrid stench of rotting flesh filled the city as the bodies of the common fallen were left unburied.

That morning, the maids brought flowers. Dried flowers, fresh flowers, oils that had been made from flowers. They filled the scribe's rooms to cover the scent of death that soiled the grand city of the paun.

But the bright scent of the blooms didn't banish the stench of decay, not from my seat by the window.

Death himself swam around me with every gust of wind off the Arion Sea. Death would not let us forget what had been lost in Cade's foolish uprising.

I stared out the window as the sun crept high in the sky, bringing a warmth that would only ripen the horrible stench. I couldn't see any of the bodies from my perch on the third floor of the library. I could peer over the wall that surrounded the scribes' home and into the square with its pretty little fountain that had been left untainted by the flames. If I stood on the windowsill, I could catch a glimpse of the merchants' shops that had been burned, but Death did not mar my view.

"You should eat." Taddy held a plate out to me.

A healer had stitched the worst of the wounds on the boy's face, but his left eye was still swollen to barely more than a slit.

"You should eat, miss." Taddy dared to take a step closer, holding the plate right under my nose.

I wanted to smack it out of his hands and scream that my eating should be the least of any paun's worries. But the boy looked so sad and earnest, I didn't have strength to do anything but take the plate and give him a nod.

Taddy pulled a chair closer to me before claiming his own plate from the tray. He took a few bites of roasted meat before looking back up at me.

"Eat, miss."

I took a deep breath, trying to convince my body I was alive enough to eat. The scent of decay rushed into my lungs.

Taddy furrowed his brow as I shuddered. "At least take a few bites of the bread."

The plain bread I could manage.

Taddy smiled, wincing at the movement of his swollen cheek.

The door to the scribe's bedroom opened, and two women in healer red came out. They kept their heads close together, murmuring words I couldn't hear as they crossed through the sitting room and out into the corridor beyond.

"He's all right," Taddy said after the door to the hall had shut. "They would have said something if he wasn't all right."

I wanted to go into the bedroom and see the scribe. See what they'd made of him. If they'd left him as the man I'd known or turned him into another paun monster.

But I'd been counting the ones bustling in and out of his room. There was still a sorcerer in with him.

I made myself finish the rest of my bread.

Taddy had taken the plate away and tried to offer me another meal before the sorcerer finally left the scribe's bedroom.

Every bit of my body ached as I unfurled my limbs and climbed down from the windowsill.

None of the healers had even tried to come near me, and I hadn't found the will to tend to my own wounds.

I was too hollow.

Finding the supplies I needed. Undressing myself. Making myself look at the damage Cade had done.

The pain I could bear. I'd felt worse before. But my loathing of the Guilds and revulsion at Cade's contamination drove me into a numbing madness that left no room for reasoning through the necessary tasks. I was grateful for the void my hatred offered.

Taddy followed close behind me as I crept toward the scribe's bedroom door.

I hesitated before touching the doorknob as the foolish notion that the sorcerers had plotted to keep me away from him swept past my reason.

No shock of magic shot through me as I twisted the knob and stepped into the room.

He lay on the bed as though he'd fallen asleep. The sorcerers had banished the bruises and cuts from his face, leaving him without a mark, despite all the damage Cade's chivving bastards had done when they'd beaten him.

His chest rose and fell in a steady, calm way, like the sorcerers had stolen his cares when they'd stolen his wounds.

"I'll get you a blanket then," Taddy whispered.

I didn't tell my feet to move, but they carried me to his bedside. I grazed the back of his hand with my fingertips. Not because I thought he'd feel my touch, just so I could convince myself he was still alive.

I leaned over him to whisper in his ear. "Wake up, you chivving paun."

His breathing didn't change.

"You have to wake up." I rested my cheek against his.

He would have reached for me if he could. Or blushed. Or stammered as he tried to pretend he hadn't fallen in love with me.

He didn't move at all.

Hopeless fear dug deeper in my chest.

"I will not let you leave me. I am not done with you, scribe."

I went to the wide couch in the corner where Taddy waited for me with a blanket. I curled up on the fancy upholstery while Taddy slept on the carpet.

I would flee to the windowsill again when the paun came back to check on their precious head scribe. They would preserve the heir of the Lord Scribe, use all the magic and might the Guilds possessed to keep him alive.

But I was the one who had saved Adrial Ayres's life. I would not let the paun steal him from me.

2

THAM

His shoulders had grown numb to the pain of swinging the ice axe. His hands clenched the handle so hard, his fingers could no longer move.

He couldn't let go. He would never let go. He would keep swinging the axe until the gods stole the breath from his body, or until he found her. There were no other choices.

He would not leave her, no matter how badly the others begged.

Elver's shoulders sagged as he staggered a step back, leaving only Tham's axe cracking against the wall of ice. Elver's panting breaths grated against the rhythm of Tham's swings.

Tham pounded the axe into the endless ice even harder.

"Careful," Elver wheezed. "We've got a limited supply of tools. We can't afford to keep breaking them."

Tham took a breath, forcing his arms back into a steady swing.

"You need a break." Elver coughed the words as he reached for his waterskin. "Tham, drink something."

"Everything all right?" Kegan called from the main passage where the dogs had been penned away from the men's work.

"Just trying to get him to drink," Elver said.

"Tham, take a chivving drink." Kegan stomped down the narrow passage they'd managed to carve through the ice.

It only reached forty feet.

He'd been pummeling the ice for the gods only knew how many days, and he'd only made it forty feet.

But forty feet should have been far enough. She'd just slipped through the wall of ice, been pulled into the blue like it wasn't even a solid thing.

He'd tried to dive after her. He'd begged whatever magic lived in the ice to give her back. He'd prayed to the common gods, Dudia, and Saint Dannach himself. But the ice kept her trapped. Somewhere in the mountain, hidden by the blue.

Carving his way through the ice was the only choice he had left. Even if he had to dig his way to the heart of the mountain range, he wouldn't stop. He would find her. He would not let his war with the ice end until he had her back. In his arms. Breathing. Alive.

She is alive.

He roared his rage at the mountain as he turned back to the wall he'd been battling through.

Inch by inch.

He would find her.

His hands had bled through his bandages again by the time Kegan dared to try and make him pause.

He touched Tham's shoulder. "Go clean your hands and eat something."

Tham struck the ice again.

"The wall will still be here once you've eaten," Kegan said.

"You can't hope to reach her if you're dead." Elver stepped sideways, blocking the part of the wall Tham had been striking. "Food, water, bandages." Elver reached for Tham's axe. "I'm not half so scared of you swinging that axe at my head as I am of having to explain to Mara that you died of exhaustion."

The sound of her name drove pain through Tham's chest.

"Go." Kegan wrenched the axe from Tham's grip and turned to strike the wall.

Tham clutched his bleeding hands to his chest, forcing his fingers to curl into tight fists, needing the burst of pain to keep him from screaming.

The steady pounding of the axes rattled through his brain as he left the roughly carved tunnel and stepped into the smooth passage of ice that led up the slope to the outside world.

Storms could be raging just beyond the passage. Or the gods might have burned the mountains with the fury of Tham's grief. He never bothered climbing far enough to see.

The outside world meant nothing now.

Tham could not leave the halls of ice. He had too much experience with magic. Leaving a place like this might mean never finding a way back in.

Kegan and Elver had tried to convince him to go to Whitend and ask for aid from the villagers. But he couldn't, they couldn't, not when she was still trapped in the blue.

Her eyes had been wide with fear when the ice had swallowed her. She'd been reaching for him, but he couldn't save her.

I will find you. I swear I will find you.

He thought the words over and over as he climbed up to where the passage of smooth ice widened enough for Kegan to put up a pen for the dogs. The supplies were laid out on the sled. Water, next to hardtack, beside a roll of bandages and a bottle of tonic for cleaning wounds.

Elle whimpered as Tham sank to the ground.

He stared into the white dog's charcoal-rimmed eyes.

Elle whined and sniffed the air.

Tham closed his eyes, trying to imagine a hint of Mara's scent filling the tunnels.

The pain in his chest sliced deeper, cutting all the way up into his throat so he could hardly breathe.

He made himself drink the water, forcing himself to swallow past the fear and rage that threatened to break him.

He unwrapped the pulpy mess of his hands as he chewed through the hardtack. The tonic stung as he dripped it onto the places where his skin had torn free. The Healers Guild had brewed the concoction to keep infection away, but it couldn't regrow the skin he'd lost. Nothing but a sorcerer could do that.

Tham shut his eyes, forcing away the unfathomable thought that a sorcerer's presence could have saved Mara.

A sorcerer would have doomed their journey from the start. Kept them from making the true maps to preserve a record of all the places they'd found magic the Sorcerers Guild would gladly destroy.

Tham had come with Mara on this journey in search of undiscovered magic. She'd dedicated everything she was to creating the true maps, risking her life with every step. Choosing to risk death with every journey.

Wishing for a sorcerer would mean wishing Mara's choices away.

He couldn't do that. He had no right.

He would just have to keep digging. He would find her. He wouldn't stop until he found her.

The sudden silence yanked Tham from the blackness that had swallowed him. He opened his eyes and leapt to his feet, racing toward the tunnel they'd carved with the bandage only half-wrapped around his hand.

His boots slipped on the ice of the floor as he bolted into the tunnel. He caught himself on the raggedly carved wall. His hand left a smear of blood behind.

"Tham, I—" Elver began.

Tham shoved him aside, not caring for anything but seeing why they'd stopped. Needing to know if they'd found...

She is still alive. I will find her alive.

Tham took a breath before letting his mind understand what Elver and Kegan had uncovered.

Solid stone cut through the ice, blocking their path forward.

Tham pressed his hands against the stone, wishing he had the power to crumble the whole mountain.

"You said she fell through the wall in this direction." Kegan spoke in an even, bracing tone. "And we've kept our path true. If whatever magic is in the ice pulled her straight back, we'd have stayed right in line with her. But she isn't here. Mara didn't get pulled straight back. And if she didn't go straight, there's no way of knowing which direction the magic carried her."

Tham yanked the axe from Kegan's hand.

"We can't carve through stone," Kegan said. "You'll break the rest of the axes, and we won't be able to dig at all anymore."

"Maybe we shouldn't." Elver backed away a step. "You've said yourself this is magic we're dealing with. None of us possess magic. This is the stuff of gods and sorcerers, not lowly men."

Tham tightened his grip on his axe, letting the pain of his unbandaged palms anchor his mind to reason above the blinding panic that threatened him.

"I'm not saying we should abandon Mara." Elver clutched his axe to his chest. "I just think we need help. Digging until we die won't save her. But maybe someone in Whitend can, or a sorcerer, or the Lord Map Maker."

"I can make the run for Whitend," Kegan said. "It'll be more than a week there, and at least the same coming back. But if she's still—"

Tham couldn't hear the rest of Kegan's words over the screaming in his mind.

The sound wasn't Tham's own voice, but hers.

Afraid. In pain. Abandoned.

She knows I'd never leave her.

He swung the axe at the ice around the stone, carving toward the side of the great rock.

I'm coming. I promise I'll find you.

"Tham," Kegan said.

He sliced the axe into the ice, breaking a chunk free.

"Tham!" Kegan shouted.

Tham pressed his palm to the place where the rock met the ice, letting his blood leak onto the stone.

"I won't ask you to abandon her," Kegan said. "You could no more do that than slice out your own heart and hope to live. We have supplies. I'll stay here with you and keep digging if that's what you want. But if bashing through the ice isn't helping, then maybe we should try something else. Maybe going to Whitend is what saves her."

The screaming in Tham's mind faded, stealing her voice from him.

I will find you. I swear it.

"If you decide attacking the mountain isn't going to bring Mara back, then tell me, and I'll race for Whitend. And if I didn't consider you a friend, I wouldn't offer it, but"—Kegan let out a rough sigh—"if I need to head for the Sorcerers Tower, I'll do that, too. I'll appeal to the Guilds Council if that's what it takes. I don't fancy the pain it would cause, but if we have to bring the might of the chivving Guilds up here to get her out of the ice, then I say we let the white mountains burn."

Tham pressed his forehead to the stone. The scent of wet sediment filled his nose, as though the mountain was trying to convince him a grave was the only place that could offer peace.

"I'll clear up this debris," Kegan said. "We've got to melt more for water anyway."

Tham dug his nails into the rock, fighting against the words he didn't dare say.

"Cut around the stone then?" Elver said.

Tham pushed away from the rock, leaving a bloody handprint behind. He wrapped the ruined bandages around his hands, protecting the axe from the worst of his wounds.

"Did she know?" Elver stepped up to Tham's right, studying the ice they needed to carve through. A moment passed before Elver spoke again. "What I mean is, did Mara know you loved her?"

She knows.

I'm coming. I swear I will find you.

He swung the axe, cracking through the ice that had stolen his heart.

Twice more, he lost minutes to sleep as they chipped their way around the stone.

It wasn't a boulder that had sunken into the ice as Tham had dared to hope, but a wall that had been carved from the mountain's stone.

They'd met the edge of it first, like finding the corner of a building. Tham's rage drowned out his desperation as the human hand in the wall's making became more apparent with every passing hour.

The stone hadn't been placed in their path by chance or fate. Men had carved the swirls that looped along the wall. Men had taken their time creating the pictures of the bears that crept across the bottom of the image.

Men had stolen his heart and dragged her through the ice.

Tham would find those men, rip their limbs from their bodies, and let their spilling blood melt the ice as he forged a path to reach her.

The promise of slaughtering his enemies kept him chipping away as they uncovered a door made completely of stone.

The carving was perfect, with lines where the door should have swung open, but the stone offered no handle or keyhole. No way to shove the door aside.

He didn't know how long he stood staring at the door, waiting for an ice monster to come out and swallow him. Hoping a beast would devour him if it meant being able to see her again.

"Something like this doesn't just exist," Kegan said. "Magic forged this passage. The people in Whitend must know who made this and how long ago. If they can tell us how to get through…"

Tham fell to his knees. His axe tumbled from his hands.

"You've got to rest, Tham," Elver said. "We'll get you some food and water. We'll take a moment. Clear our heads and figure out a way through this."

Tham leaned forward, bracing his bloody hands on the door. Tears streamed down his cheeks, falling onto the ice beneath him.

"I swear I will find you." He pressed his forehead to the door. "I will burn the mountains to find you. I will tear the gods from the stars if they defy me. I will find you."

He shut his eyes, forcing his pain behind the silence that protected him. He picked up his axe and stood.

"I'll get the sled ready," Kegan said. "See when the light might allow me to leave."

Tham ran the axe's blade along the edge of the stone door.

"That ice axe won't cut through stone," Elver said. "Kegan can bring us back proper tools. A miner's pick, maybe."

Tham thrust the edge of his blade into the crack.

"Tham, you've got to—"

"I will not leave!" Tham screamed at the stone, pushing against the axe with every ounce of strength he had left. "I will find you."

A crack shuddered deep within the stone.

He pushed harder, bellowing the fury too strong for him to contain.

Blue light sliced through the stone at the edge of the door.

Elver ran forward, ramming his shoulder against the stone, adding his weight.

"Chivving cact of a demon's spawn." Kegan planted both hands on the door and screamed through his teeth as he pushed.

The sliver of light widened, growing as the stone door ground slowly open.

As the gap grew, Tham pulled his axe from the crack and rammed his shoulder against the door with the others.

I swear I will find you.

The door scraped open another inch.

Ignoring the pain, Tham crushed himself through the narrow gap.

"Tham!" Kegan shouted.

Bright blue light bathed the tiny space in front of him, the glow seeming to come from everywhere at once. Tham stepped forward, his axe hanging forgotten at his side.

A wall of perfectly smooth ice blocked his path. The ice shone with a brilliance that could only be born of magic.

"Tham."

A hand gripped his arm but didn't hold him tight enough to keep the glow from drawing him closer.

The light in the ice glittered and shifted, promising something. Maybe danger, maybe beauty. But whatever happened to him through the ice didn't matter. This was the path she'd followed. He knew it. His bones screamed it.

"Don't!"

Tham leaned against the wall of ice. But the wall did not block him.

The ice pulled him in, carrying him into the blue as though he were sinking into the sea.

Blinding lights flared before him as a weight pressed against his chest, forcing all the air from his body.

I will find you.

3

MARA

The blue light would have driven Mara mad if her fear hadn't been strong enough to burn away every other thought.

The ice walls of her prison shone a constant blue. The light never changed. Never offered any hint of what time of day it might be or how many days had passed. If she hadn't been able to cover her head with the thick furs they'd laid out on the bed, she might not have been able to sleep. And she did have to sleep.

It was only then—when she slipped away into awful nightmares—that they brought her food and water. Each time she drifted off, she'd wake up to find a fresh tray in the corner.

She never managed to see the person who brought the food, no matter how hard she tried.

She'd pretended to sleep, but somehow, they seemed to know she was still awake. Lying still and listening for footsteps wasn't enough to trick her captors into showing themselves. She'd fallen asleep in the corner where the fresh tray usually appeared. She'd woken up to find her food waiting for her on the bed.

She'd screamed. She'd battered the walls with the metal tray. She'd clawed at the ice until her fingers bled.

She only knew they'd noticed her poor attempts at escape

because bandages and ointment had appeared with her next ration of food.

They'd taken her pack, her knife, her criolas, everything but the clothes she wore. They'd locked her in a room that might as well have been made of solid stone.

There is a way out of this, Mara Landil. You are going to find a way out of this.

She pulled her chilled hands from beneath the fur blanket and dragged them down her face.

"You're going to get back to him, Mara," she whispered to the empty room. "He'd never stop looking for you. You don't get to sit around feeling sorry for yourself while Tham is fighting to reach you."

She swallowed the flutter of panic in her chest, tamping down the frightened voice in her mind that wondered how long she'd been trapped in the ice and what the people who had taken her might have done to Tham.

"There is a way out of this." She climbed off the bed.

The bed itself was made of a metal frame, strung across with rope and topped by a feather mattress—all things that seemed to imply whoever was holding her wanted her to be comfortable. Or planned on keeping her for a long time.

The bottoms of the metal legs had been sunken down into the ice, and the frame of the bed built so she couldn't rip it apart.

Still, Mara knelt beside the bed, staring at the metal trapped in the ice, searching for a bit of inspiration.

"What I wouldn't trade for a flint."

If she could set the bed on fire, perhaps the room might melt. If she were choking on smoke, maybe someone would try and save her. They had given her bandages for her hands. That had to mean they wanted her healthy.

Mara ran her thumbs over the scabbed tips of her fingers, trying to remember what had happened between when she'd been pulled through the ice and when she'd woken up in her cell.

They'd made her comfortable. Kept her alive.

The beginnings of a terrible and desperate plan formed in Mara's mind. Tham would be furious with her for even considering it. But waiting patiently for her captors to free her wouldn't get her any closer to reaching him.

She blew on her hands, coaxing enough blood into her fingers for them to be able to move nimbly.

The knots in the ropes that supported the feather mattress had been tightened by time and use.

Mara hummed to herself as she picked at the knots. The tune was one she'd heard from Tham. A song whose words were lost to him, stolen by the time he'd spent trapped on a ship, bound to a cruel captain. He'd survived a childhood of pain and fear.

She was his home. She was his safety. She would not let the ones who'd captured her steal the little happiness Tham had found.

"You're stronger than they know, Mara Landil," she whispered.

Her scabs had cracked back open by the time she managed to untie the first knot in the rope. She took a deep breath, forcing herself to be grateful for the cold air sweeping into her lungs, before crawling to the far side of the bed where the other end of the rope attached to the iron frame.

She'd barely examined the knot before a rumble in the corner froze her in place.

Biting back her smile, Mara turned toward the wall, ready for her captors to finally show themselves, whatever punishment their wrath might bring.

But the wall didn't open to allow her jailors to enter. The room had begun to shrink, the far wall drifting toward her, stealing the little space her cell granted.

Mara leapt to her feet, lunging toward the wall, pushing against it with all her might. Her boots slid out from under her, offering no traction against the smooth ice of the floor.

Clambering up onto the bed, she braced her toes against the metal frame and leaned forward, meeting the still-moving ice. She shoved against the wall, screaming her rage and fear though there was no one but her to hear the echo of her voice.

"Why are you doing this?"

The ice devoured everything up to the edge of the bed before stopping.

Mara froze for a heartbeat, then another. But nothing happened. Her cell stayed the size of her bed.

Panic joined the anger pulsing through Mara's veins.

"Let me out." Mara banged her fists against the ice. "Let me out! At least be brave enough to show your slitching faces! Why are you keeping me in here? What do you want from me?"

Mara's breath shook in her chest as she waited for a reply that didn't come.

"You chivving cowards! Locking me in here, hiding while you keep me trapped. I will find a way out of this, and you—"

The ice shifted again, closing in around her.

"No!" Mara planted her hands against the walls that pressed in on either side of the bed. "Stop it." She pushed with all her strength, screaming with fury as the open space shrank enough to pin her arms against her chest.

"I'm sorry!" Mara shouted. "Make it stop. I'm sorry."

The walls stopped.

The light within the ice grew, gleaming so brightly Mara wished she could shift her hands enough to shield her eyes.

"You will get out of this, Mara Landil. You will find a way to get back to Tham." Her heart raced as she gasped in air, trying to convince herself she wasn't suffocating. She pressed her forehead to the ice. "Just let me get back to Tham. Please."

She lurched forward as the ice pulled away from her, drifting back toward the edge of the bed. She leaned against the wall, pushing it away though she had little hope her efforts could battle whatever power altered her cell.

The ice slowed as it moved beyond her bed, retreating toward where it had always been before.

Mara leapt off the bed as soon as there was enough space for her on the ground, keeping her hands pressed to the ice, worsening the wounds on her fingers as she searched for a weak spot she might shove through.

Her gaze was so fixed on the wall, she saw nothing but the red of her own blood staining the blue until her toe ran into something that shifted.

A foot poked out of the ice.

The wall kept pulling back, revealing the rest of a leg, and a dark-skinned hand covered in blood.

The cuff of a black coat.

A Guilded Soldier's coat.

"Tham? Tham!" Mara knelt beside him, trying to feel for a pulse in his wrist as the wall kept moving. Her hands shook too badly to find any faint hint of life beneath his skin. The blood on his hand had dried, but the wounds looked fresh.

She grabbed his arm, trying to wrench him free from the wall, but the ice wouldn't let go of its prize.

The wall slowed as it moved across his chest.

Mara pressed her hand to his ribs, holding her breath as she waited for his chest to rise and fall. Or for the thump of a heartbeat. Any sign she hadn't lost him.

His ribs rose. A slight shift. That tiny hint of life ripped a sob from her throat.

Her hands matched the movement of the ice, feeling the rest of his chest, his neck, his face for damage. There were no wounds on his head, but his eyes were closed.

"Tham." Mara trailed her fingers along his cheek. "Tham, it's me. Wake up. Tham!"

He didn't move, didn't flinch.

He couldn't hear her. He'd never lie so still if he heard that sort of terrible fear in her voice.

She pressed her cheek to his face. Warm breath tickled her chill skin.

"It's all right. You'll be all right. I'll get you warmed up." Mara grabbed the blankets off the bed, choosing the cold of the floor over risking hoisting his body and worsening any injuries she couldn't see. "I've been waiting for you."

It wasn't until she'd tucked the blankets around him that she noticed the tray on the far side of his body. Their captors had left more food than usual, more water, too, along with a kettle of something and more bandages and balms.

Mara closed her eyes and willed her heart to calm.

"We'll get a little water in you. And I'll bandage your hands." She touched Tham's cheek. His stubble had grown out longer than he'd ever allowed it. More like a beard than a bit of scruff. "I've missed you, my love." She kissed his forehead. "I won't let them separate us. Not ever again."

4

ADRIAL

The scent of flowers lured Adrial from the blackness that surrounded him. He took a deep breath, wanting to catch more of the luscious aroma.

His ribs didn't hurt as they expanded. It seemed rather wrong that they shouldn't hurt, but he pushed the thought aside, more concerned about the flowers.

No, not the flowers.

He tried to slog through the fog in his mind. Each thought came slowly, threatening to drift away as he tried to catch hold.

The flowers. The scent of the flowers.

No.

The fragrance wasn't important. It wasn't the blooms. It was the girl.

The girl who had the scent of flowers in her hair.

Ena.

Fear shot through Adrial's body.

He discovered he could move his hands as he gripped the soft sheets beneath him, and that his eyes could open as he blinked at the shadows on the dark ceiling above him.

"Ena." He tried to say her name, but the dryness of his throat wouldn't allow any sound to come out.

"Head Scribe." A pudgy face mottled with bruises loomed over Adrial. "You're awake, sir."

Adrial took a breath. The air grated down his throat.

"Water, sir?" Taddy asked.

Adrial managed a nod.

Taddy disappeared from view.

Adrial tried to push himself to sit up, but his arms didn't seem ready to bear his weight.

"Just a moment, sir." Taddy supported Adrial with one arm while shoving another pillow behind him. "You've got to sit up to drink." The apprentice laid Adrial back against the pile of pillows. "That's better, sir."

The panic in Adrial's chest smothered his mortification at needing his apprentice's aid.

"Start with a small sip." Taddy held a cup to Adrial's lips. "Best to start slow. Choking makes everything worse."

Adrial took a sip of the water. The chill of it rushed down his throat and past his lungs. He opened his mouth to try and speak.

"One more, sir." Taddy pressed the cup to Adrial's lips again. "You've been out for a long while. I'm sure you're parched."

The head scribe obeyed his apprentice.

"Ena." The word rasped free from Adrial's throat.

"There, sir." Taddy pointed to the shadows beside Adrial's bed.

Fear and hope swooped through Adrial in equal measure as he tried to turn and look.

"Let me help." Taddy put an arm behind Adrial, propping him up so he could peer into the shadows.

A couch had been dragged right up next to the bed. The thick blanket draped over her hid everything but her hair. The blue and purple of the strands seemed to glow in the flickering lamplight.

Heat burned in Adrial's eyes. "She's not hurt?"

"She was." Taddy laid Adrial back down. "All of us were."

"But she's here." Adrial twisted, trying to turn so he could see her again. He needed to watch her, to make sure she was breathing.

"She is, sir." Taddy shifted the pillows, angling Adrial so he could see the pool of Ena's hair shimmering in the dim light. "This is the first time she's properly slept all week."

"All week?"

"It's been a week since the attack, sir."

Adrial tried to dig through the blackness, searching for where he could have lost so much time.

"There've been healers and sorcerers tending to you even at night." Taddy made Adrial take another sip of water. "I'm supposed to call them now that you're awake."

"No." Adrial lifted his arm enough to take Taddy's wrist. "Don't call them. I don't want her to leave."

"Oh." Taddy wrinkled his bruised forehead. "They don't make her leave, actually. It wouldn't be safe, you see."

"Why? What's happened?"

"Out in the city? Nothing much. They caught the men who beat us. And some others, too. There were heads on pikes from what I've heard, but I never went to see. I stayed in here with you. The scribes' shop hasn't reopened, and Lord Gareth isn't letting any of the scribes out of the library. He's convinced there are more common folk waiting to murder us. He may be right. I've been too worried about you to fuss over not being allowed to leave the library."

"But what about Ena?"

"Oh. Right." Taddy sloshed water on Adrial's chest as he forced him to take another sip. "A lot's happened, sir. And I swear to you, I did my best. But I couldn't let them leave her on the street, not when she was all bloody. She wasn't moving. She was so still, I didn't think she was alive. And then once we got here, I had to make sure she could stay. I didn't mean to assume, sir, but

I thought if you woke up and couldn't find her, you might panic. And I don't mean to offend, but it seems I was right."

"Taddy, I'm honored you've stayed beside me, and you're right, I would have panicked if I couldn't be sure she was safe. But I need to know everything that's happened. I'm sure I'll be grateful for all you've done."

"I know about sitting by a sick bed. My grandmother was ill for a long time. That's why I'm good at the pillows and the water."

"I meant about Ena."

"Right." Taddy pursed his lips. "Right. Well, I was on the ground. And I thought you were dead, and Ena had killed those men, and then she was on the ground and they were hurting her. And then the soldiers came. She'd gone to get them, I think. The soldiers were looking for you, and I don't know how else they could have found us.

"Then Cade ran and the soldiers wanted to bring us here, and I told them they had to bring Ena as well. They didn't like that. They said it wasn't their job to care for rotta. That's the word they used sir, I'd never call her a rotta otherwise. So, I told them you'd given your oath as the Head Scribe of all Ilbrea that she'd be protected. I think they might've just felt sorry for me since I was clinging to you and sobbing, so they brought us all here.

"There were fires and soldiers everywhere, but they got us to the library. Then Lord Gareth came and he didn't want her here either. He seemed to think she might have been one of the people trying to kill you, and there was a fair bit of blood on her that wasn't hers. But I said she'd saved your life, and…" Taddy looked up at the ceiling as though praying for aid from Saint Alwyn herself. "And I said you'd used your last breath to order me to protect her. And that since she'd been seen fighting to keep you from harm, sending her onto the streets might get her killed."

"Good, Taddy. You did very well."

Adrial leaned back on his pillow. He wanted to reach out and touch Ena so badly. Just to feel the texture of her hair or the warmth of her skin. Anything to convince himself they'd truly both survived the horrors of the rebellion.

"The thing is, sir, Lord Gareth was still going to send her away. He said there were safe places for her outside the library. So, I told him…I told him…"

"Told him what, Taddy?"

"I told him you were in love with her. Desperately in love, actually. Like in the old fairy stories. That you never looked half so happy as when you were looking at her. That if you were going to fight to survive, it wouldn't be for the Guilds or even your family. If you were going to live, you'd be doing it for her. And he couldn't send her away. He'd be ripping your heart from your chest. And why would any man fight to survive if the person he loved had already been taken from him?"

Adrial shut his eyes.

"I'm sorry, sir," Taddy whispered. "I know you've got every right to be angry, but if it helps any, I am suffering from a rather nasty concussion. So please don't get rid of me."

"I'm not angry, Taddy." Adrial opened his eyes. "How much of that did Ena hear?"

"I don't know, sir. She was just in the other room, but she doesn't talk much. So, I don't know if she was in a fit state to hear. She killed those men. She did it to protect us, and I'm glad she did. But getting so much blood on your hands, I don't know how a person heals from a thing like that."

Images of tearing flesh and red-tipped knives flashed through Adrial's mind. "You should sleep."

"I need to get the healers," Taddy said. "It's my job."

"Just promise me they won't make her leave." The words tumbled from Adrial before he could stop them. He sounded like a fool. He was the head scribe, the one who should be offering comfort to the child who'd been so badly beaten half his face still had a horrid purple tinge.

Adrial should be braver. He should be stronger.

He was not strong enough to face her disappearing into the darkness.

"I promise, sir. The Lord Scribe had tears in his eyes when he said she could stay." Taddy set down the cup and slipped out the door to the sitting room.

Adrial shifted just enough to be able to see Ena. Her chest rose and fell, but not with the slow rhythm of someone sound asleep.

Is she trapped in a nightmare, or does the whole world torment her now?

"Ena?" Adrial said, barely louder than he and Taddy had been speaking. "Are you awake?"

Her shoulders tensed. She pulled the blanket tighter around herself but stayed silent.

"Are you all right?" He twisted, trying to reach for her. The pain that had been absent from his ribs radiated through the rest of his body. He bit back a moan.

She was on her feet in an instant, her blanket tossed aside, her hand pressed to his shoulder to keep him from moving.

"Ena." Adrial reached up, laying his hand on top of hers.

She didn't recoil from his touch or scream at him for being a useless man who couldn't even manage to defend himself.

She didn't speak either.

"I'm so sorry," Adrial whispered, "and so glad you're here."

A bustle of sound came from the sitting room as Taddy led in two healers.

"He's just woken up," Taddy said. "He's talking and knows where he is. He's also held down some water nicely and doesn't seem to be having any trouble breathing."

Ena slipped her hand out from under Adrial's and sank away into the shadows at the edge of the room.

"Please don't go," Adrial said as the healers stepped up to either side of his bed.

"Head Scribe, it's nice to see you awake." The older of the two healers took Adrial's wrist in her hand.

Ena shifted in the shadows, heading toward the door.

"No. Please, Ena." Adrial tried to pull his wrist from the healer's grip. "Please stay."

Ena didn't look back as she slipped out the door.

"It's all right," Taddy said. "She doesn't ever stay in the room when there are people here. I'll make sure she eats a bit."

Taddy gave Adrial a crooked, pained smile before following Ena out of the room.

"We weren't expecting to see you awake so soon." The older healer pressed her finger to Adrial's wrist. "We sent for the sorcerer who's been tending to you. Of course, he doesn't stay here during the night."

The two healers exchanged a glance.

"I'll check your hip, if you don't mind." The younger healer tossed back Adrial's blankets without waiting for him to respond.

Heat crept into Adrial's face as the healer shifted the thin underclothes someone had dressed him in. She peered at his hip, a crease forming between her eyebrows.

He chanced a glance down.

His hip still didn't look the way a normal hip should. The odd nobble where the muscles worked so hard to hold him up on the ruined joint showed even while he was lying on the bed.

Fear surged through him as he remembered blinding pain shattering his hip and crashing into his spine.

He swallowed before daring to speak. "Is it going to be worse than before?"

"Hmm?" The older healer felt along the sides of his neck.

"My leg." Adrial kept his voice calm. "Will it be harder to walk on than it was before?"

Both healers paused their inspection to look at one another.

"That's not for us to say." The older healer went back to prodding his neck. "The sorcerer was charged with tending to your bone damage."

"And did the sorcerer seem pleased with their work?" Adrial asked.

The younger healer ran her fingers along the strange angles of his hip once more before looking to the door. "I've never met a sorcerer who isn't pleased with their work."

"I wouldn't worry too much." The older healer lifted the lamp from the table and held it close to Adrial's face to peer into his eyes. "You won't be up and about for a while yet. You'll have to lie still for another day or two at the very least. Best to be sure you're rested. For now, just be happy you're alive. If your leg isn't what it should be, we'll work on that once we can get you up and moving."

"Right." Adrial took a deep breath, tucking his fear away. "Thank you both for your care."

"It's an honor to work on the head scribe." The younger healer covered his hip back up.

"My apprentice and the inker," Adrial said, "have you been tending to them as well?"

"The apprentice will be fine," the older healer said. "We had a bit of worry with his head, and he's got a few stitches in his face, but he'll recover."

"And the inker?" Adrial shifted to sit higher against his pillows.

"The common girl?" The younger healer glanced toward the door. "We were never ordered to see to her."

"Right." Adrial dragged a hand down his face, weighing his worry over Ena's health against any slim hope of her agreeing to allow the Guilded healers to touch her. "I'll let you know if she needs your services."

The healers exchanged another glance.

"People who are used to the streets are better off without our aid." The younger healer straightened Adrial's pillows, tilting them so he wouldn't be able to see the couch where Ena had slept. "When a mutt is beaten, they'll lick their wounds on their own or die. It's the best way with commoners, too. It keeps the blood of the strong going and weeds out those too weak to serve the will of the Guilds."

5

ADRIAL

Taddy had come in to bring him a bit of broth as soon as the healers left, but Ena had stayed in the sitting room. Silent and completely out of Adrial's reach.

If it hadn't been for Taddy's whispered, "She's perched in her window again, sir. She usually doesn't move for hours when she gets up there," Adrial would have thought Ena had disappeared. Faded into the night like a wonderful shadow he'd somehow dragged into his nightmare.

By the time he'd gotten up the courage to try calling out and begging her to come to him, the sorcerer had arrived. The hours of painful prodding and the unnatural heat of magic being worked on his flesh lasted until dawn.

The sorcerer tucked Adrial in before leaving, pulling the blankets all the way up to his shoulders as though Adrial were no more than a sickly child.

Adrial had accepted the ministrations without complaint, clinging to his gratitude for having been so well cared for by a sorcerer when even the Guilded healers didn't seem keen on tending to the common folk.

Fatigue that dug all the way down into his magically mended

bones dragged Adrial deeper into his bed, but the aching worry in his chest made him fight against the inviting embrace of sleep.

"Ena," Adrial called as soon as the door to the hall closed behind the departing sorcerer. "Ena, are you awake?" Silence thundered in his ears. "Ena, I'm sorry." Gritting his teeth against the inevitable pain, Adrial tossed his covers away. "Please, at least let me see that you're all right."

He shifted his legs toward the side of the bed, gasping as pain streaked from his hip to his shoulder.

"What are you doing?" Ena stood in the doorway, her arms wrapped around her middle, her face hidden in shadow.

"Checking on you."

"Two healers and a sorcerer spend a week tending to you, and you risk their work to check on me. You're chivving well lucky they kept you alive." Ena strode to the bed and held up the blankets as though waiting to tuck Adrial back in. Deep purple bruises stained her cheek and wrapped around her throat.

Pain cut into Adrial's chest. "They aren't the ones who saved my life."

"I wouldn't mention that to the paun. They take great pride in having saved the head scribe."

Adrial eased himself back onto his pillows, trying to keep his pain from showing on his face. He needn't have bothered. Ena kept her gaze fixed firmly above his shoulder as she draped the blankets over him.

"It's you who saved me, Ena. I know that." Adrial took her hand, holding it as gently as if she were made of spun sugar, offering no opposition if she chose to pull away. "I'm so sorry Cade hurt you. What you did to save me—"

"You wasted." Ena yanked free of his touch. "All you had to do was hide. I left you someplace safe. The soldiers were on their way."

"I could hear Taddy screaming." Adrial's words hitched in his throat. He swallowed before daring to trust his voice again. "I heard those men laughing and beating him. I know what you gave, how much you sacrificed to keep me safe, but—"

"Sacrificed?" The word came out low and dangerously even. "How much I sacrificed when I lifted my skirts for Cade? Is that worse to you than the men I had to kill to stop them from beating you to death? Slitting a throat is not an easy thing to do, scribe."

"I'm not saying it is."

"Paun are always so eager to judge a woman for spreading her legs to defend her kingdom. But a man who cuts down innocents to protect his, they'll write songs in his chivving honor. Letting Cade inside me left no larger a scar on my soul than the three lives I had to end to save yours."

"Three?" Adrial wished he could swallow the word. It hung so heavy in the air, like a curtain drawing closed between them.

"It might be four." Ena fixed her gaze on the lamp in the corner. "I stabbed one of them well enough he should have died from his wounds, but I didn't actually see him fall."

"I'm so sorry. You shouldn't have had to fight anyone. I never wanted you to carry the weight of ending a life."

"It's a weight I've grown accustomed to."

"Ena—"

"The beasts would have died anyway." Ena touched the bed, her hand within easy reach of his, as though she were daring him to bat her away. "They beheaded Cade and his lot. Put their heads on pikes right outside the cathedral. I went to see it for myself. I had to be sure he was dead."

Adrial reached for her, barely grazing his fingers against hers.

"They would have killed Taddy." Ena looked down at their hands.

Adrial dared to twine his fingers through hers.

"They would have killed you, too," Ena said. "Paraded your body through the streets to show everyone their rebellion had been worth the cost in common blood. They would have been right. There are thousands who would gladly die to see such a high-ranking paun fall. And the common folk who cheered your death wouldn't even have known they were celebrating their own doom."

"If my death could have spared you any pain, I would gladly have faced my end." Horrible images flashed before Adrial's eyes. He tightened his hold on Ena's hand as fear squeezed his heart. "I saw Cade with his hands around your neck. He was killing you, and I couldn't do anything. I couldn't even move. I was trying to help Taddy. I thought you were already out of the city. I never—"

"Don't. Telling you to hide while a child's being murdered would be too much coming from anyone. I have no right to ask it of you. But I need you alive, scribe. This city—" Her voice caught in her throat.

Adrial carefully drew her toward him, as though he were a man trying to comfort a raging storm.

Impossible to subdue. Impossible to refuse.

Ena sat on the bed and leaned closer to Adrial, letting him wrap his arms around her.

The warmth of her cheek against his neck, the murmur of her breath against his skin, dulled the edges of his pain.

"There are bodies in the streets." Ena shifted nearer to him, lightly laying her arm across his chest. "I can smell them from the window."

"Cade and his men?"

"No. They were hauled away, but the rest that died, they're just lying out, rotting."

"What?" He held Ena tighter.

"The Lord Scribe shut down the scribes' shop. There's no one to write the burial papers. The soldiers are guarding every crack anyone could use to slip out of the city. There's nothing for any of the common folk to do. The corpses have just been left in the streets."

Adrial pressed his nose to Ena's hair, trying to convince

himself he was imagining the foul odor lurking beneath the scent of flowers that filled his room.

"The healers won't see to any common folk," Ena whispered, "so more have died of their wounds from the fighting. The city is packed tight together. If people aren't allowed to bury their dead—"

"The losses will continue to spread."

Ena sat up, pulling free from Adrial's embrace. "You have to speak to Lord Gareth. You have to make him reopen the shop. None of the other paun chivving care that most of the common folk in Ilara hadn't even heard of Cade's rebellion. The paun are punishing innocent people. The Guilds ignoring the people they rule as the common folk suffer and die is nothing less than a slow massacre. You have to help us, scribe, or a fire will start in the streets. And its rage will be enough to devour every person in the city, tilk and paun alike."

Adrial touched Ena's cheek. She leaned into his hand, letting him tuck a bit of bright blue hair behind her ear.

I cannot waste what I was unfairly given.

"Where's Taddy?" Adrial asked.

"Sleeping in the sitting room."

"Wake him up, ask him to collect a wagon box for me."

Ena leaned forward, brushing her lips against Adrial's forehead. "Thank you." Her fingers trailed along the bottom of his chin before she ran from his room.

Adrial took a steadying breath and tossed back his blankets, gritting his teeth against the pain he knew would come from daring to move.

Footsteps thumped through the sitting room, and the door to the hall closed with a thud.

Adrial shut his eyes, counting on the blackness to protect him against the worst of the pain, as he shifted his legs over the side of the bed and forced himself to stand. His legs trembled beneath him. Agony seared through his bad hip as his balance faltered.

"Careful." Ena wrapped her arms around him, keeping him upright. "I've already told you, you're not allowed to die."

"I'm fine." Adrial held her close, savoring the feel of her in his arms for one more moment. "Can you find me my robes? I can't write the papers if I'm not in scribe white."

Ena backed slowly away from him, eyeing his hip as though wondering if it might shatter.

"It's not that bad," Adrial said. "No worse than getting over an illness, really."

He was grateful she didn't make him sit back down or tell him it would be better if he ordered another scribe to do the work for him. That he should send a man who wasn't a cripple, who hadn't lain on the ground while an evil monster tried to kill her, out into the city to help the common folk.

A wince found its way to his face as he tried to pull off the long shirt someone had dressed him in.

"Careful. From the mutters I heard, that sorcerer had to mend most of your ribs." Ena grabbed the hem, sliding the garment up over his head, leaving Adrial bare-chested before her.

Adrial glanced down at his shoulder. The same red scar still marred his skin. The sorcerer hadn't mended the horseshoe shaped marks on his side, either.

Ena touched the scars on his ribs. "If they knew how strong you are, they wouldn't have tried so hard to heal you."

"Really?"

"A good man is a dangerous thing."

"Do I really deserve to be called a *good man?*"

Adrial's heart stopped as Ena met his gaze. He waited for her to yell or scream, or even drive a dagger into his gut.

"For eight days, mothers have had to watch their babes rot in the street, and not a single, chivving paun has lifted a finger to help them. The scribes haven't allowed the dead to be buried. The healers didn't bother to try and save the common folk who have died since the fighting ended. If you help even one of the fallen be buried with a bit of decency, you'll be a better man than any of the other Guilded."

"I'll do whatever I can." Adrial touched her cheek, careful not to hurt the bruises that mottled her skin. "A paun life is worth no more than a common one, and a paun death is no more tragic, either."

Ena looked away from Adrial, fixing her gaze on the ground as though afraid of what he might be able to see in her eyes.

"I am not the only one in the Guilds who thinks that way." Adrial let his fingers rest on the side of her neck, below the marks Cade had left when he'd tried to murder her. The warmth of her skin against his dulled the throbbing in his hip. "I'm just the only one who has you making sure they know how horrible things are for the common folk."

"You're wrong."

The door to his sitting room banged open.

"Sir. Sir, I've got a wagon box, but I don't—" Taddy froze in the doorway of Adrial's bedroom, his eyes wide and his mouth stuck open.

A rush of panic blazed through Adrial's gut. He pulled his hand away from Ena's skin. But not touching her didn't change the fact that he was close to naked.

For the briefest moment, a hint of a smile touched Ena's lips.

"Help me into my robes, Ena?" Adrial's voice wobbled in his throat. "Taddy, we're going down to the square. Make sure we're well stocked in the parchments necessary for burial papers."

"Burial papers?" Taddy turned his back on them as Ena lifted Adrial's crisp, white robes over his head.

"The scribes' shop may be closed, but that doesn't mean life in Ilara stops," Adrial said. "It is our duty to serve the people of this city."

"But the Lord Scribe doesn't want any of us leaving the library," Taddy said.

"The square is barely beyond the gates," Adrial said. "The

scribes' guards will be able to watch over us without having to leave their posts."

Ena fastened the closure at the neck of his robes.

"Do you want me to fetch Scribe Tammin?" Taddy asked. "You're still healing, sir. She could go out there for you."

"I won't ask someone else to defy the Lord Scribe." Adrial took a step toward his boots, trying to hide his wince as pain stabbed into his hip.

"I'll get them," Ena said.

"But, Head Scribe," Taddy said, "didn't you just say you weren't really going against the Lord Scribe's orders?"

"It's a small defiance." Adrial sat on the bed, grateful for the moment of relief as he pulled on his boots. "But it must be done."

"Shall I get someone to help you down the stairs?" Taddy said. "You're supposed to stay in bed, but the Lord Scribe didn't actually issue an order against your moving, so helping you wouldn't be breaking a rule."

"I'll be fine, Taddy." Adrial stood again, feeling less vulnerable with proper shoes on his feet.

"I'm coming with you," Ena said.

"But you can't." Taddy's face paled as his eyes went wide again.

"Just to the gates," Ena said. "I understand the bargain I've made."

Taddy mouthed for a moment.

"Come on, then." Ena wrapped her arm around Adrial's waist. "Best to get the burial papers written as quickly as you can. This early in the day, those grieving families might have a chance of getting their fallen in the ground without having to let them rot on the street for another night."

Ena tightened her grip on Adrial as they followed Taddy through the sitting room and into the hall.

For a moment, Adrial wanted to tell Ena he could walk on his own. But he liked having her close to him. He could still feel her warmth, though none of their bare skin touched. He could feel that she was alive and well, even if a gnawing fear in his gut still whispered she had injuries that might never heal.

By the time they'd made it down the long corridor of scribes' chambers and to the stairs, his need to be near her to keep his heart calm had been joined by a gratitude for her help as his ribs ached from so much breathing and the pain in his leg shifted from a stabbing to a fire that seemed determined to burn through his bones.

"Will you make it?" Ena whispered too softly for Taddy to hear.

"As long as you don't let go of me."

"I've done too much to risk you falling, scribe."

Their descent was slow, Adrial only bending his good leg, taking each painful stair one at a time.

"I'm sorry," he murmured when two scribes appeared at the bottom of the steps. "I should be able to do this on my own."

"You were nearly beaten to death." Ena spoke loudly enough for the scribes below to hear. "You're the only one who's been brave enough to help the people of this city. Anyone who judges you as weak for needing help down the stairs is a worthless, chivving slitch."

One of the scribes gasped.

"Did I offend them?" Ena shifted to the side, helping Adrial move out of their way, but both scribes bowed and backed out of the door at the bottom of the stairs. "Nice of them."

Ena tilted her head toward him as they kept moving down, almost as though she wanted to be sure that anyone else who came through the door would take note of Adrial's arm wrapped around her shoulders.

Taddy stopped at the base of the staircase and turned to look up at Adrial. "I don't want to cause a fuss, Head Scribe. But how are people going to know to come to you to get burial papers written?"

"The common folk haven't seen a hint of scribe white in more than a week," Ena said. "Word will spread."

"I hope you're right," Taddy said. "It would be a pity to risk angering the Lord Scribe and then not have anyone turn up for our help."

"They're desperate," Ena said. "They'll come."

Taddy took a deep breath, as though steeling himself, before pushing the door open.

A stench worse than anything Adrial had ever imagined pummeled his nose. He opened his mouth to speak and gagged on the taste.

"You get used to it," Taddy said. "Your nose starts to forget the smell is even there."

"How many bodies does it take to taint the air like this?" Adrial said.

"It depends on if they're common or paun," Ena said. "The paun were all buried the day after the battle."

A horrible sickness rolled through Adrial's stomach as they stepped into the courtyard by the stables. He breathed through his mouth, hoping to make the nausea go away, but the feeling only worsened as he saw the line of soldiers and scribes' guards standing in front of the open gates.

Twenty scribes' guards stood behind twenty Guilded soldiers, all of them armed with swords.

They think the people are our enemy.

"Good morning, Head Scribe." One of the scribes who'd given them the stairs bowed to Adrial.

"It's wonderful to see you up." The other blushed as she looked toward Ena.

"I can't lie in bed when the people of Ilara need our help," Adrial said.

The two scribes shifted closer together as though trying to shield themselves.

Adrial couldn't tell if they wanted to hide from him or from Ena.

"When rumors spread about my being out of bed, be sure to whisper back that I left the library to help the common folk," Adrial said. "I understand what happened during the rebellion better than most. But I was attacked by a few evil men. Innocent people who are mourning their dead should not be forced to pay for Cade's crimes."

"Yes, Head Scribe." The two crept around him and bolted up the stairs.

"Everyone will know before midday." Taddy pushed the door shut behind them.

"I just hope they remember what I said." Adrial gritted his teeth against the pain and started toward the gates.

None of the soldiers or guards glanced toward them.

"If half those men had turned their hand to digging graves, the dead would be buried, and there wouldn't be whispers of a new illness making its way through the common sections of the city," Ena said.

"Cade's dead, and he's still hurting people." The terrible urge to take Ena back to his rooms and hide her far from the dangers the rebellion had left in its wake worsened the sickening feeling in his stomach.

"Will you really blame the dead instead of the living who refuse to help?" Ena asked.

"I'm so sorry." Adrial forced himself to keep moving forward. "If I had been awake, I could have helped sooner."

"There are hundreds of scribes who didn't get a scratch from Cade," Ena said. "Not a chivving one of them so much as lifted a pen to help."

The guards didn't notice them until they were only ten feet away.

One of the guards turned, looking from Adrial, to Ena, to Taddy, and back again before bowing. "Head Scribe."

"I'm going out to the square." Adrial pulled his arm from around Ena's shoulders and tipped his chin up in a way he hoped would make Allora proud.

"The square, sir?" The guard furrowed his brow, studying Adrial as though worried he might have lost his mind.

"My apprentice and I have work to do," Adrial said. "Kindly step aside."

"Sir, it's not safe," the guard said.

"I'll stay within view of the gates," Adrial said. "I have complete confidence in your ability to protect me. Do you doubt the training of the men who fight beside you?"

"No, sir. But—"

"Come, Taddy." Adrial spoke over the guard. "We have work to do."

The guard tensed his jaw before stepping away. "Make a path for the head scribe."

None of the other soldiers or guards so much as whispered as Adrial passed by.

"I'm afraid you'll have to stay in the library, miss."

Adrial turned to find the guard holding up a hand to block Ena's path.

"I am well aware of the Lord Scribe's edict." Ena curtsied to the guard. "And grateful for the protection of the almighty Guilds."

She gave Adrial a nod before turning on her heel and striding back toward the door to the stairs.

A brutal feeling of being exposed in a way he hadn't felt when he'd been unclothed upstairs replaced the revulsion in his stomach.

"Do you need help, Head Scribe?" Taddy asked softly. "If you drape your arm over my shoulders, I can help you and carry the box."

"I'm fine, Taddy." Keeping his steps as even as he could, Adrial ventured out onto the street.

The square wasn't far from the gates, not a long walk at all. And the space wasn't large. On a fine summer day, any more than thirty people made the square seem crowded. Since the fountain was in the center of the square, walking that far to take a seat would be an easy thing. Hardly more than the hallway Adrial had already traveled. And the basin of the fountain had a wide stone rim. As soon as he got to the fountain, he could sit to do his work. Just a few steps, and he could take the weight off his burning leg.

Adrial ran the comforting words through his mind over and over as he ground his teeth against the pain that now raged from his knee to his neck. But as hard as his mind shouted that the distance was small, his body seemed convinced he was trying to climb the eastern mountains.

He'd wound his mind so tightly up in trying to push past the pain, Adrial didn't realize people had started staring at him until Taddy's shoulders crept up toward his ears as he stopped beside the fountain and looked around the square.

Adrial followed his apprentice's gaze.

Everyone in sight had frozen to gape at the head scribe.

Four soldiers stepped beyond the library's gates, their hands on their swords as they glowered at the people creeping closer to Adrial.

"Head Scribe," Taddy said.

"Set out my supplies, Taddy." Adrial lowered himself onto the rim of the fountain, grateful for the lingering nighttime chill of the stone seeping through his robes.

Taddy pulled out a writing board, a pen, ink, and some parchment.

"Scribe," a man called to Adrial from twenty feet away. He held his hands open at his sides, as though wanting to be sure the soldiers knew he carried no weapon. "May I ask what you're doing?"

"I've come to write burial papers," Adrial said.

A woman ran out of the square.

"Will you be here long?" the man asked. "I have a neighbor who needs to bury her husband, but she hasn't been able to purchase the papers."

"Go tell her I'm here," Adrial said.

The four soldiers stepped farther away from the gates.

"Tell whoever is in need that I'm here." Adrial unscrewed the top of his inkwell. "It's time to bury the dead."

"Thank you, scribe." The man hurried away.

Adrial looked up toward the library. The balcony outside the great room had filled with scribes. All of them froze when they realized Adrial was looking their way.

Lord Gareth will skin me alive for this.

Adrial looked up higher.

A flash of color caught his eye.

Ena sat in his window, the light glinting off the brilliant hues of her hair.

"Sir," a woman said.

He forced his attention back to the square.

"I'd like to buy burial papers for my daughter." The woman swallowed hard, as though fighting back tears. "She died in labor two days ago."

"I'm so sorry for your loss," Adrial said. "We need to start with her full name given at birth."

He glanced back up to his window.

Ena pressed her palm to the glass and gave him a nod.

6

MARA

The cold of the ice didn't seep into their pallet. It hadn't since the first time Mara had slept beside Tham on the floor of their ice prison.

When she'd woken up that time, there had been a mound of extra furs with the food and water that had appeared. She'd laid out the bedding and carefully shifted Tham to sleep in the warmth their captors had granted.

She had to think of it that way. Tham was sleeping, exhausted from finding his way to her. He needed rest.

Simple. Fixable.

He would sleep. Then he would wake up and hold her. They would find a way out together. She only needed to let him rest.

Mara changed the bandages on his hands. She spooned the pungent tea her captors left on her tray into Tham's mouth. She drank the tea herself to make sure it wasn't the brew that kept Tham from waking up.

She kissed his face, and told him stories, and screamed and cried.

"You'll wake up soon, my love." Mara pressed her tear-soaked cheek to his. "I'll be here when you do. I promise I'll keep you safe."

She kissed his forehead, savoring the warmth of his skin against her lips. Carefully tucking the furs around him, she crawled into the pallet to lie by his side.

Hours passed. Or maybe it took days for her to drift to sleep.

The shifting of the room didn't wake her, but the proof of the walls' movement waited in the corner when she finally opened her eyes.

She'd kept them closed for as long as she could. Lying with her hand on Tham's chest, feeling the gentle rise and fall of each breath he took, she could pretend she wasn't locked in a prison made of ice, held captive by someone who possessed magic she didn't understand.

With her eyes closed, she could almost fool herself into believing she was in her bed in the Map Master's Palace. She'd managed to convince Tham to spend the night with her. Soon, he would kiss her to wake her up. She would beg him to stay longer, but he would say no, they couldn't risk anyone finding out the female map maker had a man in her bed. He would climb out her window and disappear into the early morning darkness.

Dawn would steal him from her.

She'd lie in her bed as the warmth faded from the place where he'd slept, missing him even though she knew he'd come back when the sun set.

But the blue light creeping through Mara's eyelids didn't change. The sunrise wasn't going to steal him from her. The ice already had.

She clung to the front of Tham's shirt.

"I'll get you back." She rested her forehead against his cheek before finally opening her eyes.

Without meaning to, she looked to the corner where her tray always appeared.

"They've trained their caged dog well." Mara slipped out from under the furs, tucking the blankets around Tham to keep in their shared warmth.

Food, water, bandages, salve, a pot of tea—all the things her captors had made a habit of bringing her. But the bit of white parchment tucked between the two cups, *that* her jailers had never sent before.

She looked from Tham to the tray, trying to judge the distance between the two.

They'd never tried to take Tham from her. Not since they'd left him in her care.

They'd never sent her a letter, either.

Tucking her toes into the crook of Tham's arm, Mara lay on her stomach, reaching across the ice floor toward the tray.

Her fingers grazed the lip of the cold metal.

She glanced back at Tham. The walls hadn't moved. The blue gave no hint of wanting to creep in and steal him.

Mara inched forward, grabbing the lip of the tray and sliding it toward her as she scrambled back onto the fur.

She froze, watching the walls, waiting for them to close in around her, not moving until she was certain the ice would stay still. She laid her hand on Tham's chest, making sure he was breathing before finally lifting the parchment off the tray.

A promise for a promise.
> *I'll give you your mate. You give me the truths I seek.*
> *Lie to me, and you will never see him again.*
> *I offer you my word, Ilbrean.*
> *Now give me yours.*

Mara read the letter twice before shutting her eyes, trying to imagine herself somewhere away from the unrelenting blue light. A quiet stone room where she could think and breathe. Where she was surrounded by secrets that would see her and her family hanged.

The truth of those secrets holds no value here.

What truths could someone in the white want from me?

There is no secret worth losing Tham.

I swore on my life I would protect Lord Karron's secrets. I never promised I would sacrifice Tham.

Mara leaned down, kissing Tham on the cheek. Her lips brushed against his ear as she whispered, "I'm sorry, my love."

She waited for a moment. The foolish part of her, the part that believed that the sort of happy endings from fairy stories were possible, expected Tham to wake with a gasp and tell her not to give her word to any unseen demon hiding in the ice. A promise given in a place fed by magic was more dangerous than facing Death himself.

It was a foolish choice. One the gods would punish her for.

Tham didn't move.

Mara shifted the furs, freeing Tham's arm. She laced her fingers through his.

"You have my word." Mara looked to the place where the tray had appeared. "I will give you whatever truth you ask for if you heal Tham."

Mara's heartbeat thundered in her ears as she waited for a flash of magic or for the ice to consume her.

A breath passed, and then another, before the wall started to shift, so slowly, Mara thought she might be imagining it. A ridge appeared in the wall, like a doorway forming where there had only been a solid plane of ice. The door sank back, as though the walls around Mara's prison were three feet thick.

Keeping Tham's hand in hers, Mara knelt between him and the growing door.

A sword. She needed a sword. Or an ice axe. A knife at the very least.

Mara tightened her grip on Tham's hand. She would fight without a weapon. She'd fight with her teeth and fists. She'd bite and scratch their way to freedom.

The blue of the doorway shimmered as a figure appeared in the ice.

Raising a hand as though pushing aside a curtain, the figure stepped free of the blue and into Mara's cell.

The woman was young, near the same age as Mara. Nothing in the beauty of her pale face seemed to betray her as a murderer. Her white-blond hair had been tucked up into a crown of braids with perfect curls surrounding her face. No blemishes of blood or battles marred her sky-blue dress.

Allora would approve.

The woman moved toward them, her gaze fixed on Tham.

"Who are you?" Mara shifted, blocking the woman's line of sight.

The woman stepped around Mara and reached for Tham.

"Don't touch him." Mara knocked the woman's hands away. A stab of cold shot up Mara's arm. She gasped, clutching her hand to her chest as the pain spread to her lungs. "I won't let you hurt him."

"I offer a show of good faith, and you reject me?" the woman said.

"Good faith after you've kept us locked in here?"

"Perhaps you're not ready for my help. That is your choice." The woman frowned and looked to Tham. "Though I don't know how much longer he'll survive. It would be a pity to let him die. He carved his way through our ice, violating the sanctity of the mountain trying to find you. I suppose I shouldn't have allowed my sympathies to be swayed by his devotion."

The woman walked back toward the door made of solid ice. "Enjoy watching your mate die, Ilbrean."

"How do I know you won't hurt him?" Mara asked as the woman reached for the ice.

"A promise for a promise. What more can you ask of me?"

"If I tell you whatever you want, you'll let us both go?"

"I'll save his life." The woman looked back to Mara, a hint of something dangerous glinting in her sapphire-blue eyes. "Would you like to try and bargain for more, or would you like to keep your mate alive? The mind can only take the frozen darkness for so long before madness sets in. If he slips that far, even I won't be able to cure him."

Tears burned in the corners of Mara's eyes.

Tham looked peaceful, like he slept without fear or worry.

"Magic like yours can't be trusted." Mara forced her fear and tears behind her anger.

"Magic like mine is as pure as the winter lights compared to any soul or power that drifts north from Ilbrea."

Mara leaned down, kissing Tham's forehead. "Heal him. Wake him, and I'll tell you whatever you want to know. But if anything happens to Tham, I will kill you even if I have to rip your throat out with my teeth."

The woman laughed, the warm sound bouncing around Mara's cage as though the mountain itself had decided to mock her.

"You're very lucky, you know?" The mirth disappeared from the woman's face as she knelt on Tham's other side. "We don't take kindly to intruders."

"We never meant to intrude."

"Are you going to start lying to me before I even begin to save your mate's life?" The woman froze, her hand hovering over Tham's chest.

"We're explorers. Map makers. We had no idea there were people living in the white mountains."

"You recognize magic when you see it, yet you had no idea we existed?"

"Heal him, and I'll tell you about our journey."

The woman folded her hands in her lap.

Mara stared at Tham's face, trying to picture him awake. "There are secrets worth dying for, especially in Ilbrea."

"Then shall I let you and your mate die together?"

"Ilbrea's secrets are not worth Tham's life." Mara brushed away the heat of a tear on her cheek. "There is magic in the wild. It lives in rocks, and mountains, and the Arion Sea herself. I've seen wild magic more than once, but in Ilbrea, we have to pretend it doesn't exist. Spreading that sort of knowledge would be too dangerous." She imagined the warmth of Tham's arms around her, the blissful feeling of comfort and safety she would give anything to protect. "Tham and I, we'd heard stories of magic in the white mountains. We were sent on the journey north to see if there was any truth to the legends."

"The Ilbreans have dared to venture into the white seeking magic?"

The blue of the walls deepened.

"No." Mara leaned over Tham as though she might be strong enough to keep the mountain from crumbling on top of him. "The journey was sent to search for any people living in the mountains. The Guilds Council wanted to be sure the northern border of Ilbrea was secure before the Princess's wedding next spring. No one else on the journey was looking for anything but a path that might lead to a northern settlement that could threaten Ilbrea."

"Then your journey succeeded. You found us."

"No, we didn't. We found a glimmer of wild magic. We lost most of our party to an avalanche. We went looking for a member of our journey who fled into a storm. We followed a tunnel, trying to find him. Then you captured me. You pulled me through the ice. You locked me in this room. We never found you. We never attacked you. You brought us here. You wanted us here."

"Did I?"

"Yes. Now heal Tham. If anything happens to him, I will die before you get another answer out of me."

"There's the bit of honesty I was hoping for. It wasn't so difficult, was it?" The woman trailed her fingers along Tham's cheek. "He's dead, you know?"

"What?"

"The one you came looking for. His frozen corpse was tied to a sled."

Bile rolled up into Mara's throat. "His name was Vance."

"We would have left his corpse out there, but the dogs were so cold." She pressed her fingers to Tham's lips. "They wouldn't have survived the storm. Innocent animals don't deserve terrible deaths at the hands of incompetent masters."

"Thank you for taking care of the dogs." Mara held tight to Tham's hand, battling her need to shove the woman away from him.

"It would have been simpler if we'd left them to die. They haven't proven to be the best trained beasts. But they are friendly, and I couldn't have forgiven myself if I'd denied them mercy."

"Have you found anyone else from our journey?"

The woman stroked Tham's Adam's apple. "The two who dug with your mate? Yes, we've found the others who helped him desecrate our home."

"Desecrate? Weren't they—"

Tham gasped, his chest rising off the floor as he dragged in air.

"Tham." Mara slipped an arm beneath him, catching his head as he choked in a second breath. "You're all right. You're fine. I'm here. I'm right here."

Tham blinked, his gaze drifting across the ceiling before finally settling on Mara's face. A tiny smile lifted one corner of his mouth. His lips moved as though he wanted to speak before another round of coughs seized his lungs.

"What's wrong with him?" Mara looked to the woman.

She stood up and moved back toward the ice-made door.

"You have to help him," Mara said. "He needs medicine."

"The ice froze him from the inside out," the woman said.

"That's not a thing one recovers from in a day. He'll need time to rest."

"But he'll heal?" Mara shifted her grip, helping Tham sit up straighter as another round of coughs shook his body.

"Of course." The woman smiled. "You did not come here to invade our home. You did not come here to steal our magic. You are only unfortunate travelers in need of our aid. What sort of monster would I be if I didn't provide the best my home has to offer while your mate heals? I always keep my promises. Be sure you do the same, Mara Landil."

Mara held Tham closer as dread trembled up her spine.

"Be ready for my next visit. We are going to become the best of friends. I have so much to learn from you." The woman stepped through the ice and disappeared.

Pressure on Mara's arm lured her out of her fear.

Tham gripped her wrist, his lips moving as he tried to form words. Worry pinched his brow as he looked into Mara's eyes.

"You're all right. I'm here," Mara said. "We'll be okay. We're together. We can get through anything as long as we're together."

Tham reached up, touching one of Mara's curls.

"I knew you'd come for me." Mara brushed her lips against his. "I knew you'd never stop looking."

7

ADRIAL

My Dearest Adrial,

I hate myself for not having seen you. I should have been by your side while you healed, keeping vigil, making sure you were safe and didn't forget how desperately loved you are and how horrible the world would be without you. But being certain of my place did not change my situation, and my visiting you was deemed impossible.

I know you, Adrial. I know even if you resented that I wasn't there when you woke, you won't be angry with me. I promise you, I'm angry enough with myself for both of us.

I didn't learn you'd been injured until the evening after the attack. I'd sent a letter to the library, wanting to make sure you were all right. I had only just started to panic as to why you hadn't answered when a sorcerer told me you'd been placed in their care after receiving grave and violent injuries.

I tried to come to you, but the sorcerers wouldn't allow me to leave the palace. I appealed to the King himself, but he begged me to consider my own safety. With so many commoners angry at the Guilds, the future Queen of Ilbrea would be an excellent prize for the vile men who wish to destroy our city. I told him I didn't care about my safety. You are my family, and you needed me.

The King still forbade it.

He has been very careful to keep me safe. I have ten soldiers that follow me everywhere. Though the palace has hundreds of men patrolling the grounds, my guards stand outside my door even while I sleep. If I am in the same room as Princess Illia, between her soldiers and mine, it feels as though there is an entire army lurking in the shadows.

Father has come to the Royal Palace more than once, trying to see me. I still haven't been able to force myself to face him. He sent a letter asking me to come home, promising the Map Master's Palace high on the cliffs would be safer than the Royal Palace just beside the city.

The Royal Palace is so protected by moats and bridges and walls and sorcerers, I'm not sure father's right. But, if I am truly honest, I think I'd feel safer in his home. From so high above, it always seemed as though the problems of Ilara were small enough to be conquered.

Living in a palace with sorcerers constantly haunting the halls, soldiers everywhere, and the anger of the city smoldering just beyond our gate, it seems as though the world might catch fire at any moment. I am not such a fool as to believe I would be strong enough to douse the flames. Knowing I wouldn't be able to help makes me feel utterly useless. It's been a very long time since I saw myself as a defenseless creature. I hate it.

But as much as running away to the cliffs should feel like retreating to a sanctuary, I know that's not what I would find. My father's house is a tomb to me now. I cannot be the girl who lived there such a short time ago. Even if I could, I would never choose to be her again. I would not survive the pain.

I have given so much of myself and my life to the Map Makers Guild, and I did it all willingly, gratefully. I was happy to serve my father's noble cause. But losing Niko is too much. I can't breathe when I think of it.

My lungs disappear, and my heart shatters, and all that remains is a broken and defenseless fool who was too stubborn to accept happiness. I will never know what could have been, but I do know what I can't survive. Going back to my father's house, letting the map makers take anything more from me, would kill me.

My certainty of my choices has not eased my fear of losing my father's love. I abandoned him. I am no longer the daughter Lord Karron needs. Mara will have to take my place when she comes home. I hope I will not lose her love as well.

There is too much sorrow in this world, sweet Adrial. Too much pain. I cannot face the darkness if I have lost all the people I hold most dear.

I beg you to still love me as you always have.

I am sorry news of my engagement to the King didn't come to you from me. Please blame my grief.

Forgive me for not being beside you when you woke and for the thousand other trespasses you've never mentioned. You are the best of us all, and I do not want to lose you.

Be well, Adrial,

Allora

Adrial read the letter for a third time as the tea he'd abandoned in his cup chilled. He needed to see Allora. As much as she worried over him, her injuries were graver than broken bones and lost blood. He'd need a carriage to reach the Royal Palace, which would be a harder thing to manage than just walking through the gates and daring the soldiers to stop him.

He looked to the open window where Ena sat perched on the sill, looking out over the city.

The stench had begun to clear. From what he'd been told, the last of the bodies had been buried.

The wind picked up, blowing Ena's hair away from her neck. The imprints of Cade's hands had begun to fade from around her throat. The bruises on her face had lightened to a pale green. But there was something, perhaps it was the set of her shoulders or the look in her eyes, that made her seem far from healed.

Adrial folded up Allora's letter and tucked it into his pocket.

A letter from our future Queen.

"What is it?" Ena looked toward him.

"Nothing."

"You're not a good liar, scribe." Ena hopped off the windowsill, wincing as her feet touched the ground.

"You're right then. Not nothing. Just too many things to say at once." Adrial ran a hand over his hair. It needed cutting. One more piece of order that had slipped away from his little world.

Ena took a roll from his breakfast tray and began pacing the length of his sitting room. "I have time. All I have is time. You can talk for hours if you like. I'll be right here."

"Do you not want to be?" Adrial shifted to stand.

Ena shot him a glare, and he settled back into his seat.

"Someone's got to protect you," she said, "and I don't trust a single one of those slitches with swords they've got at the gates. But by the gods this place is a cage."

"I'm sorry."

"It's not your fault." Ena set the roll back on the tray and started braiding her hair. "You're not the one who locked me in this tomb."

"No one's locked you in."

Ena gave a rueful laugh.

"The door's unlocked." Adrial stood, not sitting back down even when Ena scowled at him. "The guards at the gates won't stop you. I'll see to it."

"You slept for too long, scribe. You missed so much." Ena twisted her braid behind her and climbed back up onto the windowsill. "The Lord Scribe allowed me to stay for your sake. But I'm too much of a hazard out in the city. Too many people want me dead.

"I went to the cathedral square to make sure they'd killed the right monster. When I came back, the dear Lord Scribe made it quite clear the Guilds will not risk paun lives rescuing a lowly rotta like me. If I walk out the gates again, I'm not allowed back into the library."

"He can't mean that."

"Oh, but he does. As long as I want to protect you, I have to stay locked in this chivving stone cage. Trapped in a tomb. Surrounded by paun."

"But Lord Gareth can't mean to keep you from working." Adrial dared to step closer to Ena. "What about your shop?"

"What shop? Cade broke everything I had, and even if there was anything left, I can't go back there. I'm capable of defending myself, but not against a mob."

"A mob?"

"Cade and his men are dead. The fact that I killed some of them didn't die with the chivving bastards. There are plenty of common folk in Ilara who would like to see my head on a pike."

"Ena—"

"I could disappear into the shadows where none of them would find me, but hiding is a wonderful way to starve."

"I would never let that happen." Adrial reached for her hand. "You saved my life. You killed those men to protect me. I'm sorry helping me cost you so much."

Ena threaded her fingers through his. She leaned back against the edge of the window, her gaze fixed on their hands as though she were waiting for something to happen.

"Cade was a chivving fool. His rebellion did nothing but hurt the common folk. The blood on his hands is more tilk than paun. After the pain they caused, I would gladly have killed Cade and his men even if you hadn't been in danger. Sliced through their guts and not felt a bit of regret."

"It's not fair for you to have their blood on your hands."

"Do you think I even notice the stain?" Ena looked up, meeting Adrial's gaze.

"Ena, how many..." Adrial swallowed, trying to find better words. "How many times have you had to defend yourself?"

She drew him closer, leaning toward him until her cheek brushed against his as she whispered, "If you knew all the blood that coated my hands, you would never want to touch me again. I have been death and vengeance and so many things that would terrify you. But that girl cannot be here. She cannot exist in the Guilds' library. There are things you can't know. If you try to find out, I will have to run, and you will never see me again. Choose your questions wisely, scribe. Please."

Adrial froze, his heart hammering in his chest as the scent of her flooded through him. "I don't know what you've been before. I don't know who taught you to fight, or what you've had to do to survive. But I do know I'm grateful you're here. And I would forget how to breathe if I lost you."

Ena kissed his cheek, lingering with her lips against his skin. "Then I'll stay for as long as they let me."

"Let you?" Adrial shifted back enough to look into Ena's eyes. A tendril of blue hair had fallen across her face.

"Do you think Lord Gareth will let your rotta guard dog prowl in your room and sleep on your couch forever?"

"You're not a guard dog." Adrial reached up, his hand trembling as he tucked her hair behind her ear. She didn't flinch at his touch.

"You're up and moving now. He'll grow weary of my lurking soon if he hasn't already. When he throws me out, you'll be on your own. Please don't be foolish enough to think you're safe because you're trapped amongst paun. A man like you will have enemies no matter who surrounds him. I promise you, there is a knife to your back even if you don't know who wields the blade."

"What?"

Ena tightened her grip on his hand. "You need to find a few guards, men you can truly trust. You need eyes and ears everywhere in this library. You can't keep believing the best of people. You can't stake your neck on me being here to protect you."

"But you can't leave. Where would you go?"

"I have no idea. I can't go back to any life I've ever known." Ena let go of his hand, pulling away from him, pressing her palm to the black stone pendant that hung around her neck. "I've tried to sort through it a hundred times, but every place I've been is closed to me. Choosing any of those paths would kill me. I'll have to go south, farther than I've ever been. If I can make it that far, I might have a chance of surviving the shadows."

"But you shouldn't go anywhere. I'll find a way for you to stay here. I'll talk to Lord Gareth."

"Convince him to let your guard dog keep pacing in your rooms?" Ena hopped off the windowsill and went back to the tea tray. "I'll go mad. And madness in someone like me is a very dangerous thing."

"No." Adrial limped to the tea tray, lifting the pot away from her, trying to hide the trembling of his hands as he poured her a fresh cup. "There won't be any pacing or any tomb. I'll work something out. I'll make sure you're happy."

"You think the Lord Scribe will let you just tuck me in a comfortable corner? I think that would be the epitome of being a kept woman. I'm still prowling in your chambers, and you're well off your deathbed. I don't belong here, scribe. I'm running out of time."

"No. You're not. I promise, you're not. I will work something out." Adrial added the herbs to the tea. The spoon clinked an odd rhythm against the cup as he stirred with his still-trembling hand. "Just promise me you won't climb out the window or disappear." He pressed the tea into her hands.

"How else am I supposed to leave this place? I'd rather slip away on my own than wait for scribes' guards to haul me out through the gates and dump me where a horde can kill me."

"Just give me a day." Adrial smoothed the front of his robes. "Maybe two. I will find a way for you to stay here."

"You're panicking, scribe." Ena sipped her tea.

"You're right, I am." He gulped down the rest of his cold tea.

"You go take a bath. A nice, hot bath. I have an excellent tub. I'll have clothes sent up. Something nice and clean and new. Which I should have done before, but I'm hopeless. And thoughtless. And I apologize. Oh, and frie. I'll have frie sent to you. Good frie. Frie and a bath, wouldn't that be nice?"

Ena furrowed her brow as she bit her lips together. A glint of laughter gleamed in her eyes.

He hadn't known how much he'd missed that glint until seeing it again pummeled him in the stomach.

"Don't mock me. I thought you'd left once, and you might as well have carved out my soul. So just take a bath and give me a moment, and I'll fix this." He set down his cup and hurried out into the hall, shutting the door to his rooms behind him.

He paused in the corridor, reason catching up to him in the absence of her intoxicating scent. He closed his eyes.

"You're a fool, Adrial Ayres," he whispered to the empty corridor. "Dudia help you, you are a fool."

He let out a long breath, but his heart wouldn't stop hammering in his chest.

He wanted Ena to be happy. He wanted Ena to be safe. He wanted Ena to stay where her smile could wrench the air from his lungs.

He wanted Ena.

Even if she could never want him in the same way, even if she only ever thought of him as a good man worthy of her protection, if he could convince her to stay, at least he'd be able to talk to her and see her. Make sure she was taken care of.

Visiting her every day was infinitely better than nothing.

"By the Guilds, I'm a chivving fool." Adrial hurried down the hall, heading toward the great room as quickly as his bad leg could manage.

Day by day, the pain had gotten better. He wasn't quite as quick as he'd been before the attack—the normal ache he'd felt for years had gained a sharper edge—but he was sturdy enough to move on his own. And the pain was a secret he could manage.

He smiled and nodded at the scribes he passed as he made his way down the stairs and through the corridors that led to the heart of the library.

Rumors had been spreading while he'd been secluded in his rooms. He didn't know what the stories might be, but from the wide eyes, averted gazes, reverent bows, ducking into shadows to hide from him, and flurry of whispers following in his wake, he could only assume that, whatever the tales might be, there was more than one version and definite opinions had been formed as to which account might be true.

He kept his gaze fixed on the polished wooden door at the end of the corridor as the back of his neck burned with the gazes of all the people he'd passed.

The feeling didn't fade as he stepped into the great room and closed the doors behind him.

Sunlight poured through the skylights above the rows of tables where the scribes worked. The massive room could have swallowed ships, and the levels of books surrounding the space made it feel more like a place Dudia might visit than the Guilds' cavernous marble cathedral had ever managed.

He didn't pause to reverently wonder at the vast stores of knowledge the volumes contained. His fear that he'd made such a fool of himself Ena had decided to be done with him and already disappeared from his rooms gnawed at his gut.

She'll still be there. She'd have to slip away. She can't leave until dark. I have time. I haven't lost her yet.

Dudia, please don't let me have lost her yet.

Keeping his pace steady as he walked down the center aisle, Adrial tried not to look like a man filled with panic. The scribes he passed set down their work to bow to him. He offered them polite nods, pretending his heart wasn't racing as though it were about explode.

He stopped beside the last set of tables in the row, where the apprentices had all stood to bow to him. Most of them hid their hands behind their backs as though terrified Adrial might notice a stray drop of ink marring their fingers. Adrial gave them the sort of kind smile he would have appreciated from the head scribe during his days as a terrified apprentice.

"Taddy." Adrial waved his apprentice forward from the back corner of the group.

Taddy puffed up his chest as he stepped around his fellows. "Yes, Head Scribe." The boy gave an unnecessarily low bow.

Adrial took the nearest pen and paper. "I need to send you with a note to the kitchen and another to…" He froze with his pen hovering above an apprentice's inkwell.

"Yes, sir?" Taddy asked.

"Whomever it would be that can find clothes." Adrial wrote two quick notes on the paper, careful to keep his writing pristine even in his haste. "We owe someone a very large debt neither of us can ever repay. But we can at least begin to show our gratitude."

"Absolutely, sir." Taddy gave another low bow as Adrial handed him the notes. "I'll see to it right away, sir." He bowed again before hurrying off toward the kitchen.

"Back to your work." Adrial gave the remaining apprentices another nod before stepping up to Lord Gareth's door.

The same image of a pen that marked Adrial's arm stretched across the double doors of the Lord Scribe's office.

Adrial paused for a moment, trying to weave the thin threads of a plan together in his mind, but he had nothing besides an utter sureness that Ena leaving would tear his heart from his chest. And that if there were even a chance of someone hurting her for killing Cade's men, he had to protect her.

You can't protect anyone. You're nothing more than a cripple scribe, Adrial Ayres.

He shut his eyes, shoving the terrible thought aside before knocking on Lord Gareth's door.

"Come in," Lord Gareth called.

Adrial squared his shoulders before stepping into his mentor's study.

Lord Gareth sat behind his wide desk with four stacks of paper in front of him.

But it wasn't the clutter of the papers that sent a new flare of worry through Adrial's gut. Scribe Travers Gend stood beside Lord Gareth, his towering form casting a shadow over the withering leader of the Scribes Guild.

"Adrial." Lord Gareth's face brightened as he waved Adrial closer. "How good to see you up and about."

"Thank you, sir." Adrial stepped so near the desk he could have snatched Lord Gareth's papers out of Travers's reach. "I am feeling much better. The healers and sorcerers have taken excellent care of me. I'm looking forward to getting back to work."

"You shouldn't rush." Lord Gareth tapped his finger on his desk as though displaying his point. "I need you whole and healthy, Adrial. Going out into the square, risking your life...such things cannot be allowed."

"I was very safe, sir," Adrial said. "And, as you requested, I took time to recover from the excitement of going out to tend to the burial papers. But I am your head scribe, and there is work that needs to be done."

"Your work has been handled." Travers's smile did not reach his eyes. "I've been assisting Lord Gareth. There's no need for you to rush your convalescence. We're doing very well without you."

"There is no rushing," Adrial said. "I am quite well, and the world does not stop for one man to rest. The city is in disarray, and Apprentice Baiton informed me the pages I'd completed for Princess Illia's vellum were taken when the scribes' shop was ransacked."

"I still find it hard to believe the people would destroy our shop," Lord Gareth said. "These are dark and terrible times."

"Helping Lord Gareth to lead through such dangerous tribulations will be straining. Are you sure you're fit for it, Head Scribe? You wouldn't want to risk your delicate health." Travers glanced down at Adrial's bad leg.

"I'm a scribe," Adrial said. "My work requires a steady hand and a good mind. I do not need to win a foot race to be the best man for my job. Lord Gareth, I have some rather pressing things to discuss with you that may not be fit for an underling's ears. Would you mind dismissing Scribe Gend?"

"Of course," Lord Gareth said. "Thank you for your work, Scribe Gend. Your assistance will no longer be necessary. Report to the head of folio for your assignment tomorrow."

"Of course, Lord Scribe." Travers bowed. "It's been an honor." He bowed again, not acknowledging Adrial before walking out the door and into the great room.

"Be careful of that one." Lord Gareth kept his gaze on the closed door. "I had hoped, in working more closely with Scribe Gend, I would discover the better side of him, or help him to realize that every place within our Guild holds great value. I'm sorry to say I believe my efforts were wasted. He's a good scribe, but ambition can rot a man's soul. I fear you may have to spend the rest of your life with that one clawing at the back of your robes."

"I'm not afraid of him, sir."

"I'm not sure if that deserves congratulations or pity." Lord Gareth waved Adrial to a chair beside his desk. "Now tell me the truth, have you really fully healed, or do you simply have an aversion to a snake sitting in your seat?"

"My leg isn't quite what it was before, but it's getting better all the time. Other than that, I'm well, and I can always sit while I work."

Lord Gareth tapped his lips as he looked back toward the

door. "Your healing is a blessing from Saint Alwyn. I don't think you understand quite how close we came to losing you."

"Honestly, sir, I thought I had died. I would have if Ena hadn't saved me."

"Yes, the inker did save you. Which makes things all the more difficult." Lord Gareth furrowed his already wrinkled brow. "I am not a well man, Adrial. The horrible things that have happened over the last few months—the attack on the start of the journey, the riot—they took a terrible toll on me. Losing my heir might be enough to kill me."

"Lord Gareth, I'm so sorry." Adrial pressed his palms to his knees to hide the shaking of his hands. "I never meant to endanger myself—"

"No one can blame you for being attacked. You ran from a mob, dear boy. Then that inker saved your life. And in doing so, I firmly believe she may have saved my life as well. And, in saving us, she preserved the future of our Guild. She's a remarkable girl."

"She is"—Adrial searched for the right words—"everything you could hope for a person to be."

"But she is not a scribe, and this is the scribes' library." Lord Gareth's cheeks wobbled as he shook his head. "To have a friend by a sickbed is one thing, but now that you are well enough to work, the situation must be reconsidered. We cannot allow a commoner to continue living in the library."

"Sending her back out into the city is too dangerous. It would be no better than throwing Ena to a pack of hungry wolves."

"I don't want that girl's death on my conscience. Especially knowing how much we owe her, and how deeply you care for her."

Adrial waited for heat to rise to his cheeks as he met his mentor's gaze. But the hollow fear lodged in his lungs had stolen his shame. "If something were to happen to her, it would do more damage to me than any injury I've ever sustained. There would be nothing left of me. I have to make sure she's protected."

"Unfortunate, but I can't say I'm surprised." A hint of a smile brightened Lord Gareth's eyes. "Lord Karron is quite fond of you. Perhaps we can move her to his estate. It's well guarded, and, as it is a private home, he can open his doors to whomever he chooses without answering to the rules of a Guild as we must."

"I think I have a better idea, sir." Adrial leaned forward in his seat. "I have to restart the vellum for Princess Illia, and I'll need to move quickly. Ena doesn't have a shop anymore, but I need her to make the ink. If we can find a place for her to work here on the grounds of the library, she would be protected by the soldiers and our guards."

"And as someone in service to the Scribes Guild, it would be well within reason to have her room here, especially as the city is still in chaos."

"Exactly, sir."

Lord Gareth pursed his lips. "If I were a more reasonable man, or a heartless one, I would say no. Even the most enticing of distractions can easily become dangerous. I've laid the hopes of my Guild upon you as my heir."

"I know, and I would never do anything to endanger—"

"But I'm not just the Lord of my Guild. I'm an old man who fondly remembers the whims of his youth. I don't want you to reach my age and be sitting in this chair without any memories besides the smell of books and parchment. Do you really care for her?"

"Yes, sir."

"Beauty and suffering go hand in hand, and heartbreak can be more painful than having your soul ripped in two. But that is the way Dudia made the world, and even a man of books deserves to experience more of life than recording everyone else's journey. I'll agree on one condition."

"Anything, sir."

"Be careful. We are men of paper, and that girl is fire. If you're not wary of the flames, she will burn you up."

8

ALLORA

Sunlight rained down upon the palace gardens, coating every-thing in a cheerful glow. The reds and pinks of the flowers outside Allora's window seemed to taunt her in a hateful way. Death and fire filled the world, but the delicate blooms still survived.

I should have them all torn up. Or burned. Let ashes take the place of petals.

She could ask the King to torch the flowerbeds. Her betrothed might even say yes if he thought it would truly please her. But such a request would draw unwanted attention. The last thing she needed was even more eyes watching her.

"Lady Karron?" Agatha said. "Would you like to walk through the gardens?"

"No. Thank you." Allora stepped away from the window's unrelenting cheer, but the inside of her sitting room offered no darkness for her to hide in.

She'd been placed well away from the King's sleeping quarters to avoid any palace gossip, but her rooms were still decorated in the style the royal Willocs favored. White, silver, and gold adorned every surface. The chandelier in her sitting room had been fully lit, though the curtains were drawn back to let the bright sunlight pour in.

In her good moments, Allora could remember to be grateful for all the care the maids put into tending to her. The meals they brought and lights they lit. Though they never met her gaze, they still seemed to smile a bit as they bustled in and out of her rooms, like they were happy she was to be their new Queen.

"We have quite a day planned." Agatha reached into the pocket of her abundant, red-trimmed skirt to pull out a little, leather-bound book and pencil. "You have another fitting, of course."

"Of course." Allora paced beside Agatha's seat near the unlit fireplace. For the effort it cost, she might as well have been fording a river.

"Creating an entire wardrobe for a queen will take time. Nothing you've worn before can be used once you're married."

"Of course." Allora touched the green skirt of her dress. She was still Lady Karron of the Map Makers Guild. It was still her place to wear the green. But soon, the King's white and gold would swallow her old life.

It's a pity dresses can't swallow grief.

Agatha tapped her pencil on her book. "There's more wedding planning to be done."

"Naturally."

"The King has requested you join him for an afternoon stroll."

"Yes."

"There is also a dinner scheduled for tonight."

Better to be busy. Better not to have time to think.

"I'll need a carriage today as well," Allora said.

"A carriage?" Agatha frowned.

"If one can't be arranged, I'm more than happy to walk to the library."

"Ahh." Agatha pursed her lips in a way the matron might have believed looked like a smile. "Traveling to the library isn't safe, Lady Karron."

"Then surely we shouldn't be having dinner guests." Allora stopped pacing just close enough to Agatha that the matron had to crane her neck to look up at her. "If it's too dangerous for me to go out into the city, it's too dangerous for guests to be traveling here."

"The guests are not the future Queen of Ilbrea." Agatha stood, making the difference between her and Allora's heights less noticeable.

"You're right, I am the future Queen of Ilbrea. And I will be taking a carriage to the library. Will you arrange the carriage for me, or shall I walk to the stables and speak to the grooms myself? I know where the stables are. I am quite capable of functioning on my own."

Agatha closed her leather book and tucked it back into her pocket. "Lady Karron, I am afraid there can be no carriage."

"Why?"

"I've been gentle, as I know you've had a trying time, and you need a soft hand. But—"

"I am not a child. I will not be treated as such." Allora swept past Agatha toward the door.

"Lady Karron—"

"Trail in my wake if you must." Allora opened the white door, not allowing herself to shudder as she touched the golden doorknob.

Ten soldiers waited in the corridor. All of them armed. All of them silent as they watched over her.

Allora didn't speak to them as she strode past. She didn't even need to glance behind to be sure they were following—the ten armed men did not move quietly. The thumping of their boots had become her constant companion whenever she dared to leave her room.

The flock of soldiers outside Princess Illia's chambers bowed as she passed.

Allora offered them a nod but didn't slow her pace.

"Lady Karron, if there's something I can do for you—" Agatha puffed as she caught up to Allora.

"I'm going to see the King," Allora said. "I don't think you should visit my betrothed on my behalf."

"You're supposed to walk with him later, Lady Karron."

"I should only see the man I am to marry once a day?" Allora cut down the steps toward the public part of the palace, giving gracious smiles to the Guild members waiting in the entryway to see the King on official business.

A hint of guilt slithered through Allora's determination.

The city of Ilara had been attacked. People had died. Shops had been sacked. Homes had burned. If the Guild members in the entryway had business with the King that would aid in mending the city, then her taking the King's time was selfish.

It's not, Allora, a voice that sounded like Mara's whispered in the back of her mind.

She turned down the corridor, passing by more soldiers stationed between paintings of sweeping landscapes glorifying the beauty of Ilbrea.

The doors to the throne room had been set with silver and gold etchings, creating a scene of the first Willocs arriving in Ilbrea. On a normal day, in a normal time, the chandeliers above would have glittered off the marble of the arches and the images on the doors in a breathtaking way.

But the mass of soldiers outside the throne room cast shadows across everything, the armed men in black uniforms looking like Death's own minions sent to haunt the palace.

"I'm here to see the King." Allora announced to no one in particular.

"He's quite busy," Agatha said.

But a soldier had already stepped forward to open the door.

"Of course he is, Agatha. He's the King." Allora gave a nod to the soldier before striding into the throne room.

King Willoc sat on his golden throne on a dais carved of white marble. A man in sailor blue and a woman in healer red stood below him.

Allora kept quiet, cutting behind the pillars that lined the sides of the long room, keeping carefully out of sight, waiting until she was ready to catch the King's eye.

Others waited for their turn to speak to the King. Some in fine merchant's silks. A few in healer red. There were no scribes in white, and Allora was the only one wearing map maker green.

"There's nothing else for it," the King said. "If we're asking the sailors to patrol and protect the docks on their own, they have every right to ask for healers to be stationed with them the same way they are at the soldiers' barracks. These are dark times. Our city has been wounded. By working together, we will heal more quickly and prevent the vile disease of malcontent from spreading."

"Thank you, Your Majesty." The sailor bowed.

"As you wish, Your Majesty." The healer bowed.

Neither representative was the head of their Guild, but such small matters didn't require the full might of a council meeting. The King could be allowed to allocate a few healers on his own.

The healer and sailor walked the length of the throne room side by side, neither of them glancing down to see the subtle art beneath their feet.

The swirling mosaic on the floor had been created cleverly enough one might not see it unless they really looked. The difference in the colors between the white, gray, and pink marble blended into the beauty of the space.

The magnificence of the throne room would be better for a wedding than the Guilds' cathedral, and easier to protect as well. If only the sorcerers would allow tradition to be broken.

"Lady Karron." A sorcerer stepped around a pillar. She wore a bright smile, as though she'd known exactly who she'd been about to stumble into and what Allora had been thinking.

Allora forced her features into a pleasant expression as she studied the woman's face, searching her mind for a matching name.

The sorcerer's dark eyes and hair seemed familiar. She was older than Allora, so chances of their never having crossed paths was slim.

"Ciara Clery." The sorcerer bowed. "We've never been properly introduced."

"It's lovely to meet you, Sorcerer Clery." Allora stepped around her to continue toward the King.

"Just Ciara, please. Do you have business with the King?" Ciara asked.

"Quite important business. Haven't you heard? I'm to marry him."

A man in merchant's clothing stepped out to stand before the King. "Your Majesty." He bowed too low to have been properly educated. "I've come to beg for relief. The continued barricades and excessive searches at the city gates are ruining my business."

"Is that so?" The King leaned forward in his seat. "More so than the fires that ravaged the city?"

"Well, no, Your Majesty," the merchant said. "But if there could be a way to let carts carrying goods pass into the city unencumbered."

Allora stepped out through the pillars and into the center of the room. Though she stood a good twenty feet behind the now stammering merchant, the King's gaze flicked immediately to her.

"My darling." The King stood, stepping around the merchant, smiling as though he were truly pleased to see Allora. "To what do I owe this indescribable pleasure?"

"I hate to interrupt the work of ensuring the protection of commerce in Ilara." Allora gave the merchant a nod and sympathetic smile. "But may your future bride beg a moment of your time?"

The King took her hand, brushing his lips against her

fingers. Glee glinted in his teal eyes as he spoke to the room without looking away from Allora. "You'll have to excuse me. I cannot deny myself the joy of a moment alone with my future bride."

Allora pressed her lips into a coy smile, one the people would expect from a girl who delighted in being chosen to marry the King.

He placed Allora's hand on his arm and led her to the back of the room where a small, easily overlooked door hid in the corner. A soldier stepped forward to open the door for them.

I will never grow accustomed to being surrounded by so many.

"You can wait outside, Agatha." Allora barely glanced over her shoulder as she dismissed the matron, not wanting to give the woman time to argue.

She didn't look back until a soldier closed the door behind her. Agatha had been wise enough not to try and follow.

The chamber was smaller than Allora had expected it to be, without the glinting golden decorations that were so prominent in the rest of the palace. The low table, couch, two chairs, desk, and wardrobe were all made of plain wood and unadorned upholstery.

"Alone in a room with so many lurking just outside the door?" The King led Allora to the couch at the center of the room. "What rumors will spread through Ilara?"

"Are we still to be married in a few weeks' time?" Allora sat, smoothing her skirts as she pretended not to notice the King judging how close to her he should sit.

"If we were to call off the wedding now, I believe Lady Gwell might summon the force of the sea to drown all Ilara. The sorcerers have been putting a great amount of effort into our union."

"It seems odd the sorcerers are spending so much time on a ceremony that requires no magic."

"The sorcerers are the guides and guards of the Guilds. A

royal wedding is of great interest to them." The King pulled a cord that had blended perfectly with the wall.

"I don't want to steal too much of your time—"

"Please do." The King took Allora's hand. "Sitting with you is infinitely better than listening to that fool ask me to endanger the city so his merchandise can pass through the gates more quickly."

Allora met the King's gaze. "Do you think of me as a child?"

"Of course not." The King wrinkled his brow. "I wouldn't marry you if I did."

"Do you think I'm foolish or simple?" Allora laid her hand on the King's cheek. The warmth of his skin brought no thrill of delight.

"No."

"Am I a prisoner?"

"Why would you think that?" The King pressed her palm to his cheek, solidifying the touch.

"I need to go to the library. I need to see the head scribe. I have been kept inside by soldiers and sorcerers for weeks. When the palace gates were still firmly shut, I did not argue. But if you are taking audiences in the throne room, if we are having dinner parties, the only reason I can see for the sorcerers insisting I stay trapped within the palace walls is that I have become their prisoner."

The King took her hand and kissed her palm. "Whatever you need from the scribes, someone else can collect for you."

"I need to see Adrial Ayres. He's as good as a brother to me. There has been so much loss and chaos. I need to see him alive and well with my own eyes."

Click.

Allora gasped, pulling away from the King as a panel in the wall popped open. A maid stepped out of the shadows, keeping her gaze down as she gave a low curtsy before placing a tray of chamb and berries on the table.

"You have lost too much." The King spoke as though the maid

weren't in the room. "I don't want to cause you any more pain, but you are to be my wife. If someone wanted to inflict further damage on Ilbrea, you would be the perfect target."

"You've said as much before." Allora waited while the maid closed the panel behind her, leaving the wall appearing to be solid. "But I will be your wife for the rest of my life. If I'm not allowed to leave this palace, then I am a prisoner, no matter how beautiful my cage."

"The sorcerers won't allow it." He poured two glasses of chamb.

"The sorcerers are not the King. Brannon, please." Allora's heart stopped as she waited to be shouted at for having been so brazenly familiar.

"How wonderful to hear you say my name." He passed her a glass of chamb. "I hear it so rarely."

"Once we're married, you'll hear it more often. But being your wife doesn't mean I won't have others I care for. Adrial almost died. I could have lost him. I need to go to him."

Brannon stared at the bubbles rising in his glass. "I'll have an escort arranged. There will have to be a sorcerer traveling with you, there's no way around that. Not while there are still demons hiding in the shadows."

"Thank you." Allora took his hand.

"Drink your chamb. You'll have to leave straight from here, before Lady Gwell finds out what we've planned."

"Would she be bold enough to make a fuss?"

Brannon leaned forward, trailing his fingers across the line of her chin before kissing her forehead. "I am so grateful to have found a wise and wonderful woman to marry. But there is much you have yet to learn about the ways of the royals. Our lot is not as simple as that of the other Guilds." He set his still-full glass on the table and went back out to the throne room.

Allora's chest deflated, as though someone had torn out the

part of her that held the pretense of bridal joy, leaving her hollow and exhausted.

Better this than being trapped in a house filled with ghosts.

She'd finished the chamb in her glass and poured another before the door to the throne room opened again.

Sorcerer Ciara Clery entered, followed by a grim-looking Agatha.

"I can see to Lady Karron on my own." Ciara waved Agatha away.

"Lady Karron has a very busy day." Agatha pulled her leather-bound book from her pocket.

"And I am sure you will rearrange all her engagements beauti-fully." Ciara curtsied to Allora. "This way, Lady Karron."

She pressed on yet another portion of the wall that seemed to be solid but very easily opened into a door.

"Are all the walls in the palace hollow?" Allora asked.

"I haven't seen them all," Ciara said. "But I have been shown a few of the more subtle ways in and out of the palace in my time protecting the King, and now you."

"Agatha"—Allora cut around the matron, ignoring her reddening face—"I hope you have a lovely morning."

Ciara stepped into the passage ahead of Allora. "Apologies for breaking custom, but your safety is my highest priority."

As soon as Allora entered the passage, Ciara flicked a finger, shutting the door behind them.

The corridor, which was narrow enough for Allora's skirt to touch both walls, had no light of its own. Only the gleam coming from Ciara's palm gave Allora any way to see.

"It seems the palace holds many secrets I'll have to learn." Allora kept her face calm, refusing to betray even the slightest hint of her trepidation at being in such a confined space with a sorcerer.

"I doubt even the King knows every mystery this palace hides." Ciara started forward, moving slowly, though the ground

MYTH AND STORM | 77

remained smooth and flat. "The Lord Map Maker does have an advantage there. He built his home and knows all its secrets. The Royal Palace has been passed down through generations of Willocs. Many of its mysteries have been lost to time."

"There are no secrets in my father's home." Allora trailed a finger along the wall. There was no grit of disuse covering the stone. "Or hidden passages."

"Then think of how lucky your children will be to grow up in a palace that offers so many intriguing things to discover."

Allora pressed her palm to the wall, letting the stone steady her as she walked.

"That is why you must be so protected." Ciara turned toward Allora, holding her light between them. "Giving hope to Ilbrea by the King gaining a queen is a lovely thought, but it's the children you will bear that truly matter to the future of our great country. The sorcerers must keep you safe so the King may have heirs."

"If Dudia wills it."

"Dudia has nothing to do with it."

Ciara turned and strode down the hall, leaving Allora in the darkness.

9

ADRIAL

"It's not much. In fact, I'm quite sure it's not right at all." Adrial moved slowly down the steps from the scribes' living quarters, carefully staying steady enough Ena wouldn't feel the need to help him. "And if the whole thing is useless, you have my sincerest apologies."

"From the sounds of it, scribe, you really think you've done a chivving awful job. Are you sure it wouldn't be better if we just went back up to your room and had tea?"

Adrial could hear the smile in her voice. He wanted to turn around and bask in the beauty of her mocking, but if he stopped now he might crack, lose his nerve and scrap the whole idea.

"We can't have tea," Adrial said. "This is much more important than tea."

"A bit of intrigue?" Ena dashed around Adrial, blocking him from the door at the bottom of the stairs. "Will we be leaving the library?"

"No."

"Pity. We should go up to Lord Karron's cliffs. I'd like to see Ilara from above one more time before I leave. Make sure all the wounds it's given me are small enough for me to carry."

"You can't leave."

"It's inevitable, scribe. I won't be allowed to lurk much longer."

"I might have a solution. And I would very much like for you to see it. Please, Ena."

"I suppose I should indulge you as you did help the common folk." Ena pushed open the door and reached for Adrial's hand. "Come, scribe. Show me your solution."

She took his arm as he stepped outside, staying close as they cut across the courtyard like being near him was the most natural thing in the world. She tensed as one of the soldiers by the gates looked their way.

"You're all right." Adrial spoke softly. "They've been ordered to keep you safe."

"A chivving demon who protects you isn't any less of a demon. Letting a monster close enough to keep you safe only makes it easier for him to attack when he decides he wants your flesh."

"If I were the monster, I would be more afraid of you."

"You're smart for a paun."

Adrial led her toward the stables, cutting along the side of the building to a door just beyond the last of the horses' stalls.

"Did you buy me a pretty pony?" Ena said. "It would be a shame to keep an animal trapped inside stone when it should be running free."

"I didn't buy you a horse." Adrial held the door open for Ena, letting her look around for a moment before following her inside.

All the grooms stopped their work to bow to him.

"Such reverence," Ena whispered.

Adrial gave the grooms a nod before heading to the very back of the stables where a set of stairs led to the loft that had, until recently, belonged to the head groom before he'd married a scribe and moved inside the library proper with his wife.

"If everything is wrong, know that I can and will fix it." Adrial led Ena up the stairs, trying to focus on his balance while his stomach bounced and twisted as his nerves convinced him he'd made a horrible mistake that would drive Ena away from him for good. "It's just a starting place."

They reached the door at the top of the steps.

He didn't let his hand tremble as he grabbed the handle. Biting his lips together, he stepped inside and held the door open for Ena.

She walked into the room and stared silently around the space.

Adrial had done everything he could in such a quick time. The old furniture had been cleared away, making space for a big worktable in the center of the room. He'd had shelves placed along one wall and left the other side open for things that needed to be hung from the rafters. Mortars, pestles, knives, pots, jars, spools of twine, every tool he could think of her needing had been gathered on the table. The windows had been carefully polished so the morning light brightened every inch of the well-dusted space.

Ena walked across the room, trailing her fingers along the table as she headed toward the door at the back of the workshop.

Adrial tucked his hands behind his back to hide their shaking as she stepped into the bedroom. He'd had a new bed put in and the little tub scrubbed out. He'd requested wildflowers be placed on the bedside table. Fresh sheets had been used to make the bed. He'd made sure all the clothes he found for her had vibrant colors. A ruby-colored skirt couldn't make up for the one she'd lost, but at least it was cheerful. He'd purchased stacks of clothes for her. Maybe too much. Maybe he shouldn't have displayed them all on the bed.

Ena stepped back out of the bedroom holding a bundle of blue blooms. The shade looked perfect against her hair.

"What is all this?" She pointed her bouquet at the worktable.

"Your new shop, if you want it." Adrial closed the door to the stairs behind him. "It's not safe for you to live in Ilara proper, but here, you can have your own space and be protected. Whatever other tools you need, I can help you find. You can make the ink for the Princess's vellum, and you'll be well paid for your work. You can stay within the library grounds without feeling like you're spending all your time pacing in a cage."

"A cage is a cage, scribe, even if you have something to keep your mind off the bars trapping you." Ena set the flowers on the table. "And even if I wanted to stay, I can't make ink if I'm not allowed to leave the library. I'd need to gather ingredients, and I can't do that stuck in here."

"I can have someone else go out and collect everything for you. You can make a list, and I'll see that you have all of it."

"All of it?" Ena reached for him.

The world seemed to stop as Adrial walked forward and took her hand.

She leaned close to him, her chest brushing against his as she whispered, "Have you forgotten the waterfall so quickly?"

"I will never forget that. And I know this isn't what you want. It's not what I want, either."

"You don't want me here with you?" Ena leaned back just far enough to look into his eyes. She tilted her head and her hair shifted, revealing the side of her neck where the faint remnants of bruises still marred her skin.

"Not like this." Adrial reached up, grazing his fingers across the marks. "I want you to be free. I want you to run in and out of the city whenever you like. I want you to race the storms so not even the wind can catch you. My soul would shatter if I never saw you again, but the last thing I want is for you to be trapped in a cage."

"But if I stay in Ilara, this is my option."

"Only for now. They will make the city safe again."

"Do you really believe that?" Ena turned away from him and pressed her hands to the top of the worktable.

"Cade and the violence he started tore a hole in Ilara. The wound he left is festering, but we will find a way to heal."

"Cade didn't leave behind a wound. He lit a fire, and it will consume us all."

"Wound, fire, it doesn't matter. It will get better. I will make things better."

Ena touched the dark stone pendant at her neck before looking to Adrial. "You have a better chance than anyone I've known. I won't be the only one to see that. Being needed for the world to change is a very dangerous fate to hold."

"Then stay in Ilara. If you think I can make a difference, help me, because I don't know what to do."

"Not everyone wants things to change. It won't be a peaceful transition. People will try to stop you. They'll try to hurt you." Ena took his hand, lacing her fingers through his.

A thrill raced up Adrial's arm as their palms pressed together.

She pulled him closer, wrapping their hands behind her back. She looked into his eyes, her mouth mere inches from his.

"I'll stay here to protect you. I can't promise how long I'll last, but I'll be here as long as I can."

"Thank you."

She rested her forehead against his shoulder, leaning into their embrace.

He laid his cheek on her hair, savoring her scent.

"Which color would you like first, scribe?"

"Any one you like. All the pages were lost. I have to start back at the beginning."

"A red filled with fire, then." She turned her head to look up at him.

"Perfect."

A thunder of footsteps pounded up the wooden stairs.

Adrial tried to let go of Ena's hands, but she held on tighter, keeping him close to her.

"Don't want to be seen with me?" Laughter glinted in Ena's eyes.

The door banged open, and Taddy tore into the room.

"Head Scribe"—his eyes went wide—"oh...sorry, Head Scribe."

Ena kissed Adrial's cheek, sending a fresh blush to his face before letting him go.

"What is it, Taddy?" Adrial straightened the front of his robes.

"Lady Karron," Taddy said, "she's come to see you. She rode in a royal carriage, and she brought a whole flock of soldiers and a sorcerer with her."

"Where is she?" Adrial asked.

"She asked to be brought to your sitting room even though she's going to be the Queen soon. I'm having tea sent up, and I ran to get you, but I don't know if there's anything else I should be doing because she will be the Queen."

"Did you say *the Queen?*" Ena picked up her flowers.

"Yes," Taddy said. "She's marrying the King in a few weeks."

"Well, if *the* future Queen of Ilbrea is here, I suppose you should go, scribe." Ena pulled one of the flowers from her bouquet and tucked it behind her ear. "What pleasure could I possibly offer that royalty can't?"

Taddy's face turned bright red.

"Out. Both of you." Ena shooed them toward the door. "I have to organize my shop."

"Right." Adrial tried to ignore the pang of regret in his stomach. "You'll bring me a list of everything you need?"

"Just be sure to send someone who actually knows the difference between one flower and another to collect my supplies. Not all purple petals work the same."

"I'll make sure they're the best." Adrial bowed to Ena as he backed toward the door. "I look forward to being able to use your inks again."

Adrial had stepped onto the top stair when Ena spoke again.

"Scribe, thank you."

He looked back.

Ena had begun organizing her shelves, turned away from Adrial like she hadn't said anything at all.

"Thank you for staying." He shut the door and hurried after Taddy before his face could properly catch on fire.

"I'm glad she's not leaving," Taddy said as they cut across the courtyard.

"She's a very talented inker. And she saved both our lives."

"It's not just that, sir. You're happier when she's around."

"I am, Taddy." Adrial allowed himself a smile. "I truly am."

A line of soldiers guarded the door to the scribes' quarters. They let Adrial and Taddy pass without trouble. Two more soldiers waited at the top of the stairs with another pair flanking the door to Adrial's sitting room.

"Taddy, will you check on the tea?" Adrial asked.

His apprentice's shoulders sagged.

"You can bring the tray up yourself, if you like," Adrial said.

Taddy bolted down the hall toward the kitchens.

"He's a good apprentice," Adrial said to the soldiers. "Just gets a bit eager sometimes."

Neither of the soldiers responded.

"Right, then. I'll just…"

It's only Allora. In your own sitting room.

Adrial stepped between the soldiers and opened his door.

"Adrial." Allora stood from her seat, reaching for his hands. "Are you all right? I've wanted to come and see you. I promise I have."

"I know." Adrial hid his limp as best he could as he crossed to her. "Ilara is still settling down after the terrible violence, and you are to be our Queen soon enough."

"That doesn't make me care for you any less." Allora brushed his hair away from his face, studying him as though checking for lingering damage. "They told me the sorcerers had cared for you. If you were injured badly enough to be asleep for so long—"

"Sometimes, a forced slumber is the best means of healing."

Adrial turned toward the unfamiliar voice.

A dark-haired woman in purple sorcerer's robes stood in the corner.

"The sorcerers who use magic to heal will often intentionally keep their patients asleep," the woman said. "It makes their work easier and gives the afflicted a better chance to heal."

"I am grateful for whatever they did to help me." Adrial bowed to the sorcerer. "I should have died on that dark street. I now owe my life to several people."

"Including that inker?" Allora sat back down, leaving a place for Adrial to join her on the couch.

"Especially Ena." Adrial glanced to the sorcerer, hesitating before sitting with his back to the woman. "The soldiers wouldn't have found me if she hadn't told them where I was. And I'd have been dead before they arrived if she hadn't defended me."

"Then I owe her a debt," Allora said, "as loath as I am to admit it. But please promise to be careful with that one, Adrial. Wild animals may be beautiful, but they are also prone to bite."

"I…" The tingle of the sorcerer's gaze on the back of his neck made Adrial pause. "I've heard a similar warning before. But I have experienced enough pain to know where it is likely to come from and when it is worth the risk."

"My sweet, Adrial." Allora took his hand. "I've missed you."

"Tell me how you are," Adrial said. "How is life at the palace?"

"It's beautiful and lonesome. I have everything I ask for. I spend my days in fittings for gowns some women would murder to own. I am protected by Ilbrea's finest soldiers. I am very fortunate, though I can't help but miss the companionship of our little clan."

If Adrial hadn't known Allora for so long, he might not have noticed the sparkle of unshed tears in her eyes.

"I miss them, too," Adrial said. "Do you think they would allow me to come visit you at the palace?"

"Who is they?" Allora asked. "My soldiers or your scribes' guards?"

"It would be safer for the head scribe to come to the palace than to risk Lady Karron traveling through the city," the sorcerer said. "While the head scribe is a valuable asset to the Guilds, he does not rate the same profile with the masses as does the future Queen."

"Thank you, Sorcerer Clery." Allora gave the sorcerer a nod.

"I've asked you to call me Ciara," the sorcerer said. "After all, you and I will be spending so much of our time together."

"Of course." Allora's smile did not reach her eyes.

"I'll ask Lord Gareth if he might allow me to visit you at the Royal Palace," Adrial said. "It's been a long time since I've seen the gardens on the grounds."

"Tell Lord Gareth to request a sorcerer for your guard, Head Scribe." Ciara stepped closer to them. "It would allow you a greater level of security, and the Sorcerers Guild is happy to aid in your protection."

"That's very kind of you," Adrial said, "but I would hate to bother Lady Gwell."

"It would be no bother," Ciara said. "I can give the order to provide you an escort myself. I am Lady Gwell's second. Assigning a guard is well within my purview."

"You're Lady Gwell's second?" Allora said.

"Why do you think I've been granted the honor of ensuring the protection of our future Queen? Lady Gwell is waiting to announce my ascension until the next council meeting. But my place has already been confirmed within the Sorcerers Tower."

"Congratulations," Adrial said.

"What happened to Sorcerer Roo?" Allora asked.

There was a slim moment when Adrial thought he saw a hint of a smile flash through the sorcerer's eyes.

"I suppose they have been keeping it quiet," Ciara said. "Lady Gwell forbade the Sailors Guild to speak of it, and sorcerers rarely converse with those outside our ranks. The ship Sorcerer Roo was sailing on has been lost at sea."

"What?" Allora said.

Adrial gripped her hand, trying to stop the horrible way the room had started tilting.

"The voyage is over three weeks late in returning and hasn't been sighted anywhere," Ciara said. "We can only assume the ship has sunk and must consider all aboard lost."

"Kai." Saying his friend's name stole all the breath from Adrial's lungs. "Kai was on that ship."

"Then he was a brave sailor and will be honored for his sacrifice to the Guilds." Ciara gave what might have been mistaken for a sympathetic nod. "They went out to test an experimental improvement to a sail. Everyone on the ship knew the risk before leaving port. They are heroes to the Guilds. Their lives were not lost in vain. The work—"

"They're not dead," Allora said. "If you haven't gotten word of a shipwreck, they aren't dead."

"Lady Karron," Ciara said, "many ships are lost at sea without any trace."

"No." Allora stood, yanking Adrial to his feet to stand beside her. "I lost Niko. He was killed in the eastern mountains. His party searched for him, and we know he's gone. They sent confirmation. They wrote me a letter. He lost his life in service to the Guilds. You can't say Kai is dead without even searching for his ship."

"There is nowhere to search, Lady Karron," Ciara said. "I'm afraid you don't understand how these things work."

"You don't know Kai!" Allora shouted. "He could swim across the Arion Sea and survive. He was born to live on a boat. The sea itself would shelter him before taking his life. I know, I've witnessed the miracle of it myself. If the Sorcerers Guild won't look for Petra Roo, then I will have the King send a search party for the sailors. You do not write members of the Guilds off as dead just because it would be difficult to find them."

"Yes, Lady Karron." Ciara bowed.

"It was lovely to see you Adrial, but apparently I have urgent business with my future husband." Allora leaned in to kiss Adrial's cheek. "Tell my father." She whispered the words so softly, Adrial almost thought he'd imagined them. "I look forward to visiting with you at the palace."

Allora strode out of the room, the rustling of her skirts not quite hiding the anger betrayed by her heavy footsteps.

"It was a pleasure meeting you, Head Scribe," Ciara said.

"You as well. Thank you for protecting Lady Karron."

Ciara had left the room and closed the door behind her before Adrial had even finished speaking.

10

KAI

"It doesn't matter what you chivving well want." Kai gripped the beam in the captain's cabin, refusing to let his rage steal his footing, even as the ship lurched. "We're going to run out of fresh water. We're going to run out of food. We were only outfitted for a five-day journey!"

Petra Roo sat in the chair behind the captain's desk, the chamb in her glass not spilling despite the storm tossing the ship. She lifted her glass, studying the bubbles, not responding to Kai.

"Sorcerer Roo." Kai dared to venture a step closer. "The captain will not leave his post to come speak to you. Do you understand what that means?"

"That he's chosen to send his second to beg me to allow the ship to return to port." Sorcerer Roo sipped her chamb.

"That the ship is in so much danger, the captain needs to be on the deck," Kai said.

The wood of the hull groaned, as though wanting to aid in Kai's plea.

"The ship is in danger?" Sorcerer Roo said. "From this storm?"

"We're in the southern storms." Kai took another lurching step forward, planting his hands on the desk, looming over the second-in-command of the Sorcerers Guild. "More ships have been lost here than any other place the Ilbrean fleet has sailed."

"And we're still afloat." Sorcerer Roo leaned back in her seat as though she hadn't a care in the world. "The sail has held. The hull has held. Do you know why, Sailor Saso?"

"Because the gods aren't chivving well done with us yet." Kai spoke through gritted teeth.

"The gods mean nothing. They have done nothing to aid this ship. My magic holds up the sail. My magic keeps this ship afloat."

"Your magic is not stronger than the sea!"

"You are in no position to judge me or the might of the Sorcerers Guild."

A shout came from the deck.

Kai gripped the edge of the desk, willing himself not to wonder if another sailor had gone overboard. The fury of the storm wouldn't allow rescue or recovery. Anyone who fell into the waves would be lost forever. No body. No hope of survival.

"You're right," Kai said. "I am in no place to judge the power you hold over this ship. I cannot hope to fully understand what the Sorcerers Guild is truly capable of. But I know the sea, Sorcerer Roo. There is a worse storm coming in from the east, I can feel it cutting through the waves that are already battering us. We need to head north now, before the new front arrives.

"We have to make for the ports of Pamerane. We need fresh water and food. We need to get out of the cycle of the southern storms before not even your power can hold this ship together. You've proven your point. The sail the sorcerers provided is stronger than anything made by non-magical means. The Lord Map Maker's journey to the southern islands will be more likely to succeed with sorcerers on board the ship and controlling the sails."

"I've been saying that for weeks." Sorcerer Roo set down her chamb.

The ship lurched starboard. Sorcerer Roo's glass still didn't spill even as Kai stumbled and a fresh round of shouts came from the deck.

"Let us sail north," Kai said.

"We can make it farther. We're nearly to the southern islands. We'll pick one and go ashore. Find an artifact, something to bring the King that will prove how useless the Sailors Guild is without the aid of magic."

"This ship was not fitted to reach the islands. We have to go back."

"The matter is not up for discussion. This ship will continue south."

Kai tamped down his rage. "Have you ever been shipwrecked, Sorcerer Roo?"

"Of course not." She stood without wavering, walking to the cabinets without letting the rocking of the ship affect her gait.

"I have. Having a ship break apart beneath your feet is a chivving awful feeling. Just remember to relax. When you hit the water, find up before you start swimming. Grab hold of whatever debris you can, and don't even start counting time. If you know how long you've been adrift, you're more likely to let go of the slim safety you've found and drown."

"How very shocking." She refilled her glass of chamb, frowning at the overabundance of bubbles coming out of the jostled bottle.

"You're condemning good sailors to their deaths. You may not believe the gods control the sea, but know that whoever greets you after you drown will count the lives lost on this journey as murder."

"Murder? I've hardly raised a hand to any of you."

"Letting good men drown for your own chivving pride is just as bad as driving a knife into an innocent man's back." Kai headed toward the cabin door. "The gods know the truth of it even if you're too foolish to see the depth of your own evil."

Bowing his head against the rain, he shoved the door open and stepped out onto the deck.

The howling of the wind and groaning of the hull surrounded him as the rain pounded down, blurring his vision. He glanced back into the captain's cabin, where Sorcerer Roo sat in her magically made domain of peace.

"Chivving slitch." Kai spat the rain from his mouth and slammed the door shut. He bent into the wind, grabbing onto the railing to drag himself up to the poop deck.

The captain stood at the helm, bracing himself against the storm.

He should have been shouting orders to the crew or screaming at the gods.

But they'd been trapped in the storm for so long, there were no more orders to shout, and the one to blame for their fate sat in the cabin below the captain's feet, sipping the captain's chamb.

"Did we lose another?" Kai shouted in the captain's ear.

"Yes."

"Who?" Kai scanned the men on the deck, searching through the rain-blurred figures, trying to spot who might be missing. Some of the sailors were below, resting as best they could before charging back into the battle against the storm. He couldn't remember whose turn it had been to hide from the rain.

"We don't know yet," the captain said.

Kai swiped the rain from his eyes, searching through the shadows again.

There, near the bow, gripping the rail as though preparing to fight the storm singlehanded—

"What did the chivving sorcerer say?" The captain braced the wheel as a massive swell raced toward them.

Kai staggered as the ship took a hit from the sea as though the fist of a god had pummeled their hull.

"To keep heading south," Kai shouted. "She wants to reach the islands, sir. She's not going to let us change course."

Lightning split the sky.

Kai looked up toward the sail, waiting for the sorcerers' magic to falter and their pretty purple sail to catch fire and doom them all. But the lightning stayed away from the sail as though chivvying Sorcerer Roo had given the sky a command.

"She's sending us to our deaths, and she doesn't even know it." Kai hated to shout the words, but it was the only way to be heard over the storm.

"The sorcerers have damned us all." The captain pounded his fist against the wheel. "We've no way out of this."

"Turn the ship around, sir. If the sea is going to take us, I'd rather be lost following my captain's commands than obeying any sorcerer. We are sailors, sir. We follow only the Sailors Guild. Let us die as free men."

The captain shut his eyes for a moment, as though trying to block out the storm, or perhaps just to pretend he were anywhere else.

"Bring her around!" the captain bellowed. "All hands, bring her around. We're heading north!"

A tired shout of something like hope came from the men on the deck.

"Thank you, sir." Kai gripped the railing with both hands, fighting against the tilting of the ship as he hurried to join the other men on the line.

"Grab the line!" The shout carried through the darkness.

The sailors dashed through the rain with more vigor than they'd had in weeks.

"What's happening?" Sorcerer Roo's voice sliced through the storm.

The men froze under the sorcerer's glare.

She stalked toward them, the rain not touching her, an eerie light glowing around her, allowing all of them to see the smile that curved her lips. "I thought I heard someone say to turn the ship north, but that can't be. My orders are to continue south."

"Do as your captain commands," Kai shouted to the men as he backed away from them. "Sorcerer Roo, the captain has made the decision to change our course."

"The captain has no right to make any decisions." Sorcerer Roo followed Kai, the same awful smile still on her lips. "I think the men would agree." She looked toward the sailors who fought desperately to manage the lines against the will of the wind.

"He's protecting his men," Kai shouted, pulling Sorcerer Roo's gaze back to himself.

"They are the Guilds' men. They are *my* men. Your captain is nothing but a nuisance. A boil to be burned away." The air around Sorcerer Roo began to sizzle, turning the pounding rain to steam that surrounded her like a shroud.

"You can tell Lord Nevon that when we return to Ilara." Kai backed toward the starboard rail. "But if we don't turn north now, none of us will ever see land again."

"You will see land again when I allow it. You are only alive because I have not yet chosen to kill you." Her shroud of steam began to crackle and spark.

"Your magic is very impressive." Kai grinned as though he were trying to lure a girl into a dance instead of a chivving monster away from the men fighting to save their ship. "It makes me wonder why Lady Gwell would send her second out on a sailing run. If she's made you this determined to reach the southern islands, maybe she was hoping you wouldn't make it back. Has the Lady Sorcerer decided to replace you? What did you do to earn her ire?"

"You're trying to convince me to hurt you." The sparks surrounding her merged together, forming a flame in her palm. "Do you think your death will convince me to sail north?"

"No, miss. Just counting on you not knowing how to change our course back to south once we're heading north."

"You arrogant rotta filth." The flames in Sorcerer Roo's hand grew. "Lord Karron should have left you—"

Crack.

Kai froze, waiting for the deck to split beneath his feet.

Sorcerer Roo staggered sideways. The flames in her palm flickered.

Crack!

She lurched forward, tumbling headfirst over the rail and plunging into the sea.

Drew stood in her place, panting, a board clutched in his hand.

"Drew, what did you do?" Kai stared into the sea, waiting for the sorcerer to fly back out of the depths and kill them all. "What did you do?"

"Did she hurt you?"

"No." Kai couldn't pull his gaze away from the fury of the waves. "We have to fish her out."

"We have to help get the ship turned around. Kai." Drew gripped Kai's arm. "You don't come back from going overboard in a storm like this. Not even magic can save a monster from the sea."

Kai looked at Drew, searching his face for some sign of a spell sent to punish his friend.

"We've got to get on the line." Drew pitched the board into the waves. "We're getting out of this chivving storm."

Kai followed Drew back to the pack of sailors battling the sea.

He fixed his mind on the ropes, the sail, the speed of the wind, the strength of the waves. That battle, he had prepared for. Had spent his life training for.

"Winds worsening from the east!" The shout carried over the deck.

His dread of the sorcerer below the waves, of what one life might cost them all...that foe, he would face once they escaped the storm.

He let the line drag against his palms. The pain burned away all worries beyond the wind.

11

MARA

Flowers flourished in the frozen courtyard outside their window, the pale pinks and lavenders seeming impossible against the ice that surrounded the blooms. The benches in the garden, the base of the flowing fountain, the footpaths, the ever-glowing roof of the cavern high above—all of it had been formed of ice by some magic Mara had yet to understand.

The room she and Tham had been locked in for days had been built of ice as well. The wood of the bed, table, and chairs offered a hint of normality, as did the fur blankets and rug. But the fire burning in the sculpted ice hearth stole any hope Mara had of ignoring the magical making of their chamber.

Tham draped a fur around her before she could begin to shiver.

"You need to stay warm." He kissed the top of her head.

"I've started getting used to the cold." She wrapped her arms around him, nestling him into her furs. "I can see my breath fogging in front of me, but my fingers don't go numb."

"I'm not sure I could ever get used to the ice." Tham held Mara close, surrounding her with his warmth. "Or the unchanging light. Day should always be followed by night. How do the people here survive without it?"

"I'm not sure they know it should be different." She pressed her ear to his chest, letting the steady rhythm of his heartbeat ease the horrible fear that gnawed at her gut.

He is alive. He is alive, and I will not let them take him from me.

"You should go back to bed," Mara said. "Rest."

"No."

"We've been in here for days. Pacing won't change anything. There's nothing more for us to see out our window. Sleep while you have the chance."

"I've slept enough for a lifetime."

"You've been ill."

"I've been healed." He let go of Mara and walked across the fur rug to the flames dancing in the impossible, frozen hearth.

"Being healed doesn't mean you don't need rest." Mara pressed her palms to the sides of her legs as she walked, trying to mute the unfamiliar swishing of her skirts as she joined Tham who stared into the flames. "I almost lost you, Tham. Whatever horrible thing kept you asleep nearly stole you from me."

Mara let the silence hang in the air for a moment, waiting for Tham to tell her what shadows still made him shake when he slept and what fear made his fists tighten like he was aching for a weapon in his hands.

"If they wanted to murder us while we slept, they would have done it already," Mara said. "We can't get out. We've no chance of finding where they're holding Elver and Kegan."

"Or if they're even awake." A darkness passed behind Tham's eyes. "Or alive."

"We'll figure out how to help them." Mara took Tham's face in her hands. The texture of his beard still felt foreign to her fingers.

Their captors had let them bathe and had provided them new clothes. They'd given Mara fur slippers to protect her feet from the chill of the floor and a finely stitched, gray dress, embroidered with a white pattern of ice crystals along the bottom. They'd given Tham a jacket, pants, and thick fur boots. Purchasing the garments in Ilara would have cost a good amount of gold. Such gifts would never be offered to prisoners of the Guilds.

But their captors didn't seem concerned with the cost of keeping Mara and Tham as prisoners. Food, drink, soap, clothes—everything had appeared inside their door. However, their captors hadn't been foolish enough to give Tham a knife or straight blade to shave with.

Mara shut her eyes, pushing her panic and anger behind her gratitude.

He's alive, and we're together. We'll escape together.

Tham took her hand and kissed her palm. He met Mara's gaze and gave her the tiniest nod.

"If you're feeling too well to need more rest," Mara said, "perhaps we should ask our hosts for a book to read. Or a tour of their home. The courtyard outside is so lovely, there's got to be more wonders to see."

Tham squeezed her hand.

Mara swallowed her nerves. "I'm not exactly sure how we should ask for anything. Everything just appears when we sleep. Should we try to fall asleep and see if we wake up outside this room?"

Tham gave a laugh only a stranger might think was real.

"I suppose that is foolish." Mara headed toward the window. "It would be rude to make whatever poor soul they have watching us carry us around while we sleep. I wonder how they chose who would have the bland duty of guarding us, just waiting for us to nod off so they could deliver food without us seeing them."

"I'd have given the task to a young one. Someone desperate to prove their worth."

"Or as a last chance for a getch who isn't very good at being a guard." Mara leaned against the window frame. "Waiting to flit in like a fairy in a children's story. Our guard is a legend in the making. I wonder how many myths were born of this place?"

The courtyard below their window was empty, as it had been for as long as Mara and Tham had been locked in their ice chamber.

"My curiosity is overwhelming. I think I might just shout out the window and see if anyone knows if there are legends of the fairy-like ice guard who brings trays of food while people sleep." Mara looked to Tham. He didn't speak, but he didn't try to stop her either as she leaned out the window and shouted, "Does anyone know how our guard was chosen? Does it have to do with the magic in—"

"Do not shout."

Tham grabbed Mara, tucking her behind him before she could fully turn to see who had spoken.

"Disturbing the peace within the palace is unwise." A man in a pale blue uniform stepped farther into the room, past the place where their food tray appeared every morning.

"Oh." Mara sidestepped to stand next to Tham, her arm pressing against his. "My apologies. If I'd known we were in a palace, I never would have dreamt of causing any commotion."

"It is a privilege to be a guest of the Regent," the man said. "We can easily move you both back to the cells."

Tham's arm tensed.

Mara fought the instinct to take his hand. "We're guests? I hadn't realized. Are all the Regent's guests locked in? Does the Regent make a habit of not greeting their guests?"

The man narrowed his eyes.

"Again, I apologize if I've caused offense." Mara offered the man a smile and a nod. "Where we come from, Tham and I would be considered prisoners. You would be our jailer. The Regent would be our captor. And keeping us locked in this room, away from the others in our party, would most definitely be described as an act of hostility toward the Guilds of Ilbrea."

"You aren't in Ilbrea," the man said.

"Clearly," Mara said. "But now that you've kindly come in to speak to us, tell your Regent I request an audience."

The man shifted his glare between Mara and Tham for a moment before turning around and walking into the wall of ice.

Mara didn't breathe again until his figure had disappeared through the blue.

"I'm afraid neither of us was right," Mara said. "They seem to have chosen our guard for his lovely disposition."

Tham kissed Mara's cheek before whispering in her ear, "Allora would be so proud."

ALLORA

"You seem to be quite confused, Agatha." Allora allowed King Brannon to keep leading her down the shaded garden path. "Please permit me to clarify. There are things I find far more important than the minutia of my wedding dress."

Brannon placed his hand over Allora's, tightening her grip on his arm.

"But, Lady Karron," Agatha said, bustling up to walk just behind Allora's shoulder, "we have scheduled this walk so you and your betrothed might discuss the details of the wedding."

"What details am I meant to fuss over now?" Allora focused her gaze on the white bark of the trees surrounding the path rather than glance back at the woman's face and risk it becoming even more difficult to keep her anger from her tone.

"There is no need to fuss, Lady Karron," Agatha said. "Though you do need to decide what symbolism you would like to carry with you in the embroidery on the train of your gown. There is also the question of exactly what flowers you would like adorning the royal carriage. Then, of course, the flowers for the cathedral itself."

Brannon guided Allora off the path and to a bench sheltered by trees dripping with pale purple petals.

"You also must choose what entertainment you would like for the festivities once the guests retire to the palace for the celebration after the ceremony," Agatha pressed on. "The decorations need to be chosen. The placement on the grounds is also a pivotal decision, as it will affect what options you have for the grand display. Of course, fireworks are a very suitable choice. The sorcerers have also suggested they might put on an exhibition of a more magical making."

Allora sat and looked beyond Agatha to Ciara and the soldiers following their party. "Ciara, would you mind coming here for a moment?"

Ciara ignored Agatha's huffing as she made her way to the bench. "Lady Karron. Your Majesty." She bowed deeply.

"Ciara, Princess Illia is to wed Prince Dagon of Wyrain less than two years after the King and I are to be married," Allora said.

"That is correct, Lady Karron," Ciara said.

"The last thing I want is for Princess Illia to feel shunted aside as though I have stolen something from her by being married first," Allora said. "Her wedding needs to be the event the elite of Ilara remember, not mine."

"But you are marrying the King," Ciara said.

"I am marrying a recent widower in the wake of a deadly riot," Allora said.

Brannon squeezed her hand.

Allora slipped out of his grip, her heart leaping into her throat as she brazenly placed her hand on his knee.

"I'm sure whatever we use for the wedding will be lovely," Allora said. "But please ask Princess Illia what she would prefer for her wedding. If she would like fireworks, we will have the sorcerers' display. If she would like roses, we will have lilies. Let her choose first, and I will gladly use whatever options are left. I do not want to create strife with my new sister as I enter into my marriage."

"You are very wise, Lady Karron. I will request a list from the Princess, and we will make our plans accordingly." Ciara bowed.

"Now that we've finished the wedding planning," Brannon said, "would you all give me some time alone with my betrothed?"

Agatha's face reddened. "Yes, Your Majesty." She bowed and walked away with the stiff gait of one who longed to stomp but knew better than to dare.

"Your Majesty." Ciara bowed and waved to the soldiers.

The men fanned out, forming a circle around the bench, giving enough room that Brannon and Allora could speak without being heard, but not nearly enough for the illusion of solitude to be complete.

Ciara waited until the soldiers were all in place before walking down the path, stopping just within sight.

The purple of her robes shone like a beacon. Though, whether the imposing color was a threat or a promise of safety, Allora didn't know.

"It's very kind of you"—Brannon placed his hand on top of Allora's—"deferring to Illia's choices on the wedding plans. You don't have to."

"She's finally excited to be marrying Prince Dagon. I refuse to let our wedding taint her joy. Illia will be leaving her home. Let her last memory here be perfect. Besides, I care very little for the wedding ceremony."

Brannon lifted her hand, pressing her fingers to his lips. "Are you regretting your choice to marry me?"

Allora took a deep breath, testing her soul for cracks before speaking. "No. I don't regret it. And I appreciate the value of pageantry in maintaining the stability of the Guilds within Ilbrea.

The people need to see you as powerful and me as perfect. But what is embroidered on the hem of my train will only be remembered for a week, and even then, only by the people who bothered to notice."

"You are more sensible than anyone gives you credit for." He reached up, grazing her cheek with his fingers before brushing an imagined stray hair behind her ear.

"How can I fuss about wedding plans when my friend is missing?" Allora leaned into his touch. "Tell me you've done something to find Kai's ship. Tell me there will be a search."

"I've spoken to the Sailors Guild—"

"And?"

"They've gladly agreed to mount a search. They've asked for the map makers' aid. Lord Nevon and Lord Karron are coming to meet with me this afternoon. If all goes well, the search party will set sail within the next two days."

"Thank you, Brannon." Tears burned in Allora's eyes.

He leaned forward, kissing her forehead. When he backed away, he left barely any space between them.

"If I earn half the devotion as your husband as you give to your friends, I will be a very lucky man."

"Kai is family. I know he's alive. Thank you for helping me find him."

"It's the sailors and map makers who will be doing the real work." He looked to their joined hands. "Allora, your father will be here in a few hours. He's requested to see you."

Allora tipped her chin down. She was so near Brannon's shoulder. It would be easy to lean against him and let him offer the support she so desperately needed.

"I'm not ready to see him. I'm not ready to beg his forgiveness or demand his apology. I…"

"You don't have to explain." Brannon tipped her chin up. "I will offer my apologies first."

"You?"

"I stole his daughter, the jewel of his home. I may be offering you a kingdom, but that won't lessen the sting your father feels."

"You're a good man, Brannon Willoc."

"I only hope to be the sort of king and husband that will make you glad to have placed your faith in me."

He leaned forward, brushing his lips against hers.

Allora's breath caught in her chest as he pulled away just enough to meet her gaze with his teal eyes before leaning back in and kissing her in earnest. He placed one hand on her waist and tangled the other in her hair, drawing her closer.

She laid her hands on his chest, trying to find the joy in feeling his heart racing beneath her palms. She focused on the feel of his lips—strong and confident as he kissed her—searching for the pleasure that should come with being touched by a handsome man. The deeply craved thrill of being desired. Of having a man lose himself in the wanting of her.

It's not right. It's not him.

He shifted away from her lips, kissing the side of her neck, and the hollow of her collarbone. He slid his hand from her waist to her ribs, freezing just shy of touching her breast.

He rested his forehead against her neck for a moment, taking a shuddering breath before lowering his hand back to her waist.

"You are magnificent, Allora." He sat up, his gaze locked on her lips. "The wedding ceremony may not matter much to you. But I think we will find joy in our married life."

Allora touched his cheek, drawing him closer. She let her lips brush against his as she whispered, "Go, Brannon, before the soldiers all die of shock."

He kissed her one more time, lingering for a moment before standing as though ready to end their meeting on the price of grain.

"I look forward to our next walk." Brannon bowed. "And for

what it's worth, you will be a lovely bride even if they dress you in a sack." He strode down the path toward the palace.

Half the soldiers followed in his wake. The other half tightened their circle around Allora.

Like a noose tied for my own protection.

"Lady Karron." Ciara breezed back down the path. "Would you like to stay in the gardens for a while longer? Or would you prefer for me to have someone run ahead and order your lunch to be prepared?"

"I'll stay out here. I don't fancy going back to the palace at the moment."

"Of course." Ciara bowed. "I must say, Lady Karron, as upset as poor Agatha may be at a lack of movement on the wedding plans, at least we've made strides toward joyful prospects for the wedding night."

"Ciara." Heat rose in Allora's cheeks.

"There is nothing to be embarrassed about, Lady Karron. The King will be visiting your bed as often as is necessary for an heir to be conceived within the first month of your marriage. The task of such virulent coupling can either be traumatic or pleasurable."

"The intimacy between the King and me is a private matter that you will have no knowledge of or say in." Allora stood, heading down the path as the foolish notion that she might actually be able to escape the sorcerer told her to flee.

"That is quite wrong, Lady Karron."

A barrier, like a hand knocking into her ribs, blocked Allora's path. Her chest ached as she backed away from the invisible spell.

"Do not use your magic on me," Allora said.

"Your duty as a wife will be done," Ciara said. "By force or by choice, it makes no difference to us. It is best that you understand these expectations now. It will ease your wedding night."

"I will be the Queen of Ilbrea." Allora rounded on the sorcerer. "I will not be bullied or abused by you or anyone else."

An ice-cold touch forced Allora's chin up before wrapping around her throat.

"I have heard those words before, Lady Karron. Do not make the same mistakes as your predecessor. It would be unwise to risk enduring a similar fate."

13

NIKO

I had never thought of the darkness as an enemy. Nighttime gave me the peace to dream of pleasure, and shadows held mysteries for me to explore.

Now, I fear the darkness will be my undoing.

I don't know how long I've spent in the black. I don't know how far belowground the mountain has forced me.

If the compass on my arm holds true, I could be directly beneath Ilara right now. But there is no path for me to climb up to you.

I am trying. I swear on everything I am, with every step, I am trying to come home to you.

Knowing you are waiting for me is the hope I cling to.

Yours in darkness and in light,

Niko

14

MARA

I miss the wind whipping through my hair. I miss the magic tickling the back of my mind as it draws my maps.

Mara sat across from Tham, sipping the tea that had appeared with their tray of food for the day.

Tham took his time, carefully portioning out their meals, saving the dried meat and cheese for later in the day, choosing bread and fruit for their breakfast. In all the time they'd been locked in their ice chamber, they'd never run out of food. Still, Tham rationed everything, and Mara knew enough about the dark and hunger-filled years of his life before he'd joined the Karron clan to not question his morning ritual.

When he finally began to eat, Mara let her ankle press against his. A flare of joy sparked in her chest as a hint of a smile lifted the corners of Tham's eyes.

I miss discovering new places. I miss finding magic where none should exist.

She reached across the table, pouring Tham a second cup of tea. He caught her hand, kissing her fingers before letting go.

Such a simple thing. A quick touch. A tiny show of affection.

I miss knowing I'm a part of the Map Makers Guild. I miss helping to build the Guild's legacy.

I'd trade it all to share breakfast with him every morning.

Mara touched the place on her arm where the sorcerer had marked her with the symbol of the Map Makers the day she'd been accepted into the Guild. She could feel the magic of the compass even through the fabric of her sleeve.

"Mara?" Tham said.

"When we get back to Ilara, I'm going to spend a day sitting by the Arion Sea." Mara pressed her face into a smile. "Just watch the waves and smell the salt in the air. Will you sit with me?"

"If you want me to."

"I always want you beside me." Mara sipped her tea, trying to drown the growing knot in her throat.

"We could go north of the city." Tham leaned toward her, offering his hand. "There are some beautiful places where no one will see us."

"But what if—" A shimmer in the wall silenced Mara.

Tham sprang to his feet, looking to the place where their guard had appeared once before.

Mara palmed her fork, hiding it in the folds of her skirt as she stood.

The woman who'd woken Tham stepped out of the ice. She looked from Mara to Tham before smiling. The expression did not reach her sapphire eyes.

"It's good to see you've both recovered so well." The woman stepped farther into the room. "It takes some people a very long time to regain any sort of strength after the ice has filled them."

"We've been well cared for," Mara said.

"Of course," the woman said. "I made sure of it."

"What about the other two from our journey?" Mara cut around the table to stand beside Tham, keeping the fork hidden in her skirt. "Have they been living here, too?"

"No." The woman walked toward the window, not looking at Tham or Mara, even as she passed within inches of them.

"Where are they?" Tham asked.

"One is still ill from the ice. He's not fit to be in a room on his own. And the other"—the woman looked back to them, as though not wanting to miss their expression—"is not currently amenable to any arrangement that would allow him to be moved out of his cell."

"He's still in a cell?" Mara asked.

Tham gripped her wrist, keeping the hand that held her poor weapon hidden.

"He's given me no choice," the woman said. "The city of Isfol is our sanctuary. It is a place of peace. Having rumors flying on the breeze that an enemy is living within our safe haven? I'd rather have your compatriots' blood on my hands than risk panic spreading amongst my people."

"Are you the Regent?" Mara asked.

"My father is the Regent. I am a lowly princess who has yet to seize her rightful throne." The Princess met Mara's gaze. "Ilbrea is not the only kingdom that hobbles its women."

"That's a pity to hear, Your Highness." Mara curtsied. "I'm sorry we were never properly introduced when you visited my cell."

"I didn't introduce myself to your dogs, whom I so graciously rescued, either," the Princess said. "I fed them and put them in kennels where they would be properly taken care of."

"I appreciate the comforts you've provided us," Mara said, "and our dogs. But since I am capable of speech, I would like to know who I am speaking to."

"Princess Ronya Kian of the Ice Walkers," Ronya said. "Daughter of Regent Ture Kian. If you had any business being in the white mountains, both of our names would terrify you."

"I've been told many things should terrify me," Mara said. "They rarely do."

"There are two sorts of people who lack fear in the face of monsters," Ronya said. "Heroes and fools."

"How clever," Mara said.

Tham tightened his grip on Mara's wrist as he shifted closer to her, placing his shoulder in front of hers.

Not every battle needs to be fought, a voice that sounded like Allora's whispered in Mara's mind.

"I would like to petition for our freedom and the freedom of the others in our party," Mara said. "I'll negotiate with you, if you like, or with the Regent, if I must."

"Negotiate?" Ronya laughed. "What will you negotiate with? The sleds we've already taken? Will you offer to let me keep your dogs? You won't make it back to Ilbrea without them."

"If you want gold, the Guilds will pay for our safe return," Tham said.

The Princess studied Tham, starting with his boots and working her way up. She gave a sly smile when she finally reached his face.

Mara tightened her grip on her fork.

"I have no taste for your Guilds' gold, Ilbrean," Ronya said. "My duty is to protect my people. And secrecy has long been our most valuable defense."

"We won't ask the Guilds for payment, then," Mara said. "We can go straight to the Lord Map Maker. We lived as his wards, and Lord Karron's discretion can be trusted."

"I hope I am never foolish enough to rely on the discretion of someone vouched for by a stranger," Ronya said.

"Tell us what our freedom will cost," Tham said.

"I thought I had made that clear." Ronya fixed her cold gaze on Mara. "I want to get to know you. I want to know all about you and Ilbrea. Such a fascinating country just south of our mountains. So many questions I'd like answered."

A wave of ice ran up Mara's back, as though frozen fingers trailed along her spine.

"I would be happy to tell you about Ilbrea," Mara said, "as soon as we can see Elver and Kegan. I want to make sure they'll be ready for the journey home."

Ronya laughed and stepped closer to Mara.

Tham tensed, letting go of Mara's wrist, reaching an arm in front of her as though preparing to block an attack.

"Silly Tham." Ronya bent and kissed the back of his hand. "If I'd wanted to hurt Mara, I would have let her watch you slowly die as the ice destroyed your veins. I wish you no harm. In fact, I would like nothing better than to call you a friend. But, despite the kindness that fills my heart, I cannot risk the safety of my people by allowing strangers who have discovered our home to wander back into the outside world."

"So you'll keep us trapped?" Mara said. "Will you move us back to my cell, or will we be kept here?"

"That all depends on you." Ronya let go of Tham's hand and headed toward the door made of solid ice. "Come along." She beckoned them over her shoulder. "Leave the cutlery behind. Any hint of you trying to arm yourselves, and I'll have to let the ice take you."

She laid her palm on the door but didn't pass through the solid surface as she had before. The ice shifted under her touch, pushing open as though it were a normal, wooden door.

"Are you coming?" Ronya asked. "Or would you like me to leave you to rest for a few more days?"

"We're very well rested." Mara stepped around Tham and laid her fork back on the table.

"Perfect." Ronya walked out into the corridor.

Mara looked to Tham. He nodded for her to go first.

It was their way. He would be able to see any threats lurking in front of her and protect her from any attack that came from behind.

Mara glanced toward the door before reaching for Tham's hand. "Please."

His fingers grazed her palm before he took her hand. A thrill rushed through her chest as the warmth of his skin pressed against hers.

Tham gave her another nod, and together, they walked into the corridor.

Eight guards in pale blue uniforms waited just outside their door. Tham tensed, but none of the men reached for the swords or daggers at their hips.

"They'll be coming with us," Ronya said. "We can't risk you getting lost. Isfol is a labyrinth that has claimed the lives of many poor souls who had too much faith in their own wits."

"We appreciate your protection," Mara said.

"You have yet to realize how fortunate you are." Ronya turned and strode down the corridor.

The hall had been built of the same blue ice as everything else Mara had seen since being captured, but the makers had spent much more time in the construction of the corridor. Arches filled the spaces between the doors, each niche adorned with a relief carved into the wall itself.

Mara tried to take in as many of the images as she could while distracted by all the things she longed to shout at Ronya and the pounding of the guards' boots thumping along at her heels.

The reliefs seemed to tell a story. Or, if not a complete story, the artist had been given a specific theme for their designs.

A woman cradled a baby in her arms. The child reached away from her mother, as though hoping to tear the stars from the sky.

The mother and child stood on a mountaintop as a storm raged around them. The mother gave her child as an offering to appease whatever god had created the terrible storm.

The mountain swallowed the baby, but the child didn't die.

The ice at the heart of the mountain changed the child. She grew into woman, a warrior who rode on the back of a wolf.

"Kareen," Mara whispered.

"What did you say?" Ronya held up a hand to stop their party before turning to look at Mara.

"The legend of Kareen. One of the women who lives in Whitend told me the story. This one looks like her." Mara stepped closer to the image to get a better look.

A bird circled over the woman's head. She held a spear, its tip pointed toward the sky.

"Kareen," Ronya said. "I don't think I've heard the story the mud dwellers invented. It's not surprising their tales mimic ours. That's the problem with histories that involve magic—the truth of them drifts so quickly into legend. Then everyone starts to claim your people's birth as their own origin story."

"I'd like to hear your version of the legend if—"

"The true version of our history," Ronya cut across Mara.

"Of course," Mara said. "I apologize. I would like to learn about the history of your people."

"So you can lessen your chances of our deciding it might be safe to allow you to run back out into the world?" Ronya grazed her fingers across the image of the woman before continuing down the corridor.

"In hopes of understanding why you're so afraid." Mara looked to Tham as they followed.

His jaw tensed.

Mara could see the movement even through the shroud of his beard.

"Do not make the mistake of confusing fear and wisdom," Ronya said. "The Regent will not look kindly on such foolishness."

Ronya turned down another corridor. Wide windows lined one side of the hall, offering Mara her first true glimpse of Isfol.

The massive cavern contained an entire city. There was no opening for sunlight to peer through. No hint at all of a path that might lead to the outside world.

Mara shoved aside her disappointment and turned her focus closer to the palace.

A thick wall surrounded the grounds, and just beyond the gates, the city proper began.

The houses were made of the same ice as the palace. Against the beautiful blue of the buildings, the vibrant colors worn by the people of Isfol seemed almost garish. What looked like a row of shops filled the road just beyond the palace gates, but there were no horses pulling wagons of goods. Dogs and sleds seemed to be the mode of transport favored on the roads of ice.

In the distance, just before the buildings blocked Mara's view, a bridge spanned over a river of deep blue water.

Mara reached for her hip, ready to use her sorcerer-made scroll to create an image of the city. But she had no scroll. No magic tickled the back of her mind.

A pang of grief dug into Mara's chest.

"Follow the Princess," one of the guards ordered.

"Sorry," Mara said.

Tham let go of her hand and wrapped his arm around her waist, keeping her close to his side as they hurried after Ronya.

"I'm not useless," Mara whispered.

"I'd never think you are," Tham said. "But I've been locked up for weeks, and I need a solid reminder of why now would be a deadly time to try and fight back."

Mara placed her hand on top of Tham's, tightening his grip on her.

A sweeping staircase led up from the end of the hall. Men and women who weren't in any sort of uniform stopped on the steps, lowering their gazes as Ronya passed.

The members of the court had chosen tempered versions of the brazen colors the people outside the window had worn. Delicate greens, soft reds, and pale purples seemed to be the favored hues.

Ronya didn't acknowledge her people as she climbed the stairs.

As soon as their princess had passed, the people lifted their heads and turned their interest toward Mara and Tham.

I wish I'd braided my hair.

Mara swallowed her laugh at the absurd thought. A well-dressed captive was still nothing more than a primped prisoner.

At the top of the steps, two columns of guards in white uniforms flanked a massive entryway. The ice doors had been pushed aside, offering a view into the chamber beyond.

A man in sapphire-blue robes sat on a throne built of twists and swirls, as though it had been carved by the northern wind.

Icicles hung from the vaulted ceiling, the blue lights dancing within them casting the room in a cold glow that made the whole scene seem more like a dream than a threat.

The eight guards that had accompanied them from their room surrounded Tham and Mara as they approached the throne.

"Papa." Ronya reached for her father's hand, offering no reverence but a kiss on his cheek.

"Your Highness." The Regent gave his daughter a nod.

"These are the guests I've been telling you about," Ronya said.

Anger burned in Mara's chest.

"Mara Landil and Tham Karron." Ronya smiled at Mara and Tham. "Both were on a cartographer's journey when they lost their party to a storm."

The Regent looked to Mara and Tham. There was kindness in his blue eyes, and the lines creasing his face seemed to fit someone accustomed to smiling.

"Southerners," the Regent said. "We so rarely see anyone from below the mountains, let alone two Guilded Ilbreans."

"It is an honor to meet you, Lord Regent." Mara stepped away from Tham just enough to curtsy. "Your city is beautiful."

"Indeed it is," the Regent said. "But it is nothing, nothing compared to the true wonders the mountain holds."

"Then I wish we'd come to Isfol under different circumstances," Mara said. "I would have loved to explore the marvels of your home."

"But you should," the Regent said.

"I'm afraid our time here—" Mara began.

"Will be entirely monopolized by me." Ronya gave a bashful laugh as though she were embarrassed for creating an inconvenience. "Mara and I are already becoming such good friends, and I've always wanted to learn more about Ilbrea. She's sworn to tell me every last detail of her homeland and the Guilds. The gods smiled on Isfol when they brought a Guilded map maker to our door."

KAI

Pain throbbed from his feet to his head, each part seeming to choose a different moment to pulse, making it impossible for Kai to decide where he had been injured worst.

The glistening of the waves dug into his eyes. Breathing made the grit in his throat catch fire. His shoulders screamed their protest with each pull on the oars. The blood on his ribs had long since dried, but the pain in his side hadn't ebbed.

None of it mattered. Not really. Not anymore.

There in the distance. Land. Real, proper land.

The coast of Pamerane.

Vast stretches of sand, then palm trees rising up along the gentle hills to the north. A few islands reached toward them, inviting Kai to let the boat drift to their shores so he could stop rowing. Just ram the boat into the beach and finally rest.

But the islands were too small. Land like that might not have fresh water. If they stopped somewhere without water, they'd never leave. If Kai stopped rowing, he'd never find the strength to start again.

He swallowed the pain in his throat and blinked away the grit in his eyes, fighting to focus on the shoreline.

"Let me take a turn." Brody winced as he pushed himself to sit upright.

"Rest." The word crackled in Kai's throat.

"You're not the only man on board," Brody said.

Kai glanced to the four other men in the boat.

Five. Five sailors in the boat he rowed. All of them injured. All of them far past exhaustion.

Six sailors crammed together in the boat rowing a hundred yards to the east.

Eleven men.

They'd left Ilara with sixty.

"I'm fine." Kai pulled the oars harder.

Don't think. Don't think about them.

Waves crashing against the hull. The mast cracking, smashing through the deck. The crew abandoning ship. Rowing for the edge of the storm. All the surviving sailors had gotten into the boats. Even the captain.

Cold slicing into Kai's bones as they fought against the sea. Rowing. Wind and waves and rowing.

"Kai."

Boats disappearing. Only Kai's and the captain's had made it to clear waters.

The others were gone. All of them gone.

"Kai."

A hand gripped his arm.

Drew knelt in front of him, red still staining his face even though the slice on his scalp had finally stopped bleeding.

"Let me take a turn," Drew said.

"I'm fine." Kai tightened his grip on the oars.

"You're not the only one who's going mad," Drew said. "And you dying from exhaustion won't do the rest of us any chivving good. Now let go of the oars and give me the seat."

"No, we're almost there. I can see a split on the shoreline. I can see fresh water cutting down."

"You guide. I'll row." Drew spoke softly. "We've lost enough. Don't make me mourn you, too."

The pain in Kai's arms doubled as he made himself let go of the oars. He didn't fight as Drew gripped his elbow, guiding him to sit in the bottom of the boat with the other men.

Not men. Survivors. We're the survivors.

Kai dug his knuckles into his eyes.

You've been shipwrecked before. You've been lost at sea before.

He fought to make his body relax, trying to force himself to find gratitude. He should be thanking the gods for sparing him from another storm.

It doesn't make surviving any easier.

His breath pinched in his chest.

I've survived too many times. It should've been me. I should've drowned.

"Where's the water?" Drew's voice cut through the horrible words screaming in Kai's mind. "Kai, where's the water?"

Kai forced himself to breathe. Forced his eyes to open.

"There." He pointed. "Just west of the rocky rise."

"You have better eyes than me." Drew squinted toward the shore. "Keep watching for anything closer."

Kai searched the shore as Drew rowed them toward salvation.

Water. Find water.

A straightforward task. Something he could do to help his crew.

To make sure we don't lose any more.

It should've been me.

Why am I still breathing?

Even the men who'd been passed out managed to rouse themselves as they neared the beach.

"I can see it," Brody said. "Kai's right. There's a waterfall."

Kai looked to the captain's boat, trailing behind them, but heading the same way.

The southern storms still raged on the horizon, their constant churning like an oath from the gods, vowing to destroy the fools who dared try their hand against a might stronger than any man.

But the storms hadn't chased their boats. Of the sixty who'd sailed into the storm, the gods had chosen to set eleven of them free.

Eleven. So few.

So many gone. So many families that would have to grieve.

Embracing the pain in his legs, Kai jumped into the water as the bottom of the boat began to scrape the rocky sand.

The warmth of the sea seemed like a betrayal as he dragged the boat up to the edge of the beach. The men all staggered out, heading straight for the falls that cut down the rocks of the outcropping before joining the salty sea.

"No one else would have spotted that." Drew helped Kai drag the boat all the way up onto the sand.

"They would have."

"Come on." Drew began limping toward the falls, favoring his left leg.

Kai didn't know when Drew had hurt his leg. It had all been too dark. There had been too many fearful shouts as the mast came down. The roaring of the storm had pounded in his ears.

Someone had been hit by the falling mast. Their end had been quick. Kai would never know which sailor the gods had granted such a mercy.

"Come on, Kai." Drew turned back. "You'll do the captain more good once you've gotten a bit of water in you. You know I'm right."

Kai looked back to the captain's boat one more time before forcing his feet to move.

"Let me help you." Kai wrapped his arm around Drew's waist, taking some of the weight off Drew's injured leg.

"It's not that bad," Drew said as they slogged through the sand toward the falls. "My foot got caught in a rope when we were lowering the boats. Nearly twisted my ankle in two before I got free. Not too bad a price to pay, though. If I'd stayed stuck, I would've gone down with the ship."

Kai stifled the pain that flared in his gut.

"We'll make a splint for it," Kai said. "Hopefully, we'll find a healer soon."

"Any idea where on the Pameranian coast we've landed?"

"Farther east than we want to be." Kai stopped, taking a moment to study the landscape. "The port cities for trade with Ilbrea are in west Pamerane, out of reach of the southern storms. It's all mountains and chain lakes there, none of these rolling hills."

"Do you think we'll be walking or rowing west from here?" Drew limped toward the falls, gripping Kai's shoulder, forcing him to move as well.

"For the sake of your ankle, let's hope the captain agrees to row."

16

MARA

The servants slipped in and out of the courtyard, delivering fresh tea and new trays of sweets, though neither Ronya nor Mara had touched any of the food laid out for them.

Mara pitied whoever ran the palace kitchens, how they must be panicking as their princess and her guest refused to eat the food delivered to them. Still, Mara couldn't bring herself to touch any of the cakes.

Tham had been forced to stay locked in their room. He'd looked ready to tear the palace down, but Mara had to risk going without him. A simple note from the Princess—*Remember your promise, Ilbrean*—had driven enough terror into Mara's heart to make her agree to leave Tham behind.

Only for a little while. Sit through this abominable tea, and you'll be back in his arms.

Mara looked to the trees that grew beside the courtyard walls. The beauty of their pale bark and emerald leaves brought her no comfort.

You don't belong here, Mara Landil.

"Are all Ilbreans this stubborn, or is it only you?" Ronya tipped her head as she studied Mara.

"There is a great variety of people in Ilbrea," Mara said. "There are some who crumble like dirt and others who endure like stone."

"Is that what you're doing?" Ronya asked. "Are you enduring, Mara?"

Mara laced her fingers together in her lap. "I'm a prisoner in your lovely palace. I've been a prisoner of the Ice Walkers for weeks."

"*Prisoner* sounds so dire." Ronya beckoned one of the servants. "Think of yourself more as a well-protected guest. I've told you before, many have gone astray in Isfol and been taken by the ice. I'm only keeping my friend safe."

The maid curtsied to Ronya, carefully averting her gaze from Mara.

"Wine, please," Ronya said, "and be sure the surprise I arranged for dear Mara is ready."

The maid curtsied again before slipping away.

"Is the surprise my freedom?" Mara asked.

"Don't be so dramatic. It's boring."

"If you're bored, then tell me why you wanted me out here." Mara gripped her hands together, forcing her voice to stay pleasant and calm. "I'm sure you have much more important matters to attend to, Your Highness."

"You have more important matters to attend to as well. You and Tham." Ronya grinned. "I simply adore you together. So passionate, yet so careful. I'd think you'd be happy to be locked in a room with your mate. You do seem to enjoy your time together."

"You've been watching us?" Heat flashed in Mara's cheeks.

"You already knew that. Why else would you be so carefully restrained?"

"How curious that the Princess of the Ice Walkers likes to spy on her *protected guests*."

The maid returned with a tray bearing a decanter of wine and two glasses that seemed to have been made of the same blue ice as the city of Isfol.

"Let us toast to our friendship." Ronya filled both glasses.

"No, thank you."

"Are you refusing the wine or my friendship?" Ronya held a glass out to Mara. "I should warn you, either answer could be equally dangerous."

"Tell me why you wanted me out here, and maybe I'll agree to drink." Mara made no move to accept the glass.

"I wanted to chat. I want to learn all about our neighbors to the south, and what better way to do so than by befriending someone who's already promised to give me whatever truths I ask for because if she refuses, she forfeits her mate's life?" Ronya leaned closer to Mara.

Mara stayed frozen, rejecting her instinct to back away.

"I am trying to do this in the most pleasant way possible. I could have you pinned to the ground while I force wine down your throat until your stomach explodes. I could torture Tham to make you talk. I could execute the other two from your ill-fated journey as an afternoon amusement. Instead, I offer you exquisite wine in a lovely garden. Accept my kindness, or I will be forced to change tactics."

Mara gritted her teeth as she relaxed her hands enough to pull them apart. "Thank you for the wine. How do you grow fruit in the ice?"

"The same way we grow everything else." Ronya passed Mara a glass. "The ice feeds the plants as it feeds our people. It's how Isfol survives."

"Fascinating."

The stem of the wine glass held the same chill as everything in Isfol, but the cold didn't bite into Mara's fingers as she sipped the sweet liquid.

"What do you think?" Ronya drank from her own glass.

"It has a thicker sweetness than Ilbrean chamb." Mara took

another sip. "Almost like honey."

"I've always wanted to try chamb."

"If you never let anyone who finds you leave, I'm afraid you'll never have the chance."

"Be nice, Mara." A hint of danger glinted in Ronya's unnaturally blue eyes.

"You might very well prefer frie to chamb." Mara smiled. "It burns on the way down."

"Fascinating." Ronya trailed her finger around the rim of her wine glass.

"There are many"—Mara shifted in her seat, willing herself not to scream—"fascinating things about Ilbrea. Have you spoken to Kegan and Elver? I'm sure they could tell you wonderful things if you'd bring them here."

"Don't be dull. You'll only anger me."

"My apologies, Your Highness." Mara took another sip of her wine, swallowing the scream that burned in her throat. "What would you like to know about Ilbrea?"

"Is the Ilbrean Princess really to marry the Prince of Wyrain?"

"Yes, it was announced at Winter's End." Mara gripped her glass. "Their marriage will strengthen the bond between Ilbrea and Wyrain."

"Did the Princess choose this marriage for herself?" Ronya stared at Mara, studying her again.

"I've only met the Princess a few times, so I can't say for sure. But I doubt the marriage was Princess Illia's idea."

"Your King sold his sister for a little security. How utterly pathetic."

"How is marriage amongst royals decided here?"

"Eat a sweet, and I'll tell you." Ronya held a plate out to Mara.

Mara took the smallest of the red cakes and shoved the whole thing into her mouth. The rich sweet still held warmth from the kitchen fires and offered a bit of spice she hadn't expected.

Ronya pursed her lips, as though hiding her smile. "When the time arrives, any who wish to vie for my hand will come to the palace. They will be allowed to present themselves and display whatever attributes they believe would make them a good partner for me. My advisors will sieve out the rabble, and I'll choose my mate from those deemed worthy."

"That seems like a very kind system."

"I'd kill anyone who tried to make me marry against my will. I rather think you'd do the same."

Mara caught herself on the verge of agreeing. "Princess Illia is doing her duty to Ilbrea. Her people are grateful to her. What other Ilbrean gossip interests you, Your Highness?"

"A woman as a map maker. I'd thought such things weren't allowed in the south."

"It's uncommon but not forbidden." Mara took a large swallow of her wine. "Women may join the Soldiers, Sailors, and Map Makers Guilds, but they give up their right to marry. A wife can't be running off on adventures. It would be unbearable for her husband."

"That explains so much. Does Tham not think he could—"

"Is this what you want to know?" Mara set her glass down on the table, sloshing her wine onto the tray of sweets. "You brought me out here so you could question how Ilbrea treats its women?"

"Temper, temper." Ronya beckoned a servant to clear the mess away. "I was promised answers to my questions."

"What happens between Tham and me is none of your business," Mara whispered through gritted teeth as the maid refilled her glass of wine and whisked the tray away.

"I just find it shocking that a man who would carve through a mountain of ice to find you would refuse to marry you simply because you'd be running off to map the world's wonders."

"He would have married me ages ago if it were allowed. But no one in Ilbrea can know we're together. If word spread, I would lose my place in the Map Makers Guild, and the Soldiers

Guild would send Tham so far away, I'd never see him again." Mara loathed the heat that burned in her eyes.

"Such cruelty from the glorious Guilds." Ronya set her glass on the table. "I'm embarrassed to say I didn't expect it. This has been such an enlightening chat. I think you've earned your surprise."

"What enlightening thing have I said?" Mara's mind raced back through the conversation, searching for anything that might have been a betrayal to her country.

"Sweet Mara, Ilbreans treat their women as less than men. They are wives and trinkets. They are valued for the life their organs can produce but not for the contributions they can offer society." Ronya gave a wicked grin. "I can now be sure that half of Ilbrea's population is of no threat to me. Then weed out the old and the young, the rebels I'm sure lurk in the shadows of such a vast country, and our enemy to the south is much less frightening than it might appear."

"Ilbrea is not your enemy," Mara said as Ronya stood. "Release us. Allow us to take an ambassador to Ilara, and you may find Ilbrea to be an invaluable ally."

"Why would I seek friendship with a country that treats their women in such an abominable way? Should I request an audience with the Guilds who would view me as inherently less than their precious King Brannon?" Ronya nodded to the servant waiting in the far corner of the courtyard. "I will not beg for favors from those who would keep my dear friend Mara from marrying her devoted mate."

Mara bit the insides of her cheeks, swallowing the words she longed to shout.

"You may doubt my friendship now," Ronya said. "But in time, you'll come to treasure what I offer."

A howl and a yip drew Mara's attention to the corner of the courtyard.

The servant tripped, grabbing onto a tree branch to stay upright, as a dog tore past her, charging straight for Mara.

"Elle?" Mara began to kneel but not quickly enough.

The sled dog launched herself at Mara, knocking her to the ground. Elle panted and whined as she licked Mara's face with gleeful enthusiasm.

"Oh good." Ronya stood over Mara. "Your guards had heard you mention missing one of the dogs. This one seemed the friendliest of the team, so I'd hoped it was her."

"This is Elle. She slept in my tent during the journey." Mara managed to prop herself up on one elbow, using her other arm to defend herself against Elle's affection.

"She can stay in your room with you," Ronya said. "The guards will ensure her needs are cared for."

"Thank you." Mara sat up and bundled the still-panting dog in a hug.

"I look forward to our next meeting. Tell Tham I hope he remains in good health. The ice dug so deeply into his veins, there is always a risk of lingering damage we can't foresee."

Mara froze as Ronya reached down and patted Elle's head.

"Don't fret, dear Mara. The best healers in Isfol work at the palace. I'll make sure they take excellent care of Tham. That is, after all, how friendship works. We look out for each other."

"Of course." Mara held Elle close, guarding the dog from anyone who might drag her away.

"Perhaps next time we meet, I'll give you a more thorough tour of the palace. Or maybe we should walk out into the city. Isfol has so many wonders I would just love for you to see." With one more grin, Ronya strode away, leaving Elle and Mara alone.

"It's all right." Mara kissed the top of Elle's head. "Everything will be all right. I can protect both of you."

17

KAI

"I don't think I've ever been so happy to see a foreign port." Drew leaned against the side of the boat, a true smile on his face as he stared at the city of Soumid.

"If you're this happy to reach a port in Pamerane, you'll lose your chivving mind when we make it home to Ilara." Brody punched him in the arm.

"Too right, I will," Drew said. "I'm going to down a barrel of frie and sleep for a week."

The other three chuckled their agreement.

Kai gripped the oars, rowing toward the nearest of the docks, grateful to have something to excuse him from having to celebrate along with the others.

The beauty of Soumid couldn't be denied. The city itself was sheltered in a cove, with docks on the east and west sides, reaching out into the sea where the depth was great enough for large ships to safely port.

Beyond the harbor, the city had grown up the slopes surrounding the cove, carving out levels for the buildings to perch on. The richest in Soumid had claimed the highest points in the city, building their stone homes with towers and turrets that cast imposing silhouettes in the dimming evening light.

"Think the captain will be able to get the shipping laxe to put us in proper rooms for the night?" Sean looked to Kai.

"I don't know any of the shipping merchants in Soumid," Kai said. "I've only been here twice. Wouldn't get my hopes up for a warm greeting, though. We'll be lucky to be given food and a roof."

"They trade enough with Ilbrea," Brody said. "The captain should be able to get us something decent from a merchant in exchange for a reward from the Guilds when we get back to Ilara."

Kai slowed the pace of his rowing as the sounds from the docks reached their boat.

Men shouted orders as workers loaded crates of goods onto a ship. A bell rang somewhere on the docks, probably signaling that two strange boats had been spotted rowing up to the eastern pier. A few Pameranian soldiers patrolled the wharf but not enough to make Kai worry about being hauled off and tossed in a cell as soon as they stepped on land.

"How does it feel to be home, Kai?" Sean asked.

"Home?" Kai looked up at the stone buildings. The windows gleamed as the people began lighting their lamps for the night. "I was born in Pamerane, but my home was as different from this as it is from Ilara."

Six soldiers stepped out onto the pier, all of them watching the boats approach.

"Be careful here." Kai kept his voice low as the captain's boat thumped into the dock. "Most people in Pamerane aren't fond of Ilbreans. The laxe might help us, but only because merchants will help anyone who'll bring them gold."

"I've been to Pamerane before," Brody said. "Everyone was welcoming."

"I'll bet you had coin to spend then," Kai said.

The soldiers stepped up to the edge of the pier, blocking the captain from climbing out of his boat.

"Why don't the people in Pamerane like Ilbreans?" Sean asked.

"If you'd spent centuries having to deal with the Guilds, would you like us?" Kai said.

"We're seeking sanctuary in your harbor," the captain said. "I am a captain of the Sailors Guild of Ilbrea. Our ship was lost to the southern storms. I'm here to negotiate for the safe transport of my crew and myself back to Ilbrea. The Guilds will gladly pay a reward to the one who delivers these sailors home."

The soldiers glared down at the captain for a long moment before one of them finally spoke.

"Stay in your boats. Granting you sanctuary must be the harbormaster's decision." The soldier walked away, his boots thumping on the pier.

The rest of the soldiers stayed, glaring down at the Ilbrean sailors.

Kai rowed his boat to stop right alongside the captain's.

"Five days in these boats." The captain spoke in a carrying voice. "We'll be very grateful to whoever grants us food and shelter for the night, won't we, Kai?"

"Of course, captain." Kai matched the captain's tone. "The Guilds will generously reward all those who help us. Lord Karron will want to thank those kind people as well. He'll be sailing this way soon enough. Even after being the Lord Map Maker's ward for so long, I still find his generosity overwhelming. He's always treated me like a son. Fathers are extremely grateful for the safe return of their children."

"I can imagine." The captain nodded.

"When we get back to Ilara, we should have a ball at his palace," Kai said. "Lady Karron will want to celebrate. What better way to welcome ourselves home than with the best chamb gold can buy?"

Drew raised an eyebrow at Kai.

If five armed soldiers weren't looming over them, Kai would have laughed.

Everything he'd said was true. Lord Karron would gladly pay well for their safe return, and Allora would want to hold a massive party. But Kai had never cared about the Lord Map Maker's wealth, and flouting his riches to strangers felt as unnatural as a fish trying to show off its feathers.

The lot of them fell silent, waiting in the gently bobbing boats.

Kai tried to think of something else to say that might ease their time in Soumid as a breeze swept across the sea, bringing welcome relief after a day spent in the southern sun.

He tested the weight of his boots. He'd hidden his coin in the hollowed-out heels as soon as Sorcerer Roo had insisted they sail for the southern storms. The habit gained from the darker days he'd spent at sea had served him well. He had enough coin to buy himself a bed for the night, but that would mean separating from the rest of the men.

A bribe would only be valuable if he knew who to pay, and he wasn't familiar enough with Soumid to know who'd be worth his coin.

Strains of faint music carried beneath the renewed rounds of shouted orders coming from the team loading the ship nearby.

With luck, they'd be home in Ilara in less than two weeks.

Kai would see his family. Let Allora coo and worry over him.

His longing for his own bed and the company of friends made waiting for the harbormaster all the harder.

Lord Nevon would be furious with the Sorcerers Guild for the atrocious actions of Head Sorcerer Roo. There'd be a war within the Guilds Council.

It was high time the Guilds pushed back against the sorcerers' grab for power. Still, Kai didn't cherish the thought of being so close to the center of the trouble.

But he'd been the second in command on the ship Sorcerer

Roo had decided to commandeer. He'd been standing right in front of her when she'd been sent over the rail.

He'd be questioned by the Guilds Council. All of them would be.

A weight settled in Kai's chest, pressing against his lungs. He looked to the captain, who sat watching the Soumid soldiers watching him. There was no way for them to talk, not with so many around. He looked to Drew.

Drew had fixed his gaze on his own palms. Worry creased his brow.

The rest of the crew all looked somewhere between exhausted and elated.

There'll be time. Arranging a ship back to Ilbrea won't happen tonight. Relax, the demons aren't breathing down your neck.

Yet.

It took nearly an hour for the soldier to return, walking at the heels of the harbormaster.

With his black hair carefully combed, his beard perfectly trimmed, and his gray coat tailored to fit a royal, the harbormaster had the look of a man who wanted nothing less than to offer shelter to eleven Ilbreans who hadn't seen clean clothes or soap in more than a week.

The harbormaster stared down into their boats, his mouth pinched in a tight smile that did nothing to distract from the loathing in his eyes.

"You lost your ship to the southern storms?" The harbormaster addressed the group.

"Yes." The captain stood in his boat.

"And I should take pity on fools who decided to face the southern storms this early in the season?" the harbormaster said.

"My name is Captain Devlin," the captain said. "I am a Guilded sailor of Ilbrea. I didn't make the choice to sail my ship into that storm. My Guild didn't choose to send me, either. I'd be pleased to tell you the whole awful tale once I see my men fed and given a place to rest."

The harbormaster continued to glare.

"Helping us return to Ilara will earn the right people a huge profit," the captain said. "Would you like to be one of those people?"

Kai tightened his grip on the oars, resisting the urge to speak as the harbormaster's pinched smile twisted into a frown.

"It would have to be a fine story for a captain to offer to tell a stranger why he abandoned his ship," the harbormaster said.

He abandoned his ship to try and save the sailors still under his command, you slitch.

Kai forced himself to breathe and let go of the oars. He pressed his shoulders down and fixed an expression of gratitude on his face.

"Have provisions brought to warehouse seven." The harbormaster looked to the soldier who'd gone to fetch him. "They can stay there."

The soldier gave a nod and strode down the pier.

"You'll have a complement of soldiers watching you," the harbormaster said. "I've no guarantee you're Guilded or even Ilbrean."

"Will this help?" Kai rolled up his right sleeve. He stood, stepping as close to the harbormaster as his boat would allow.

Each of the Pameranian soldiers raised their hand to grip the hilt of their sword.

"No tricks here, fellows." Kai held out his arm, displaying the curling breath of wind the sorcerers had burned into his skin the day he joined the Sailors Guild. "Have you seen a mark like this before?"

"All that it means is that you were, at one point, accepted into the Sailors Guild." The harbormaster tucked his hands behind his back and raised his chin, almost as though he were tempting Kai to ignore the armed soldiers and take the easy attack.

"Then at least you can agree we've come from Ilbrea." Kai made himself smile.

"Take them to the warehouse and keep them there," the harbormaster said. "Do not allow them access to the city."

"Thank you for your hospitality." The captain gave the harbormaster a nod.

The harbormaster didn't acknowledge him before turning and striding away.

"Welcoming, isn't he?" Drew whispered.

"All of you on the pier," one of the soldiers ordered. "Now."

"Gladly." The captain climbed out of his boat first, placing himself between the soldiers and his men.

Kai waited until the rest of the crew had made it onto the pier before joining them.

A rolling dread swept through his stomach as his boots struck the wooden planks.

As different as his village was from Soumid, Kai had been born in Pamerane. This was his true homeland.

It doesn't feel like coming home.

Kai glanced back toward the boats as the soldiers marched the sailors up the pier. The boats were the only true asset the ship-wrecked Ilbreans had. And they'd just left them bobbing in a foreign port.

Brody leaned close to Kai. "I thought you were exaggerating about them not liking Ilbreans."

"Did I ever tell you how I became a sailor?" Kai kept his voice low.

"Lord Karron paid your way," Brody said.

"He paid for me to join the Sailors Guild, but I was on ships long before that."

Sean dropped back to walk beside Kai.

"Despite how Soumid looks, life is hard in Pamerane," Kai said. "When I was little, my family was starving. My mother brought me to a port, hoping to find a way for me to earn some food. An Ilbrean captain offered to buy my labor from my mother. Paid her good coin, and as a member of his ship's crew, I'd be fed."

"Sounds like the captain was a generous man," Sean said.

"He was a slitch who liked to hit when he was in a bad temper," Kai said. "But he kept his word to my mother. I always had at least a little to eat. Of course, she doesn't know that. I haven't seen her since the captain took me away."

"I'm sorry, Kai," Brody said.

"It was all a lifetime ago," Kai said. "But things like that are why people in Pamerane don't like Ilbreans. We swoop in, throwing about gold and offering salvation. But help from an Ilbrean always comes with a heavier price than you'd think. Folks here won't go so far as to refuse Ilbrean coin, that's a luxury they can't afford, but if you've nothing to pay—"

"They'd rather see you locked in a warehouse." Sean shook his head. "How quickly do you think we can make it back to Ilbrea?"

"Only the gods know that," Drew said.

Their party's pace slowed as they neared a cluster of warehouses. The smallest one, whose paint had long since peeled leaving the exposed wood to rot, had twelve soldiers standing out front.

All of them tensed as the Ilbreans approached.

"Maybe we should have rowed home," Drew said.

"Do not attempt to leave," one of the soldiers ordered. "Anyone caught trying to flee will be moved to the prison."

"Lovely." Kai gave the soldiers a smile and nod, as though he weren't dreading being held in captivity. "Thank you for your hospitality and protection."

The smell of rotting wood and poorly shoveled animal dung crashed into Kai's nose as he stepped into the warehouse. The filth on the three high windows blocked out most of the light. Several long-forgotten crates lurked in the corners.

Before Kai could finish studying his new home, the soldiers closed the door, throwing everything into thick shadows.

The scrape of a bolt sliding into place came from outside.

"Welcome to chivving Pamerane," Drew said so only Kai could hear.

"Better Pamerane than Ilbrea." Kai sat on the filthy floor. "Have you ever witnessed the true wrath of the Sorcerers Guild?"

"I've always managed to avoid that honor," Drew said. "But Sorcerer Roo forced us to keep sailing into that chivving storm—"

"And it's her fault she slipped and fell overboard." Kai locked eyes with Drew, gripping his friend's arm and offering his solemn vow. "Accidents happen on ships. Especially when someone isn't used to the violence of an angry sea."

Drew held Kai's gaze for a moment before nodding.

"That the chivving slitch brought about her own death is the least of our worries," Kai whispered. "Telling the Guilds Council that the Sorcerers Guild overstepped and caused the deaths of most of our crew—that's where the danger comes."

Drew scrubbed his hand over his mouth. "Then what under the gods are we supposed to do? Pretend we decided to take a pleasure cruise into the southern storms?"

"I've no chivving clue."

18

NIKO

I dreamt of you last night.

We were sitting on the cliffs at your father's estate, enjoying the afternoon sunlight. I could feel the warmth of the sun touching my face. I've spent so long trapped in the darkness, craving even a hint of sunlight. But having you beside me brought infinitely more joy than even the bright, open sky could offer.

I held your hand as we looked out over Ilara, watching the sun sparkling off the Arion Sea.

We didn't speak.

Maybe I should've tried. Maybe I would have gained some relief by telling you how desperately I love you instead of huddling in the black, scrawling the words on stone like a madman.

The grief that punched through my lungs when I woke nearly broke me. I lay in the cold darkness, wishing I would sleep forever if only I could fall back into that perfect dream.

But I cannot give up. I promised I would come home to you, and I will do whatever the gods demand to keep my word.

I will come home, Allora.

I will sit on the cliffs with you. I will hold your hand as I beg you to be my wife.

I will never give up fighting for the joy I will find when I have you by my side again.

You are all the hope I need to survive,

Niko

MARA

Elle crouched on the foot of the bed, growling at the maids as they laid out new clothes on top of the blankets.

Both maids kept glancing at Elle, their shoulders tensing, their faces paling, looking as though they'd like nothing better than to flee from the room and never return.

Elle gave a low bark.

"Hush, Elle," Tham murmured.

Elle went back to growling.

Part of Mara wanted to pull Elle from the bed and bundle her into the corner to save the maids the fright. But the more practical part of Mara, the part that had moved from panic to bitter anger at having been held prisoner in the icy palace for so long, took twisted pleasure in the maids' fear.

With any luck, word of Elle's temper would spread through the palace staff, and the servants would have something to whisper about besides mocking the two Ilbreans who had been locked up for ages without finding their compatriots or making any attempt to escape.

Escape and go where? Even if you could make it out of the palace, you don't know how to get out of Isfol, and without proper equipment, you'd never make it to Whitend, let alone Ilara.

Tham brushed his hand against Mara's, offering her an anchor to drag herself back into the moment.

Mara met his gaze, wondering for the thousandth time if he had the ability to read her thoughts and had spent years hiding his talent from her.

"The—" one of the maids began, giving a frightened squeak and backing away from the bed as Elle's growl grew louder.

"Elle," Tham said.

Elle huffed and laid her head on her paws.

"Thank you. The…" The maid let out a long breath, keeping her gaze fixed on Elle. "The, eh…Her Royal Highness has requested for you both to dress in the fine new wear she, in her generosity, has provided. She wishes for you to be appropriately attired for the day's activities and promises you will find much gratitude for her—her kindness."

"Did she make you memorize a speech to bring us clothes?" Mara asked.

"It was my honor." The maid curtsied. "If we could please assist you in dressing, then we could—"

"Run away?" Mara said.

"Yes, miss," the second maid said.

"I can dress myself." Mara stepped closer to the bed, truly looking at the clothes for the first time—layers of petticoats and a green gown with billowing sleeves and a low enough neckline to make an Ilbrean lady blush.

"It laces up the back, miss," the first maid said.

"Tham can help me." Mara touched the gown. The fabric held the promise of wool's warmth and the softness of silk's texture.

"If you please, we were ordered to help you." The first maid looked to Elle. "We won't be allowed to leave until we're done."

"You can't open the door on your own?" Mara asked.

"Neither of us has that gift, miss." The first maid bit her lips together.

Tham looked to Mara, giving her the choice.

Mara gritted her teeth and dug deep down into her soul, searching for sympathy for the terrified maids. "Fine. You can help."

She began unlacing the front of the dress she still hadn't become accustomed to wearing. Too much fabric. Too much restriction of her movement. Too many generations of Ilbrean traditions screaming in her mind that a woman who'd joined the Map Makers Guild had given up the protection of femininity and with it, the necessity of wearing skirts.

The maids reached into their pockets, pulling out bundles of combs and powders.

"Are you planning on prettying Tham up?" Mara wriggled out of her dress and snatched up a petticoat before the maids could stop her.

"We've been given orders, miss." The maids exchanged glances, seeming to have a silent war as to which one would be forced to continue.

"The Princess wants me primped up like a getch of a doll?" Mara dragged the petticoat over her head.

It's not worth the fight. Belligerence won't get you closer to freedom.

"Primp me, if you must." Mara tied the petticoat around her waist. "But stay well clear of Elle. She's a wonderfully loyal dog who's quite capable of sensing my displeasure."

If Mara hadn't known Tham, she might have missed his breath of a laugh as he gathered his own clothes and went to the back of the room to change.

In an act of loyalty no animal had ever before shown, Elle stayed with Mara rather than trotting over to bask at Tham's feet. Elle watched as the women dressed Mara in the fine green gown, pulling the laces tight enough to display Mara's less than ample breasts.

They then sat Mara down and tutted over how best to manage her mane of red curls.

"Just shove some pins in it," Mara sighed. "Trust me, you'll save yourselves a lot of angst."

Once her hair had been abandoned as an impossible cause, they painted Mara's face, giving her rosy cheeks and alluring eyes.

"Where exactly is the Princess taking us?" Mara asked as the women stood back to judge their work.

"No idea, miss." The first maid patted cream onto Mara's lips. "But you look lovely. Fit for wherever the Princess takes you."

"Perfect." Mara stood and went back to the bed, barely resisting the temptation to throw herself face first onto the fur blankets. "Then I assume you can leave."

"Yes, miss." The second maid looked to the place where the door usually appeared. "Someone will come for us, miss."

"Maybe it's the hair," the first maid whispered to the second. "Maybe we didn't do it well enough."

"You're not going to make it please the Princess." Mara pulled off her fur slippers and reached for the new, black, fur-lined boots the maids had delivered. "As a girl, I spent years with people trying to ram my hair into a respectable order every day. It caused my scalp plenty of pain, and all that fussing never once worked. I have hair that's meant to be flying in the wind as I run off on adventures. I'll never look suited for any sort of grace or fashion. Aren't I right, Tham?"

"She is." Tham stepped forward, wearing an all-black suit, as though someone had been trying to make him feel at home in a vague mimicry of his uniform as a Guilded soldier.

Without a sound, the ice of the wall shifted, changing into a door that could be opened.

Two guards stepped into the room, followed by Ronya.

Both maids dropped into low curtsies their princess ignored.

"I don't know which pleases me more," Ronya said. "How

lovely you look for our little excursion, or finding out how long you and Tham have known each other."

"What *excursion* will you be taking us on?" Mara stood, brushing out her skirt, wishing her layers were at least five pounds lighter.

"I've definitely decided I'm much more interested in how long you and Tham have known each other." Ronya pursed her lips.

"We met when we were barely more than children." Tham moved to stand beside Mara, placing a hand on her waist. "We've tried not to be parted ever since."

"How delightfully romantic," Ronya cooed.

"It is." Mara forced her voice to stay cheerful. "I will never know why the gods sent Tham to find me. But I will always be grateful."

"The gods?" Ronya furrowed her brow. "I thought the Guilds believed in one god and a pack of saints."

"Dudia is followed by the Guilds," Tham said. "The common folk believe there are many gods."

"And what do the gods all do?" Ronya asked.

"No one knows," Mara said. "Common folk don't spend much time worrying about it either. You just pray to the lot of them and hope for the best."

"And this is what you believe even though you're sworn to the precious Guilds?" Ronya asked.

"Is this really what I had to be primped up for?" Mara said.

Tham tightened his hold on her waist.

"Has her temper always been this bad?" Ronya looked to Tham.

"No," Tham said. "It used to be worse. Now her anger only flares like fire when she means it to."

"You sound like you fell in love with a wild beast," Ronya said.

"Her wrath is a beautiful thing to behold," Tham said. "The world can be changed by the right person's fury."

"Coming from a man who sliced his way into a mountain, I'll

have to assume you're telling the truth." Ronya waved the maids toward the door without looking at them. "We should be off on our little adventure, then. As much as I enjoy chatting with Ilbreans, I wouldn't want to risk Mara's rage. The dog stays behind." Ronya strode toward the still-open door. "It would be too much for her."

"Stay, Elle." Tham rubbed Elle's back. "We'll be back soon."

"Such faith from the soldier," Ronya laughed.

"What exactly does our adventure entail?" Mara took Tham's hand, keeping him beside her as they followed Ronya out into the corridor.

"The beginning of your adjustment." Ronya led them in the same direction they'd traveled to reach the Regent.

"What *adjustment?*" Mara asked.

"You've been so well-behaved, I think it's time we alter our arrangement," Ronya said.

"In what way?" Mara studied the ice-carved images they passed. She'd seen them more than once, and the pictures hadn't changed. But between the warmth of Tham's hand in hers and trying to understand the full story of the woman who had sacrificed her child to the ice, she had enough to distract her from the anger still pressing against the back of her lungs.

"I've told you more than once, you can never return to Ilbrea." Ronya cut into a smaller corridor, heading away from the throne room.

"Yes, we're to be prisoners for the rest of our lives." Mara didn't manage to keep the bite from her tone.

"Ah, but that's where you've misunderstood." Ronya stopped, turning to face Mara so quickly, Tham tensed as though they were about to be attacked. "You can never return to Ilbrea. I can't endanger my people in such a horrific way. But I don't want you to be prisoners. If I have to lock you up for the rest of your lives, then it would be kinder to simply execute you."

"Is that what you've done to Kegan and Elver?" Mara asked.

Tham shifted sideways, placing his shoulder just in front of Mara's.

"The ice might revel in tasting the blood of Ilbreans, but I am not so crude. I don't fancy having to kill my new friends, Mara." Ronya shook her head, sending her perfect blond curls bouncing around her face. "However, there is a path to your happiness that would be beneficial to the Ice Walkers."

"And what would that be?" Mara asked.

"You could build a life here." Ronya turned and continued down the hall. "Isfol is a magnificent city. I think, in time, you would grow to be grateful to call it your home. And your unique knowledge would be an asset to my people."

"You're going to set us free in the city?" Mara tamped down the hope that bubbled through her anger.

"Of course not. I'm generous. Not a fool."

Two rows of white-uniformed guards waited at the top of a staircase that cut down to a massive set of double doors. As one, the guards bowed to Ronya then closed in on either side of their party, flanking Mara and Tham as they walked down the steps.

"Trust must be earned," Ronya said. "And, as I hold your lives in my hands, you have too many reasons to lie to me. To try and fool me into believing you're friends of Isfol when really I'd be setting monsters loose in my own city."

"Then it seems you'll have to keep us locked in our room until we die naturally," Mara said.

"On the contrary." Ronya headed straight for the massive doors. "I think the most prudent path would be to allow you to see exactly what prizes can be gained by winning my trust. I have so much to offer you, dear Mara. In time, you'll be begging to stay by my side as my closest friend and advisor."

"I don't know if I'm suited to be a friend and advisor to a princess," Mara said.

"I'll be Queen soon enough." Ronya waved a hand, and the ice doors opened without any of the guards touching them. "Are you more suited to be the confidant of the Queen?"

Ronya stepped outside and stopped, as though she knew full well the view would steal Mara's breath away.

Rows of white-leaved trees stretched out toward the open palace gates. Flowers, whose petals looked to be cast of silver, sparkled in the blue glow that radiated from the dome of the cavern. Fields of pale-green moss grew beyond the trees, and gardens with flowers of light-blue and pink dotted the lawn.

"The view is quite different when you see the grounds from here. None of the windows in the palace truly do the gardens justice." Ronya led them down the steps, nodding to the well-dressed gentry that bustled out of their path.

"Your home is quite lovely. I don't think anyone could argue with that." Mara stopped, casting aside her pride to kneel near a flowerbed for a closer look at the silver flowers. She reached out, carefully caressing a bloom.

The petals had the same soft texture as an ordinary Ilbrean flower.

"How?" Mara looked to Tham. "By all logic, this is completely impossible."

"If you only believe in Ilbrean standards of botany, then I'm sure you're right." Ronya beckoned them forward.

"The ice should prevent plants from growing." Mara trusted Tham to lead her forward as she kept her gaze fixed on the white leaves of the trees that hung over the path. "There's no sun here, either."

"Are these the brilliant things they teach map makers?" Ronya laughed.

"The easiest answer would, of course, be magic," Mara said. "But that would be too simple a solution."

"You don't think the Ice Walkers possess magic?" Ronya asked.

"I'm quite certain you do." Mara dragged her gaze from the trees as they neared the gate. "The way doors appear and walls move is proof enough of magic for you to be sure we could never tell anyone in Ilara what we found here."

"Is that so?" Ronya stopped just inside the gate, rounding on Mara and Tham.

"The Sorcerers Guild will not allow knowledge of magic outside their control to spread," Mara said. "They hoard all Ilbrean children who show signs of magic, forcing them to go to the Sorcerers Tower whether they like it or not. Any hint of magic existing in the wild is suppressed. The Sorcerers Guild will destroy any evidence of such wonders and the source of the magic itself if they can.

"If you were to let us go, we could never tell anyone in Ilbrea what we found here. If we tried, we would be considered heretics. The Sorcerers Guild would dispose of us." She took a tentative step closer to Ronya. "At best, they'd execute us for some crime they made up. At worst, we'd just disappear. We don't know what happens to the people who vanish after angering the sorcerers, but any sympathetic heart would pray those people are dead."

"The Sorcerers Guild is so terrified of the truth of magic?" Ronya looked up toward the peak of the massive cavern.

"Yes." Mara tightened her grip on Tham's hand as she dared to take another step forward. "Which is why letting us go is no threat to you. We could never tell anyone about the Ice Walkers. The Sorcerers Guild would kill us for you."

"Then you should be even more grateful for the life you're going to build here," Ronya said. "Magic does not belong to its purveyors. It's larger than any country or clan, larger even than Ilbrea's precious sorcerers. You shouldn't wish to go back to such close-minded, possessive hoarders. Things are better here. Our magic is for everyone."

"But we don't—"

Tham squeezed Mara's hand as he cut across her. "Are you saying everything in Isfol was created by magic?"

"I can't just tell you our secrets." Ronya laughed and beckoned them to follow her out onto the streets. "You're explorers. Handing you the answers would lead you straight to boredom."

My captor has no right to understand my heart. A fresh flare of anger broke through Mara's wonder, but stepping out onto the street dulled her resentment.

Mara had managed to catch glimpses of the city through the palace windows on the rare occasions she'd been taken from her room. But seeing the sea of buildings made of ice from inside the palace and walking down the bustling street were two entirely different things.

The people of Isfol, dressed in their brightly colored clothes, all stopped to bow to their princess, but none of the citizens seemed shocked to have royalty walking among them. The guards stayed behind Ronya, flanking Mara and Tham, as though only concerned with their prisoners attempting escape and not worried at all about their princess being attacked.

Rebels would have nowhere to run. There isn't a place for malcontents to hide from their ruler.

The hue of the ice that made the buildings stayed the same as they traveled farther into the city, the color unchanging no matter the size or shape of the structure, but the people seemed to have found their own way to break the monotony of the blue.

Richly colored tapestries hung outside the shops, woven into images that displayed what they sold.

A patisserie had a pink and purple image of a cake. A clothier, a man and woman posing in fine apparel.

Mara peered over the heads of the people they passed, trying to peek into as many shop windows as she could.

"Whoa!" The call came from up ahead followed by a round of barking.

A dogsled skidded to a stop in front of their party. The musher hopped down from his perch, bowing deeply to the Princess. "Apologies, Your Highness."

Ronya nodded to the man and skirted around the sled.

Mara peeked down into the crates the musher had been hauling. Bottles of wine had been packed in with wool.

"The glass bottles," Mara whispered to Tham. "I hadn't thought of it before. Glass bottles means they have a glass blower. That kind of heat—"

"Means there are enough mysteries in Isfol to keep an intrepid map maker entertained," Ronya said.

Mara chewed the inside of her bottom lip, her desire to ask a thousand questions warring with her loathing of implying Ronya was right. Mara could spend ages exploring every secret Isfol had to offer. And if she could do it while walking through a beautiful city, proudly holding Tham's hand…

Ronya turned left, leading them down a street that seemed to be populated by homes rather than shops. Tapestries still adorned the fronts of the houses, but they were woven into brightly colored patterns rather than images. No two banners were alike, almost as though the families within had been given designated patterns to distinguish who lived where.

"As beautiful as the city is and as well guarded as we keep the secrets of Isfol," Ronya said, "our home is not without its dangers. You cannot be allowed to roam without guards."

"In case we find an escape?" Mara asked.

"You couldn't." Ronya cut down a street barely wider than an alley.

Two guards stepped in front of Mara and Tham, walking almost shoulder-to-shoulder as they followed Ronya.

"Even if you trusted your gods to somehow ferry you to the outskirts of the city, which you'd be foolish to even dare attempt," Ronya said, "you could never leave the mountain. Even Tham and his ice axe couldn't carve you a path out of our home, no matter how badly he let his hands bleed."

It was Mara's turn to tighten her grip on Tham's hand.

The narrow road opened up into a little square with a stone statue at the center.

The figures hadn't been carved of marble or any of the other coveted materials Ilbrean artists fancied. The stone was plain gray, yet the shock of something being made of anything but ice was enough to make the figures astounding.

A man and a woman stood side by side, their hands locked together, their chins raised as though looking toward a brilliant future. But the ground around them had been carved in jagged, fang-like spikes, giving the base of the statue the look of a vicious mouth determined to devour the pair.

Ronya stopped in front of an unassuming, one-story structure.

The building had no colorful banner marking it as important, but Ronya and all the guards assumed a solemn air as though they'd entered a sacred place.

"The people try to record as many as they can"—Ronya touched the wall, running her fingers across the notches carved into the ice—"but there are some poor souls whose names are never marked down."

Mara leaned closer to the wall, studying the texture.

Words. Tiny words carved into the ice. Hundreds and hundreds of names.

"What happened to them?" Mara asked.

"The ice is a living thing," Ronya said. "It grows and changes just like everything else in the world. The palace lies at the heart of the mountain—things shift very slowly there. The ice allows us to protect our home. But the outskirts of the city, the shortcuts that sometimes lead to entirely different places, the twisting passages that lead to hidden wonders...all of them change. These poor people were caught in the metamorphosis. Once swallowed by the will of the ice, there is no coming back."

"But the ice swallowed me," Mara said, "and Tham."

"It wasn't the ice that drew you in," Ronya said. "That was

done by our guards to protect the people of Isfol from your invasion. You were pulled in and out of the ice quickly. You were given tonics to prevent any lasting ill effects. Those who stay in the ice for more than a few minutes are changed forever."

"If we are to be constantly surrounded by guards, I don't think we'll have to worry about wandering the wrong way," Mara said.

"The warning isn't just for your future." Ronya pressed her palm to the names carved into the wall. "It would be unkind if I didn't prepare you."

Ronya bowed her head and closed her eyes for a moment before leading their pack farther down the narrow street and out onto a road bordering the river that flowed through the city.

People pressed their backs to the buildings, making way for the Princess to pass.

A few boats drifted along the river, their passengers looking more like merry makers than workers. The boaters all tucked their chins, silencing their laughter in deference to the passing royal.

Mara studied the peoples' faces, searching for some sign of fear or loathing, any hint of despair that might combine the benevolent princess Ronya seemed to be with the scheming captor that had stolen Mara's freedom.

Ronya stopped in front of a building with tapestries of deep blue flanking the entrance. With a wave of her hand, the door opened, sending the people inside scattering out of her way.

An older woman with her thinning hair tied up in a bun was the only person to step into their path.

"Your Highness." The woman bowed. "We weren't expecting you today. Are you well?"

"Yes, thank you," Ronya said. "These are two of the Ilbreans."

The woman looked up, her eyes shifting from curiosity to pity in an instant.

"It's time they see him," Ronya said.

"Of course, Your Highness." The woman bowed again. "This way, if you please."

Doors lined the hall that cut into the heart of the building.

Mara tensed as a pained moan carried out of one of the rooms.

"What is this place?" She tucked herself closer to Tham, not allowing her mind drift into wondering how quickly she could run with all the layers of her skirts trying to tangle around her legs.

The sound of muffled sobbing came through another door.

"Your Highness," Mara said, "why are we here?"

The woman stopped in front of a door that looked just like all the others. "We will continue to do our best for him." She gave a deep bow before opening the door and stepping aside. "It is not our way to ever give up hope."

"Thank you for your service." Ronya gave the woman a nod and stepped into the room.

A bed and a chair had been fixed to the floor, just as Mara's bed had been in her cell. A ball of clean sheets had been tossed into the corner, seeming out of place in the barren space.

But the white fabric began to stir, and a head of matted hair appeared. The poor creature had been huddled around a chain that attached its leg to the wall.

"I've brought them to you." Ronya spoke in a calming tone. "Just as I promised. Would you like to see them?"

The matted hair shifted as the creature turned its head.

It wasn't a beast.

Not an animal. Not fur.

An overgrown beard, caked in filth and food, covered most of his face.

The man looked up at Mara and Tham.

"Elver," Tham whispered.

Recognition drove a dagger into Mara's gut. "What's happened to you?"

"Run! It's coming. Run! You have to run!" Elver's eyes grew wide with terror.

"Elver!" Mara reached toward him.

"Death. He's here." Elver yanked on his chain. "It's time for you to die. Dead, dead, dead, you'd be better off dead."

Tham grabbed Mara around the middle, lifting her out of the way as Elver dove toward them, hands outstretched, ready to kill the people he had so recently called friends.

"Why won't you die!"

KAI

He rubbed his palms together, letting his calluses grate against each other as he tried to ignore the sudden silence. Shifting his weight onto his toes, Kai tested the grip of his boots on the beam one final time before leaping into the air.

A gasp carried from the crowd as he stretched his arms high, reaching for safety. A familiar pain shot from his palms to his shoulders as he caught hold of the rope.

The spectators thirty feet below cheered as he steadied himself. Looping the rope around one foot, he waved at the horde of soldiers.

"So much applause for such a little thing!" Kai twisted, wrapping the rope around his torso. He let go with his other hand, gritting his teeth against the growing bruises on his ribs as he spiraled down, tumbling to the ground, landing in a crouch that gained the loudest cheers the Pameranian men had ever offered.

"Thank you, thank you!" Kai bowed to the soldiers gathered in the warehouse. "Though my antics can't begin to repay the generosity we've been granted in Soumid, please know that we are grateful and will remember your kindness as we begin our journey back to Ilara in the morning!"

Kai bowed again, and the soldiers gave one final round of applause.

Keep smiling. You know you should.

Kai shook the hands of the men who came up to him, letting them examine the calluses on his palms, assuring them that launching himself at a rope high in the air was not something he'd learned to do while drunk.

Kai glanced to the corner of the warehouse where the captain had made his nest in their prison, which still stank of decay and animal dung despite the sailors having lived in the wretched space for more than a week.

The captain still hadn't returned from his final meeting with the harbormaster.

He'll be back. You'll have time.

You should have been bold enough to speak sooner. Smart enough to think through the danger sooner.

"Don't know if you're brave or foolish." A soldier gripped Kai's arm as though testing his muscles.

"It's a mixture of both, honestly." Kai tensed, letting the soldier feel the firmness of his arm. "And I've never minded heights, so that helps."

"You should quit the sea and make a living entertaining. There are a few troupes that travel along the coast, playing at parties and festivals." The soldier leaned close, as though offering Kai a sliver of precious advice. "They make a fair amount of coin. And I've seen their camps. Even a king would envy the fun they have. Pleasure to fulfill everyone's tastes." He gave Kai a coy smile.

"Kai would never quit the sea." Drew clapped both Kai and the soldier on the shoulders. "Besides, he's a Guilded sailor. He'd have to be released from his bond by the Lord Sailor."

"Alas, tis true. Though next time I make my way to Pamerane, I might have to win my way into one of those camps." He winked at the soldier and shook his hand. "May the storms bring gentle rains."

The soldier looked from Drew to Kai before giving a nod and fading back into the group.

"Any sign of the captain?" Kai kept his smile for the soldiers as he spoke quietly enough for only Drew to hear.

"Nothing," Drew said. "He'll turn up soon enough. He hasn't got a choice."

"No, he hasn't." Kai waved as the soldiers started leaving.

"None of this feels right." Drew scrubbed his hands over the hair on his chin, which had grown thick enough to be considered a reasonable beard. "We're setting sail tomorrow, and we haven't seen the ship. We should be loading supplies or checking the rig—"

"It's not our ship," Kai said. "The only thing we're supposed to do is graciously board and stay out of the way."

"And hope the sailors are competent enough to get us home."

"They deal with the outskirts of the southern storms at the best of times. They can make the journey to Ilara." Kai gave one last nod as the soldiers closed the door, locking the sailors back in.

"Funny how they're our friends when you entertain them and our wardens when your little show is over."

"Kai, they left us some frie!" Sean called from the corner.

"And that makes the ache in my shoulders worth it." Kai bowed Drew toward the rest of the sailors who had all gathered around the bounty left by the soldiers.

Kai hadn't started performing nightly stunts to gain goods from the guards. He'd been caught climbing through the rafters while looking for a way to the roof and spun a tale about enjoying leaping around high places to save himself from being thrown in the Soumid prison.

The food and drink the guards brought to pay for the entertainment Kai offered had provided a balm for the men who'd been locked in the dark for so long. The excuse to explore every rafter and loose shingle had been the advantage Kai truly needed.

"You should perform for the King when we return to Ilara." Brody passed Kai a flask of frie. "Maybe they'll put a rope up for you at next Winter's End."

"I think the King can find better entertainment than my pitiful act." Kai took a swallow of frie, enjoying the burn as it sank past his lungs. The stuff had less flavor and more sting than the Ilaran version, but prisoners couldn't afford to be picky.

The men sorted through the bread, fruit, and cheese the soldiers had left, offering Kai the biggest portion since he'd been the one to earn the bounty. Kai refused, taking one of the smaller rations, unsure his stomach could bear even that amount.

He carried his supper to the far side of the warehouse, sitting against a crate to watch the door.

"Do you want to brood alone?" Drew sat beside him without waiting for an answer. "The harbormaster won't let the captain miss the ship tomorrow. He'll be back."

Kai made a noise close to a growl and bit into his bread. It had been stale for at least two days.

"The harbormaster is probably busy upping the price he wants for getting us home." Drew handed Kai his cup of water. "They're negotiating as we speak."

Kai took a sip, forcing down the bread stuck in his throat. "I know the captain will be back. The harbormaster has his heart set on gaining Ilbrean gold, and he won't get any if he doesn't deliver the captain safely back to Ilara."

"Then why do you look like you're preparing for an attack?"

"I've been circling through it over and over the whole time we've been locked in this rotting warehouse," Kai said. "We've got to tell the Guilds what Sorcerer Roo did. If we let the Sorcerers Guild keep pushing as they have been, they'll be running the Sailors Guild before Princess Illia's wedding."

It was Drew's turn to give a throaty growl.

"People have to know." Kai passed the water cup back. "Lord Nevon has to take a stand against the Sorcerers."

"Seems like you've figured it all out."

"I know what needs to happen. I just don't know how to accomplish it without all of us ending up dead, or worse." Kai shoved away the rest of his food. "They have the ship's manifest. They'll know who all of us are, and the Sorcerers Guild won't have any trouble silencing the survivors. Or their families. Or the barman they spoke too loudly to. It's a chivving mess, and we're all chivving doomed."

"Then I wish the soldiers had left us more frie."

"I need to talk to Lord Karron." Kai planted his palms on the ground, fighting the urge to leap to his feet and climb to the beams again just to burn off a bit of the anger tensing his limbs. "If anyone could think of a way to push back against the sorcerers and survive, it would be him."

"Then go to him as soon as we reach the docks in Ilara."

"If he's in the city, I'll race to him."

"Then breathe, Kai. There's nothing to do now but eat this stale bread and wait to get on the ship come morning."

"You're right." Kai gripped Drew's shoulder. "It just still feels like disaster is prowling closer."

Kai stayed staring at the door as the others shifted from eating to talking about getting home, to sleeping on the worn blankets the harbormaster had kindly provided his Ilbrean guests.

Drew brought Kai his blankets before making his own pallet on the floor nearby. Even as the others turned out the few lamps they'd been granted, Kai couldn't bring himself to sleep.

There had to be a way.

They could summon as many Ilarans as would gather. Bring them all to the cathedral square and shout what had happened for the people to hear. The survivors of Sorcerer Roo's horrid expedition might still be killed, but at least the truth wouldn't die with them.

Or they could go in front of the Guilds Council and give a full account of the journey. The council members couldn't all be gotten rid of for knowing the truth. Not even the Sorcerers Guild would dare to be that brazen.

But the crew would still be in danger, ripe for the sorcerers to pick off one by one. And if the sorcerers truly wanted to torture the crew, they could go after the men's families. Some of the crew had wives, children...

Chivving cact of a demon's spawn.

Lord Karron had spent years collecting information that displayed the evil of the Sorcerers Guild. Building a plan. Keeping records. Creating a place to store extra copies of whatever evidence he found so if the sorcerers killed him, the truth wouldn't follow him to his grave.

But how could Kai hold back the truth of his ship's doom when the fate of his Guild hung in the balance? He didn't have time to squirrel away evidence in hopes of someday getting the chance to speak the truth about the Sorcerers Guild.

He needed a faster plan.

The door slid open, letting in a waft of fresh air and a strip of starlight.

The captain's silhouette appeared in the doorway. He bowed to the soldiers before stepping into the warehouse. The door slid shut behind him.

Kai leapt to his feet, crossing to the captain before the man's eyes had adjusted to the dim light.

"Sir, I was starting to worry the harbormaster wouldn't send you back before morning." Kai kept his voice low enough not to wake the sleeping crewmembers.

"The bastard wanted to renegotiate his prize for returning us to Ilara." The captain headed toward his claimed corner of the warehouse.

Kai followed behind. "You agreed on a price a week ago."

"The slitch has an itemized list of all the costs he's incurred while keeping us in this warehouse. Insists we negotiated for ship passage home, not for our keep in Soumid."

"How much is he charging for our lovely accommodations?"

"As much as we'd spend at the finest inn in Ilara." The captain sank down onto the crates the crew had cobbled together to make him a bed. "From the cost of the food we've been eating, Lord Nevon will think we've had twelve feasts a day."

"Pity the harbormaster never sent us an invitation to the festivities."

"He also charged a Guild Lord's ransom for the letters I've sent to Ilara." The captain took off his coat, folding it up to make a pillow. "Enough to buy a farm in the south and spend my—"

"Letters, sir?" A jolt of cold panic knocked into Kai's spine.

"Six of them." The captain yanked off his boots. "Three to the King, three to Lord Nevon, all distributed to boats that have headed north since we've been trapped in our luxurious accommodations. Both the King and the Lord Sailor will know exactly what happened in the southern storms before we dock in Ilara. Hopefully, that will soften the blow of the trunk of gold the harbormaster is demanding from the Guilds before we're allowed to set foot on land in our own chivving country."

"The letters will beat us there." The cold trickled down Kai's spine, numbing his legs, stealing his confidence in his own limbs.

"They'd better, or I've wasted a hoard of the Guilds' chivving coin."

"Sir, we can't get on that ship."

"What?"

"We'll find another way back. We'll march across the mountains if we have to, but none of us can board that ship in the morning."

"Kai, have you lost—"

"That ship will never make it to land." Kai knelt in front of the captain. "The King is always guarded by sorcerers. As soon as he opens the letters you sent him, the truth of what happened in the southern storms is as good as in the Lady Sorcerer's hands."

"The King needs to understand the villainy of Sorcerer Roo's actions before we dock. He needs to know—"

"Know what, exactly?" Kai glanced over his shoulder to the other men. "That a letter, supposedly sent by you, is accusing the Sorcerers Guild of horrible things? Until we arrive in Ilbrea, there's no way to prove the letter came from you. Or that your words are true and not the ravings of a man who gambled in the storms and lost his crew."

"You push too far, Sailor Saso."

"Until we stand before the Guilds Council, there's no way to confirm the truth of your story. The Sorcerers Guild will never let our ship reach Ilara."

"You credit too much power to the purple lady."

"Boarding that ship is suicide, sir." Kai shut his eyes, wishing for the thousandth time he could have one of the Karron clan beside him, doing the things that didn't suit his skills. "I have seen the wrath of the Sorcerers Guild. I have witnessed the torment they inflict on those who dare to defy them. You are our captain, you are in charge of this crew, but I have seen a darker side of the demons that dwell in the Sorcerers Tower than you've endured. Violence and vengeance are what they thrive on. I am begging you, sir, please believe me. This is not a journey mere men can survive."

The captain stayed silent for a long moment, his gaze sweeping over the darkness as though he were counting the men he could not see.

"It is our duty to the Guilds to sail for Ilara," the captain said. "We must return to the Lord Sailor's side as quickly as the gods will allow and stand with him as we face the sorcerers. Anything less would be a violation of the oath we swore to the Sailors Guild."

"We should find another ship. If the sorcerers are expecting—"

"There will be no other ship. We've worn through the harbor-master's good will. If we don't sail for Ilara tomorrow, we'll be thrown in prison for the debt we owe for our food and lodging."

"Then we sneak out and go on foot. The mountains—"

"Are too hazardous to cross. And even if we survived the journey through the mountains, we would end up at the southern end of Ilbrea. We're boarding that ship in the morning."

"If we die, the truth will die with us." Kai sank back onto his heels as the cold in his legs drifted away, leaving behind anger that burned through his limbs. "If that ship doesn't make it to Ilara, the Sailors Guild will crumble under the force of the sorcerers' will."

"My decision is final. I will not be swayed. You're dismissed, Sailor Saso."

"Yes, captain." Kai gave a nod and stood, backing away as the captain lay down on the crates that were his bed.

Kai gripped his hands together, willing the anger surging through his body to calm enough to allow him to think.

He shut his eyes, picturing himself in the sitting room at the Map Master's Palace, his favorite people surrounding him. The late afternoon sun streaming in through the wide windows that looked out toward the cliffs. The scent of fresh-baked sweets filling the air. The comfort of knowing the people he called family were with him.

He imagined himself pacing behind the couch where Mara sat at a comically respectable distance from Tham.

The captain's wrong, Kai thought. *He's dooming the Sailors Guild. No one will survive that voyage.*

They might. Tham furrowed his brow. *The sorcerers would have to reach the ship before it nears Ilara. That means finding the right ship and attacking on the open water where they're at a disadvantage.*

The Lady Sorcerer won't care if she has to smite the crew as they step onto the docks. Mara looked up at Kai, fear and grief filling her eyes. *The sailors won't survive, no matter how much innocent blood the sorcerers have to spill to kill them.*

I should rouse the crew, Kai said. *We can sneak out without the captain and—*

And end up in a Pameranian prison? Allora took Kai's hand. *You're a good man, Kai. A clever one. I know you want to protect your crew, but there's no chance of you getting all those men out of the warehouse, let alone beyond the city and through the mountains.*

I can't just leave them here! Kai shouted. *They are my crew. I can't let them sail to their deaths.*

You could be wrong. The sorcerers might not attack, Tham said. *The men who sail back to Ilara could have the safer journey.*

After all we've survived, I can't believe that's true. Grief sank into Kai's gut.

You have to go, Kai. You don't have a choice. Allora held Kai tight. *It's bigger than the crew of one ship. It's the future of Ilbrea. Someone needs to make sure the truth reaches Ilara.*

I can't. Allora, I can't.

It's a horrible sacrifice we're asking you to make. Adrial kept his gaze fixed on his palms as he spoke. *Surviving can be a truly terrible wound to endure. But you know we're right. And we know you're strong enough to carry the burden.*

I'll be going against my captain's orders. A painful hollow grew in Kai's chest. *I'll be tossed out of the Sailors Guild.*

You won't. Tears glistened in Allora's eyes. *None of them will make it back to Ilara to report you.*

Sunrise is coming, Kai. Niko appeared by Allora's side, wrapping his arm around her waist. *Go. You're running out of time.*

A stone pressed against the front of Kai's throat as he gazed at his family for one more moment before opening his eyes and facing the darkness of his rotting prison.

He looked back toward the captain, studying his silhouette,

watching the steady rise and fall of his chest for a good minute before heading to the other side of the warehouse.

He passed Sean, who had proposed to the girl he loved before leaving on this journey, and Brody, whose wife was expecting their third child.

He stopped in the corner where the poor cut of the wood allowed him to climb up to the beams.

For the good of Ilbrea.

He shut his eyes again, trying to silence the battle between guilt and anger that made his hands tremble too badly to climb.

He turned away from the wall, cutting through the sleeping figures to the blankets Drew hand laid out for him. It only took him a minute to toss his coat, flask, and uneaten food into the thickest of the blankets and tie the whole thing into a bundle he could carry on his back. He grabbed a rope, looping it over his shoulder. He tested the weight of his boots, making sure the coin he'd stashed in the heels hadn't been stolen by the gods.

Pausing to study the shadows, he searched for any hint of movement before creeping to Drew's side.

He crouched down, clamping a hand over Drew's mouth and pinning his shoulders to the ground as he whispered in his friend's ear. "Wake up, and don't make a sound."

Drew moved to swing for Kai's face.

"It's Kai, you slitch. Stay quiet."

Drew dragged in a shaky breath as he lifted Kai's hand away from his mouth.

"Do you trust me enough to do something chivving awful we'll both regret for the rest of our lives?" Kai whispered.

"What under the stars are you talking about?"

"I'm leaving now. Climbing out through a weak point I found in the shingles and making a run for the edge of the city before dawn."

"Why would you—"

"I don't have time to reason through the whole chivving mess again. I'm going. I don't want to leave you behind. Come with me."

Drew shut his eyes, laying his head back on the ground.

"Stay safe, friend." Kai gripped Drew's hand, holding on for a heartbeat before forcing himself to stand.

The walk back to the wall seemed too short, but Kai didn't let himself study the shadows of the men he was abandoning.

You could be wrong. They might outlive you.

I pray the gods are kind enough to let them all *outlive me.*

He focused on the strain in his hands as he climbed the wall. On finding the niches where he could fit the toes of his boots. He wished the climb were harder, something to make thinking of anything else impossible.

Near the top of the wall, the wood sagged beneath his weight where neglect and rain had rotted the planks. He shifted his weight from side to side, waiting for the gods to crack the wall and send him tumbling to the ground, shattering his limbs and stealing his chance of escape.

The wood refused to break.

He glanced to the beam about two feet to his left, gauging the distance in the darkness before looping one arm over the top. He held his breath as he let go of the wall with his other hand, leaving himself vulnerable as he dangled thirty feet in the air.

Tightening his grip, he swung his legs up, wrapping them around the beam before swiveling to sit on top of the wood. He took a deep breath, shaking out his hands before inching forward.

The shingles he'd managed to loosen were in the very corner of the eaves. He lay flat on his stomach, twisting his neck to see what he was doing as he pried the shingles free. He shoved the chunks of rotting wood into the gap where the wall met the roof so the debris wouldn't fall to the floor and wake the men, destroying his escape.

The sorcerers will destroy Ilbrea.

That's why you're doing this. You're not a chivving coward. You're defending your Guild. Your country.

His fingers were nicked to bleeding by the time he'd made a hole in the roof large enough to slip through.

You'll run out of darkness if you don't go now.

Twisting his shoulders, he pushed his head through the hole. The cool night air filled his lungs, shifting the moment from nightmare to reality. He planted his hands on the roof, gritting his teeth against all the words he should have said.

There wasn't time.

It wouldn't have made a difference anyway.

Something caught on his back. He wobbled on the beam inside, his heart shooting up into his throat as he spread his arms wide, bracing himself on the roof.

Sense returned as he regained his balance. He reached behind with one arm, pulling the rope over his head. He tried again to push himself forward, arching his back to give the bundled blanket he carried room to fit through the opening.

He didn't properly breathe until he'd made it all the way onto the roof. He sat on the worn shingles, wondering if they'd give out beneath his weight.

Most of the lights in the city had been dampened for the night. The only lit path led up to the mansions at the top of the rise. He'd need to climb up that way. Get beyond the fancy estates and north of the city before morning. Then continue north. Find a way across the mountains and into Ilbrea.

Then stand against the Sorcerers Guild.

"Give a fellow a hand."

Fear shot through Kai's chest at the whispered words.

Drew's head poked out of the roof. "Not all of us climb like chivving spiders."

NIKO

Time has little meaning without light. It seems Lord Karron should have taught me that. Though, I'm not sure even the Map Master understands what life becomes when days stop.

For a while, I tried counting the days by how often I needed to sleep. But I never know how long I've slept for. Hunger isn't a good measure of time, either. The food we've found, mushrooms and moss, aren't like any food I'm accustomed to. I think I need to eat more often here than I did aboveground. Somehow, the mountain always provides.

I've slept thirty-six times. I've written thirty-five messages to you you'll never receive. Perhaps these letters are a sign I've begun to lose my reason. But at least when I see your face again, I'll be able to say I wrote you every time I thought we'd reached a new night. I don't know if it's day or night now, and I'll have no paper proof these letters ever existed. But you'll know I thought of you.

Every night. Every day. Every step. You are why I cannot surrender to the darkness.

I will come home to you,
Niko

ALLORA

My Darling Bride,

It is not traditional for the groom to write to his bride mere hours before their wedding, but I would like to think I have come to know you well.

I want this to be a joyous day for us both. I don't want any worries to weigh heavy on your heart as we stand together in the cathedral. So, I will tell you this now.

There is still no news of Kai's ship. They have continued scouring the coast and will soon reach Pamerane. If they've still found no sign of wreckage when they pass out of Ilbrean waters, they will request that the Pameranian Navy take up the search while our party sails west. They will start at the Southern Citadel and sail north along the Barrens.

Lady Gwell herself has placed the full might of the Sorcerers Guild behind the search. Sorcerers have been boarding every ship that docks in Ilara, questioning the crews in hopes of finding some hint as to the fate of Kai's ship. I have been assured of their thoroughness. No trace of information will slip by. I cannot imagine more capable hands than Lady Gwell's. With her ensuring the hunt stays on the right path, my hopes are high that we will know more very soon.

This is not the news I wanted to give you. But there is nothing else that can be discovered today. So please, put this from your mind. Enjoy our wedding, secure in the knowledge that the search has not been abandoned. We will continue to look for your Kai, you have my word.

I will see you in the cathedral, my Queen. We will make our vows before Dudia and the Guilds and begin our life together.

I may not always be able to instantly fulfill your every need, but know that I want you to be happy. You will never be ignored.

As I protect Ilbrea, I will protect you.

Your loving husband,

Brannon

Allora read the letter for the fourth time as the women bustled around her, fastening the hundred buttons down the back of her gown, painting pink on her cheeks, and adding yet more pins to her hair.

Your loving husband,

Brannon

He would keep searching for Kai. He could have said no. He could have already abandoned the search. But for her sake, he persisted.

He's a good man.

A maid carried away Allora's green dress. The last Map Maker green she would ever wear.

He's not the right man.

"It's time for the veil, Lady Karron." Agatha climbed onto the stool beside Allora.

Three women carried the lace of the veil. The sorcerers must have helped for such a piece to have been created so quickly.

Allora longed to tear the veil from their hands and shred it. Destroy the sorcerers' perfect work and with it any pretense she would become the Queen they demanded she be.

She folded Brannon's letter and turned so Agatha could pin

her veil in place. The lace held unnatural weight, pressing down on her, smothering her.

Logic screamed the weight was imagined, but she could feel it either way.

She'd wear the veil. She'd go to the cathedral and give her vow. The women would take off the veil. The women would take off her dress.

Then Brannon would take her to bed.

She knew the intricacies of what would happen. Mara had explained everything to her ages ago.

The longing Mara felt for Tham. The needs her body demanded be fulfilled. The ecstatic pleasure that brought her back to Tham's arms over and over, despite the danger such trysts posed to Mara's place in the Map Makers Guild.

Mara loved Tham. Their bodies completed each other's.

Allora did not love Brannon. She did not long for him. But she would be his wife. He would visit her bed.

He would kiss her, and touch her, and enter her.

"No joyful tears yet, Lady Karron." One of the women dabbed below her eyes. "You must let them see you in a perfect state before succumbing to emotion."

"Of course," Allora murmured.

She would carry his child, give birth to the next ruler of Ilbrea.

If she did not conceive, he would come to her bed again and again.

It doesn't matter. I will be his wife. He will visit me anyway. He will always touch me. He will long to be inside me.

She pressed her hands to the front of her dress, not allowing them to tremble.

"The carriage is ready," a soldier said.

The gaggle of women chatted and worried as they chivvied Allora out the door.

Brannon could not be blamed for wanting to bed his wife.

He'd done nothing wrong in asking Allora to marry him.

He is innocent. I am the one who is guilty of using him to flee my grief.

I will welcome him. I will not make him suffer for my broken heart. I am strong enough for that.

I will have to be strong enough for that.

The palace servants lined the entryway. They watched Allora descend the stairs. All of them looked happy. Each and every one.

They are glad to have a new queen and mistress. I cannot betray them. I will not be a shadow that haunts these halls, trailing misery behind her.

She let out a slow breath, tucking the life she had dreamt of aside, folding it up in the tatters of her soul and hiding it in a corner of her mind where she would only look at it when she was alone and her grief could not harm anyone else.

Pressing a demure smile onto her lips, Allora nodded to the servants, every bit the shy bride they needed her to be.

The younger girls grinned like they would have giggled if such things could be allowed in front of the future Queen.

The bright light of a joyful morning greeted her outside.

Soldiers and sorcerers on horseback waited to escort her. Lilies and deep green vines dripped over the sides of the glittering golden carriage that would carry her to her wedding.

"Agatha," Allora said.

"Yes, Lady Karron." Agatha rushed forward, gripping her little leather book.

"The carriage is lovely. Thank you."

It took three women to arrange Allora's dress and veil inside the carriage, carefully placing everything so she would be able to step out in front of the cathedral in perfect order with only the Lord Soldier's hand for support.

"We'll see you at the cathedral." Agatha closed the carriage door, leaving her alone.

Her father should have been riding with her. He should be with her, holding her hand, keeping her calm.

But they hadn't spoken. She'd been too angry and too ashamed of running from her heartbreak.

The carriage began to rumble forward.

"Stop." Allora pounded on the roof. "Stop!"

"Whoa."

The carriage rocked back as it stopped.

"Lady Karron, what's wrong?" Agatha opened the door, a look of terror on her face.

"Have a soldier ride ahead," Allora said. "Have him find my father, beg him to greet me at the carriage."

"Yes, Lady Karron." Agatha bowed.

"Then come back. I can't ride alone. You can sneak out the far side of the carriage once I've gone up the cathedral steps."

"As you wish, Lady Karron." Agatha bustled away.

"I can do this," Allora whispered. "I can be Queen. I will not fail my people. I will be the Queen of Ilbrea."

23

ADRIAL

Faint strains of music floated under the murmured conversations that filled the cathedral. The musicians had been hidden in a corner behind a trellis of pure white flowers, as though it would be a horrible offense to admit the music was not, in fact, bursting into being at the stars' sheer joy at a royal wedding.

Each of the Guilds had arranged themselves by the appropriate spoke of the seven-pointed star inlaid in the white marble of the floor. A few mingled outside their group, but most kept to their color, leaving clusters of purple, white, green, red, black, and blue all standing before the silver and gold of the Royal Willocs.

King Brannon and Princess Illia kept close together, both of them radiating joy as though they hadn't stood in the exact same place to bury the fallen Queen not so very long ago.

"You look pale." Lord Gareth furrowed his brow as he studied Adrial. "Are you unwell?"

"No, sir." Adrial bowed. "Though you're probably right about my pallor. To be completely honest, I think it's all the time I've been spending on the vellum. Coming here in the carriage today was the most sunlight I've seen in weeks."

"You're not the first I've heard that from." Lord Gareth tapped his wrinkled lips. "The scribes have all become restless. The courtyard is not nearly large enough for a few hundred people to receive the proper amount of exercise and sunlight required to maintain health."

"You are correct on both fronts, Lord Gareth," Adrial said.

"The city has been calm long enough, perhaps we might consider easing the restrictions on the scribes' movement. There would have to be guards, of course. And no one would be allowed out after dark."

"Absolutely, sir." A tiny spark of hope shot through Adrial's chest.

If the scribes were allowed to leave the library, he could take Ena out riding. Not as far as the waterfall, but she could collect some of her own supplies. She'd been well beyond peeved when the man Adrial had hired to find her ingredients had come back with the wrong flowers for the third time in a row.

Adrial could spend the day with Ena, riding beyond Ilara. Enjoying the sun and each other's company.

Movement toward the front of the cathedral caught Adrial's eye.

A soldier cut quickly toward the cluster of map makers. The soldier bowed to Lord Karron before speaking beneath the crowd's chatter.

Lord Karron froze for a moment, his jaw tensing in what anyone who didn't know him might take to be anger, before nodding and striding across the room and out of the cathedral.

"I hope there's nothing wrong," Lord Gareth said.

"I don't think so," Adrial said. "If I'm not mistaken, something might finally be very right."

The bell on top of the cathedral tolled once. The sound reverberated around the space, silencing the crowd.

Adrial glanced back toward the image of Saint Alwyn on the scribes' stained-glass window.

Please, let this day be one of peace and forgiveness. Let my friend's heart begin to heal.

The music fell silent as Allora and Lord Karron stepped through the cathedral doors side by side, Allora's hand resting on top of her father's as it was meant to be.

Lord Karron's face held a look of duty and promise. Allora's lips curved up in a tiny smile, befitting the Queen of Ilbrea.

They stayed in the doorway for a long moment, letting all present bask in the glory of Allora's beauty. Her blond hair had been woven into what looked almost like a foreshadowing of the crown she would soon wear. Tiny golden stitches peeked through the pure white of her dress, letting the light radiate off her gown as though she were a star come to grace the mortal world.

She wore a thin necklace of diamonds, forgoing the more opulent royal jewels. The simplicity seemed fitting for someone marrying a recent widower. Besides, she didn't need glittering gems to be sure everyone present would be telling all of Ilara how beautiful their new Queen had been at her wedding.

Allora gave her father a nod, and Lord Karron led her slowly forward. She looked to each Guild as she passed. She caught Adrial's eye as she acknowledged the scribes.

He hoped the joy on her face was real.

She looked to the other side of the cathedral, nodding to the flock of red-robed healers. She turned again, recognizing the sailors, then stopped in front of the map makers.

She let go of Lord Karron's arm. He reached up and touched her chin, looking into his child's eyes one more time before she would become his Queen.

Allora left him in his place with the map makers before acknowledging the soldiers and finally the sorcerers.

She stopped again in front of the King, bowing to the man who would soon be her husband.

The cathedral doors closed.

The King stepped forward and bowed to Allora before kissing her hand. Pride radiated from him as he led her up to stand by his side.

The whole cathedral seemed to exhale at the same moment as the perfect image of their King and future Queen drove the breath from their bodies.

Lady Gwell stepped away from the other sorcerers to stand in front of the King.

"It is my honor to join togeth—"

Bang!

The ground shook.

Lord Gareth wobbled and lurched forward.

Adrial stumbled sideways, trying to catch Lord Gareth while looking for whatever had nearly knocked him off his feet.

"My Lord!" Adrial shouted over the panicked voices, reaching for Lord Gareth, missing his arm as the old man fell to the ground.

A rumble and a crack sounded from above.

Adrial looked up. The dome of the cathedral looked wrong, misshapen.

"Move!" one of the soldiers shouted a moment too late.

The ceiling above the healers crumbled, raining massive chunks of the marble dome onto the flock dressed in red.

"No!" Adrial's scream didn't break through the chaos.

He grabbed Lord Gareth's hand, trying to yank him to his feet as the damage spread around the dome, collapsing a hail of stone onto the map makers. Pain shot through Adrial's spine as something heavy hit him in the back, knocking him forward. He fell, his vision blurring as his temple struck the floor.

Lord Gareth's hand slipped out of Adrial's grip. Someone grabbed Adrial under his arms, lifting him to his feet and shoving him toward the corner of the cathedral, out from under the still-falling dome. They pressed Adrial against the wall, mashing his face to the cold, trembling marble.

A crackle cut over the cries of pain and fear.

"We can make it to the door!" a woman shouted near Adrial's ear.

"Not yet," Adrial's protector said.

The sound from above grew to a high-pitched rasp of stone grinding against stone before the whole building shook as the remains of the dome collapsed.

It was all over in less than a minute.

The noise of the falling debris stopped. The screams of the survivors seemed to triple.

"Allora." Adrial tried to wriggle away from his protector. "Allora."

"Wait," his protector said.

Adrial hated the unfamiliar voice for speaking so calmly.

"Lord Gareth." Adrial didn't stop trying to break free. "Where's Lord Gareth?"

"We have him, Head Scribe."

That voice Adrial did know. He managed to turn his head enough to see Scribe Natalia Tammin.

In all the time they'd worked together in the scribes' shop, he'd never once seen Tammin's eyes filled with such terror. She held Lord Gareth against the wall, sheltering him with her own body just as Adrial was being sheltered.

"We need to get them out," Tammin said. "Before the rest collapses."

"Let's go." Adrial's savior kept one hand on his arm and one on the back of his head as he herded him toward the cathedral doors.

The golden doors stood open now. The doorframe hadn't been damaged. Soldiers poured into the ruins of the cathedral.

Adrial glanced back. For a moment, he thought he'd gotten blood in his eyes. He blinked twice before realizing the blood had been painted on the cathedral floor.

So many bodies crushed. So much blood spilt.

Dust still drifted down from above, looking almost like snow.

Beauty does not belong in this pain.

"Allora." Adrial pulled against his savior, trying to turn enough to see the far side of the cathedral. "Lord Karron. I can't leave them."

"We have to keep moving." The man steered him toward the door.

"I can't leave them!"

"Lord and Lady Karron are with the sorcerers," the man said. "They're on their feet and well protected. Keep moving, Head Scribe. You have to get to safety and out of the soldiers' way."

"Thank you." Adrial let himself be forced out of the cathedral and back into the sunshine.

Common folk had gathered at the far edges of the square, held back from a closer view of the catastrophe by soldiers with drawn swords.

"Adrial!" Lord Gareth shouted as Tammin and a scribes' guard lifted him into a carriage. "We must wait for Adrial."

"We have him." Tammin reached for Adrial's hand, dragging him the last few feet to the carriage.

The scribes' guard lifted Adrial up and into the carriage before banging on the wall. "Go!"

The carriage charged forward, knocking Adrial into his seat as it whisked them away from the cathedral square.

"We have more room!" Adrial shouted out the window. "We can fit more people!"

"It doesn't matter." Lord Gareth wheezed as he leaned back in his seat. "They won't risk waiting. They have to secure us in the library before our guards can help anyone else." He dabbed at the blood near his mouth with the sleeve of his white robes. "I've told you before, Adrial, part of protecting the Scribes Guild is allowing yourself to be protected. Even when you wish it weren't."

"I don't even know the name of the man who saved me."

Adrial touched his temple where he'd cracked his head against the floor. His fingers came away red.

"You've never met Declan Farrell?" Lord Gareth said. "I suppose you might not have. He's a good scribe."

"I'll have to thank him for saving my life." Adrial shifted in his seat, wincing as pain radiated from where falling marble had struck his back.

"It wasn't your life he cared about. It was the life of the head scribe."

"Keep the gates secure!" The shout carried from outside as the carriage began to slow. "We need a healer for the Lord Scribe."

"Send wagons to gather the other wounded. All scribes who are able to move should be brought back here," another voice added.

The captain of the scribes' guard yanked the carriage door open. "We need healers."

"You won't find any." Lord Gareth reached out to take the captain's hands. "They were hit first. They'll have lost many from their Guild and those that remain will need to tend to the seriously wounded."

"You are seriously wounded, sir." The captain lifted the Lord Scribe from the carriage. "Get him to his room and find a healer. I don't care what it takes."

Two guards ran forward to carry Lord Gareth.

The captain reached back into the carriage for Adrial.

"I really am fine." Adrial stood, hunching over to make his way to the door.

The captain took his arm as he stepped down onto the cobblestone.

With a shout from the driver, the carriage pulled away to loop around the courtyard and race back out onto the street.

"We need to get you to your room." The captain spoke over the rumble of the carriage's wheels.

"Please see to someone else," Adrial said. "I got a bump on the head, but I assure you, I am perfectly fine."

"You've blood on your head and on your back, Head Scribe," the captain said.

"The entire dome of the cathedral collapsed," Adrial said. "I will survive my injuries without aid, many others will not. I have every reason to believe the Guilds were just attacked in a most horrific way. I will see myself to my room and have my apprentice bring me what I need to wash my wounds. You see to the protection of the library and organize what help you can for the wounded who are still stuck inside the cathedral."

The captain stared into Adrial's eyes for a moment, as though looking for signs of an invisible injury, before nodding and turning back to his men. "Straff, get to the kitchens. Have them start boiling water and collecting anything that can be used as a bandage. Vale, ride to the healers' compound, beg them to send what help they can."

Adrial cut through the guards as quickly as he could, keeping his gaze fixed front, trying to make sure no one would stop him and declare him an invalid.

"Adrial."

He looked toward Ena's voice, swaying as his head protested the sudden movement.

She ran to him, taking his face in her hands and peering into his eyes much as the captain had.

"What happened to you?" She took hold of his arm, guiding him away from the door that led to the scribes' chambers.

"The dome of the cathedral collapsed," Adrial said. "It must have been an attack."

Ena's steps faltered for a moment.

"Who was hurt?" She tightened her grip on his arm, quickening her pace as she led him toward her workshop.

"Almost everyone." Adrial's voice shook. "I think the sorcerers protected the royals. It was awful. There are so many wounded."

She shifted to walk behind him. "Your back's bleeding."

"I think part of the dome hit me. I fell. That's when I hurt my head. Another scribe pulled me out of the way."

"How did it happen?" She stayed behind him on the stairs to her workroom, keeping a hand on his lower back as though afraid he might fall.

"I don't know. Lady Gwell had just begun the wedding ceremony. There was a bang, and the whole place shook. Then the dome started falling on us. Almost like a wave. The healers were hit first, but the damage spread. The stone couldn't hold its weight."

"Chivving gods and stars." She pushed him into her shop and locked the door behind them. She took Adrial's face in her hands again. A hint of fear had replaced the usual glint of teasing in her eyes. "Tell me you're all right and mean it."

"I'm fine." Adrial pressed her hands to his cheeks. "A little blood spilt, but no real damage done."

Ena tipped her chin down, her shoulders relaxing as she took a breath before pulling her hands away from him.

"Good." She grabbed a stool from the corner and set it beside her worktable. "Take off your robes and let me see how bad the damage on your back is."

"It's fine."

"*Fine* can go horribly wrong if you let a chivving wound fester." Ena pulled three jars down from her shelf. "And don't tell anyone I'm doing this unless you want to see me hanged."

"Hanged for what?"

"Robes. Off." She reached under the tabletop and pulled down a wooden box, though Adrial couldn't tell how the box had been held in its hiding spot.

"What's that?" Adrial stepped around the stool to reach for the box.

"I will slice the clothes from your body if you make me." She smacked Adrial's hand away before striding to her bedroom.

"I believe you." He unfastened his robes, taking a sharp breath through his teeth as the fabric pulled away from the wound on his back. Squinting against the pain, he eased his robes off. A good portion of the pristine white had been stained a horrible red. He'd bled more than he'd thought.

Ena came back out of her room with a bundle of bandages.

"Sit." She grabbed a bowl of water and a stack of cloths from near the stove.

"You don't have to clean it for me." Adrial sat on the stool. "I can go up to my room and take a bath."

"A bath won't save you from infection." Ena dipped a cloth into the water. She wrung it out and stepped behind Adrial's back. "We'll get it cleaned up so I can properly see the damage done."

"You shouldn't have to tend to me. You've already saved my life once."

"Depending on the sort of infection that could make its way through your filthy wound, I may very well be saving your life again. Don't worry, scribe, I've seen far worse than this and it's never damaged my feminine wiles."

A groan escaped Adrial as she touched the cool cloth to his back and pain radiated down his spine.

"Just breathe." Ena spoke in a soothing tone. "A little pain now will lessen the hurt of healing."

"I believe you." He gripped his knees and tried to ignore the throbbing heat of his wound.

"The whole dome fell?" She wrung out the cloth before wiping more of his blood away.

"All of it. It was over so quickly, I barely had time to think. I don't understand how this could have happened. There were soldiers everywhere."

Ena stepped in front of him and tipped his chin up. Her fingers lingered against his skin for a moment before she began cleaning the blood from the side of his face. "I don't think it would have been that hard if you had the supplies and daring."

"What do you mean?"

"The dome was heavy. That amount of stone doesn't want to be hovering in the air. It wants to fall. All you have to do is let it. The black powder they use in the mines would work. Pack explosives in at the base of the dome and up one of the seams. Create a crack, and the whole thing would come down."

"I've never seen a place as well protected as the cathedral was today. We were surrounded by an army."

"Wouldn't have had to put the explosives up today." Ena set down the bloody cloth and opened one of the jars. The scent of its contents stung Adrial's nose.

"What is that?"

"Liquor stronger than homemade frie." Ena dipped a fresh cloth into the jar. "This part will be awful."

Spots danced in Adrial's eyes as she pressed the cloth to his back, working the liquor into the wound. The burning dragged an involuntary groan from his throat. "How could they have placed the black powder if not today?"

"Use your sense, scribe." She pressed another round of liquor to the wound. "It would be easy to climb to the dome at night. All you'd need is a rope and a distraction to keep a tired soldier busy for a few minutes. Pack in the powder, leave a patch big enough for a skilled archer to target, and climb back down. Once all the paun are crowded together, you're one well-shot flaming arrow from ridding the world of a whole mess of evil men. Chin up."

Adrial raised his chin, closing his eyes as she cleaned the wound on his temple. "You came up with that very quickly. Have you thought about bringing the cathedral dome down before?"

"All the Lord Paun gathered in one place? Of course I have. I've imagined hundreds of ways to destroy the cathedral with all the paun inside. Kill the monsters and watch the Guilds crumble to ash." Ena unscrewed the second jar, whose contents gave off a much gentler, calming aroma. "You really should have stitches on your back. It would heal faster and keep it from scarring too badly. But if the healers insist on looking over the head scribe, there would be no way to lie about my helping you if I'd stitched you up."

"Have you ever stitched skin before?" Adrial turned toward her. A shock of pain shot through his back.

"Are you looking for more reasons for the Guilds to hang me? Do you want a nicely written list?"

"The Guilds wouldn't hang you for helping me."

"You know so little of your own people." She scooped pale lavender ointment from the jar. "This'll help stop the bleeding. Don't let the pleasant scent fool you, it'll sting worse than the liquor."

"Lord Gareth would thank you for helping me."

"The penalty for being an unguilded healer is death." Ena rubbed the ointment into the wound on Adrial's back.

He arched his spine, instinctively fleeing what felt like hot coals searing his skin. He pounded his fist against his knee.

"The dome collapsed above the Healers Guild first." Adrial spoke through the pain, trying to force his mind to focus outside his body. "They were the worst hit. Their ranks have been decimated. With the number of wounded that will be coming back to the library, someone who's stitched skin before would be a hero for helping."

"A hero right up until the rope's around my neck." She rubbed more ointment onto his back. The second round didn't burn so horribly. "I risked my life even mixing this ointment."

"Then why did you do it?"

She dabbed the ointment on his temple. The heat of it sliced right behind his eyes.

"Because even though the streets have been quiet for weeks, that doesn't mean we're anywhere near peace. Cade began a rebellion. It was poorly planned, and the paun blood shed wasn't worth the common lives lost. But he did win in one way. You can relax. I'm done with that bit of torment."

"How did he win?" Adrial resisted the urge to turn and watch Ena work at the table.

"Denying the common folk burial papers, refusing to send healers to help the injured tilk...those who tried so hard to ignore the sins of the Guilds can't pretend anymore. The paun laid their evil in the streets for all to see when they let the common corpses rot."

"They shouldn't have done that. Most people in Ilara had nothing to do with Cade's rebellion. The Guilds should have helped them."

"That they should. Bend forward a bit."

Adrial tipped forward a few inches. An odd tickle sent a shiver up his spine as Ena sprinkled powder onto his back.

"The soldiers are the easiest enemy for most common folk to point to," Ena said. "They're the ones that steal your land and shove a blade through your gut. But the healers are a special kind of monster.

"The soldiers come and demand a farmer's taxes, letting him starve as payment for having a Guilded healer nearby. Then the farmer's child gets sick, and the healer demands more coin to help the farmer. The farmer can't pay. All his coin has already been taken by the soldiers, so the healer lets the child die."

"That's horrible."

"It happens all the time. The healers should be the ones to bring hope and comfort, but they can't even be bothered with a bit of mercy. After the rebellion, the Guilds were fool enough to forget to pretend to care for the people of Ilbrea. I doubt it was an accident the dome collapsed above the healers first. If the red paun are so willing to let the common folk die, why should the common folk let the healers live?"

"Ena, I'm—" Adrial swallowed the apology he wanted to give. "If there were some way to erase the damage the Guilds have done to you, I would do everything in my power to make it happen."

"I know." She tipped his face to the side and sprinkled powder onto his temple. "Why do you think I'm risking my neck to be sure you don't get an infection? Stand up. Let me get a bandage on your back."

The pain wound its way from Adrial's spine to his hip as he forced himself to his feet. "How did you get all this anyway? You've been trapped in the library for weeks, and there haven't been any healing supplies on the lists of things you've had me gather for you."

"Do you really think you'd know which plants are for healing and which are for inks?" She lifted his arms and began wrapping a bandage around his ribs. "Besides, if the scribes truly wanted to keep me locked in here, they wouldn't have made the library walls so easy to climb."

"Ena." Adrial grabbed her hand. "You can't climb over the library walls."

"I promise I can." Ena winked. "It's really quite easy."

"If they catch you climbing back into the library, they could think you're attacking and kill you. If they catch you in the city—"

"I'll be banished from the library?" Ena kissed his wrist before pulling her hand free. "There are plenty of people in the city who want me dead. As long as I value my own survival, I promise I'll never let anyone catch me."

She wrapped the bandage around his ribs several more times before tucking the end in and finishing it off. "Come back in the morning, and I'll change this out for you. If a healer wants to see you before then, excuse yourself for long enough to take the bandage off. It'll make you bleed again, but fresh blood will help cover my work."

"Thank you, Ena." He reached for her. His blood tainted both their hands.

"Come and wash up." Ignoring the stains, she took his hand, leading him to the tub in the bedroom. She knelt beside the worn metal basin to work the giant pump handle.

Adrial hadn't thought through her not having a tap she could simply turn to have hot water brought up from the furnaces tended to by the servants in the library's basement. "If you ever want a hot bath, you can come to my room."

"Are you trying to seduce me, scribe?" She began scrubbing her hands with a brick of pungent soap. "Come on. The cold water won't hurt your delicate hands."

"I know." Adrial gripped the lip of the tub to lower himself to the ground. The thought of climbing the stairs to his room exhausted him, yet Ena had climbed the library walls. He couldn't even imagine how such a feat could be done. "How do you get over the walls?"

"You shouldn't ask a girl to give up her secrets." She handed Adrial the brick of soap. "But don't worry, the library isn't vulnerable to a horde creeping over the walls. It takes skill to make the climb. There is no open path for invasion."

"How often do you leave?" Adrial sat back on his heels as his mind raced to places he did not want it to go.

"I doubt that's something you really want to know."

"Ena"—Adrial scrubbed the red from around his nails—"Ena, you were so quick in thinking up a plan for how to collapse the cathedral's dome. And, if you've been leaving the library, and I know you're a brave climber—"

"Are you asking if I brought down the cathedral dome?"

"Yes." Adrial scrubbed his hands harder, letting the soap sting his skin.

"Did I bring down the dome with you beneath it?"

Adrial glanced to Ena. She sat on the floor beside him, drying her hands with a clean cloth.

"If everything you've said about the wrongdoings of the Guilds has been learned from personal experience, then you would have reason enough to attack." Adrial ran his hands under the cold water, wishing he had another task to give him a reason to keep his gaze away from her.

"You're right. I have plenty of reasons to gleefully watch every paun in Ilbrea burn. If I had black powder and some fighters to stand with me, I would gladly risk the noose to watch the healers bleed." She held the cloth out to Adrial.

"Right." He dried his hands, carefully inspecting each of his fingers to make sure he hadn't left any of his blood behind.

"But I'm alone in Ilara, and such a feat would take more than one." She held a fresh cloth under the tap.

"Absolutely. It was a foolish question."

She wrung out the cloth, then placed a finger under his chin, drawing him closer to her. "Do you really believe I'd bring the dome down on your head? Do you think I would throw you away like that?" She dabbed away the powder that had fallen onto his cheek.

"I think you understand that some things are bigger than one person's life."

"Freedom from the Guilds will cost thousands of lives." She laid the cloth on the rim of the tub.

"Then my death would barely be noticed in the final tally." Adrial looked to her just in time to see a flicker of hurt in her eyes. He laid his hand on top of hers. "I'm sorry. You've just helped me yet again, and I've said something hurtful. I'm a foolish getch. Please forgive me."

"*Getch*. Such a low word from the head scribe." She took his hands, helping him to his feet.

"Can you forget I ever mentioned it?"

Ena stepped near him, laying her head on his shoulder and letting him wrap his arms around her. "Why do you let me stay here when you know I want the Guilds to burn?"

"Because I'm a selfish and horrible man. As much as I love the Scribes Guild and am grateful for my place in it, I wouldn't be able to breathe if you were gone, and I'm too cowardly to put myself in that sort of pain."

"Lies." She nestled deeper into his arms.

"It's the truth. And I suppose I hope that maybe if you keep pushing me in the right direction, I might make my Guild into something you won't hate."

"I don't believe in fairy stories, scribe."

"Perhaps you should. I've seen several impossible things happen in my life."

"I suppose I have as well."

They fell silent for a moment. He rested his cheek against the top of her head. His heart fluttered as the beauty of their stillness overwhelmed him.

He froze as she eased away from him, readying himself to be shouted at for having pushed the boundaries of their friendship too far. But she only shifted enough to look into his eyes as she wrapped her arms around his waist.

"If I were going to crush a pack of paun, I would make sure you weren't there. I'd lock you up and keep you safe while I slaughtered the monsters. I've lost too many people. Your life is not a sacrifice I'm willing to make." She pressed her lips to the scar on his shoulder. "You're the only one I have left."

Adrial held her tighter as the rattle of wagon wheels and shouts of panic drifted in through the windows.

24

KAI

A warm wind carried the scent of the storms from the south. Gray gathered at the edge of the horizon, but none of the people in the tavern seemed to care. They danced and laughed and drank, as though positively certain the storm wouldn't touch their portion of paradise.

The Tiller's Tree was as unlike an Ilbrean establishment as Kai could imagine a place being. There were no proper walls to begin with. Heavy beams held up the roof, but the sides had been left open, giving both the view of the mountains rising above them to the north and the ravenous bugs a chance to do their work.

The people in the Tiller's Tree were both less afraid and less lawful than any crowd in Ilara. In the hour Kai and Drew had spent sweating in the shade as they nursed their foul liquor and ate their supper of meat and fruit, there had been two brawls and one dice game that took over the entire center section of the establishment.

Kai studied the people around him, finding a woman with dark curling hair like his. He rolled up his sleeves, displaying his forearms, which had the same rich hue as the man at the bar who protected the coin the owner of the Tiller's Tree collected. The scrawny man with the scar on his neck had the same color eyes as Kai.

Kai took a gulp of his liquor, letting it burn away the strangely blurred sense of belonging and regret growing in his gut.

In Ilara, his dark complexion was rare enough to be unique in a tavern crowd.

In the Tiller's Tree, someone could easily mistake the people around him for his blood relations.

I could very well have distant family in this drunken horde. I wouldn't even know.

"You all right?" Drew leaned closer to Kai, not pulling his gaze from the southwestern corner of the tavern, where a cluster of men with knives at their hips had gathered.

"Fine." Kai took a long drink from his cup, letting the cheap liquor scour his throat. "Just wishing things were different."

The smash of breaking glass carried over the rumbling voices of the armed men.

"How do you mean?" Drew shifted forward in his chair.

"If we hadn't left against the captain's orders to risk our hides crossing the mountains into Ilbrea, I'd have liked to head farther west. See if I could remember how to reach the place I was born."

"Going there would be a safer bet than chancing the mountains."

"We're not doing this for safety. We're protecting the Sailors Guild."

"You're past your last chance!" A voice shouted from the pack as the chatter of the armed men grew louder.

"Would have been nice if you'd told me that before I followed you." Drew eased himself to his feet. "My allegiance is to the sea. Not to any Guild."

"You can't tell me you wouldn't have come." Kai rose to stand beside Drew, slipping the last of his food into his pocket and resettling the tied blanket that was his pack onto his back.

"Don't rub it in." Drew shouldered his own bag. "Since you finally owned up to having enough coin for food—"

"Always hide your coin in your boot when a storm is coming. Being shipwrecked without a scrap of silver is a mistake a man only makes once."

"Thank you for that wisdom. Have you got enough hidden for a decent room before we get ourselves killed trying to cross through the mountains?"

A roar of anger carried from the cluster of knife-wielding men.

"We should go." Before Kai could move, one of the men had grabbed another, tossing him into the air. The flying man screamed as he fell, smashing through a table before hitting the ground.

"Why here?" Drew took Kai's elbow, steering him farther from the fight as the sound of metal striking metal came from the pack of men. "Why under the chivving stars are people in this tavern losing their chivving minds?"

"Something in the liquor?" Kai ducked as a chair flew past his head. "Though I can't see how that would benefit the establishment."

"It's not the liquor," a female voice said.

Kai glanced down, searching for the woman who'd spoken.

A girl with bright red, curly hair sat at a table, calmly eating her meal as a terrified scream carried over the shouts from the brawl.

"Good to know." Drew tightened his grip on Kai's arm, trying to drag him away.

"It's the mountains." The girl pointed behind her to the vast range that swallowed the northern horizon. "They drive men mad."

"I've heard of many strange things being attributed to odd corners of our world, but I've never heard of a mountain range being blamed for brawling." Kai pulled against Drew's grip, staying beside the girl.

"Let the mountains catch you in their grasp, and you'll find nothing but madness." The girl pulled a string from her pocket and tied back her hair. "Think of the brawling fools as the mountains warning people away. Things get worse the farther into the forest you dare to venture."

"Do many people heed this warning?" Kai asked.

"I'll burn your whole village!" The shout came from the far side of the pub, followed by a coughing gurgle that sounded as though someone had been stabbed in the gut.

"Have you ever known anyone who's crossed through the mountains?" The girl finally looked up at Kai. Her eyes were filled with calm skepticism, completely lacking the playful flirtation he'd expected to find.

"I've heard stories of people making the journey from Pamerane to Ilbrea on foot. There's no way to do that but through the mountains.

"Rumors?" the girl said. "Such an excellent source to gamble your life and sanity on."

"Enough, all of you!" A woman stood on top of the bar, banging metal pans together.

Kai flinched, wishing there were a respectable way to cover his ears.

Four men came out from behind the bar, each of them carrying a wooden bat, all of them heading straight toward the brawlers.

"I don't fancy bloodshed with my meal." The girl stood. "If you choose to cross through the mountains, may peace embrace you in your grave. That would be the kindest fate you could hope for. If you want to be smart and take a ship around to Ilbrea, the nearest port is five days that way." She pointed southwest and walked away.

"Come on, Kai." Drew yanked on Kai's arm, trying to drag him in the other direction.

A crack and a scream came from the brawl side of the pub.

"Why would you think we're trying to cross through the mountains?" Kai jerked free from Drew's grip, then grabbed Drew's arm and dragged him along after the girl.

"Am I wrong?" the girl asked.

"No," Kai said.

"Really, Kai?" Drew growled.

"But I haven't been caught in some mountain-spawned rage, either," Kai said as they reached the edge of the pub and stepped out into the midday sun. "How do you explain that?"

"I don't care about explaining anything," the girl said. "I've finished eating, so I'll be on my way."

"If you know so much about the mountains, what's the safest path to cross from here?"

The girl studied Kai, glaring at him for a moment before heading onto the dirt road that led to the center of the village.

"Come on, miss." Kai chased after her, keeping a tight hold on Drew's arm. "You don't want our deaths on your soul when a little advice might have saved us."

"Your deaths are none of my chivving concern. I've already given you my advice." The girl pointed. "Port. Five days that way."

"We can't go by sea," Kai said. "Please. I can tell just by looking at you, you know about those mountains."

"Why's that?" The girl rounded on him.

"Long answer or short?" Kai grinned.

Drew made a noise somewhere between a sigh and a growl.

"You spoke of the mountains making men mad without any fear," Kai said. "So, either you don't believe it, or you've forged a truce with whatever keeps everyone else out of the mountains. Between your hair and the way you speak, I thought it safe to assume you weren't from Pamerane. Then, you said *chivving*, which confirmed it for me.

You come from Ilbrea. Either you crossed through the mountains to get here, or you paid a massive amount of gold to come to Pamerane by sea only to head north to the mountains that drive men mad."

The girl tensed her jaw.

"If we assume you aren't a fool, logic assures me you've made it through the mountains at least once." Kai bowed.

The girl stayed stone-faced.

"Any advice you have would be greatly appreciated. We're heading into the mountains today, and I'd rather not walk straight to our deaths." Kai let go of Drew's arm and reached forward, offering to shake the girl's hand.

The girl's gaze flicked down to Kai's outstretched hand. "A man like you would be smarter to sail."

"The sea is not a possibility for us," Kai said. "Please."

The girl reached for Drew's hand.

Drew glanced to Kai, a look of something between annoyance and murder in his eyes, before he shook the girl's hand.

"I'm going into the mountains today." The girl spoke to Drew as though Kai no longer existed. "I can't guarantee your safety, but you're welcome to walk along behind me."

"We don't have anything to offer," Drew said.

"Perhaps you can pay me with the story of why you're forbidden from the sea." The girl hung onto Drew's hand for another moment before letting go and stepping back. "North of the village center, there's a patch of palms that grows with red leaves. I'll be leaving from there in one hour. If you're not there, I climb on without you. If you slow me down, I climb on without you. If you annoy me—"

"You climb on without us?" Kai cut in.

"I lead you down the wrong path and watch you die with joy in my heart." The girl turned and strode away.

"What's your name?" Kai called after her.

She didn't answer.

"You can't be considering this." Drew spoke in a hushed tone, as though afraid the girl could hear him even as she walked behind a palm-thatched home and disappeared from view.

"She's made it through the mountains." Kai clapped Drew on the back. "We're better off with someone who's survived the journey before than we are on our own."

"She didn't even ask for gold. There's something not right about her."

"Most definitely." Kai draped his arm around Drew's shoulders, coaxing him north. "A girl we just met in a brawl-filled pub agreeing to travel through the mountains with two strange men. There is something very not right about her. Just think of it as a way to make the journey more interesting."

25

MARA

One right. Past the shop with a goat on the tapestry. Then left. Cut through the narrow alley between the blue-marked house and the orange-marked house.

Mara followed the familiar route, wishing for the hundredth time she had a sorcerer-made scroll to draw her map as she walked. She would have settled for a pen and some paper she could use to create a map by hand while huddled in her room at night. But she hadn't a chance of scribbling notes of her explorations without the guards who lurked in her bedroom walls handing Ronya reports of Mara's search for the secrets of Isfol.

The guards were always watching. Constantly spying. Making sure Mara could never forget she and Tham were well-kept prisoners.

Better kept than Kegan, still locked in a cell you can't find. Better off than Elver, haunted by the monsters that claw through his mind.

Mara shook the thoughts away, not allowing herself to tumble into that particular spiral of guilt. Helping Elver was far beyond her power. The healers would have to tend to mending his mind. Mara's talents lay in a very different direction.

The sound of children's laughter came from around the next

corner on the right. That path led to a line of smaller houses, where workers seemed to live.

Mara turned left instead, heading toward the northern edge of the town, where the wealthier Isfolians dwelled.

A team of dogs appeared up ahead.

Mara stopped, pressing her back to the nearest house, offering the sled team the road. The musher slowed his dogs, giving himself time to get a good look at Mara, Tham, and the pack of six guards that trailed behind them on their daily walk.

The guards stepped back out onto the road as soon as the sled had passed. Mara waited, watching the dogs disappear before continuing onward.

A left at the estate with the tall turret. In her five times passing the home, Mara had never once been able to spot how a person might be able to see out of the icy tower. But then, why would a turret be necessary in a city that couldn't be attacked?

If there was no way into the heart of the mountain that wasn't controlled by Ronya, the elite of Isfol would have no reason to have built their homes as though they were preparing for an enemy to invade.

Mara's heart beat more quickly as the sounds of the river began to rumble through the quiet streets. She slowed her pace, peering down every alley, searching for any new discovery that might offer enlightenment.

The pale green leaves of the trees peering over the walls of the estates hadn't changed. There were still seven birds on the gate of the home that had a giant, eagle-shaped fountain blocking Mara's view of the front door.

Cutting between the garden walls of two homes, Mara reached the edge of the river that was, by all non-magical reason, impossible.

Though the water should have frozen in the constant cold of the cavern, it flowed south just as it always had in the time Mara and Tham had been allowed to explore the city.

But not everything had stayed as consistent.

Today, the bridge between the garden walls reached diagonally across the river. Two days ago, it had spanned straight across.

Eight days ago, she'd found the bridge by walking up the road running along the river.

Seven days ago, the path along the river's banks had disappeared, leaving the neighboring homes butting right up against the water's edge.

At five days, the people of Isfol seemed to be avoiding the river as the water continued to widen.

Three days, the guards had urged her to explore some other section of the city, far away from the changing banks.

But the missing road hadn't been stolen by a surge of the river. And other, more frightening changes had appeared as well. The magic behind the reshaping of Isfol had quickly become undeniable and, though Mara hated to admit it, horribly intriguing.

Since the first change in the river's banks, the bridges had begun shifting their locations during the night, cropping up in unexpected places that would drive anyone trying to get anywhere mad. As the water grew wider, the streets surrounding the homes beside the river had narrowed, allowing the existing houses to be packed closer together. Landmarks Mara had used to guide her path disappeared, though none of her guards would tell her what became of the people whose homes had ceased to exist.

Yet in all the changes the ice had made, the bridge between the garden walls had appeared every day. Taking on different forms, but always leaving a way to cross the water.

One day, the bridge had been so narrow, only a brave person would have risked balancing their way over the river. The next, the bridge had stretched wide enough for two sleds to comfortably pass, not that even a single sled could have cut down the alley to reach the water's edge.

If some magic were reshaping Isfol to its will, the logic of the garden bridge's consistent placement was beyond Mara's comprehension.

Mara held tight to Tham's hand as she studied the place where the bridge met the bank. Not because she feared the ice or even falling into the river. Clinging to Tham gave her an anchor, a bit of reason that could whisper over the voice in her head that shouted for her to toss caution aside and race across the bridge to find what waited on the other side.

You can't escape if you're dead, Mara.

She squinted across the river. On the far side, the bridge joined seamlessly with a wide street. The near end of the bridge reached all the way to the western wall of an estate, butting up against the sheer surface in a way that made it impossible for handcarts or dogsleds to use.

"It must be maddening." Mara spoke loudly enough for the guards to be sure she wasn't trying to hide her words from them. "Waking up in the morning, trying to reach the bakers, spending an hour wandering lost just so you can find a loaf of bread."

She bent double, peering beneath the bridge.

"Do you feel it?" She whispered while her face was hidden from the guards.

Tham squeezed her hand in response.

She closed her eyes, focusing on the texture of the air around her. Beneath the crisp cold, something else touched her cheeks. A tingle that caressed her skin, as though she'd found herself too close to the heart of a lightning storm.

Magic. Faint traces of it, but enough to stand out.

Mara paused before running her hand along the edge of the bridge. Her fingers couldn't detect any hint of its magical making—no unnatural warmth, no energy that stung her fingers—though the truth of there being magic behind the nightly changes in the city was undeniable.

"What a wonder." Mara examined the place where the bridge melded with the garden wall. "The very ground beneath your feet changes, and Isfol just carries on."

None of the guards replied.

Mara looked to Tham, tipping her head toward the bridge.

He took a moment, studying the road across the way before nodding.

Lifting the skirts she was still forced to wear, Mara stepped up onto the bridge.

The ice stayed silent and firm, giving no indication of being unable to hold her weight. Mara shifted back and forth for a moment before nodding for Tham to follow.

A roughness covered the arc of the ice, allowing enough grip for a person to walk without slipping into the water. Still, Mara kept her pace slow, searching for something to mark the bridge as special and worthy of being remade night after night.

Mara had made it less than five feet before the guards began climbing up behind her.

"I suppose you're used to it." Mara offered the guards a smile. "The city changing all the time. I would have been lost to the ice before my teens if I'd grown up here. Knowing there would always be new bridges to explore, I don't think anything could have kept me from wandering off."

None of the guards spoke.

"Are there any records of the changes the city has undergone?" Mara asked. "Not necessarily every shift, but something that shows Isfol's development over time?"

One of the guards glanced to the eldest of their pack before speaking. "There are some maps people have created in an attempt to decipher the changes, but the study of those records is exclusive to the royal scholars. We couldn't take you to see them."

"Pity," Mara said. "As a map maker, I would be well suited to help riddle out the patterns of the shifting ice."

"Unfortunately, you are not a scholar," the eldest of the guards said. "Nor will you ever be."

"Many people told me I'd never be a Guilded map maker, either. Yet here I am." Mara kept her tone bright and friendly, charming in a way that would have made Allora proud. "Next time I chat with the Princess, I'll have to ask her what steps might be taken to raise my standing enough to see the maps. After all, I am going to be here for the rest of my life. I might as well have a goal."

"You would do well as a scholar," Tham said as they reached the peak of the arc. "And they would be lucky to have you."

"And what about you?" Mara asked. "How would you fill your time in Isfol?"

"Is your safety guaranteed?"

"Yes." Mara slowed her pace as they neared the end of the bridge.

"I'd work in the dog kennels. Care for the pups, train them. Learn to properly run a sled."

"Careful, come home smelling like too many dogs and Elle will be thoroughly jealous."

"I'd bring her with me." Tham gave a small smile. "It would be good for her to get out and run."

"She would love that." A tiny hint of something strange flickered through Mara's heart. Almost like hope for a joyful future. But fleeting. Sadder.

A fool's wish for a future she could never accept. Not if it meant staying a prisoner and abandoning her family in Ilbrea.

"I would have to petition the Princess for pants," Mara said. "I'm so abominably tired of skirts. If you gave every woman in Ilbrea a week in pants, I don't think you could ever get them to coil themselves in skirts again. It would cause a rebellion if the Guilds were foolish enough to try."

The bridge ended on a street lined by ordinary-looking homes. Mara studied the hangings on the fronts of the houses. The patterns of colors hadn't changed from the day before.

"I'm not sure I agree with you," Tham said.

"Really?" Mara stepped down onto the street. "Would you like to try wearing skirts and see how you fancy layers of fabric tangling around your legs?"

"Not at all. But I don't think you'd have a hope of convincing Allora to give up her ball gowns."

"Fine, then. Dresses will still be permitted on formal occasions, just not as daily wear." Mara stepped aside, allowing the guards to join her and Tham on the road.

The breeze changed, touching Mara's cheek, leaving a chill across her skin.

"Perhaps you should be a diplomat instead of a scholar." Tham kept by Mara's side as she crept back toward the edge of the water, following the breeze. "Work to change the rules women endure."

Mara trailed her fingers through the air, searching for the cold current.

From the north. Starting low. Close by to create the correct angle.

"How are women outside the palace treated in Isfol?" Mara glanced back to the guards. "The only one I've truly spoken to is the Princess, so I've no sense of what ideals normal women are made to suffer."

The younger guards looked to the eldest.

He sighed before speaking. "Women are the givers of life and protectors of the young."

"Are they allowed to be scholars?" Mara ran her hand along the edge of the bridge.

"Of course," the eldest guard said.

"Guards?" Mara knelt beside the bridge.

"No," the eldest said.

"Pity." Mara glanced back at the guard. "I had true hope for a moment."

"Women can only join the guards with special permission from the Regent," the eldest said. "It is a guard's duty to sacrifice their life for Isfol and the crown. The womb of a woman is worth more than the entire life of a man. If a woman is determined to become a guard, she can seek the Regent's approval, but choosing any other life is encouraged for the good of the Ice Walkers."

"That's not as desperately horrible a reason as I assumed you'd offer. I apologize for misjudging you." Mara squeezed Tham's hand before slipping free to duck beneath the bridge. "I have so much to ask Princess Ronya when she calls for me again. The ways in which societies hobble their women is one of our favorite topics."

The cold wind stirring beneath the bridge cut through the layers of Mara's clothes.

Mara touched her hip, reaching for her criolas before remembering its absence.

She shut her eyes, weighing pride against practicality.

They are your jailors, not your peers.

She opened her eyes and crawled toward the deepest of the shadows. The wind lifted her hair from the back of her neck.

A deep pool of black sliced through the shadows beneath the bridge.

"You weren't here yesterday," Mara whispered to the darkness. She reached toward the swatch of black.

The cold of the wind carrying up from below stung her fingers.

"What lies beneath Isfol?" Mara called to the guards.

"Whatever the ice chooses to place under us," the eldest guard said.

"Have you been ordered to kill us if we explore below the city?" Mara asked.

"We have been ordered to keep you safe," the eldest said.

"In that case, do you have a light I could borrow?" Mara said. "My requests to have my criolas returned have been ignored, and I have every intention of crawling into this dark hole. A bit of light would definitely aid in my safety."

"May I encourage you to come out from under the bridge and stroll back to the palace?" the eldest said.

"You may try all you like"—Mara twisted around and pressed her feet into the black—"but unless you intend to forcefully carry me, your efforts will be wasted."

The sound of stone striking stone came from beyond the bridge, followed by the quick hiss of a newly birthed flame.

"Don't burn yourself." A guard passed the light to Tham, who passed it on to Mara.

She had never truly appreciated the worth of her criolas, not until that moment.

The Isfolian light was a flat, palm-sized stone with a flame burning in the center like a rock-based candle.

Mara could very easily have burned herself on the flames or stifled the fire by dropping it. She most definitely couldn't tuck the light into her pocket when she needed both hands.

"I hate appreciating the Sorcerers Guild," she whispered as she glared at the light.

"Are you sure?" Tham crawled under the bridge to kneel beside her.

"About crawling into this hole or despising the sorcerers?"

"Do you really have to ask?"

"No, but I find humor aids my nerves when everything we say is overheard by guards." Mara scooted forward, reaching the light into the darkness.

The shadows shifted in the flickering light. The space widened beneath the opening, creating a tunnel a person could walk down.

Mara held the light lower. "It looks like the ground is barely six feet below us. I should be able to hop right down."

"I'll be with you," Tham said.

Mara set the light beside her and twisted, lying on her stomach so her feet dangled over the open air.

Tham held tightly to her wrist, bracing his feet against the underside of the bridge as Mara lowered herself down.

She held her breath as the world above disappeared, leaving only the flickering light casting shadows on Tham's face as he guarded her from tumbling into the black.

Her toes touched solid ground. She eased her weight onto her heels, freezing for a moment, listening for any cracking or groaning of the ice, before shifting her weight back and forth.

"It's solid," Mara said.

Tham let go of her wrist and passed her down the light.

The single flame left much to be desired as she studied the shadows around her. The tunnel reached back farther than she could see. The ground, while not the well-laid roads of the city, seemed solid enough to be cautiously trusted.

"You can come down," Mara said.

Tham landed beside her a moment later.

"I believe we've discovered why the bridge keeps reappearing in the same place," Mara said. "It's rooted to this passage."

"But the tunnel wasn't here yesterday." Tham tested the ice before stepping forward.

"Maybe it was still forming," Mara said. "Like a seedling waiting to break through the surface."

"Step forward, both of you." The eldest guard appeared above them.

"Why?" Mara asked.

"Unless you intend to crawl out of there and go back to the palace, then you're forcing your guards to follow you into this braidic darkness you've found," the eldest said.

"Braidic?" Mara said. "What a funny word. Should I ask the Princess what it means?"

"There's no reason t—"

"To follow us? You're right. Tham and I are perfectly willing to go alone." Mara crept down the tunnel. "While we may not be Ice Walkers, we are nowhere near helpless."

"We have orders from Her Royal Highness." The smallest of the guards dropped down into the tunnel. "We are to follow you."

"Wonderful." Mara pressed her face into a careful smile. "In that case, please do keep up. I have a love of exploring, and with the way the ice changes, I'll have to get as far as I can in this tunnel today. This passage might not exist tomorrow."

26

NIKO

You and I have long known the horrors the Sorcerers Guild inflicts to hide the existence of magic outside their control. I fear even we did not know the extent of the lies that surround us.

Everything the Guilds teach us is wrong. There are things down here that can only be explained by sorcerer-wielded magic.

We found an abandoned city in the darkness below the mountains. Not stone hovels or crude dwellings. Proper houses and streets. The stone of the buildings grows right up from the ground. The magic in the city's making is undeniable, but I've found no other clues as to who once called this place home.

The city is empty, though I can't tell why. Everything made of wood has started to decay. I have found no proof as to whether the doors of the stone homes were kicked in or simply fell victim to time.

Of the homes we've explored, we've only found the bones of one poor soul, when there should be thousands if the city had been emptied by an illness. We've found evidence of a stable, but no trace of the horses that would have lived there so long ago.

The city seems haunted, and every instinct tells me we should run. This kind of darkness is not meant for men to survive. Perhaps it was different when this place was filled with living people, but with the darkness pressing in around the single light we carry, I cannot convince myself that specters do not lurk just out of sight.

If Dudia made ghosts of all the people who once dwelled here, I am surrounded by an army of the dead, a horde that possess magic I could never hope to defeat.

But I'm still glad I've found this place, even if the people who built it fled from some unspeakable evil. Even if Dudia sends all their spirits to haunt me.

Those who dwelled in this darkness must have found a path that led down here. And if their bones aren't here, they must have found a way out.

There is another passage into this place. This city is proof that one must exist. We only have to find it.

As much hope as this brings me, questions still swirl through my mind. What horror could have driven so many to give up the light and build their homes this far underground? How much does the Sorcerers Guild know of these people? How far would they go to destroy the magic that created this home in the heart of the mountains?

I'm not sure I want to know the answers.

Do not lose faith in me.

I will find a way out,

Niko

KAI

"It's not a comfortable bed or even a hot bath I miss the most." Kai stopped speaking as he reached forward and grabbed a branch, using the tree to pull himself up a steep and crumbling portion of the slope.

"Are you waiting for me to ask what you do miss most?" Drew kept climbing in front of Kai, not slowing his pace or glancing behind to make sure Kai was still following.

The girl climbed thirty feet ahead of them, cutting through the trees quickly enough to make Kai grateful that her red hair stood out so well against the deep browns and vibrant greens of the forest. She kept a steady pace, never seeming to tire or mind the slopes, even with the weight of the pack on her back. Despite the sticky warmth of the forest, she kept her sleeves rolled down to her wrists and her hair loose around her shoulders.

"I wasn't aiming for you to ask." Kai ran a few steps, ducking beneath a low-hanging branch to walk right on Drew's heels. "But now that you have—"

"Wonderful," Drew said.

"It's the people I miss most," Kai said. "My family, of course, and friends. But I miss being among strangers in Ilara, too. Just sitting in a tavern, drinking. Or dancing in the square after my family's all abandoned me on Winter's End."

"We'd better be home by Winter's End." Drew stumbled over a root. "We've spent days trudging through the mountains. I've no chivving clue how close we are to reaching Ilbrea. The only thing I'm quite certain of is that I made the right choice when I chose to live my life at sea."

"Don't be in a foul mood." Kai paused, listening beyond the sounds of Drew's inelegant movement and the rustling of the underbrush around the hem of the girl's skirt.

Something stirred to their left—in the trees, farther away than Kai could see through the dense forest.

"Decided you'd rather die in this forest than keep walking up this chivving mountain?" Drew called over his shoulder. "I wouldn't blame you."

"I'd never give up." Kai's legs twinged their protest as he took the slope at a run to catch up to Drew. "I was only appreciating the beauty of the trees. Finding the joy in our journey. Just think, every horrible step we take through this muggy mountain range is a step closer to home. We'll make it to Ilara before winter begins, and I promise I'll buy you a cask of frie to help ease the memories of this adventure."

"It'll take a lot more than one cask." Drew pressed his back to a tangle of branches, holding it aside for Kai to pass.

"What about you?" Kai called up the slope. "Do you prefer frie or that odd, burning liquor from the Tiller's Tree?"

The girl didn't speak. Or slow her pace. Or acknowledge Kai had spoken at all.

Kai glanced back, circling a hand at Drew.

Drew frowned before speaking. "If you were to have your choice, would you prefer frie or terrible Pameranian liquor?"

"I'm not fancy enough to be picky about such things." The girl's voice was nearly swallowed by the trees.

"Drew," Kai said loudly enough to frighten a bird off its perch high up in the trees, "if I were to want to buy our guide a cask of something as a gift of gratitude for her leading us through the mountains, would she prefer frie or pam—"

"Talking between you two is almost as tiring as climbing through these chivving unending mountains," Drew said.

The girl laughed.

"Blame her." Kai pointed up the slope. "You know I'll talk to anyone."

Drew shot Kai a look that would have scared most men. "Kai would like to know if you'd prefer he buy you frie or liq—"

"If I'm taking anything as a gift, it'll be chamb," the girl said.

"What name should I address the gift to?" Kai called.

"Gods and stars," Drew murmured before shouting, "What name should Kai address his gift to?"

The girl laughed again but didn't answer.

"It was worth a try." Kai clapped Drew on the shoulder. "She'll have to give in and tell us her name eventually."

"No, I really don't think she will."

Kai let the conversation die as the girl led them to a place in the mountains where rocks grew up out of the slope in a sheer wall fifty feet high.

The girl cut west.

Kai fought to listen past the swish of her skirt sweeping through the underbrush, trying to find a hint of the sound he'd heard before.

Nothing.

The quiet brought him no comfort. Tension crept up Kai's spine, adding a new ache to his body.

I'd sell my ears for a proper weapon.

The rock wall had crumbled near the western edge. Kai scanned the rubble, choosing two large stones, heavy enough to be hard to hold one-handed.

"Drew," Kai whispered, passing one of the poor weapons to Drew.

"How kind." Drew took the stone.

"Just humor me." Kai quickened his pace as they began climbing again, keeping closer to the girl than he usually bothered.

Her skirt snagged on a twig that broke with a sharp crack.

Drew's breath grated in his throat. He'd need more water soon. They couldn't risk becoming ill from dehydration.

Birds called in the trees to the east.

There.

To the west. The same sound as before. Something cutting through the brush. It had mimicked their path, keeping the same distance from them.

Kai sprinted to the girl's side.

She reached for the knife at her hip.

"Something's following us." Kai kept his voice calm, soothing. "I've thought it for a while, but I'm chivving sure of it now."

The girl didn't change her pace.

"Do you know of an animal in these mountains that would follow alongside us for hours?"

The muscles in the girl's neck tensed.

"Should I interpret that as a *no*? If a person is tracking us, we need to find out who they are and what they want," Kai said. "We can't keep letting them shadow our path, just hoping they don't mean us harm."

Drew pounded up the slope to Kai's side. "Don't tell me I need to do more talking between you two," he panted.

"I'll fall behind," Kai said. "Cut around to the west and see who it is."

The girl slid through a narrow gap between two trees.

Kai dodged through behind her and was back by her side in three long strides. "I'm willing to take the risk of going to see who's following us, but I need your word you won't leave us behind. Drew and I have no clue where we are. We don't know how to get out of these cursed mountains. If you leave us here, you'll be abandoning us to die."

She glanced sideways at Kai but said nothing.

"We won't be safe to sleep tonight if we don't know who's following us," Kai said. "Going to see who's out there is for all our good. Don't punish me for it."

The girl's lips curled into a small and vengeful smile.

"I'm going," Kai said. "If I die, I'd be very grateful if you could lead Drew all the way to Ilara."

"We'll both go see what's stalking us," Drew said. "You're not wandering off in this godsforsaken forest without me."

Kai kept his gaze fixed on the girl. "If you get him to Ilara safely, you'll be handed more gold than a common Ilbrean can earn in a lifetime."

The girl sneered.

"I said you're not wandering off without me." Drew grabbed Kai's arm. "Are we pretending no one can hear me now? I thought I'd stopped having to play these games when I grew into men's pants."

"Take him to Lord Karron, head of the Map Makers Guild," Kai said.

The girl shifted her head, looking down at Kai's boots as though battling with herself over whether or not to look at his face.

"Stay with her, Drew. We have a duty to uphold." Kai twisted away from Drew's grip and ran southwest.

"Kai!"

He didn't slow or look back at Drew's call.

The sound was probably nothing.

A person trying to stumble their way through the mountains and trusting the girl's path more than their own senses. Or maybe the girl's hint of fear had been born from knowing of a beast that would stalk men for hours, waiting for the right time to pounce.

And you're creeping after the monster with a chivving rock, you slitch.

Kai froze for a moment, listening to the sounds of the forest over the thumping of his own heart.

To the northeast, the thud of footsteps and rustling of underbrush.

Dead north, the soft shifting of branches as someone, or something, tried to move quietly.

Kai quickened his pace as he charged up the slope, keeping on his toes as though he were balancing on a beam, ready to leap into the open air, reach for a rope, and hope his strength and wits were enough to keep him alive.

In front of him, the branches swayed, shifting back into place after having been shoved aside.

Kai raised his rock to his shoulder as he slipped between the branches and caught sight of the thing that had been stalking them.

The beast's dark hair had been tangled with twigs and decaying leaves. It walked on its hind legs like some kind of manlike monster.

The thing stepped through a patch of light between trees and the sun glinted off something the creature carried.

The monster stopped, sweeping its head back and forth, as though trying to scent the wind.

Kai's heartbeat quickened, thudding in his ears as the beast turned its head.

Even the filthy beard that covered most of his face couldn't hide the fact that it was a person tracking their party.

Attack. Attack now, Kai's instincts screamed in his mind.

The man raised a mud-smeared sword.

He could be lost. He could've been stuck in the mountains for years. He could have a family who's been waiting for him.

The fate of your Guild is waiting for you. You have to make it to Ilara alive.

Too late.

The man turned, fixing his dark gaze on Kai.

With a roar, he charged.

"Wait!" Kai shouted. "We don't want to hurt you!"

The man didn't slow.

Kia pitched his rock, hitting the man in the center of his chest.

The man stumbled at the impact.

Kai took off through the trees, sprinting east.

"Run! Drew, run!" Kai darted toward a tree with low-hanging limbs. He gripped a waist-high branch that had grown as thick around as his forearm, pulling with one hand while bringing his other elbow down hard. The branch cracked but didn't break.

Kai tossed his weight forward, slamming his torso onto the branch, stumbling as it broke free. He spun around, steadying his stance as the man charged toward him.

The man didn't scream this time. From the fury filling his eyes, he had moved beyond any loathing that could be expressed by bellowing.

"We mean you no harm." Kai raised his pitiful, leaved weapon.

The man swung his sword, aiming for Kai's neck.

Kai blocked the blow, flinching as the man's sword hacked away a chunk of the branch.

"Have you been lost out here?" Kai ducked as the man swung high again. He swept his branch low, managing to catch the man in the hip.

The man didn't seem to notice he'd been hit at all. He brought his sword around, slicing at Kai's flank.

Kai dodged. His heel caught on a root as he struggled to keep ahold of his weapon. He staggered sideways, trying to find his footing.

The man grinned, displaying his blackened teeth as he drew his sword back, ready to run Kai through.

"No!" The shout yanked the man's gaze away from Kai.

Drew charged through the trees, the rock Kai had given him raised over his head.

The man giggled as he flipped his sword and ran toward Drew.

Kai chased after him, swinging his branch for the back of the man's knees a moment too late.

The man thrust his sword for Drew's gut.

Drew screamed, cracking his stone onto the man's shoulder, knocking his arm out of its socket.

The man stumbled forward as Kai's branch hit his legs, but neither blow seemed to have caused him any pain as he arced his sword, ready to slice through Drew's hip.

A glint of red shone on the blade.

The rock fell from Drew's hands as he lurched away, too slow to avoid the attack.

"Drew!" Kai's scream drowned out Drew's cry of pain. Kai raised his stick, bashing the man on the head.

Not even flinching at the blow to his skull, the man rounded on Kai, glee filling his eyes as he giggled again.

"What are you?" Kai leapt back as the man swung for his gut. "Are you a demon?"

The man spun his sword in a wide arc, as though hoping to slice Kai from the bottom up.

"Is it magic?" Kai cracked his branch down on the blade, which slashed through the wood, sending the tip flying into the air. "Is there some magic in these mountains that's infested your mind?"

The joy disappeared from the man's eyes.

"If it's wild magic that's taken hold, you could have a chance to break free." Kai dove sideways, gasping as the man's blade nicked his shoulder. "Put down your sword and let me help. Take me to whatever it is that did this to you. I've seen wild magic do strange things before." He blocked a blow from above, shielding his eyes as shards of wood rained down on him. "I am not your enemy!"

A tree branch smacked into Kai's spine, blocking his escape as the man pulled his sword back, ready to plunge it through Kai's heart.

I'm sorry. I've failed.

A crack, like lightning had split a tree in two, drove into Kai's ears.

The man froze, the tip of his sword mere inches from Kai's heart. He turned, as though looking for the source of the sound.

Kai slammed what remained of his weapon against the back of the man's neck.

The man took two steps forward before falling to his knees.

Kai shifted his weight, rearing back to attack again, but a strange light stopped him.

Shimmering a pale blue, the glow that drifted up from the man somehow seemed cold—born of a place men weren't meant to survive. The light grew as it brightened, pulling away from the man as though trying to rip him apart.

The man screamed. His sword fell from his hand.

He began to shake as the pitch of his pain swelled to a horrible, inhuman shriek. He tipped his head back, giving a final vengeful death cry to the sky before toppling forward and falling silent.

He landed on the ground at the girl's feet.

She stared down at him without any fear or pity on her face.

"What was"—Kai swallowed the sour that had somehow risen to his throat—"what under the chivving stars was that?"

The girl didn't answer.

A gasp of pain pulled Kai's attention away from the fallen man.

Drew sank down, leaning against a tree, one hand held to his side, the other pressing on his hip.

"Drew." Kai darted forward, grabbing the man's sword before

running to Drew. "How bad is it?" Kai set the sword down and pulled off his blanket-made bag.

"Bad enough I'd be thankful for that cacting awful Pameranian liquor." Drew lifted his hand away from his side, letting Kai peel up his blood-soaked shirt.

A four-inch gash sliced through Drew's flank.

"There are worse places to be stabbed." Kai kept his voice light, desperate to hide his panic. "We'll wrap it up. You'll be fine in a few days."

Dirt marked the edges of the wound. The sword had been filthy when it had gone in.

We'll clean the cut. Cauterize. Liquor.

I can't help him. Not here. I've nothing to help him with.

"Let me see your hip." Kai unfastened Drew's belt.

"He got the muscle." Drew winced as Kai shifted his pants down. "I don't think I'll be fit to trek through the mountains anymore."

"Then I'll carry you."

The sword had sliced through too much flesh. The white of Drew's hipbone broke through the red of the blood.

"Kai, I know you're a stubborn bastard, but we have to be realistic. We don't even know how far from Ilbrea—"

"I'll build a litter and drag you if I have to, so don't make one chivving mention of you not continuing on this godsforsaken chivving journey with me."

"Kai." Drew gripped his hand.

"How do you know Lord Karron?" The girl stood over them, holding the sword Kai had cast aside.

"What?" Kai shifted, planting himself between the girl and Drew, still keeping Drew's hand clasped firmly in his.

"How do you know Lord Karron?" the girl repeated.

"This is not the time," Kai said.

"Drew is dying." The girl peered around Kai to Drew. "Probably not today. But he's right, you'll have to leave him behind.

Without help, wounds like that will kill him far before we reach the northern edge of the mountain range."

"I'll keep him alive." Pain pressed on the front of Kai's throat. "I'll carry—"

"There's nothing you could do to help him," the girl said. "But I can."

"Then do it," Kai said. "I'll pay you. I'll—"

"How do you know Lord Karron?" the girl said.

"I'm his ward!" Kai shouted. "I'm his chivving ward. He took me in when I was young and raised me. He will give you gold if you save Drew. I swear on my life, Lord Karron will pay you."

"Do you know Adrial?" The girl took a step closer to them, leveling the sword at Kai's throat as she studied his face.

"Adrial?" Kai tightened his grip on Drew's hand. "Adrial Ayres? Yes, I know him. Adrial is as good as a brother to me. Lord Karron raised us both."

"You're so different from him."

"Adrial's always been a better man than me. The only fool who doesn't know that is him. Drew is a better man than me, too. If you have some awful grudge against Lord Karron's wards, fine. Kill me if you have to. But help Drew."

The girl tossed the sword up into the air.

Kai dove sideways, bracing his body over Drew's, but the blade didn't tumble back down to the ground. It hovered twelve feet in the air as though it had been placed on a shelf far out of reach of naughty children.

"Adrial Ayres helped me once," the girl said. "A lifetime ago. He saved someone I loved very much. It would be wrong of me not to help Adrial's brother. Move."

Kai eased himself to Drew's other side, trying to keep both the sword and the girl in his sight.

"You're from Ilara then?" Kai asked.

"Keep breathing." The girl touched Drew's flank. "The pain will be better if you keep breathing."

Drew gasped as the girl trailed her fingers along his side. "What are you doing to me?"

"I told you to breathe." The girl narrowed her eyes, frowning at Drew's wound as the bleeding began to slow.

"What is this? What's happening?" Drew moved as though trying to stand.

Kai pressed on Drew's shoulders, pinning him in place. "Sorry. He's never been healed by a sorcerer before."

"No. No sorcerers." Drew fought against Kai's grip.

"She's not from the Sorcerers Tower," Kai said. "The Lady Sorcerer wouldn't waste precious magic having one of her people wandering through the mountains."

Drew moaned as the skin on his side began to knit back together.

"Is that why you left Ilbrea?" Kai asked. "You didn't want to join the Sorcerers Guild?"

"I'm saving your friend. That doesn't mean I have to answer your questions." The girl trailed her fingers across the place where Drew's wound had been. "I'm not the best at healing. Someone else will need to see to him, but it should hold for now."

"Where can we find someone else to help him?" Kai asked.

"You'll have to look for someone outside these mountains," the girl said.

"If you're the only sorcerer in these mountains, what magic possessed that man?" Kai asked.

"I told you at the Tiller's Tree." The girl leaned low, her face close to Drew's hip as she pressed against the wound.

Drew screamed, gripping Kai's arm hard enough to bruise.

"Keep breathing. This is the worst of it, just keep breathing," Kai said. "So, whatever wild magic is in these mountains drifted down to mess with the minds of the men at the Tiller's Tree and drove the demon of a man that attacked us so mad he didn't notice when I hit him over the head."

"How do you know about wild magic?" The girl furrowed her brow as newly made sinew covered the white of Drew's hipbone.

Drew tipped his head back and screamed.

"The same way I ended up Lord Karron's ward." Kai gripped Drew's shoulders. "I've lived more in this world than anyone has a right to."

"Then why are you so desperate to get back to Ilara?" She pulled her hands away from the unhealed skin on Drew's hip and looked up to Kai. "Tell me. Or I won't finish my work."

"Kai, I'm not worth—"

"We were serving on a Guilded ship. There was a sorcerer onboard. She took control of the ship and forced us to sail into the southern storms. Most of our crew died. The survivors boarded a Pameranian ship. They should have reached Ilara by now." Kai swallowed past the ache in his throat. "The Sorcerers Guild knows what happened. I don't think any of the survivors from our crew will make it into Ilara alive. We're trying to get back to make sure the truth of the Sorcerers Guild's treachery doesn't die with the rest of our crew."

"You're going to stand against the Sorcerers Guild?" The girl sat back on her heels.

"We don't have a choice," Kai said. "They're destroying the Sailors Guild. Give the Sorcerers Guild enough time, and they'll destroy us all."

She looked up to the sword hovering in the air.

"You can't tell me you have any love for the Sorcerers Guild," Kai said.

"None."

"Then help us," Kai begged. "Heal Drew. Lead us to the northern edge of the mountains."

"No." The girl looked back to them. "Letting you walk back to Ilara so the Lady Demon can slaughter you is a waste of a Karron who wants to stand against the Sorcerers." She pressed her fingers to Drew's wound.

He bit his lips together, trying to stifle his scream of pain.

Kai watched the wound heal, holding his breath until both the spell and the screaming had stopped.

Drew fell forward, resting his head against Kai's shoulder as his breath shuddered in his lungs.

"You're all right." Kai wrapped his arms around Drew, waiting for his breathing to even out before looking back to the girl. "If going north is a waste of a wayward Karron, what would you do with me?"

"There are people I'd like you to meet." She stood and brushed her skirt off. "They may very well kill you, but if not, you'll be making a more powerful ally than even a king could wish for."

Kai eyed the sword still floating in the air. "I suppose we don't have much choice in this."

"None at all." The girl grinned. "You'll do as I say, or you'll die. Sometimes the gods do try and make up for all the damage they've caused."

MARA

"You really could make this so much easier on yourselves." Mara tightened the knot at her waist. "A few ice axes, and you wouldn't be stuck hauling us back out." She looked from the crevasse that had swallowed half the street to the pack of guards assigned to follow her and Tham that day.

The eldest of the guards was the same as always, but he'd been given yet another fresh batch of underlings. Whether the old ones had begged their way into other assignments or been deemed unworthy of trotting along at Mara's and Tham's heels as they ventured into every crack she could find in Isfol, she didn't really know. She couldn't bring herself to care much, either.

"You should leave some of your party up here." Mara checked the knot at Tham's waist. "As grateful as I am to have been allowed to commandeer rope, without ice axes, there's a good chance of us being stuck at the bottom of this crevasse."

"Then perhaps you shouldn't go into it," the eldest guard said.

Mara knelt, checking to be sure the cuffs of the pants she'd borrowed from Tham were tightly tucked into her boots. "If I don't go down, how will I know what's at the bottom?"

"Ice," the eldest said. "There's ice at the bottom."

"I didn't know you had a sense of humor." Mara glanced up at the guard. "And while you're probably right, you seem to have underestimated my need to press every limit imposed upon me. My dearest friend calls it a vice. But, if I hadn't tried wearing pants out of our room, I wouldn't know if the Princess would have me whipped for wearing Tham's clothes. If I hadn't refused to give back your light, I wouldn't know if I'd be beaten for cheek. If I hadn't acquired such a fine rope from the stables—"

"You wouldn't know if you'd be arrested for theft." The eldest's scowl didn't falter. "Stomp on your luck too often, and eventually it will crack."

"And I'm sure if it were up to you, my luck would have shattered long ago." Mara yanked on the end of her rope, testing its hold on the tree she'd anchored it to.

She hadn't chosen the tree nearest the crevasse. The slice in the street had been growing far too quickly to allow such a risk to be taken. The ravine had only been a crack in the road when Mara had first found it, too small for even a cat to slip into. In the three days since, the gap had grown wide enough for guards to have been stationed around the area to warn people away from the street.

Now, the nearest tree's roots were visible through the clear blue of the ice, making it a poor choice for anchoring the ropes Mara, Tham, and whatever guards dared to follow them would be using to lower themselves into the darkness.

Instead, Mara had chosen a tree more than ten feet away, right beside a house with a pale yellow and blue tapestry hanging out front.

A woman sat in the window nearest the tree, glowering at Mara.

Mara offered the woman a sympathetic smile and a nod.

"If I were charged with following someone who kept insisting on testing their limits while sliding into every hole in the ground they could find, I know I would have stopped letting me out of my room days ago." Mara turned back to her guards. "Which means it must be the Princess herself who's ordered you to indulge my explorations."

None of the guards spoke.

"I'm sorry you've been charged with trotting along behind the mad Ilbreans," Mara said. "And perhaps the next desperate message you send to Her Highness begging for your torment to end will be answered with her locking us in our room. In the meantime, my terms remain the same. I will gladly become a well-behaved charge as soon as you take me to see Kegan."

The guards stayed silent.

"Then I hope none of you are afraid of heights," Mara said.

"One of our party is ill." Tham stepped toward the guards. "Our visiting him only makes him scream. Another is locked in a cell. Alone. Abandoned. We've asked every day to see him. And you refuse. Should you ever be in our position, I hope those who call you their *guests* will find mercy in their hearts."

"Come, Tham." Mara backed up to the edge of the crevasse. "Perhaps Kegan is being held in a cell below this part of the city."

She leaned back, testing the rope one final time before stepping over the edge.

Keeping her pace slow, she lowered herself step by step into the darkness. Tham stayed a few feet above her, silhouetted by the unrelenting blue glow of Isfol.

"How long until they follow us?" Mara asked once they'd gone thirty feet into the darkness.

"I'm not sure they know how," Tham said.

A naïve corner of Mara's heart had a moment of hope as she dreamt of freedom.

"They've been herding us toward this part of the city," Mara said, taking the risk of speaking freely, hoping that for once they might not be overheard. "They started guiding us this way—"

"Right after you found the first tunnel and dared to climb into it."

"It's good to know I haven't become too paranoid." Mara swallowed past the knot in her throat. "I've missed properly speaking to you, without them listening all the time."

"I love you, Mara."

"I love you, too. There's no one I'd rather rappel into a trap with than you."

The low rumble of Tham's laugh acted like a salve, soothing the anger in Mara's chest.

"We have to find a way out of here before we both go mad," Mara said. "And this is not the path to freedom."

"We'll find a way."

Mara's toe touched solid ground.

She lowered both feet, testing the ice before daring to let go of her rope and reach for her light.

Her fingers fumbled, trying to find the right angle to strike the flint against the stone. It took three hits for the wick to catch.

Tham reached the ground beside her as the flame flickered to life, offering them a poor view of the bottom of the crevasse.

The passage they'd reached was fifteen feet wide. The jagged ice that covered the ground had been crushed along the center of the tunnel, as though something large had forced its way past.

"We've definitely been herded this way." Mara looked toward the light high above as she untied the knots around her waist. "I despise being corralled and spied on."

Tham untied his own rope before kneeling to study the ice. "If something heavy enough to flatten the ground traveled through this tunnel, there must be an easier path we could have taken to get down here."

"That would be too dull for Ronya." Mara held her light high, watching the flame flicker in the faint breeze. "Feel free to join us," she called to the guards. "We'll be heading west, toward whatever delight it is we're meant to find."

The guards high above stayed silent.

"I miss actually discovering things. It's so much more satisfying than spending all your time being manipulated into playing a princess's game," Mara said.

"No matter who starts the game, my bet is still on you winning."

Mara allowed herself the comfort of a smile as she walked into the wind, not arguing when Tham kept a step behind her.

They crept quietly along, Mara listening for any hint of their guards' descent over the crunching of the ice beneath her feet.

Minutes passed before Mara slowed her steps as they reached a small, dark something on the ground. The thing didn't move. It didn't have the texture of a pool of blood, the shadow of an animal waiting to pounce, or any other form that might have been planted by Ronya to cause fear.

Mara held her light low and nudged the thing with her toe. "A work glove." The worn leather flopped over and lay lifeless on the ice. "There's definitely an easier path down. I wonder how long it will take our guards to travel the workers' route to catch up to us."

She looked into the solid black behind them, back toward the crevasse, battling with the temptation to douse her light and drag Tham into the darkness. To run as fast as they could and beg the gods to offer them a path out of the ice.

"We can't leave Kegan," Tham said. "Or Elver."

"Or Elle." Mara bit her lips together. "I didn't know prison cells could be quite so expansive."

"The Princess controls the pathways out of Isfol. Everyone in the city is her prisoner, even if they don't know it."

"Ronya's not the only one who can open a passage through the ice." Mara continued heading west. "She may be a royal, but there are others with ice magic. We'll find someone who will let us out. We've been in worse places, and we've always made it out in the end."

"Listen."

Mara froze, holding her breath, tipping her head toward the faint sound coming from up ahead.

A steady rhythm and a low rumble.

"Digging." Tham stepped forward, laying his hand on the back of Mara's waist, as though needing to be sure she wasn't a shadow. "I know that sound. They're digging in the ice."

Mara twined her fingers through Tham's and kissed the back of his hand. "I'm right here. I won't let them separate us."

Tham pressed his lips to the top of Mara's head, taking a deep breath before whispering, "I'll tear down their mountain if they try."

"I know." Mara kissed him, savoring his familiar taste. The comfort of his strength as his arms surrounded her. The lure of his body as she leaned against him. She eased away, promising herself she'd tumble into all the joys of Tham later.

Soon.

"Let's go see what under the stars they could be digging for," Mara said.

It took another two minutes of walking for the sounds to gain enough distinction for Mara to hear the difference between the low rumble of voices and the grating of some crushing machine. The striking of the axes gained distinction as well. The workers all swung in the same rhythm, but metal met ice at slightly different times, giving texture to the *shink* of their cleaving.

In the distance, a light bathed the tunnel, coming from an opening around the bend. The glow held the same blue tinge as the city of Isfol.

The familiar tingle of anticipation began to grow in Mara's chest, but anger shoved the feeling down.

Herded. Trapped. Corralled. Prisoners. Playthings of the Princess.

The cycle of anger drowned out her wonder as they rounded the bend and the tunnel opened up into a cavern.

A team of forty workers carved away at the walls of ice, while another crew loaded broken ice onto massive sledges, and a third ran smaller chunks of ice through a hand-cranked machine on the far side of the space.

The light in the cavern came from the walls but not with the same ambient glow that bathed Isfol in its constant gleam.

Spots of radiant blue shone from within the ice. Each of the diggers seemed to be targeting their own point of light. The ice in the sledges glowed, displaying the bounty of the miners' work.

But none of it spawned any awe. Mara could only fix her gaze and anger on the tea table set in the center of it all.

Ronya sat at the table, sipping wine and smiling at Mara. She raised a hand, beckoning Mara and Tham toward her.

Tham squeezed Mara's hand as though sensing her urge to scream.

The workers peeked at Mara and Tham as they approached the Princess, but none of the miners stopped their labor.

They all knew. She set us up. She warned the workers we'd find this place.

Ronya stood as Mara and Tham reached the tea table, offering them both a gracious nod before looking to the second of the two seats.

"I'm so sorry, Tham," Ronya said. "I'm afraid I only planned for Mara to sit with me today."

"How strange." Mara pressed her lips into a careful smile. "You clearly knew when Tham and I would be reaching this cavern. You must have known we'd be arriving together."

"Of course." Ronya sat, taking the time to refill her wine glass before continuing. "But Tham is so fond of digging, I thought he might enjoy speaking to one of the miners. Perhaps he could gain some advice, should poor Tham ever need to burrow through ice again."

"I would slick the streets of Isfol in blood before Tham would ever find a need," Mara said.

"How barbaric." Ronya sipped her wine. "Don't make me regret having such a fine table brought down here just for us."

"The crews' work must be impressive to capture the interest of the Princess," Tham said. "I'm sure I would love to learn what the light inside the ice is. We lost a good portion of our original party after one of the men carved a similar light out of a ravine."

"Pity your man was so foolish." Ronya beckoned over a white-haired worker. "Show our guest the finer points of ice mining. But Edrick, remember the difference between a guest and an ally."

"Yes, Your Highness." Edrick bowed. "This way, sir. I've heard of your feat of strength when you tried to find Isfol. I'm honored to make your acquaintance."

Tham held Mara's gaze for a moment before following Edrick to a rack of ice axes and tongs.

"If anything happens to Tham—"

"You'll slick the streets of Isfol in blood." Ronya raised her glass. "Join me, Mara. We have so much to discuss."

"Unless it involves seeing Kegan, healing Elver, or setting Tham and me free, I can't say I'm interested."

"Such brave words from someone who exists at my mercy." Ronya took another sip of her wine. "Sit and chat. I command you."

"And if I don't?"

"Sweet friend, don't play the fool. It tires me. You're wise enough to know the consequences of my anger without my having to resort to crude threats. Besides, I have a gift for you if you behave."

Mara forced her jaw to relax and sat opposite the Princess. "What gift might you bestow upon me? If it's seeing Kegan, I'll be genuinely grateful."

"If I'd wanted to talk about Kegan, we could have had tea in the garden." Ronya poured Mara a glass of wine. "We're here to chat about something that can't be discussed near the palace. This topic requires a nice large space without hollow walls where spies can hide."

"You're afraid of your own spies?"

Ronya leaned forward to whisper, "Not all of them are mine."

"What an enthralling secret." Mara sipped her wine. The sweetness did nothing to drive the tang of unspoken curses from her mouth.

"Anyone in Isfol could have told you that. No, the gift I'm offering is deeply valuable information, a secret you've been dying to learn. Burning away with the loathing of not understanding. Though you've been so distracted by the fate or your compatriots, you may have neglected to actually formulate the question in your mind."

"Then please enlighten me. What is this question I don't know I have?"

"That's not how our game works," Ronya said. "If I'm going to tell you the hidden truth that will change your fate, you have to offer me something first. Fair is fair."

"What could you want from me? You've taken my freedom. You've asked me about Ilbrea at the palace without fussing about spies."

"I want a truth from you, Mara."

"I've already bargained that away." Mara gripped her glass, refusing to let herself glance toward Tham. "I've answered all your questions. Why go through the theatrics of luring me down here?"

Ronya leaned forward, and for once, the spark of battle faded from her eyes. "There are some secrets you couldn't tell, not even to save Tham. There are some horrible truths you can't admit to yourself. That's what I want to hear, Mara Landil. The secret you've buried so deeply, you risk tearing your soul to dig the memory back up. I couldn't ask you to unearth something like that with spies lurking around us. I'm not capable of that sort of cruelty."

"But you would threaten Tham?"

"There's a massive difference, even if you don't see it."

"Are you threatening him now?"

"Not directly." Ronya sat back. "But you will both suffer if you refuse me."

"What a lovely luncheon." Mara sipped her wine.

"Play along, Mara. You'll be glad you did."

Mara let herself glance at Tham.

He knelt beside the wall, hands pressed to the ice as he studied the light within.

"Your deepest secret, Mara," Ronya said in a singsong voice. "Tell me."

A truth she couldn't admit to herself. Not the maps she and the others in the Karron clan worked so hard to protect. That secret was safe. She was proud of that work, and her dearest friends all knew of the hidden scrolls.

Something deeper. More frightening to admit.

Mara shut her eyes, digging through the whispered conversations she'd shared with Allora. Both of them bundled in Allora's bed, pretending the rest of the world didn't exist.

"Tham would have been better off if he'd never fallen in love with me." She kept her eyes closed, letting the feel of the glass in her hand bind her to the unpleasant present. "Even though his captains when he was young were horrible men, he loved being a sailor. He loves the sea. He gave it up to become a soldier. So he could follow me on my map making journeys. And I can't even admit we're together. He'll never be a father or a husband or a sailor. I will never be worth that sort of sacrifice."

"I told you if you lied to me I'd take him from you," Ronya said.

"That wasn't a lie." Mara's eyes flew open. She looked to Tham, ready to run to his side to defend him.

"If I wasn't so sure you believed it, I'd have him hauled away right now." Ronya chose a cake from the tray. "You should be very grateful I'm not so cruel as to punish you for your delusions. Tham thinks you well worth any sacrifice, and he's the only one who's allowed an opinion on that subject. Now, dig deeper. It'll be worth the prize I offer."

"This is absurd."

"Don't make me regret having wine brought down."

Mara huffed and shut her eyes again, imagining herself in Tham's arms, telling him the truths she could only admit when she felt the safety of his strength surrounding her.

"I find no honor in the Guilds," Mara said. "They turned their backs on me when I was a child. They've belittled me, they've stolen the truth of magic from their own people, they've allowed the common folk to suffer because the Guilds Council can't be bothered to care. I try to blame it all on the Sorcerers Guild, but even Lord Karron deserves his share of the blame. Even as I serve the Guilds, I can't bring myself to hate the rebels who long to watch their horrible reign crumble."

"Hmm."

Mara opened her eyes, blinking in the blue light to see the pucker of Ronya's pursed lips as she swirled the wine in her glass.

"Someone like you who's fought so hard against the rules the Guilds inflict, it seems only fair you'd grow to hate them," Ronya said. "But it's still not good enough."

"I have nothing better to give." Mara spoke through gritted teeth.

"Of course you do. Dig deeper."

"No. I have given you your truth. Now give me my prize, and let us end this game."

Ronya tipped her head back and laughed. "You don't get to decide when my game ends. And you'll keep playing as long as I want because you are incapable of stopping. You'll search the city, looking for a path to escape. You'll trade secrets with me, hoping I'll divulge some weakness you can abuse. You will keep doing whatever I ask, because you know if you don't, I'll lock you in your room. And the freedom to roam I have so kindly granted puts you one step closer to finding a way to reach your little friends and slip out of Isfol.

"Giving up that freedom would mean admitting you can't escape, and that, sweet Mara, is something you simply cannot stomach. Let us not waste our time pretending you won't play my game. You risk me growing tired of your company, and if I walk away without telling you my secret, I won't give you the opportunity to gain that confidence again."

"You're enjoying this." Mara gripped her glass.

"Immensely, and that is in no way a secret. Now, shut your eyes, and think of something good before I get bored and leave."

Mara closed her eyes, leaving behind the warmth of Allora's friendship and the comfort of Tham's strength.

Back to the darkness where I am all alone. Back to the place I don't want to remember. The place I've learned to avoid even in my nightmares.

"I was sent to Ian Ayres."

"Ian Ayres?"

"The bastards' island. Where the Guilds send the women they capture as punishment for becoming pregnant outside of marriage."

"You were pregnant?" Something like glee brightened Ronya's voice.

"No, I was an orphan, which made me no better than a bastard to the Guilds." Mara fumbled her wine glass onto the table with her eyes still closed, needing to have the glass out of her hand, but not brave enough to open her eyes. "My mother died when I was a baby. My father when I was ten. There was no one to claim me, so the Guilds shipped me to Ian Ayres. I was there for two months before Lord Karron rescued me."

"If you were rescued, then it's not a secret you were there."

"People knowing I was there doesn't stop the island from tormenting me. I'll never be free of those demons." Mara dug her nails into her palms, willing her voice to stay steady. "The ships come in with the Guilds' prisoners. It seems like they're transporting horrible murderers, but it's only terrified pregnant girls. The soldiers and sailors haul the girls onto the island and sail away, abandoning them in the middle of the Arion Sea. The matrons take the girls to the birthing house. They keep them locked away until it's their time. I could hear the screams from the deliveries. There was nowhere in the children's house you could avoid the screams. Sometimes, the screams went silent too quickly, and the whole world would get cold.

"Then they'd let the pregnant girls out, make them dig the graves of the ones who didn't survive. The matrons made them stack the graves, digging over old bones. You could see the white of them mixed in with the dirt. Hundreds of bodies packed into the ground with no record of who those girls had been. We never saw what they did with the babies' bodies.

"The babies who lived were brought to the children's building. Even the ones whose mothers had survived. They always separated them. The babies' wails were almost worse than the mothers' screams. But once the children were old enough to understand words, they went quiet. All of them went quiet. It was like they knew they'd been doomed to the most terrible of lives, and no amount of screaming could stop their suffering. I was there for such a short time, and even I'd gone quiet before Lord Karron came for me."

"I never knew the Guilds were capable of such cruelty," Ronya whispered. "The people of Ilbrea have embraced a terrible sin."

"But the people don't know. I don't know. I lived on Ian Ayres, and I still can't understand." Heat pressed against Mara's eyelids as tears fought to break free. "There were so many children, so many women brought to the island. Always arriving on the ships. Always screaming. So much screaming. So many babies born. But

I only know two who have left that horrible place. Out of all of us, only two. But it was just the new mothers, and young children, and matrons living on the island. There wasn't anyone else."

Mara opened her eyes, letting her tears slide down her cheeks. "What do they do with the children who grow up? What happens to the bastards of Ian Ayres?"

"You don't know?" Ronya gripped Mara's hand.

"I can't let myself ask. I don't think I'm strong enough to survive the answer."

"The Guilds truly do deserve to burn."

"I have no darker truth to offer." Mara pulled away from Ronya. "Give me my prize."

Ronya refilled Mara's glass. "The blue light in the ice comes from ice worms. When the ice opens the tunnels, we mine the worms and distill what allows them to exist in the ice into a tonic. We feed the treatment to our infants, making them able to bear the cold. Our scholars believe the plants that grow in the ice have the worms to thank as well."

"This is the secret I bargained for?" Mara swiped away her tears.

"I'm not done." Ronya handed Mara her glass. "Drink."

Mara set the glass down.

"There's nothing in the wine you should be worried about." Ronya nudged Mara's glass toward her. "You ingested enough of the ice worms' tonic to survive here before you were ever allowed out of your cell."

"What?" Mara looked toward the glowing blue spots in the walls.

"In the tea we fed you." Ronya sighed. "The same tea that saved Tham's life. You're so bright, I really thought you would have questioned why you don't freeze here."

"You had no right—"

"To use our most precious resource to dose you with the very substance you needed to survive?" Ronya raised Mara's glass, holding her gaze, daring Mara to refuse. "None of your party would have survived being pulled through the ice if I hadn't chosen to save them."

"Then you have my thanks." Mara accepted the glass but didn't drink. "Will the tonic you so kindly forced into our bodies keep us trapped here? Can we only survive in the cold of Isfol?"

"Not at all." Ronya looked to the sledges loaded with glowing ice. "The few I've sent down to Ilbrea have all managed to adapt to the warmer climate."

"Sending spies to Ilbrea is quite ambitious." Mara gripped her glass, fighting the urge to smash it on the ground. "I'm so glad they survived. Are we quite through?"

"Your lack of gratitude is exhausting. Children, the ill, the brave souls who willingly travel through the ice to defend our city—our reserves of the tonic are meant to protect them. Helping you deprived my own people."

"Deprived? You lured us into your mine—"

"A mine that only appears when the ice allows," Ronya said. "When the mountain wills it, we are granted paths to the worms' nests. We harvest all we can before the ice closes. What we can collect is all we have until the ice opens again."

"A harvesting season. What a terrific secret."

"If the ice refused to open, all of our infants would die." Ronya's hand shook as she set her glass down. "If we cannot dose them with the tonic, they will freeze. Then our elders will freeze. One missed season, and Isfol will fall."

Mara shut her eyes, searching her heart for a spark of sympathy. "Has the ice ever refused to open?"

"No, but the time between openings grows longer, and the harvests poorer. Our mountain is losing its magic, and even I am not strong enough to save my people from the cold."

"I'm sorry." Mara met Ronya's gaze.

"The people cannot know how tenuous our fate has become.

It would cause chaos more dangerous than facing a freeze. If you tell anyone, I will have Tham executed."

"Who better to share your secrets with than a captive?"

"You're more than a captive, Mara. You're a woman with a soft heart, and you're going to help me keep my people alive. You simply haven't accepted it yet."

NIKO

Madness or monsters? The question has plagued me through two days of walking.

I can feel something lurking in the dark, staying just out of reach of my light.

I can't hear the creature or see it. But in all the times I have been surrounded by magic, I have never been so sure that something beyond the scope of normal man is trailing behind me.

Amec doesn't feel it, but he's agreed to sleep in shifts, a practice we had given up long ago. I think he might believe I'm losing my mind. Part of me fears he could be right. No man with sense would hope a monster is stalking their steps. But if there is nothing in the darkness, then my reason has truly slipped away.

How will I find my way back to you if I've gone mad?

We left the massive cavern that seemed large enough to swallow Ilara six times over several days ago. We found only one other passage leading out. The darkness is forcing us south. We've traveled so far in this tunnel, I don't know where we would be if we found our way up to the surface. Even if we were to emerge in the kingless territories, I would be grateful for a glimpse of sunlight. I'd climb through the southern mountains to get back to Ilbrea with a song in my heart. Anything would be better than this.

Being kept in this narrow tunnel often feels like the earth is trying to squeeze the air from my lungs.

But at the least the beast can only attack us from one direction. If the monster exists at all.

I hope there will be enough of me left for you to recognize the man you loved when I return to Ilara.

I will find a way to reach you,

Niko

ADRIAL

The depth of the blue sank into the parchment as though opening a tiny portal to a daring world Adrial longed to explore. The pale lavender he'd looped along the edges of the page held a delicacy that defied the human hand in its making. The scarlet edging that hinted at the tale's coming sunset brought a violence that belonged on a battlefield.

But it was the blue Adrial wished to lose himself in.

Dipping his pen into the ink again, he dug into his mind, trying find the memory that made the pigment so alluring. He drew another line, creating the edge of the river that weaved through the field.

The romance of King Gransen and his first Queen was not a tale usually highlighted in Ilbrean history, but their story seemed especially suited for Princess Illia's vellum.

Her wedding, at least, had yet to be disturbed. Allora and the King had not been so lucky.

None of the royals or sorcerers had been wounded in the attack on the cathedral. Lord Karron had survived with only a broken rib and some terrible bruising.

But four scribes had been killed. Fifteen healers, seven map makers, eight sailors, twelve soldiers. Their deaths were a terrible blow.

The bodies had long since been buried, and the wounded had begun to recover. But the harm had passed beyond the physical, and though he'd only been allowed a short visit with Allora at the Royal Palace, Adrial knew the Willocs felt the damage deeply.

A new wedding date for Allora and the King had yet to be set. The cleanup of the cathedral hadn't even finished, and arguments over plans for construction of a new space had already begun to plague the Guilds Council.

Adrial would have to sit through yet another council meeting tomorrow, where each Lord would argue their view of how the construction should be handled while all of them avoided shouting the obvious problem to the saints that guided them.

They had yet to find the villain who'd attacked them.

Adrial dipped his pen into the ink again.

The hue of the blue brought a good memory with it, far from the violence and fear of the cathedral attack.

Something dark and delicious. Not quite the current blue so prevalent in Ena's hair. A far deeper shade than the blue that had glowed from the waterfall.

"If you're going to waste all your time complaining, then go back to the scribes pool." Tammin's voice carried through the door of Adrial's private workroom.

The rumbled response from the outer office was too soft for him to make out the words.

It wasn't the blue of a night sky.

The Arion Sea as viewed from the cliffs at the Map Master's Palace.

Adrial sat back in his chair, smiling as he imagined the wind rushing past his face. The world had always seemed infinite and terrifying from so high above the city. Full of bountiful possibilities and horrific disasters in equal measure. A step too near the ledge, and you'd fall to your death, but the beauty of the view made the danger worthwhile.

"There is a purpose behind our assignment," Tammin said. "Respect the Lord Scribe's decisions and get to work."

This time, the rumbled response had a bite of anger to it.

"Alwyn, give me patience and wisdom." Adrial pushed himself to his feet, taking a moment to test the stability of his hip before going to the door.

Seven desks took up the main room outside his office, the setup much the same as they'd had when working in the scribes' shop out in the city. The wide windows here looked out over a different street, and the common folk were made to wait in the square and beg a scribes' guard to bring their request to the scribes in the workroom. But the tasks of writing out the papers that kept the city going were the same, and so, unfortunately, were the scribes that did the work.

"Is everything all right?" Adrial stayed in his doorway, looking from Natalia Tammin to Travers Gend and back again. The two stood behind their desks, glaring daggers at each other.

"Everything is fine, Head Scribe." Tammin gave Adrial a bow before sitting.

Taddy ducked closer to his desk, scribbling away so quickly, he'd have no hope of having his work approved.

"If anyone has a question as to why we are continuing to work on behalf of the people of Ilara while sheltering inside the library, I would be happy to hear their concerns," Adrial said.

Travers's jaw tensed, but he had the sense not to speak.

"It's not…" Taddy said. "Well, I wasn't talking about that, sir."

"You, Taddy?" Adrial walked down the line of desks to his apprentice. "I didn't know your voice had dropped so low."

"It hasn't." Taddy blushed. "I'm just the one that started it, sir. And I'm very sorry."

"Out with it," Adrial said.

"I…" Taddy set down his pen, hiding his ink-stained fingers behind his back too late for Adrial to even pretend not to have noticed. Taddy cringed. "Some of the other apprentices have been talking about a story—or maybe not a story, it could be true I suppose—but I told them it was all nonsense, though I wasn't *really* sure. So I asked in here, so I could get the opinions of full scribes, to see if they thought the story was true, and that's how it started."

"And it continued?" Adrial looked to Tammin.

"It continued with Scribe Gend saying we shouldn't be serving people who shelter killers that draw Guilded blood and me reminding him that we have a duty to the Guilds and to our head scribe." Tammin smiled as she shot a glare at Travers.

"Lovely," Adrial said. "Though sad that, after all the city has been through, Scribe Gend still cannot find sympathy for the innocent people who are suffering. We cannot blame the masses for the foul deeds of a few evil men."

"Is it a few men, then?" Taddy asked.

"Yes, Taddy," Adrial said. "The whole of Ilara has not turned against us. Though they could if we ignore our duty to keep the city running properly."

"Oh no, I know that part, sir. It's just, are you sure it isn't *one* man?" Taddy furrowed his brow. "One, possibly demonic man?"

"What under the stars are you talking about?" Adrial asked.

"It's a story going through some of the younger scribes," Tammin said. "They're trying to scare each other, which seems like a waste of time when we've plenty of real fears to worry over."

"Tell me the story, Taddy." Adrial tucked his hands behind his back, carefully shifting his weight to his good leg as he waited for his apprentice to speak.

"As a punishment, sir?" Taddy asked.

"As a lesson," Adrial said. "We scribes handle a huge volume of papers to maintain order for the people, but we are also the keepers of the stories and histories of Ilbrea. If you're going to be spreading ghost stories, you'd better be equipped to tell a decent version."

Taddy stood, back straight and chin high, as though preparing for a recitation. "Born deep in the shadows of the eastern mountains, the Demon's Torch seeks vengeance on Ilbreans who proudly stand with the Guilds."

"Why vengeance?" Adrial asked.

"Oh, right." Taddy blushed. "He seeks to *torment* all who proudly stand with the Guilds. They say his soul has been consumed by fire, and if you're fool enough to look into his eyes, you'll see the inferno blazing within him. He travels along the mountain road, murdering soldiers, as he hunts for the one his heart cannot forget.

"He goes into the soldiers' camps at night, setting their tents on fire and slaughtering them all, save three. He'll kill dozens of men and always manages to leave just the three alive. But always, those poor men beg for death. He questions the three, torturing them with knives and flames, always seeking information none of them have. Sometimes, he searches for a girl with raven hair. Sometimes, he hunts for a man who stole something precious. Sometimes, he searches for stones made of men's hearts."

A shiver tightened Adrial's shoulders as a child-like dread sank in his gut. He glanced toward the door, half-expecting a man with a soul consumed by fire to come charging in to kill them.

"By dawn," Taddy whispered, "even the three survivors have been released from their pain. He's hunted through camps and towns, searching for the answers he seeks, and his desperation has finally brought him all the way to Ilara. But the great capital is too large a place for even his mighty flames to consume all at once. So, the Demon's Torch will scorch us bit by bit, picking away at the Guilds until there are only three of us left for him to question."

Taddy fell silent, biting his lips together as though he'd terrified himself.

Adrial clapped and gave his apprentice a nod. "A finely told story Taddy. But it's only a story."

"I know that. And that's what I told the other apprentices. But what if..." Taddy cringed. "What if it is real? What if the Demon's Torch did come to Ilara and he's the one who brought the cathedral dome down?"

"A fire cannot replace a soul," Tammin said.

"Well, not literally," Taddy said. "His skin would all burn up. But some legends have bits of truth woven into them. And what if the bit of truth woven into the tale of the Demon's Torch is that there's a man whose anger burns like fire and he's really good at killing people and he's come to Ilara to slaughter members of the Guilds?"

"I'm proud of you, Taddy," Adrial said. "Searching for the grain of truth hidden within a legend can be a very valuable skill to have. But if there were one man who'd been terrorizing soldiers up and down the mountain road, we would have heard about it. We'd have had bounty notices pass through this very office. Something terrible happened, and searching for an explanation that fits neatly into a box is a very natural response. But the Demon's Torch is not the one who attacked us."

"Of course, sir." Taddy's cheeks pinked as he bowed. "That was the other point I made to the apprentices. One man couldn't slaughter a camp of soldiers without magic, and all magic lies within the Sorcerers Guild. The whole country would know if there were any magic outside the control of the Sorcerers Tower, so the story of the Demon's Torch is completely impossible."

Adrial tucked his hint of worry behind a proud and placid smile. "Well reasoned, Taddy."

"Thank you, sir." Taddy gave another, deeper bow.

"If everyone is ready to go back to work without snipping at each other, I have to collect some new ink." Adrial started toward the door.

"I can go for you, sir," Taddy said.

"No thank you, Taddy. I have something to give Ena, anyway."
Adrial kept his gait even until he reached the corridor beyond the
office and closed the door behind him. He took a moment to look
up and down the hall, making sure he was alone before leaning
against the wall.

He reached into his pocket, pulling out the little leather pouch
he'd carried with him for days, procrastinating like a coward
unprepared to meet his doom.

He untied the string, wanting to check the gift one more time
to be sure it was truly worthy.

Not worthy—no gift could ever be worthy of Ena—but, at the
very least, good enough he could feel pride in presenting it.

The little charm sat nestled in the silver chain of the necklace,
the tiny bird as true to his memory of the mark on Ena's side as
he could hope to create. The raven had spread its wings wide as
though ready to take flight. The feathers had been carefully
etched and the head made without any of the grotesque errors so
common in miniatures.

"Good enough." He pushed away from the wall and cut
toward the stairs that led below the main level of the library and
out to the courtyard. "It'll have to be good enough."

The man Adrial had been a few short months ago would
never have dared to bring a gift to a woman, let alone a woman
like Ena. But he'd learned quite a bit about bravery, and nearly
dying had made time seem to slip away all the more quickly.

He needed to offer her something in exchange for all she'd
done.

I'd give her all Ilbrea if I could.

He avoided meeting the gazes of the scribes he passed as he
made his way below the library and to the door that led to the far
side of the courtyard.

As he stepped outside, the bright afternoon sunlight dazzled
his eyes. He blinked away the glow, which had, for half a heartbeat, convinced him the world had been swallowed by magic.

The heat of summer had finally struck in earnest. The warmth cut through Adrial's robes, burning away the ice of the lingering doubts he fought so hard not to acknowledge.

Ena was a friend. A dear, wonderful friend who had given him indescribable amounts of joy. Even without knowing the true story of what her life had been before she'd come to Ilara, he knew she'd suffered more pain than most could survive. Her heart had been too badly scarred to be swept away in romance. Perhaps she would never again be able to feel the bursting, astonishing wonder of love that suffocated Adrial's reason.

But she didn't want to lose him. She cared for him and trusted him with secrets that would see her executed if the wrong people were told. That attachment meant more to Adrial than any romance with another ever could. He cherished her and would gladly accept whatever form of affection she offered in return.

The scars Adrial had been given as a child would never heal, and he doubted the pain Ena had suffered would ever allow her to heal, either. And, even if she ever could find love, Adrial knew he would never be the man to lure her into that exquisite danger.

Then why are you making a fool of yourself?

He leaned against the wall outside the library, shutting his eyes, wishing he'd taken the time to doubt himself in his office where no one could see him.

A gift for a friend. That simple. He couldn't allow his panic to turn the gift into something to suit his selfish ends instead of a heartfelt thanks for all she'd given him.

"After everything she's done for you, you can have the courage to bring her a token of thanks." Adrial gripped the pouch in his pocket and headed toward the stables' side door.

The scribes lingering in the courtyard seemed cheerier than usual. Even the guards and soldiers at the gates had lost some of the resigned stoicism that had plagued them since the attack on the cathedral.

Allowing himself to absorb a hint of their joy, Adrial entered the stables and ventured up the steps to Ena's shop. He raised his arm, preparing to knock before he'd actually reached the top of the stairs. As soon as his hand came near enough, he rapped his knuckles on the door, not allowing himself time to think.

"Who's there?" Ena called.

"Adrial." He waited, resisting the urge to reach back into his pocket. Panic fluttered in his chest as seconds slipped past with no sound of her movement.

"I can come back later." Adrial leaned closer to the door.

The soft thumping of footsteps and the scape of a shifting bolt came from inside the shop.

Ena opened the door a crack, peering over Adrial's shoulder before speaking. "You can come in now. Though I don't know what for. I haven't any new inks for you." There was no teasing in her tone. Her face was pale with faint purple rings around her eyes.

"Are you all right?" Adrial reached for her hand.

"I wasn't planning on visitors." She pulled the door open.

"I know." Adrial stepped into the shop, trying not to let the blissful aroma that filled the room muddle his thoughts. "I was hoping to discuss what inks I'll need after the next batch."

"Do you have a list?" Ena closed the door, sliding the metal bolt back into place.

"Are you concerned about intruders?" Worry tainted Adrial's nervous joy. "Do you not feel safe here?"

"Surrounded by soldiers?" Ena strode back to the table. "I suppose that depends on what whispers they've heard about me."

Six bowls had been laid out, each of them filled with different powders or petals. Jars, knives, strings, and leaves took up most of the rest of the surface, creating a more explicit chaos than Adrial had become accustomed to in Ena's space.

"I'd never turn you in for anything, but if you feel you're in danger here, if someone's threatened you, I'd like to know so I can help keep you safe." Adrial sniffed the contents of the first bowl. A bright tang filled his nostrils.

"Safety is a chivving lie, and you're smart enough to know it." Ena pushed the bowl aside and set parchment, ink, and a pen in front of Adrial. "Make me a list. I'll get everything on it to you as soon as I can."

"A list? You don't need more details than my poor descriptions?"

"I lost my ability to twirl in a circle and have you point at the pretty colors on my skirt the night of the rebellion. Just write it out."

"Ena, what's wrong?" Adrial reached for her.

She flinched as his fingers grazed her arm. "My pretty skirt is gone. Cade's filth ruined it. I didn't think you would forget so quickly, scribe."

She turned away from him, storming to the shelves of ink near the window.

"I will never forget that night." Adrial willed his voice to stay steady and calm. "I will never in a thousand lifetimes forget all you did to protect me. I will always be grateful."

"The gratitude of the head scribe. What a worthy gift." Ena set four jars of black ink in front of him. "Take these, you'll need them in a few days."

"I can come back then to get them."

"Take them now so you don't have to keep wandering up here." There was something in her face—the tension in her jaw, the way she didn't meet his eyes—that made her seem more afraid than bolting the door had.

"I want to come back to see you." Adrial held out his hand in front of her, letting her choose whether or not to take the comfort he longed to offer. "To see my friend. To ask what's bothering her and give help if I can."

"There is no help I need from you." She stared at his hand. "I have work to do and coin to earn. Just make your list and go."

"If it's gold you need—"

"Don't." Ena pulled her hair over her shoulder, whipping the strands into a tight braid. "I'm not a whore. I don't take coin from men."

"I wouldn't want anything in exchange." Pain tightened in Adrial's gut. "I'm your friend, Ena."

"You're a paun." She finally met his gaze. Adrial hated the pain in her eyes. "You are a good man. But you're a paun."

"And you've always known that. Something has changed. Something's wrong. Just tell me what it is."

"I'm tired. I don't want company or comfort. I just want to do my work."

"Ena—"

"Your list." She picked up the pen, holding it between them.

"Please, Ena. If you feel unsafe, tell me why. Is there something else going on in the city? Did one of Cade's men survive? Are they threatening you for living here and working for the scribes?"

Ena didn't move.

He took the pen from her and set it on the table. "Is it a soldier? Is it a commoner?"

"It's nothing to do with you."

"It has everything to do with me!" Adrial shut his eyes, wishing Dudia would allow him to skip back a few moments in time and make her forget he'd shouted. "I care for you, Ena. With everything I am. Seeing you upset makes it feel as though my heart will shatter."

"Then your heart is too weak to survive in my world." Ena spoke softly. There was something in her tone. A finality that seemed to belong to a goodbye. "Write the list in your chambers and have Taddy bring it by. I don't have time to wait while you make up your mind."

"Right." A strange cold swept through Adrial's body as he picked up the jars of black ink. "I'll have someone else bring it by if you're so busy. Taddy would want to talk to you. He's on a tear about the Demon's Torch."

"What?" Something sharp replaced the hollow quiet of Ena's tone.

"It's the new rumor on the wind." Adrial tucked the jars into his pocket. His fingers grazed the leather pouch. "A man from the eastern mountains who's tortured soldiers along the mountain road. They say the Demon's Torch has finally come to Ilara. He's the one who attacked the cathedral. Continuing his quest to find a woman he blames the Guilds for stealing from him."

Ena gripped the edge of the worktable with both hands, as though trying to stop the room from spinning.

"It's only a story." He took her waist, steadying her. She didn't pull away from him. "It's apprentices talking nonsense."

A tear rolled down Ena's cheek.

"Is it not a story?" Adrial glanced toward the door. "This man, the Demon's Torch, is he real? Is that who you're afraid of?"

"I would never fear him." A second tear betrayed her.

"But he is real? He would attack the Guilds?" Adrial held her closer, wanting to offer comfort and desperate for a way to protect her. "Ena, if he's the one who brought down the dome, you have to tell someone before he attacks again."

"It wasn't him." Ena swiped her tears away.

"Someone else will be blamed for what he did. I know you want freedom from the Guilds, but a commoner will pay with their life for what happened at the cathedral. We can't let an innocent man be punished for the crimes of the Demon's Torch."

"I swear to you, scribe. The Demon's Torch is not haunting Ilara. If he was, you'd already be dead." She touched his cheek.

"Keeping any information you have a secret means risking the wrong person being punished for the attack."

"This is Ilbrea. The innocent are punished every day. It's our fate. Now get out of my shop."

"I didn't mean to upset you."

"Leave." Ena backed away. "Have someone else bring me your list."

"I should come myself. If not today, then tomorrow. To make sure you're feeling better, safer."

"There's no need for you to come back here." Ena turned to her table. "My work does not require your presence."

"Right." Speaking the word carved a hole in Adrial's chest. "I'm sorry. I won't bother you again." He pulled the leather pouch from his pocket and set it on the corner of the table. "Please be safe. The world would be a darker place without you in it."

He stepped out of the workshop and shut the door behind him.

The walls rushed away from him, everything expanding until he was too small to be seen and the chasm of his isolation too great to be climbed out of by someone as weak as the Guilded Cripple.

KAI

The air in the forest had changed. Not thickened. Not chilled. It hadn't gained a new scent, either.

But there was something that prickled against Kai's skin. Whether the prickle was meant to be a warning or an invitation, he hadn't quite decided.

He stayed beside Drew as they cut down the slope of the latest mountain the girl had made them climb, heading east if Kai wasn't completely mistaken.

The terrain made their path slow. Drew's newly gained limp added to the arduous challenge.

Kai reached out, gripping Drew's arm before his mind had fully processed that Drew had slipped.

"I'm fine." Drew spoke through gritted teeth.

"I know." Kai kept his tone light. "Just trying to steady myself on this godsforsaken slope."

"Don't." Sweat coated Drew's brow. He kept his jaw clenched against the pain.

"Sorry, old friend." Kai let go but stayed right by Drew's side. "Will the people you're taking us to be able to help with his pain?"

The girl didn't answer.

"How much longer until we reach them?" Drew said. "If they're going to murder us, I'd just as soon they do it before we have to climb another chivving mountain."

The girl didn't answer him, either.

"It was easier when she'd at least talk to you," Kai said. "Her keeping silent for days is just plain peculiar."

"I should have dived off the ship and swum straight back to the docks in Ilara the moment I knew there was a sorcerer on our ship," Drew said. "Would've been the best chivving decision of my life."

"Come on, Drew, don't be such a getch." Kai grabbed Drew's arm as he slid again. "If you hadn't been on this cact of a demon's journey with me, you wouldn't be here to enjoy all the lovely trees we've passed."

"Kai—"

"We started with palm trees, which made for an exotic view, and now look"—Kai swept his free arm to the side, as though presenting a guest—"we're in a lovely forest of *not* palm trees. Look at their nice, thick trunks. They've got such pretty, deep green leaves, and they tower over us. The ground is supple yet firm beneath our feet. The soil positively radiates fertility."

The girl gave a low laugh.

"A better man than me would write lyrical poems about the beauty of the forest we've been lucky enough to trample through for weeks. All we need is to see a few more birds, and there won't be any way you can deny this walk has been worth being slashed twice by a possessed man," Kai said. "Some people spend their whole lives dreaming of a journey like this."

"And those men are chivving slitches." Drew's furrowed brow and pursed lips didn't quite disguise the slight smile lifting the corners of his mouth.

"I'm sure they are." Kai nodded solemnly, searching the trees for something else to prattle on about to distract Drew from his pain. "But they are chivving slitches who dream of seeing something as wonderful as that rock."

Kai pointed to the bottom of the slope where the ground leveled out, promising a bit of relief for aching legs. A black boulder sat right where the flat basin began.

"A rock," Drew said. "All my dreams have come true."

"Perhaps they have," Kai said.

The girl slowed as she neared the bottom of the slope, cutting at an angle that would lead her straight toward the boulder.

The longer Kai studied the rock, the more out of place it seemed. Ten feet tall and darker than the other stones that had hindered their trek through the mountains, not a shred of moss or lichen grew on the boulder.

"If I'm lucky enough to die surrounded by family, my final breath will be spent telling the tale of seeing that chivving rock," Drew said.

"You might be right." Kai shifted his grip on Drew's arm, slowing their pace as the girl stopped and turned to face them. "Time for a rest already?"

"You know better than that," the girl said. "Don't pretend to know or notice less than you do. They won't take kindly to it."

Kai stopped ten feet away from the girl, sidestepping to stand between her and Drew. "Any other advice?"

"Don't fight them," the girl said. "You won't stand a chance of winning. Don't try to run away or follow me. Both will end in your death."

"Are you going to leave us here?" Drew said.

"For now." The girl pulled a string from her pocket and tied her hair back.

Kai scanned the trees, searching for people hiding up in the branches. To the north, another dark boulder peered between the leaves. Squinting through the shadows, he caught sight of a third boulder to the south.

"I don't know how long it will be. But you'll need to be ready in case they choose to speak to you. Take off all your clothes, your boots, everything. Leave it all in a pile there." She pointed to a tree twenty feet up the slope. "Don't try to hide anything on your body. They'll kill you for it and not feel an ounce of regret."

"They sound like lovely people," Kai said.

"You want us to wait here naked?" Drew asked.

"Like I said, a story to tell on your deathbed." Kai shrugged out of his blanket-made bag.

"It's the way things work here. Either you'll do as I say, or you'll die. There are no other options." The girl turned and walked toward the boulders.

For a moment, it seemed as though she'd just keep moving across the flat ground of the forest, but without a shimmer or sound, she disappeared. Vanished, like they'd been following a ghost for days on end.

"Chivving, cacting gods and stars, of all the slitching—"

"Don't panic." Kai patted Drew on the back. "When facing magic, panic is usually the worst option."

"Demon spawn of the frozen chivving north, the monsters on the mountains and all their chivving myths. And chivving, cacting, blood of the Guilded paun—"

"That's the way." Kai pulled off his shirt. "Just breathe."

"Things like that should not happen! People do not just disappear into thin air!"

"I know." Kai yanked off his boots. "But think of it this way, if whoever is hiding behind those stones doesn't decide to kill us, we might get to eat something tonight besides leaves we really hope aren't poisonous."

"I should have dived straight off that ship." Drew threw his bag to the ground. "Should've gone to the nearest tavern and drunk till I couldn't remember any chivving sorcerers existed. Then found my way across the eastern mountains and settled in Wyrain. They have ships in Wyrain. I could have been a chivving sailor there."

"You'd never abandon Ilbrea." Kai took off his pants, adding them to his pile.

"I chivving well would." Drew froze, shirt off, hands on the buckle of his belt. "She walked past that boulder, and now we can't see her."

"Yes."

"Can she see us?" Drew squinted at the trees beyond the rock. "Can whoever she brought us here to see, see us?"

"Probably. Now take off your pants."

"And have a load of people staring at me naked?"

"If anyone beyond the boulders decides to stare at your naked form, it will be to thank the gods for sending such a handsome sailor on a perilous journey so he could display his manhood in the forest. Now give me your pants and I'll walk our things up the slope."

Drew winced as he dropped his pants. "Someday, sarcasm will fail you."

"But this is not that day." Kai grabbed their things, carefully choosing his footing as he climbed back up the slope.

"How long do you think she'll leave us out here?"

"Long enough to be bitten up in places you hope never itch." Kai piled their things beside a tree.

"Perfect."

"Shall we sing them every shanty we know?"

"No."

Kai picked his way back down the slope to Drew, gaining a bur in the foot for his caution.

"Either we'll be singing to ourselves or giving whoever is lurking out of sight, watching us wait like two naked slitches, a show to remember us by." Kai clapped Drew on the shoulder. "Who knows? We might even annoy them into killing us faster."

"That's the most hopeful thing I've heard in days."

"Good man." Kai took a deep breath and began to sing. "The soul of the sea stings like a vicious bee, and—"

"Those aren't even the right words." Drew smacked Kai on the chest.

"Best sing along if you want it done your way."

"It's not my way. It's the right chivving words." Drew scowled as he sang. "The soul of the sea is a heartbreaking thing—"

Kai joined in, singing as loudly as a drunk in a cheap tavern.

They sang through every song they knew and some they only remembered bits of. When Drew's hip got too painful to bear his weight, they sat beside a tree and started back at the beginning of their repertoire.

The sun had begun to fade from the sky and Kai's voice had grown gravelly by the time they reached the middle of the third round of songs.

"We should put our clothes back on," Drew said as Kai took a breath to begin *The Storm of Souls*, one of his least favorite songs, though the mournful tune was a favorite of those who lasted until dawn in the taverns.

"She told us not to." Kai took another deep breath.

"I'm not going to sit out here naked in the dark." Drew stifled a groan as he got to his feet. "If they decide not to kill us, she can pop back out past the magic stone and tell us to strip down again. This chivving mess started with a sorcerer giving us foolish orders that nearly got us killed. Now we're naked on the orders of a new sorcerer. I'm chivving tired of obeying people just because they were born with magic in their blood."

"Just give it a few more minutes." Kai stood, blocking Drew's path. "We've come so far to stare at this boulder. A few more bugs gnawing on our masts won't break us. Please."

"Don't tell me how close I am to breaking. This whole chivving journey has been damned by the gods." Drew dug his knuckles into his eyes. "I've been shipwrecked and stabbed, and now cacting bugs are chewing on my better assets. And every last chivving bit of this mess has been caused by chivving sorcerers. I can't stand any more of this madness. I am going to run away to a land without any sorcerers. I'm done with the lot of them!"

"Sorcerers themselves aren't the problem," an unfamiliar voice said.

Kai leapt forward, planting himself between Drew and the boulder.

A man with thistle-brown hair stood beside the stone, arms crossed and eyes narrowed as though trying to decide how to kill the invaders who'd been led into his woods.

"Then what is the problem?" Drew tried to cut around Kai. "Is it all of magic? Apparently *wild magic* is what made the demon of a man who ruined my hip."

"Drew, be careful," Kai whispered.

"*Careful* has gotten me nowhere!" Drew shoved Kai aside. "*Careful* has gotten me naked and singing without a drop of frie in me. *Careful* doesn't stand for a normal man in a world of magic."

"Saelk." The man stepped away from the boulder. "That's what we call your kind here. *Saelk*."

"And what do you do with saelk?" Kai asked.

"If it's not feed them and mend their wounds, then I pray to the gods you offer them a swift death," Drew said.

"It depends on the individual." The wrinkles on the man's brow smoothed. "Saelk we count as friends are our equals. Saelk we deem enemies, we torture for information. We kill most of them after we've gotten whatever little details we might find useful. Some, we save. Keep them as subjects for teaching students how to properly interrogate."

"And how do you know if someone's an enemy or not?" Kai let a smile slide onto his face as he stepped closer to the man. "I'd like to know what the parameters are if I'm risking prolonged educational torture."

"You're a Guilded sailor," the man said.

"Proudly." Kai held his marked arm forward for the man to see.

"You're prepared to stand against the Sorcerers Guild?" the man asked.

"I love Ilbrea, and I love my Guild." Kai dared to venture another step forward. "The Sorcerers Guild is a blight. If we allow the disease of their greed to spread, they will destroy everything I hold dear. They have to be stopped. I will gladly give my place in the Sailors Guild and my life to ensure the Lady Sorcerer never rules Ilbrea."

"She already does," the man said. "You're a fool if you think otherwise."

"She doesn't sit on the throne," Kai said. "As far as I'm concerned, that means we still have a shred of hope."

"Fool saelk, that's what Isla brings me." The man glanced back as though he could see beyond the boulder.

"Isla." Kai smiled in the direction the man had spoken. "What a charming name for a charming guide."

"Come," the man said. "We'll get you fed and your wounds tended. I may change my mind about you tomorrow, but I have enough faith in Isla to let you live through the night. I think we may find a way to be very useful to each other."

"Lovely." Drew took a step toward their piles of clothes.

"Leave them," the man said. "My faith in Isla doesn't go that far."

"You're a wise man." Kai beckoned Drew toward him. "Does seeing to our wounds include the massive amount of bug bites we've received?"

"That'll depend on the mood of the one who heals you." The man waited until Kai and Drew stood right behind him. "It's best to relax. Some find the sensation to be overwhelming, but the stones will not hurt you. Unless I will them to."

"Comforting," Drew whispered.

"It shouldn't be." The man stepped beyond the boulder and disappeared.

"I blame you for all of this," Drew said.

"I wouldn't have it any other way." Kai took Drew's hand and stepped forward, dragging him beyond the boulder.

A heat started at Kai's nose, almost like the burning of hope or the promise of a desire that would devour his soul. The sensation shifted down to his chest, setting a fire around his heart he was sure would melt away the man he'd been to forge him into the person the gods demanded he become.

He took another step, and the heat vanished, leaving him cold. An odd pain dug at his chest, almost like a wound carved by grief.

"Men like us do not belong in places like this," Drew whispered.

The tone of Drew's voice yanked Kai's focus away from the wonder mixed with fear that pressed against his lungs, making him look at the scene before him.

The basin of trees had disappeared, replaced by a village built of dark stone houses. Well-packed dirt roads cut between the buildings, breaking the perfection of the matching thatched rooves.

A tower rose above the rest of the buildings, reaching a hundred feet high. The joyful noise of children playing blocked out the sounds of the forest Kai had become accustomed to, the bright tone bringing relief and bereavement all at once.

The girl who had brought them to this impossible place—no, not the girl, Isla—stood in a line with seven other people. All of them were older than her. All of them had expressions ranging from displeased to suspicious.

"What is this place?" Drew tightened his grip on Kai's hand.

"Are you sure about this, Beckham?" A woman with steel-gray hair looked to the man who had invited them into the spell.

"I'm sure that any advantage we can gain against the Sorcerers Guild is worth the risk of having two saelk enter our home,"

Beckham said. "If we decide we don't trust them, we can kill them later."

"And if you decide you can trust us?" Kai said. "We have information we need to deliver to the right people. We need to get back to Ilara as soon as possible."

"For your battle, not ours," a woman with long, brown hair said.

"Take them to be healed and cared for." Beckham nodded to Isla. "The council will convene and decide what to do with the lost Ilbreans."

"Yes, Beckham." Isla bowed to him. She waited as the rest of the group filed away, heading down the widest of the dirt roads and disappearing into the chaos of what seemed, for all the gold in Ilbrea, to be a thriving village in the middle of the mountains.

"What is this place?" Kai asked.

"Your refuge. Maybe your doom, depending on how you behave." Isla beckoned them south to a narrower dirt road.

"Who are all the people here?" Kai wrapped an arm around Drew's waist, helping him keep up with her. "You can't tell me this settlement just sprang up from the ground."

"How many myths are you willing to accept as fact in one day?" Isla cut down an alley between houses, stepping around a calico cat that mewed after her.

"There is no truth you can offer that will be too much for me to bear." Kai twisted sideways, keeping his grip on Drew even when the cat swiped for his ankles as they sidled down the alley.

"Do not include me in your madness," Drew whispered.

"This is where the Black Bloods bring the sorcerer children they manage to rescue from Ilbrea." Isla stopped in front of a house with a purple door.

"Black Bloods?" Kai's steps faltered.

"The Brien Clan provides us shelter." Isla banged on the door. "They train and protect us."

"Brien?" Kai pulled Drew closer, keeping a tight hold on the one thing he could be sure wasn't madness.

"One of the five Black Blood clans. You're now working for the Brien. As training fodder or as assets in our battle, you'll be useful either way." Isla smiled and stepped aside as the purple door swung open.

A weathered man with tufted white hair peered out at them.

"New saelk," Isla said. "Beckham wants them healed and fed."

The man's glare drifted from Drew to Kai. "At least this pair won't bleed on my floor."

ADRIAL

The city seemed dark and lonesome as Adrial stared out his window. The same window Ena had sat in months ago when she'd proudly watched him defy Lord Gareth by writing the burial papers for the common folk.

He'd done well that day. As small an act as writing the burial papers had been, he'd helped people. Had genuinely made a difference in the lives, or rather deaths, of Ilbreans.

But something between then and now had gone horribly wrong.

Adrial tried to untangle it all, searching for the transgression that had destroyed his foolish joy.

He could only find one, and he hated himself for it.

Ena was his friend. Ena had trusted him. Ena had let him into her life, and he knew, *he knew* how much that had cost her.

But he'd pushed too far. By the simple act of taking their friendship for granted, he'd asked for more than she'd offered. He'd made himself another despicable man vying for her affection.

"I'm not like them." Adrial dug his knuckles into his temples.

"I could never be like them. I would never force her into anything. I would never think she owed me her...herself."

But guilt broke through the rage Adrial felt toward Cade and all the men who had come before him, trying to get Ena to lift her skirts. Seeing only the pleasure her body could offer, not the incomparable person she was.

Adrial had never touched her against her will. Never used anger or threats to coerce her.

But he'd betrayed their friendship. The affection she'd shown him had been a part of her game, the banter he'd agreed to when he'd begged Ena to stay in his life.

He'd mistaken playful teasing for mutual happiness. And, if he was brave enough to dig deep into his heart, a very small part of him had hoped that, unworthy as he was, she might someday be willing to offer him more.

From everything she'd said, Ena had no one else in her life she came close to trusting, and he'd broken that faith by valuing a lovesick dream over a precious friendship.

She could never want me. I've ruined everything for an impossible hope.

He looked out toward the sea, wishing it were Kai's ship on the horizon instead of a coming storm.

The triumphant return of his friend would ease the pain that gripped his chest, even if it wouldn't change anything with Ena. Though Kai had prolific success with romance, he wasn't who Adrial longed to ask for help.

Only Tham could be trusted with that. Tham, who loved silently and stoically whenever anyone might see the true passion of his heart.

Tham hid the best part of his soul to protect Mara and her place in the Map Makers Guild. He and Mara were happy behind closed doors, but Adrial knew how it pained his friend not to be allowed to live the truth of the love he breathed.

If Tham could hide his heart, so could Adrial.

He would find no bliss when hidden from the world, but if he could keep Ena in his life, he would never show his foolish affection again.

Anything is better than losing her.

He stood and straightened his robes, steeling his nerves against the dreaded task.

"You're not too proud a man to beg for forgiveness, Adrial Ayres." He headed for the door before his courage could fail him.

The walk through the corridor and down the stairs seemed longer than usual, and not just from the approaching storm adding to the usual pain in his hip. Dread seemed to pull him back with every step.

Best to get it done quickly. Better to know your fate.

By the time he'd made it halfway across the courtyard, he could no longer hide his limp. He kept his gaze fixed on the door in the side of the stables, hoping to avoid whispers and pitying glances.

Movement near the open gates caught the corner of Adrial's vision.

One of the scribes' guards spoke to the man beside him before approaching Adrial.

Adrial tried to hasten his pace.

"Head Scribe," the guard said.

"I'm fine." Adrial waved him away. "Just going to the inker's workshop. I can make it on my own."

"Sir." The guard took Adrial's forearm as though he'd nearly fallen.

"I know they whisper about the Guilded Cripple, but I am capable of crossing this square."

"I need to walk with you, sir, so they don't see us speaking." The guard shifted sideways, blocking Adrial's face from the view of the other guards at the gates.

"Then I appreciate your assistance." Adrial gave him a nod and continued slowly toward the stables.

"I only arrived back at the library an hour ago, sir," the guard said in a low voice. "I'm on duty for the evening. I was out in the city during the day. I saw the inker."

Adrial froze. "That's impossible."

"Keep walking, or I'll have to carry you."

"Why would she be on the streets?" Adrial made himself move forward.

"No idea, sir. I cornered her, asked what she thought she was doing going out where she could be attacked. Told her she was recklessly ungrateful after the Lord Scribe had been kind enough to offer her protection."

"What did she say?"

"She said—and pardon the words, sir, but they were hers—she said she didn't care about the Lord Paun's protection. I told her she wouldn't be allowed to come back to her shop. She told me to burn it all down if I liked, she wasn't chivving coming back."

"Where was she?" Adrial asked.

"I haven't told anyone else, sir. She looked sad and a bit desperate. There was a panic to her, deeper than what most people can endure and stay on their feet. I've been hoping that whatever way she snuck out, she'd come back in on her own, once she'd sorted herself. I'd hate for someone on the edge of despair to lose the roof over their head, even if they did insult the Lord Scribe. I'm sorry if I've done the wrong thing, sir."

"Where did you see her?" Adrial asked again.

"I wanted to tell you because you seem fond of her, and I was hoping you wouldn't turn her in for leaving or turn me in for not saying anything." They stopped beside the stables.

"I would do anything to protect Ena, just tell me where she is."

"I saw her by the cliff road to the Map Master's Palace."

"Have a horse saddled for me." Adrial tore through the door, racing toward the stairs.

"But, sir—"

"A horse. Now!"

Adrial used his hands, pressing against the wooden walls to help him climb the steps faster.

"Ena." He banged on her door before throwing it open. "Ena!"

Though the twilight was dim, no lamps had been lit. The table had been cleared and scrubbed. There were no half-ground petals or jars of powder left out for later use.

"Ena." His uneven footsteps pounded against the floor as he ran to the bedroom.

She'd left everything tidy. Everything carefully packed away. No trace of the colorful chaos she thrived on.

His heartbeat seemed to emanate from his throat as he raced back down the stairs and into the stables. The guard stood at the far end with two saddled horses.

"I'm going alone," Adrial said.

"You can't, sir," the guard said. "It's not safe in the city."

"I learned that when I was almost beaten to death." Adrial grabbed the reins of the nearest horse. Gritting his teeth against the pain, he dragged himself up into the saddle. White-hot agony sliced through his ruined hip, brutally reminding him he hadn't ridden since Cade's men had smashed his bones.

"I can't let you," the guard said. "I'll lose my place as a guard."

"Then act surprised." Adrial confined his pain to the shadows of his mind as he kicked his horse, charging through the open front doors of the stables and toward the gates. "Clear a path!"

The guards began to scramble at his shouted command before looking back to see who had ordered them to move.

Adrial kicked his horse again, not giving the guards time to stop him, sending the soldiers in front of the gates diving out of his path.

He hoped they hadn't hurt themselves. He hoped the guard who'd warned him had the sense to pretend he didn't know why Adrial had ridden away.

But none of it mattered.

Ena.

He raced through the city, shouting at the few people on the streets to get out of his path.

Ena. Ena.

He'd taken her to the grounds of the Map Master's Palace once. To the pink trees by the edge of the cliffs. That's where he'd thought their friendship had begun.

"I'd like to see Ilara from above one more time before I leave. Make sure all the wounds it's given me are small enough for me to carry." She'd told him that months ago.

But he'd thought, once she had a shop of her own...

If she'd gone up to say goodbye to Ilara from above before fleeing the city and finding some new place to build her home, he'd never be able to find her once she left the cliffs.

Or if she hadn't gone up to say goodbye to Ilara, but to cast aside her memories of him.

Or if she hadn't gone up because of him, or for the view of the city. If she'd gone up for the cliff itself. If...

Panic that would knock most people off their feet. That's what the guard had said.

"Ya!" Adrial pushed the horse faster as he reached the road that switchbacked up the cliffs.

The wind whipped against him as he tore around corner after corner. The clouds of the coming storm swallowed the stars that should have shone over the Arion Sea.

Adrial gripped the reins, trusting the horse to have the sense not to run off the side of the twisting road, but needing something to hold onto as dread filled his chest as though Dudia himself had decreed the world would soon end.

"Faster," Adrial whispered to the horse as he urged it onward. "Please, faster."

The gates of the Map Master's Palace blocked the road ahead. In the darkness, the dozen guards seemed like specters come to haunt him for some unforgiveable sin.

"I'm Adrial Ayres, former ward of Lord Karron," he bellowed over the wind before he reached the men. "Open the gates."

Two men pulled the gates open as the first bolt of lightning split the sky.

As the rest of the men rushed to clear Adrial's path, one of the guards stayed close to the center of the road. "Head Scribe, are you all right?"

"Did a woman come this way?" Adrial asked. "The inker, Ena Bairn, have you seen her?"

"No, sir," the guard said. "No one's come through the gates in hours."

"But did you see anyone on the road?"

"A woman walked up the cliff road, but she didn't come this way."

"Then she went over the wall." Adrial kicked his horse forward.

"What, sir?"

"She went over the wall!" The wind swallowed Adrial's shout.

Please let her be here. Please let me find her.

He wasn't even sure who he was begging. Dudia, Saint Alwyn, the common gods, the stars above. He would have bargained with anyone if it only meant finding her.

The rain began as another streak of lightning split the sky, throwing the trees ahead into terrifying relief.

Monsters. The woods were monsters, trying to hide the woman he loved from him.

He swiped the rain from his face as he rode down the tree-shrouded path.

Or maybe the storm and the trees were vengeance sent by Dudia to torment him, his rightful punishment for thinking himself worthy of more than he could ever deserve.

"Ena!" He saw no sign of her through the pounding rain. "Ena!"

He pushed the horse faster, cutting through the trees.

"Ena!"

A shape in the distance. A form that didn't belong along the edge of the rocky cliff.

"Ena!"

She wore no cloak. She let the rain soak through her as she looked out toward the Arion Sea.

"Ena." Adrial stopped his horse. His legs buckled as his slid down from his saddle and onto the muddy ground. "Ena, I'm sorry."

She didn't look at him as he stumbled toward her.

"Ena, please—"

"Go home, scribe."

"Please, Ena. I'm sorry. Just give me one moment to tell you how sorry I am and beg your forgiveness."

Ena coughed a laugh, but the sound changed as she choked on her tears.

Adrial reached for her, wanting to wipe her tears away before they could mix with the cold rain.

"Don't touch me." Ena pulled away from him. "Just go."

Pain pierced Adrial's chest as he stepped away from her. "I'm so sorry, Ena. I didn't mean to push the boundaries of our friendship. I swear to you, I'll never come to your shop again. I'll send Taddy with the orders. You'll never have to see me. But please come back to the library, Ena. This storm is only going to get worse, you're not safe here."

"I'm not safe anywhere." The wind whipped her hair behind her as though it were trying to tear her away. "I have been doomed from the very start. The world has taken too much from me, and I cannot keep fighting. I am too broken to keep fighting."

"You're not broken. You are the strongest person I've ever known."

Ena's chest shuddered as she fought against her sobs. Thunder shook the cliffs as though the gods themselves railed against her sadness.

"Ena, whatever's wrong, I beg forgiveness for the part I played. Whatever demons you have to fight, I will fight beside you. Just stay with me. Come home. Let me help you."

"There is no helping me, scribe."

"Ena, please."

"No, scribe."

"Ena—"

"You can't fight against Cade. You can't protect me from him."

"Cade is dead."

"His child isn't. I'm carrying that monster's child."

Even the storm seemed to quiet as Adrial tried to understand Ena's words.

"That chivving bastard will have his revenge. A simple tonic could have saved me. But I let him hurt you and break me. I couldn't think. I couldn't leave the library and abandon you. Gods, I know better. But I let it all fall apart. Now it's too late for me." She tipped her face up into the pouring rain, letting the sky drown her in its tears. "There is no help. There is no safety. The only path left for me is Ian Ayres. I will not go into that hell. I will not give a child to that demon island. I have fought too many battles to let my life end there."

"It won't. You won't be sent to Ian Ayres. I won't let them take you. Ena, look at me." Adrial reached toward her. "Just look at me. I swear to you on everything I am, I will not let them send you to that terrible place."

"Even you don't have that power, scribe." She stepped away from him, her toes brushing the edge of the cliff. "I should have died a long time ago. I've stayed alive to fight the Guilds. But I can't fight against this. I'm not strong enough. I have never been strong enough."

"I can protect you." Adrial inched forward.

"You can't. No one can. I'm out of places to run. I finally understand there is no escaping the wrath of the Guilds."

A bolt of lightning streaked toward the city. The ruins of the Guilds' cathedral seemed to glow in the darkness.

"Go, scribe." She met his gaze. Fatigue, sadness, and pain beyond his understanding filled her eyes. "You don't belong out here."

"I will not abandon you."

"You're not abandoning me. You're letting me choose the kinder fate." She looked down at the city far below. "There are some hells even I don't deserve."

"Marry me." He grabbed her hand.

She tried to pull free. The rain had slicked her skin.

He held on tighter, refusing to let her slip away.

A clap of thunder shook the ground.

"Marry me, Ena." He stepped to the edge of the cliff beside her.

"What?"

He wrapped his arm around her, blocking her from the temptation of the open air. "I am not a warrior. I cannot defend you with a sword, but I can give you the protection of my name."

"No."

"I will keep you safe." He touched her rain-slicked cheek. "If we're married, they can't send you away. You and the child will be safe from Ian Ayres."

"It's not your child!"

"I don't care. I will claim him as my own. He will have the protection of my station within the Guilds."

"Cade tried to kill you. He has already stolen my life. I will not let you sacrifice yours."

"What sacrifice? To have a wife? To give a child my name?" Adrial held her tighter, wrapping his arms around her as though he had the strength to protect her from fate's cruel claws. "That would bring more joy to my life than I've ever dreamt possible."

"Cade was a murderer. He was evil and cruel." Ena looked

toward the warehouses where Cade had nearly murdered them both. Where she'd let Cade violate her to save Adrial's life.

The cold of the rain sliced through Adrial's soul. "Cade is dead. Marry me, and this child will be ours. No one will ever need to know about Cade. The Guilds won't be able to take you from me."

Ena's sobs shook her chest.

Adrial tightened his hold on her, guiding her away from the ledge. "You don't have to fight them on your own. Not Cade, not the Guilds, not any of the shadows that haunt you. Come home, Ena. Let me fight beside you. I promise, I will stand beside you."

She wept in his arms, the anger of the storm stealing the sound of her tears.

Adrial held her as she cried, giving promises of safety and hope. But the wind stole the sound of his words as well. So he held her close, making sure she could not disappear.

ADRIAL

The pounding of the rain had slowed to a steady patter before the sun rose, but Adrial still couldn't convince himself to sleep. He needed to stay awake. He needed to make sure she was safe, that it really was Ena who lay nestled in his arms and he hadn't slipped into some kind of wonderful dream to drown out the nightmare of losing her.

She slept with her head on his shoulder and her arm draped across his bare chest. His robes had been soaked through by the storm, but he couldn't bring himself to leave her in the little bedroom behind her workshop. And she hadn't asked him to.

When they'd finally left the cliffs, he'd ridden in through the gates while she snuck back over the library wall. For the few minutes he'd had to wait for her in her shop, he hadn't been able to breathe. All the air had vanished from the world. And, if she'd changed her mind and disappeared into the storm, he didn't want the air to come back. Better to suffocate than to lose her.

But she'd slipped silently into her shop, not looking at him as she bolted the door. She'd put on a dry shift and curled up on her bed, leaving a space for him beside her as though she'd needed the comfort of his presence as much as he'd needed the solace of being able to see her and be sure she really hadn't disappeared.

The sun peeked through the windows, its beams sparkling off the colors strewn through her hair.

He tried not to think beyond the moment. He couldn't allow himself to start building a future in his mind. Those sorts of fantasies could break a man if they crumbled once the urgency of panic had passed.

But holding her, watching her sleep, this moment he could keep forever. Remember the look of her face without any anger or worry. Remember the weight of her hand as it lay over his heart. Remember the touch of her skin against his. Remember the warmth of her by his side.

A pang, like a little heartbreak, punctured his chest as she began to stir.

Adrial resisted the urge to tighten his arms around her as he waited for her to pull away.

She let out a sleepy sigh, her hand sliding from his chest to his scarred shoulder as she nestled closer to him before opening her eyes.

"You're still here." She tipped her chin up to look at him.

"I didn't want to leave you." He reached up, the crack in his heart deepening as he brushed a strand of purple hair away from her face.

She closed her eyes but didn't shy away from his touch. "It's daylight now. There's no way you'll make it out of here without someone seeing you."

"Does it matter?"

"If a horde of guards and soldiers find out you've spent the night up here? I should think so."

"But if we are—" Adrial pushed away the pain that threatened to break him in two. "If we are to be married, my being caught sneaking away would only benefit the narrative."

"What narrative?" Ena pushed herself up on her elbow. Her

hair draped over her shoulder, touching Adrial's arm as she looked down at him.

"The most beautiful woman in Ilara marrying the Guilded Cripple."

The haze of sleep left her eyes as she turned her gaze toward the door.

Adrial tensed, preparing for her to flee.

"The future Lord Scribe marrying a rotta who's pregnant with a dead demon's child. That's the story they'll be telling." She climbed over him and out of the narrow bed. "We can't do this. I was a desperate fool to even consider it."

Adrial closed his eyes, willing his heart to stay whole long enough for him to give her the help she needed.

"The common folk in Ilbrea need a decent man in the Guilds, and you're the only one I've seen." She grabbed a deep blue skirt from a hook on the wall. "I can't let you put yourself in danger to protect me."

"What danger?" Adrial sat up, ignoring the protests of his hip as he got to his feet.

"There are people in the Guilds who want to hurt you, even if you're too stuck in your work to notice." Ena yanked her skirt over her head.

"I don't see how marrying you would affect that." Adrial grabbed her bodice from the floor.

"Marrying a woman who's already well pregnant?" Ena snatched the bodice from his hand. "I've seen men killed for that."

"What?"

"Executed by soldiers for waiting too long to marry his love after slipping a child into her." Ena tugged her bodice on.

"Soldiers did that?"

"I've seen soldiers do much worse." Ena tightened the laces on her bodice, stopping with her hands near her stomach. "I've worked too hard to keep you alive. Your life is more important than mine. I can't let you throw it away."

"Marrying you wouldn't be throwing anything away." Adrial stepped out of her path as she strode across the room to her boots. "I would be gaining more than I ever dreamt I could have."

"And risking your life."

"No, I wouldn't." He dodged around her, blocking her path to the door. "The soldiers who murdered that man were beasts, and if you had their names, I would give the information to Rictor Nance and have them brought before his wrath."

"And what would the paun Nance do to his men for upholding the Guilds' chivving laws? Or is there no law punishing a man for marrying a woman who's already carrying his child?"

"There is a law, but it's not meant to be used."

"What does that even mean?"

"The law fell out of favor years before I became an apprentice to the Scribes Guild. The Guilds' purpose in creating Ian Ayres was to stop fatherless children from being born in Ilbrea. To make sure women and children weren't starving in the streets."

"So they send them to an island to be tortured instead?" Ena pulled on her boots. "Such chivving compassion from the paun."

"Ian Ayres is one of the gravest errors the Guilds have made in a long time. But they did at least realize that punishing the men who were willing to claim the children they'd helped in creating only sent more women to Ian Ayres, as most men were too cowardly to pay the penalty for what they'd done."

"Too cowardly to be murdered by soldiers, you mean."

"That law is no longer enforced in Ilara, especially not within the ranks of the Guilds." Adrial dared to step closer to her.

She stood and pulled her knife from the table beside the bed, tucking it into the ankle of her boot. "I can't risk them hurting you."

"There is no risk." Adrial took her hands, stopping her frenetic motion. "If the Guilds decided to enforce that law, a good third of the married soldiers would have to be punished. A fair batch of the rest of the Guilded men as well. At least a dozen scribes I know could be added to the list."

Ena looked toward the door.

"Please." He touched her chin, guiding her gaze back to his. "That the law was misused against any common folk is a travesty and a stain on the soul of Ilbrea. But they would never punish a member of the Guilds. It's terrible that the justice given to the Guilded is different than what the common folk endure, but it's true. I swear to you, Ena. There would be no risk to me."

She shifted her weight, as though longing to run. "You'd still be giving up too much. To spend your life bound to me. To raise another man's child." Tears glistened in the corners of her eyes. "It's too much to ask."

"I want this, Ena." He laid his hand on her cheek. She leaned into his touch. "To have you near me, to give a child my name. I would be the happiest man in all Ilbrea."

"It would be a debt that could never be repaid."

"There would be no debt. I would be the most grateful man alive."

"You're a fool." Ena laid her hand over his heart. "No man should toss away his freedom to right the damage done by a monster."

"I'm throwing nothing away." He kissed her forehead. "There's only one thing I ask."

She met his gaze. Her lips so close to his. A life beyond his wildest dreams only a breath away.

"Never tell anyone the baby isn't mine," he said. "I will raise the child. It will be born into our marriage. It will be our baby. I will be our child's father. Promise me."

"Swear to me this is what you want." A tear escaped from her eye.

"More than I've ever wanted anything."

She brushed her lips against his cheek. "Then this is our child. And not even the gods will know different."

She laid her head on his shoulder.

He wrapped his arms around her, holding her close.

She melted against him, nestling her forehead on the side of his neck, like the safety he offered was enough to protect her.

A spark lit in Adrial's gut, and a boiling joy filled his whole body.

Ena's shoulders shook.

Adrial pulled away from her, tipping her chin up to meet his gaze.

Tears spilled down her cheeks.

"Ena?"

Her face turned pink as she stepped out of his embrace, doubling over as she shook even harder.

"What's wrong? Are you ill?"

Ena coughed out a laugh as she stood up, wiping away her tears. "I can't decide who's going to be more furious. The Lord Scribe or Lady Karron."

Adrial's eyes widened as cold dread began at the tips of his toes.

"You say you're not going to be in any danger." Ena grabbed her comb, pausing for a moment to catch her breath before dragging it through her hair. "One of them may chivving well kill you."

"It'll be fine." Adrial waited for a knot of panic to form in his throat, but his blazing joy had already banished the chill of dread from his feet. "I don't care if they're angry. I'm going to marry you. I'll tell Lord Gareth this morning. Right now." He stepped toward the door.

"Wait." Ena caught his hand, turning him back toward her. She wrapped his arms around her, her body pressing against his as she leaned close to whisper in his ear. "You'll need clothes to go outside, and your robes are caked in mud, scribe."

He glanced toward the hook on the wall where his white

robes hung. A solid layer of deep-brown mud covered the bottom six inches.

"I'll make Taddy bring over a fresh set." Ena twisted out of Adrial's grip. "Wait here for an hour or two, then leave with well-pressed robes so no one will think you spent the night."

"Does it matter if they know?"

"Propriety, scribe." Ena winked then strode through the door into her shop. "We're not married yet."

He sank down onto Ena's bed.

His future wife's bed. The mother of his child. He let out a laugh as his joy grew so large he thought it would shatter his ribs.

It wasn't how he wanted it to happen. He should have wooed her, won her heart, then proposed.

But she never would have accepted. He was sure of that, just as much as he was sure that he loved her and would brave the wrath of Dudia himself to keep Ena by his side.

He was losing nothing in marrying her.

But Ena?

She was losing so much. She'd sacrificed everything when she'd given herself to Cade to save him.

He dug his knuckles into his eyes.

It wasn't fair to her. Ena deserved better than to end up bound to a cripple because she'd saved him.

She should have a husband who could defend her from every threat. She should have a choice in who and when she wanted to marry.

He circled through it over and over again in his head as he waited for Taddy, trying to find a different solution. A way to protect Ena and the baby from Ian Ayres without her having to marry him.

As the minutes ticked past, his joy changed, shifting from a blaze of exquisite happiness to the determined pride of a map maker embarking on a journey.

There was no other option, not one where she and the child

could both be protected from the cruel justice of the Guilds. Becoming a scribe's wife was not the life she would have chosen, but he would fight to make it the best he possibly could. For his wife. For his child.

A knock sounded on the door.

"Head Scribe, sir," Taddy called. "Ena's sent me with robes for you."

"Yes. Come in, Taddy."

"Right, sir." Taddy pushed open the door and stepped into the room with his eyes firmly shut.

"It's all right. I'm alone." Adrial stood, keeping his gait even as he walked over to take the robes from his apprentice.

"I thought you would be, sir." Taddy blushed as he opened his eyes. "As Ena is the one who sent me. Not that she'd be in here with you. Though this is her room. But even if she was in here, I wouldn't say anything to anyone anyway. Ena saved my life as well as yours. I'd never breathe a word that could wound her reputation."

"Your discretion is unnecessary but very much appreciated." Adrial pulled on his robes.

"Should I take the dirty ones to the laundry?" Taddy averted his gaze from the offending garment even as he pointed at the mud-covered robes.

"Yes, please." Adrial shoved his feet into his boots. "Are you behind on your work at the moment, Taddy?"

"No, sir." Taddy gave a pleased nod.

"Good. I need your help." Adrial stepped around Taddy and through the door into Ena's shop.

"Of course, sir." Taddy trod on Adrial's heels as he followed.

"I need you to run a message for me." Adrial found a pen and paper. He reached for a jar of black ink, but plain black didn't seem right. Not when there was so much joy to be found in the midst of the darkness. He plucked a sapphire-blue jar from the shelf. "Have two soldiers accompany you, and I'll need you to wait for her reply. If anyone tries to chivvy you out, tell them the head scribe asked you to stay until she responds. Unless it's the sorcerers, then leave without argument."

"Sorcerers?" Taddy squeaked.

"Yes." Adrial wrote a quick note.

It should be properly sealed.

She won't mind.

"Run this to the Royal Palace. Tell them you're to wait for a reply from Lady Karron."

Taddy's face paled.

"Don't be nervous about Lady Karron." Adrial folded the note. "Just try and avoid the sorcerers if you can."

"Yes, sir." Taddy bowed. "Of course, sir."

"I'll have a special meal sent to your room." Adrial screwed the top back onto the ink, checking his fingers for spots before straightening the front of his robes. "This day calls for celebration, and you shouldn't be left out."

"What are we celebrating?"

"In good time." Adrial headed for the door. "There's work to be done."

"You're not supposed to leave yet." Taddy chased after him. "Ena said to make sure you waited."

"You go to the soldiers at the gates and make a fuss asking for an escort to the palace. I'll walk calmly the other way." Adrial clapped him on the shoulder. "You're an excellent apprentice, Taddy. I'm grateful to have you." He held the door open for Taddy to go down the stairs.

"Yes, sir. Are you sure you're all right, sir?"

"I have never had a better day in all my life. Now get to the palace."

Adrial stayed well behind Taddy as they went down the stairs, then lingered in the stables for a moment, marveling at the beauty of the horses until he heard Taddy's voice outside.

"I have been ordered to take a message to Lady Karron."

Taddy spoke as though announcing a decree from the King. "I've been told to ask two soldiers to accompany me to the Royal Palace where I am to wait for Lady Karron to respond to the message."

Adrial slipped outside, walking calmly, not toward the door to the scribes' quarters, but toward the low door that cut under the library to the secondary entrance to the great room.

He glanced over his shoulder to check on Taddy, pausing to watch a raven soar over the courtyard.

Taddy stood at the center of the pack of soldiers, Adrial's blue-inked note held above his head as though the parchment granted him ultimate power.

Adrial tipped his face up to the sun and laughed. Lord Gareth would be happy for him, perhaps even thrilled.

And Allora, she wanted him to be happy, and he'd never felt such joy in his life.

ALLORA

"I know it's not news you expected from me now, or quite possibly ever." Adrial stood beside the window in Allora's sitting room, rubbing his thumb across the knuckle of his fourth finger in a panicked tick she hadn't seen from him in years.

"What news is it?" Allora waved the maid away from the tea tray and out of the room. "You've been jabbering for five minutes and haven't actually told me anything."

"I've already been to see Lord Gareth," Adrial said. "And he approves. Actually, he looked about ready to burst from joy and told me he was relieved. Glad to see I had taken the time to remember that I am a young man and life exists outside of papers and books. He did insist the whole thing take place at the library. And, of course, given the state of things, I can't say I disagree."

Allora chose a tart from the tray. The sweet juice of the berries paired wonderfully with the richness of the cream. They'd never had a special cook just to make sweets in the Map Master's Palace. There had never been a need for one. Of all the people who skittered through the halls serving the occupants of the Royal Palace, she was most grateful to whoever made the sweet delights for offering her a bit of distraction.

"I'm heading right up to Lord Karron when I leave here," Adrial said.

His mention of her father drew Allora back to his rambling monologue.

"It's not as though anything is required of him, but as he is the man who took me in, I want to tell him the news in person."

"My darling Adrial, I hold you close to my heart and know you to be one of the best men in all Ilbrea." Allora set the remains of the tart onto her plate and picked up the teapot. "But you sent your poor apprentice, who nearly fainted when I walked into the room, racing here with an urgent letter asking to meet me. Then, you came tearing to the palace, as though trying to panic yourself into an early grave, and you've yet to say a single thing that makes sense. Please sit, have a sip of tea, and calm your nerves. Then tell me whatever delightful news has whipped you into such a state."

"I'm getting married." Adrial beamed.

"What?" The teapot slipped in Allora's grip, spilling tea onto the floor.

"I'm getting married in two days' time. Lord Gareth has approved. The servants will be arranging everything in the scribes' gallery of the library."

"Married in two days in the library." Allora's hands trembled as she set the teapot back onto the tray.

"Yes. I know these are dangerous times, but please tell me you'll be there, or at least that you'll try." Adrial took her hand. "I want you to be at my wedding, Allora."

"And I want to be there. I want you to be happy. Though you've given me no choice but to ask, who is your bride?"

"Ena."

There wasn't a trace of doubt in Adrial's eyes. A hint of worry wrinkled his forehead, but not for the wedding. For his fear of disappointing Allora.

"Are you sure you want to marry her? The inker who climbs

through windows like a thief?" Allora took Adrial's other hand, turning him square to her. "You've said it before, she doesn't love you."

"There are different kinds of caring that make a life together worthwhile. I promise you, having Ena as my wife will bring me more joy than anything else in the world ever could."

"She doesn't belong in our world. You will be the Lord Scribe. Do you really believe her fit to be the Lady of a Guild?"

"I know her to be the strongest, most daring, most capable person I've ever met. There is not a thing in all the world she can't accomplish. I will be a better man with her by my side, and the Scribes Guild will be better for it." He squeezed her hands. "Please, Allora. Believe me. This is the most miraculous thing to have ever happened to me. Be happy for me. Come to my wedding."

"I would never miss your wedding." She kissed his cheek. "You're a part of our Karron clan. We always look out for each other, no matter what."

"Thank you, Allora." Adrial pulled her into a tight hug as he laughed with glee. "Now I have to make my poor escort take me up the cliffs to your father."

"He'll be thrilled you're happy." She wrapped a berry tart in one of the napkins and tucked it into his hand. "Give him my love."

"I will." The weight of Adrial's hidden limp seemed to disappear for a moment as he hurried to the door. "I'm getting married!"

A soldier shut the door behind him, leaving Allora alone.

She stared at the pile of tarts and the spilled tea on the floor.

She'd rarely seen Adrial bursting with such unbridled joy. Kai would have insisted they all have chamb to celebrate. Mara and Tham would have been thrilled he'd fallen in love. Niko...Niko would have taken the moment to needle Allora about how wonderful a thing marriage could be.

Allora sat in the chair closest to the window, closing her eyes and imagining all of them there with her. Niko sitting close, his scent surrounding her. The comfort of having them all together as they celebrated.

Allora reached out, allowing herself one thin moment to believe she'd find Niko beside her. Her fingers found nothing but empty air.

Niko would never sit beside her again. And when the others came home, there would be no joy. Only mourning and sorrow.

"I won't let her add to it." Allora stood and peered out the window, looking at the line of carriages that had delivered the people who had come to beg the King's favor. "She doesn't love him. He's a game to her. I will not let her ruin Adrial's life so she might have a fancy toy to play with and discard."

She kept her pace even as she went to her bedroom and dug into the drawer behind the ink stand. It would be a simple thing. A few moments of unpleasantness, and the inker would be gone forever. She pulled a leather bag from the drawer. The weight of it sank a stone in her stomach.

"You are protecting him." She slipped the bag into her pocket. "You are protecting your dear friend from a vicious beast."

Not everyone outside the Guilds is a beast, Mara's voice whispered in her mind.

"This girl is." Allora checked her hair in the bedroom mirror before cutting through her sitting room and out into the hall. The normal flock of ten soldiers stood at attention. "Where is Sorcerer Clery?"

"I'll fetch her, Lady Karron." One of the soldiers stepped forward.

"Don't bring her here, actually." Allora started down the hall. "Have her go to the King's private study behind the throne room. I'll meet her there."

"Yes, Lady Karron." The soldier disappeared from the pack

following behind her, slipping into some passage Allora was not meant to know about.

I will not be a captive in my home.

She breezed down the stairs to the sparkling entryway, smiling and offering regal nods to the few who waited below.

Sympathetic glances and bows were offered in exchange. She hadn't been hurt in the cathedral attack. The sorcerers had protected the royal family. Allora's gown hadn't even been marred by falling dust. Still, she was treated as though she'd been gravely injured by having to postpone her marriage to Brannon.

At the bottom of the stairs, she kept going straight, her gaze locked on the front doors of the palace.

"Lady Karron," one of the soldiers said.

"Yes." Allora fought the urge to quicken her pace.

"You requested Sorcerer Clery meet you behind the throne room," the soldier said. "Would you like us to escort you there?"

"I have lost neither my reason nor my sense of direction. I've simply changed my mind."

Two footmen stepped forward to open the doors.

"Shall we fetch Sorcerer Clery, Lady Karron?" the soldier asked.

"No need."

The breeze outside lifted her hair from the nape of her neck as the midday sun kissed her cheeks.

Six carriages waited in front of the palace. One in the color of the Sorcerers Guild, one healer, three merchant, one map maker.

Thank you, Aximander.

Allora strode straight to the map maker's carriage.

"Good afternoon," Allora called up to the driver.

"Lady Karron." The man began to scramble down.

"Please keep your seat," Allora said. "Is my father here?"

"No, Lady Karron. I brought Map Maker Traim."

"Well, I suppose I'll have to beg his forgiveness when we get back." Allora opened the carriage door. "I need to go on a quick errand. As the Lady of the Map Makers Guild, surely I still have the privilege of using the carriages."

"Of course, Lady Karron." The driver looked toward the palace as though he were not at all sure. "I'm happy to serve you."

"Perfect."

"Lady Karron." A soldier stepped beside her, taking her hand to help her climb into the carriage and blocking her path with the same movement. "If you wish to leave the grounds, you must speak to Sorcerer Clery."

"Am I a prisoner?" Allora asked.

"Of course not, Lady Karron."

"A child?"

"No, but—"

"Then get out of my way. Now."

Allora pushed past the soldier and into the carriage, slamming the door behind her.

"Where to, Lady Karron?" the driver called.

"The soldiers' barracks," Allora shouted back, loud enough for the panicked soldiers to hear.

She watched out the window as the carriage rumbled forward and the soldiers scrambled to find horses to chase after her. She regretted their panic, but a morning of stress for the soldiers was a trifle when weighed against a lifetime of pain for her friend.

No one stepped forward to stop her as the carriage neared the gates. Allora leaned back into the shadows, not willing to test whether they didn't stop her out of fear of her wrath or because they believed Map Maker Traim to be the carriage's passenger. A childish fear filled her as they passed through the gates and neared the bridge leading out of the palace grounds.

The sorcerers' power created the path, letting the stones hover over the wide moat far below in a way that went against all reason. Ciara would be angry Allora had fled from her guard, but would the sorcerer's ire be enough to break the spell that steadied the bridge? Would choosing to leave the palace grounds be a grave enough offense to doom Allora to drown in the water far below?

The tension in Allora's chest eased as the carriage reached the far side of the bridge and the sound of the wheels changed as they met the cobblestone street.

Allora let the cart rumble forward for a minute before knocking on the roof.

With a call from the driver, the carriage slowed.

Allora leaned out the window. "Actually, I've changed my mind. I need to go to the library."

"Yes, Lady Karron," the driver called down.

The carriage rumbled forward again.

With any luck, Ciara would be so twisted around, she wouldn't be able to find Allora until the necessary task was done.

And it was necessary. It was not cruel or hurtful, but the performance of her duty to her family.

Dudia, help me protect Adrial from the grips of such despair.

He'd be heartbroken. Devastated to have his imagined joy ripped away from him and embarrassed at having to tell Lord Gareth there would be no need for a celebration in the scribes' gallery. But a broken heart could heal much more quickly than a shattered reputation.

The carriage slowed as they reached the library's gates.

"I have Lady Karron," the driver called.

"You'll have to excuse us for checking," a man said.

"These are dark times," the driver said. "But the protection of the Guilds must come before all."

The carriage door opened, and a soldier looked inside. "Lady Karron, I apologize for the intrusion."

"No intrusion at all," Allora said. "I'm grateful for your diligence."

The soldier closed the door. "Let them through."

Allora gripped the bag in her pocket through the fabric of her dress. Five minutes, less probably, and the whole awful mess would be done.

The carriage rumbled through the gates and stopped again.

A different soldier opened the door and offered his hand with a bow. "Lady Karron."

"Thank you." Allora took his hand and stepped out of the carriage.

Six of the palace soldiers tore up to the gates, each glistening with sweat and wearing a look of something between anger and panic.

"I'm in need of your assistance." Allora kept her gaze fixed on the soldier who'd helped her step down from her carriage. "I'm here to see the inker. Do you know where her workshop is?"

"Above the stables, Lady Karron."

"Will you show me?"

"This way." The soldier gave her another bow before walking toward the long side of the stables.

Allora looked to the carriage driver. "If you could stay, I'll only be a minute, and I promise to beg Map Maker Traim's forgiveness." She gave the driver a nod before following the soldier toward the stables, ignoring the sounds of her guard assembling behind her.

The soldier stopped at a door in the side of the stables. "Would you like me to go up and fetch the inker for you? I don't know if her shop is really a fit place to greet a Lady."

"I'll be fine."

"It's just up the stairs." The soldier bowed her through the door.

"Thank you." Allora turned to her guard. "And I'm quite capable of going up the stairs on my own. I'll be right down, and then you can whisk me back to the palace before you all collapse from panic."

"Yes, Lady Karron." One of the soldiers from her guard spoke, looking as though he had other things he'd much rather have said.

Allora gave what she hoped could pass for a kind smile before squaring her shoulders and stepping into the stables.

The stench of the horses pummeled her nose and the sudden dimness stole a bit of her confidence. The soldiers were furious. Traim would not be forgiving for her having stolen his carriage. Dealing with Ciara would be no small feat.

As long as Adrial never knows.

She started up the stairs. The wooden steps had been worn down by years of use. The walls had been placed close together, looming in around Allora as though trying to prove someone like her did not belong here.

Neither does Adrial.

The smell of the horses faded as she climbed the steps. A scent almost like flowers mixed with spices filled the air instead.

Allora hated the aroma.

Is this how she tricked him? Luring him in with perfumes and outlandish colors? Dragging him away from the world he fought so hard to join?

She tucked the questions aside with the rest of the accusations she longed to scream at the common inker. But with her flock of soldiers lurking at the bottom of the stairs, she couldn't risk raising her voice. A future queen could not shout. And, even if she longed to throw propriety to the wind, the fewer people who knew of Adrial's mistake, the better.

The door at the top of the steps was made of plain wood with an iron latch, giving no sign she'd found the right place.

Then leave well enough alone. Let Adrial lead his own life, Mara's voice whispered in her mind.

"He is going to be the Lord Scribe," Allora whispered back. "I love him too much to allow his name to be tarnished."

She knocked on the door before her nerves could waver again.

"Come in," the inker called.

Allora smoothed the front of her dress before opening the door.

The scent of flowers thickened as she stepped into the workroom, their perfume surrounding her as though she'd entered a place touched by magic.

If she hadn't come on such horrible business, the shop might have been beautiful. Flowers hung from the eaves. Jars of every color sparkled in the sunlight pouring through the windows. Even the table had been turned into a colorful work of art. Splashes and pools of vibrant ink had stained the wood, though she doubted the inker had been purposeful in creating its beauty.

"Huh." Ena stopped her work just long enough to glance at Allora before going back to chopping deep-green leaves. "Should I greet you as Your Majesty? Or is there a different title for someone who hasn't quite managed to marry the King yet?"

"You may address me as Lady Karron." Allora closed the door behind her, pressing against the latch to make sure the wood stayed firmly shut against prying ears.

"Fine then, Lady Karron, what can I help you with today?" Ena gathered the chopped leaves in her hand. "More ink for the Princess's love letters? She must be a prolific writer if she's gone through the batch I already made her."

"I'm not here about ink." Allora stepped farther into the room.

"Then I'm afraid you've made a wrong turn somewhere. All I deal in is ink. Horses are in the stables. Books are in the library." Ena sprinkled the leaves into a metal pot. "Feel free to see yourself out."

"Are you always such a rude creature?" Allora clasped her hands in front of her, keeping her chin high and her face placid.

"If I say yes, will you leave faster?"

"I'm not leaving."

"Pity." Ena ran her fingers through her hair, exposing the pinks and purples that hid beneath the more visible layer of blue.

"I'd say I'd leave instead, but this is my shop, and I have work for the head scribe that needs doing."

"Adrial came to see me this morning."

Ena froze for a moment so quick, Allora wasn't sure she'd actually seen it. "What a lovely treat that must have been for you."

"I will not let you ruin him."

"Ruin him?" Ena took a little glass bottle from a shelf and held it to the light coming in through the window. "Is that what he told you I was doing?"

"That is what marrying you would do. Adrial Ayres is going to be the Lord Scribe."

"I had heard that."

"He cannot marry a commoner."

"That part I didn't know." Ena poured golden liquid from the glass bottle into the pot. "You'd think if there were a law banning him from marrying a lowly rotta like me, he would know about it as he is a scribe." She set the bottle down and looked at Allora. "Or is it not a law yet? Will you have your King write a new law banning Guilded from marrying common folk just to keep your pet scribe away from me?"

"I will do whatever it takes to protect Adrial. He has overcome too much to have you destroy his future."

"How would him having a wife be destroying anything?"

"You are not fit to be the Lady of a Guild."

"Now we're getting closer to it." Ena added deep blue powder to the pot. "You don't mind him being distracted by marriage. You might even accept a well-behaved merchant's daughter. But an untamed, filthy creature like me...how could you bear to see me standing beside your dearest pet scribe?"

"Adrial deserves more." Allora fought to keep her voice level.

"Let him decide what he wants for his future. Or do you not think him smart enough to make up his own mind?"

"He is wonderful man with a kind heart." Allora stepped

closer to the table, resisting the urge to yank the pot out of Ena's reach.

"I chivving well know that."

Shock fumbled Allora's heartbeat as though she'd just been slapped. "I'm sure he cares for you, and I am hoping you have an ounce of care for him. I am asking you to protect him." Allora reached into her pocket and pulled out the bag of gold. The weight of the coins seemed heavier than it had back in her room at the palace. "Leave Ilara. This is enough gold to open a shop wherever you like. I can have a horse meet you at the southern gate. Go. Ride away. Make a life far from here and leave Adrial alone."

Ena stared at the bag in Allora's hand. "Get out of my shop."

"I will book you passage on a boat. All the way to the kingless territories if you want to go that far."

"No."

"Then tell me what your price is. Tell me where you want to go." Tears burned in Allora's eyes. "I will send you wherever you like, but I will not let you destroy him."

"I can't leave him." Ena rammed the cork back into the little bottle.

"There are other men who would be happy to have you and other places you can live."

"No."

"I am offering you a chance to—"

"You help no one by being here." Ena slammed the bottle onto the table with enough force the glass should have shattered. "If you care for him, go back to your palace and let us be."

"You are leaving Ilara. Choose where you would like to go, or I will choose a place for you."

"The only other place for me is Ian Ayres." The inker held Allora's gaze. "If you send me to that demon's island, which one of us will be destroying him?"

The bag fell from Allora's hand as the room swayed. The clatter of the coins seemed to come from far away.

"You're lying." The two words stole all the breath from Allora's lungs.

"You have no idea how badly I wish I were."

Allora forced herself to study the inker's face. There was no mocking in her. A little anger. So much fear.

"Does he—" Allora pressed her fingers to her lips, taking a breath before daring to try and speak again. "Have you told him?"

"Of course I chivving well have. And last I saw him, he looked as though he would burst from delight. But I suppose that doesn't matter to you." Ena ripped a cluster of blue flowers from the wall. "Are you going to tell your pack of paun soldiers? They must be waiting downstairs. I'm sure they can make time to drag me to the docks on your way back to the palace. Won't cost you a single coin to be rid of me forever. How lucky for you."

"No. No one else can know." Allora's hands trembled as she smoothed the front of her dress. The familiar motion didn't stop the floor from shifting beneath her. She gripped the edge of the worktable, anchoring herself to something more solid than her panic. "Adrial's child cannot be born on the bastards' island. He'd never survive it. Not after everything he suffered before he escaped that hell. We have to protect the baby."

"If you want to protect this child, then leave us alone." Ena tore the petals from the flowers. "Let us get married in peace."

"Adrial's a good man, but he's a fool. Marrying you won't be enough to protect his standing within the Guilds. There are too many eyes on him, and rumors this high in the ranks of Ilbrean society do not fade with the seasons. Whispers would follow him for the rest of his life." Allora looked toward the door, wishing the soldiers were miles away instead of lurking at the bottom of the stairs.

"He said marrying me wouldn't put him in any danger." Ena

finally stopped working. She pressed her hands to the top of the table as though perhaps she too could feel the tipping and swaying of the room. "He said he'd be safe."

"Adrial may be brilliant, but there are some things he doesn't understand. The timing has to be considered if we want to avoid suspicion. He said he wanted to marry you in two days, that's too soon. You'll have to wait."

"We don't exactly have time to spare."

"We'll make the time." Allora stepped closer to Ena, keeping one hand firmly on the table for support. "Two days to plan a wedding is chaos. Everyone will know why the head scribe suddenly married a common inker. That's how scandals begin and rumors spread. But two weeks to plan a wedding? That's true love. A man and woman who have decided they don't want to wait to spend their lives together. That's a shining symbol of hope after so much darkness. A blushing bride and an enamored groom and everyone else in the room utterly jealous of their love story."

"The longer we wait, the harder the baby will be to hide. I'll start showing eventually, and everyone with a working mind will know—"

"By the time anyone can do more than wonder if you're about to burst or have just indulged in too much cake, you won't be in Ilara anymore."

"Where will I be?"

Allora waved Ena's question away. "The city is such a chaotic place at the best of times, and far too much for a woman carrying a child to endure. My father has a house a day's journey to the south. You'll retreat to the country for some much needed rest. There will be guards and workers, of course, but all we'll need to do is make sure one of the women tending to you has a baby of her own. Men can't tell the difference between one child's cry and another's.

"We'll find trustworthy women to care for you and the baby when it's your time to deliver. You'll stay in the countryside for a few months, until it becomes hard to tell exactly how old the baby is. Then you'll return to Ilara with no one the wiser as to when exactly the child was born."

"Is this a plan you worked out for your own use, Lady Karron?"

"No, it was for the woman I love best in the world. But we will use it for you. I will not allow them to take you to Ian Ayres." Allora let out a shaky breath. "I will not allow anyone to take Adrial's child from us."

"Thank you."

"I'm not doing any of this for you." Allora met Ena's gaze.

"And I wouldn't accept your help if it were only my neck in the noose. That doesn't make me any less grateful."

"Expect my seamstresses to come this afternoon." Allora let go of the table, testing her balance before picking up her bag of coins and tucking it back into her pocket. "You are the future Lady of the Scribes Guild. You will not be married in a common gown."

"Yes, Lady Karron." Ena gave her a nod.

"Call me Allora. We are to be family now." Allora whisked her way out the door and onto the stairs without waiting for Ena's reply. She made sure the door was closed behind her before burying her face in her hands. "Stupid Adrial. Stupid, stupid Adrial."

She wiped the tears from the corners of her eyes.

Adrial, married to the inker. Adrial, a father.

It was such an easy scene for her to picture. Adrial holding his child. Joy radiating from him as he cooed to his son. Adrial bursting with pride as his heir took his first steps and learned to ride.

Allora closed her eyes and allowed a bit of joy to grow through the panic still pounding in her chest.

At least if Ena broke his heart, Adrial would have his child to comfort him. The child would be worth whatever pain the madwoman brought along with her.

ALLORA

"It's more than just the one dress we'll need made." Allora prowled through the row of fabric the seamstresses had laid out for her. "The wedding gown will need to be done first, of course, but she'll be the wife of the head scribe and will someday become the Lady of the Scribes Guild. There will be parties and dinners and guests begging for her time."

"Will she be needing dresses for daily wear?" the eldest of the seamstresses asked, her pen hovering over her paper as she took notes on the little lap desk she had so wisely brought when Allora had warned the women they'd be charged with creating a new wardrobe for Adrial's bride.

"I wish I could say yes." Allora frowned. "But Miss Bairn is an extremely talented inker, and I doubt she'll be giving up her work. Would it make sense to have day dresses made for her if she'll only end up with ink stains on them?"

"We could make a few," one of the younger women said. "For days when she isn't working."

"I suppose." Allora made another pass through the fabrics. "But you may have to stray away from the traditional scribe white. I'm afraid if we don't offer her color, she'll toss ink on her skirts just to make things lively."

The seamstresses stared at her in horror.

"I know." Allora sighed. "My sweet Adrial is marrying a unique creature."

Allora bent down to feel the texture of the materials as the women went back to their work, folding up the fabric Allora had rejected and laying out more options.

Really, it seemed like a waste. Soon enough, Ena wouldn't be able to fit into any of the new clothes. But having a finely made wardrobe that suddenly couldn't be used would add another element of truth to the lie that would protect Adrial's reputation. Ena didn't seem like the sort to spend Adrial's coin on new clothes for married life, so Allora would just have to do it for her.

Preventing the wedding had ceased to be an option. Protecting Adrial's future had become more important than ever.

Allora caught herself smiling before she noticed the hint of joy warming her heart.

The first child of their little clan. A baby to coo at and spoil. After all the pain of his childhood, Adrial would build a family of his own.

"Save some of the larger scraps from Miss Bairn's gowns," Allora said. "The head scribe desperately wants children. With any luck, I'll be pestering you all for clothes for a child before next summer's end."

"And aren't children the greatest gift Dudia can offer?"

Allora spun toward the voice.

A portion of the wall beside the fireplace tipped sideways, allowing Ciara to slip into Allora's sitting room.

Allora dug her nails into her palms, needing the pain to assure herself she hadn't tumbled into a horrible dream where hidden doors appeared in her walls.

"Sorcerer." The seamstresses tucked their chins as they murmured the word as though they were warding off evil.

"It is traditional to knock before entering a Lady's private chambers." Allora tipped her chin up, refusing to cower under Ciara's burning glare.

"How foolish of me." Ciara closed the door in the wall, hiding any hint the passage behind existed. "I assumed, after you decided to abandon the safety so many have risked their lives to provide, you'd chosen to dispense with all the niceties of civilized society."

"I didn't abandon anything," Allora said. "I had a very important matter to tend to, so I went. It was my understanding that I'm not a prisoner in this palace, but the future Queen."

"Leave us." Ciara shifted her glare to the seamstresses.

"You do not command the women in my chambers," Allora said.

"Leave. Now." The door to the hall burst open, though the sorcerer hadn't so much as twitched a finger.

The women abandoned their fabric and fled for the safety of the hall.

The door slammed shut behind them.

"I will not tolerate—" Allora began.

"We seem to be suffering from a considerable number of misunderstandings." Ciara flicked her finger and the lock on the door twisted. "I apologize if any of that was born from my lack of clarity. I made the mistake of choosing a soft hand over well-laid expectations. It would be unfair to leave you stumbling through the darkness any longer, so please, allow me to make things absolutely clear."

"The only clarity I desire from you is the knowledge of how to block off whatever passage allowed you to enter my room."

"Sit."

A chair slid forward, knocking Allora behind her knees. She gasped as she fell back into the seat.

"How dare you!" Allora tried to stand, but a weight pressed down on her, pinning her in place.

"My use of that passage should be the least of your worries. Make the wrong enemies, and there are other, far more frightening things that may come crawling out of your walls, Lady Karron." Ciara waved a hand and all the fabric flew away to pile itself in the fireplace. "You agreed to marry the King. The King is the figurehead Ilbrea needs to maintain its power."

"The King is the ruler of this country."

"Believe what you like." Ciara sat on the couch as though she'd come for an innocent chat. "As Lady Gwell's second, it is my duty to see to the safety and productivity of this monarchy for the good of all Ilbrea. I will not have a rogue queen ruining my work."

"You've already made it abundantly clear that you plan to use me as a breeding mare. I understand the duties required of me as the King's wife. Now get out of my room."

"If you've accepted the King will come to your bed, then we are making strides in the right direction."

The weight on Allora doubled.

"But your duty goes beyond spending the rest of your life allowing the King to writhe on top of you as he pleasures himself." Ciara gave a taunting smirk.

Bile rose in Allora's throat.

"You will be a dutiful and supportive wife who stands as a shining example of what all Ilbrean women should be. You will bear the King's children as a vessel of the crown and a servant to the Sorcerers Guild."

"I am not your servant."

"You are. And the sooner you accept that, the less painful your life will be."

A crackling came from the fireplace. Smoke drifted up from the folds of the cast-aside fabric.

"You will not run away from the palace. You will not attempt to keep secrets from me. You will not give in to the temptation to whisper how the sorcerers are taking more power than they're due. You will follow our orders and keep in line. If you choose to be spiteful, history will be forced to repeat itself, and think of the grief that would cause the poor King."

Allora looked to the door. "There are soldiers in the hall who are charged with protecting me and you are bold enough to make threats?"

"Soldiers are only useful when guarding against steel and fists. If you defy the will of the sorcerers, your reckoning will not be so simple." Ciara stood, placing her hands on the arms of Allora's chair, looming over her as though ready to attack with teeth and claws. "Disobey me again, and you will never take a sip of tea without chance of there being poison in your cup. Your bath could be tainted. Your sheets, your clothes, your shoes. You will not be able to breathe without risking my wrath trickling into your lungs."

Cold trailed down Allora's throat.

"If that's the way you want to kill me, then you might as well start now. I will be the Queen of Ilbrea, not the servant of the sorcerers."

"Such brave words from a pretty young girl." Ciara tapped Allora on the nose.

Allora flinched, trying to convince herself the tingle on her skin was no more than her mind playing tricks.

"But I won't start with you," Ciara whispered. "Driving the King toward the right candidate for a bride is time-consuming. I'd hate to have to start from the beginning again. And I can't risk your health if a child is growing in your womb. No, I'd have to begin somewhere else. A bit of poison hidden in a map maker's boot. No one would even question why the Lord Map Maker's heart suddenly stopped. And the head scribe does enjoy tea, doesn't he?"

"I won't let you hurt them." Allora pushed against the weight that held her.

"Well, you know how to stop it." Ciara grinned. "Be a good

girl, and we'll never have to speak of this again. But know you are watched. Every minute, everywhere, there are eyes upon you, and they will tell me if you choose the more painful path."

"Why? Why would you do this? If you didn't want me as I am, why would you push Brannon to choose me as his wife?"

"Be careful, Lady Karron. Curiosity may suit a map maker, but it kills a queen." Ciara backed away from Allora's chair as the flames on the fabric in the fireplace flickered and grew to be three feet tall.

The panel in the wall popped back open, and Ciara stepped into the passage beyond, magically shutting the door behind her.

It took a moment for Allora to realize the horrible weight pinning her down had disappeared, replaced by the feeling of being watched from every angle as though she were on display.

A sob shook Allora's chest.

Adrial, his baby, her father.

All at risk because she'd fled from her grief.

Mara, Tham, and Kai. When they came home, they would be in danger, too. The sorcerers had always been the enemies of their little clan that fought so hard to carefully hide the true maps of the magic they'd found in Ilbrea.

Allora had always known she was risking death at the sorcerers' hands for her part in protecting the truth. She never imagined she'd be the one creating the danger for those she loved.

Tears spilled down her cheeks.

All of them. I could lose all of them.

Her sobs tore through her chest as the weight of her guilt threatened to drown her.

MARA

The swish of her gown seemed to taunt her as Mara walked down the grand staircase of the ice palace on Tham's arm.

If the hours the women had spent primping her had been annoying, then being forced into a blue and silver gown was flat-out insulting. And the way the elite of Isfol stared at her as she descended into their midst made her want to scream.

"I hate being her doll," Mara whispered.

"You're a beautiful doll," Tham said. "I'm glad you're walking on my arm all powdered with your curls pinned back."

"Tham." Mara's steps faltered and her heart tensed.

"If hundreds of enemies were gaping at my Mara, I don't know if I'd be able to control my anger. But the woman the Princess is parading around"—Tham glanced down to Mara's chest, which had been left more exposed by the cut of her gown than she would have ever willingly allowed—"this painted doll is only a mask for the woman I love. It doesn't matter who stares at you, they're not seeing anything close to the person you actually are."

They reached the bottom of the steps, and the horde drew toward them.

Thank you. Mara mouthed the words.

The tiny smile that barely curved Tham's lips bolstered Mara enough she managed to nod to the finely dressed strangers as she cut through the crowd toward the ballroom.

An unfamiliar sort of music carried over the conversations of the crowd. The tune seemed wrong to Mara's ears, the chords not fitting with what a lifetime in Ilbrea had taught her to expect.

The rest of the revelers seemed to be enjoying the music as they gratefully accepted the wine being carried by a fleet of palace servants in blue-trimmed, white uniforms.

Though Mara and Tham had only found out about the ball when the flock of women bearing finery unexpectedly entered their room, the amount of wine being poured and the presence of musicians seemed to imply that at least the palace staff had been given more than a few hours' notice before hundreds of guests had arrived.

"It seems like a celebration." Mara slowed her steps as she passed a gaggle of older women, trying to catch the thread of their gossip.

"—I'll have to pay her extra for screeching at her, or she may never work for me again," a woman in a pale pink dress said.

"I nearly claimed illness," a woman in a pale green dress said.

"The stress of it all nearly made me ill," a woman in a pale purple dress added. "It would have been far kinder—"

Mara drifted too far away to hear what mercy the woman wished she'd been granted.

At least we're not the only ones who weren't warned of the ball.

Not that Mara was fool enough to expect to be treated with whatever courtesy the gossiping women thought they deserved, but forcing prisoners to attend a ball seemed odd, even by Ronya's standards.

The musicians had moved on to a different tune by the time Mara and Tham had reached the doors of the ballroom.

Dancers filled the center of the space, weaving in and out of formation beneath chandeliers dripping with silver flowers. Clusters of people had formed around the edges of the ballroom, basking in the glow of the dozens of candle-filled sconces.

The air of excitement brought a different pitch to the chatter than the low gossip in the corridor.

Mara scanned the room, searching for whatever it was that might have given the people in the ballroom a reason to feel differently than those just outside the doors.

There were no posted notices Mara could see, nothing to provide new information. The wine on the trays appeared to be the same.

The Regent sat on a dais at the far end of the room with two empty seats beside him, but he hardly seemed interested in the dancers or in interacting with any of the revelers.

Something in the Regent's furrowed brow drew Mara toward him. The cheerful man who'd greeted Mara and Tham as his daughter's new friends now seemed weathered and worried.

"—such an exciting time."

"If there really were a reason to rejoice—"

"I only hope there will be something to eat."

Mara caught the bits of conversation as she weaved through the clusters of revelers surrounding the dancers.

Tham leaned down to whisper in Mara's ear. "Where is the Princess?"

"Wherever she is, I doubt we'll like her reason for being late to the party she demanded we attend."

Guards in white uniforms stood at the front corners of the Regent's dais, with more positioned just behind, blocking anyone from crossing at the back of the platform.

Mara slowed her pace as she approached the dais, giving ample time for the guards around the Regent or the guards trailing behind her to deter her.

The Regent's guards eyed Mara but said nothing as she stopped just in front of the throne.

"Regent." Mara gave a low curtsy as Tham bowed. "It's been so long since we've seen you."

"Mara, Tham." The Regent gave each of them a nod. "It seems you've not been idle as the time has passed. I hope you've found your new home to your liking."

Mara willed her shoulders to stay relaxed. "Isfol is a beautiful city. I've enjoyed learning more about it."

"Our history here is long." The Regent looked down at his right hand. He wore a silver ring set with a blue stone. "Most of the Ice Walkers' story seems more myth than truth when told without the burden of undeniable knowledge."

"I…" Mara paused for a moment, trying to reason through the Regent's words. "I would love to know as much as I am able about the Ice Walkers. I must admit to spending more time learning about the city than its people."

"Come with me." The Regent stood, waving away his guards as he stepped off the dais.

The chatter of the revelers changed as the Regent took Mara's arm from Tham, leading her toward the side of the room.

Mara glanced back.

Tham followed a few steps behind her, their guards trailing in his wake.

Though the music still played, the dancers had fallen out of their pattern, choosing whispering to their fellows over keeping up with the tune.

"I spent my life as a scholar before I married the Queen." The Regent cut toward the back corner of the room.

"I didn't know that," Mara said.

"I doubt there was a reason for anyone to tell you. I'm sure you never asked about me."

"My apologies." Mara dipped her chin. "I should have taken the time to learn more about my hosts."

"Why learn about your hosts when you're too busy studying

the city, searching for a chance to escape?" The Regent tightened his grip on Mara's hand.

"Sir, I don't—"

"I am not the doddering old fool my daughter would have people believe. There is a reason the throne has not been given to the Princess." The Regent kept his tone polite even as his hold on Mara's hand grew painful. "There are powers at work in this palace you cannot see. You would do best to abandon any attempt to escape Isfol."

"Isfol is not my home," Mara said. "Ilbrea is my home, and as grateful as I am—"

"Don't lie to me, girl." The Regent stopped in the far corner of the room. He pointed to an image high up on the wall. A woman kneeling as she sacrificed a child to the ice. "Ronya is more dangerous than you have even begun to imagine. Not just to the people in this palace. To anyone who stands against her. She is desperate for power, and Isfol is not enough to sustain her. Ronya's ambition is a poison."

"Which has nothing to do with me. I am her prisoner, nothing more than a plaything she can drag out and torment when she sees fit. She is bored, and I am her entertainment."

"You are an Ilbrean who has granted Ronya more power than you've realized. You were a fool to give her a scrap of information."

"About me." Mara tried to shift away from the Regent. He clamped his arm on top of hers, pinning her to his side with a strength that seemed unreasonable for an old man. "I haven't told her anything that could damage anyone but me."

"If you truly believe that, you are well beyond my aid." The Regent pointed to the next image down. A woman rode on the back of a wolf, charging down the slope of a mountain. "The ice will not stay in the north forever. If we are not careful, my daughter's greed will destroy us all."

"Why? What's she planning?"

The music changed, swelling before fading away.

"Your freedom is but a small piece in this bloody game." The Regent spoke so quickly, Mara could barely catch his words. "If you care anything for the country you left behind, you will do your duty for the survival of your people and mine."

"What duty?"

The Regent let go of Mara's arm and turned toward the dais, a welcoming smile lighting his face.

"Thank you all for gathering for this celebration tonight." Ronya stood on the dais in a white-and-silver gown. "While I know all your seamstresses and maids have been panicking, I assure you, their efforts were well worthwhile."

A round of polite laughter rolled through the crowd.

"This is, indeed, a momentous evening. It is not often the Ice Walkers find new brethren," Ronya said, "and tonight, I am pleased to welcome the newest member of Isfolian society."

She gave a nod, and a man stepped up onto the platform beside her.

His hair had been carefully cut and his face cleanly shaved. He wore sparkling white and silver to match Ronya's own gown. But the changes in his appearance didn't hide the man Mara had known.

"Kegan." Mara started toward the platform.

One of her guards grabbed her arm, holding her back.

Tham stepped in front of Mara, as though waiting for Kegan to turn against her and attack.

"Kegan Whelan has renounced all ties to Ilbrea. He has joined the Ice Walkers, and we welcome him gladly." Ronya looked to Mara. "He has already proven his worth to our people, and with his aid, we shall greet a new era of greatness for Isfol." She raised her glass. "To the promise of our future."

KAI

"We'll begin organizing your party to head north tomorrow." Beckham furrowed his brow and tented his fingers beneath his chin. "While getting to know you has been a pleasure, lingering here in the bastion would not be wise."

"Of course." Kai kept a smile on his face even as the woman fitting his new pants tucked a pin too far north for his pleasure. "The sooner we can reach Ilara, the better."

"Yes, yes." Beckham nodded and began to pace the bit of space left empty by the four seamstresses that had invaded the bedroom Kai and Drew had been sharing since arriving in the Brien's settlement. "Our people will be able to travel with you as far as the southern gate of the city. Once you reach that point—"

"We'll have to part ways." Drew stood with his arms to his sides and a grimace on his face, as though he hadn't noticed the two women fussing around him were making him finer clothes than he'd ever owned. "Traveling undiscovered to the Map Master's Palace won't be easy, and you can't risk your people."

"It's not a matter of risk." Beckham waved a dismissive hand at Drew. "It's a matter of maximum potential impact from all those who stand against the Sorcerers Guild. While our home here is impressive, we have no resources to waste."

"We understand." Kai shot Drew a warning smile. "And in exchange for your hospitality, we'll spread the word of the sorcerers' evil, preparing the people of Ilara for a time when the sorcerers of the bastion are ready to rise up and stand against the Lady Sorcerer."

"I know we're asking too much of you." Beckham continued to pace, as though the movement might aid in his performance of worry. "A bit of shelter and allowing you to travel with our people hardly seems payment enough for asking you to speak against the most powerful force in Ilbrea."

"Oh, really?" Drew pulled his arms away from the women.

"It seems as though you're asking too little," Kai said quickly. "It's our duty to speak against the Sorcerers Guild. The shelter you've given us, your magical mending of Drew's wounds—"

Drew coughed a laugh.

"Even if the Lady Sorcerer herself should torment us, we'd still owe you a debt," Kai pressed on. "And that's something neither of us will forget."

"The mountains blessed us when they delivered such allies to the bastion." Beckham bowed. "Come, ladies. Finish the sewing elsewhere. Our Ilbrean friends need rest. The plotting of a perilous journey begins in the morning."

"Yes, sir," the women murmured as one.

Beckham bowed his way out the door while the women stripped Kai and Drew of the half-finished clothes.

"Thank you. You've been far too kind." Kai held the door open for the women, offering each of them a bow and a chance to blush as they hurried away.

"You're a cad." Drew threw Kai a pair of pants as soon as he'd closed the door.

"You no longer have a limp." Kai yanked on his pants.

"Don't goad me."

"Are we not stating obvious things?" Kai asked. "Sorry, I thought we were."

"Obvious things." Drew buckled his belt. "Obvious things like them perfectly healing my wounds. Them feeding us and giving us better chivving ale than I've ever tasted."

"I really should have you up to one of Allora's parties."

"We've found ourselves in a magically hidden village filled with sorcerers the Guilds haven't claimed." Drew chucked a shirt at Kai's face.

"I'm glad you've come to accept that fact." Kai pulled on the shirt.

"And now they've decided they're just going to let us leave?" Drew whispered. "Complete with an escort of sorcerers and newly stitched chivving clothes?"

"Apparently." Kai shoved his feet into his boots.

"Are you that foolish, Kai Saso?" Drew grabbed Kai's arm, spinning him around.

Kai straitened up, meeting Drew's glower, their faces inches apart.

"Are you asking if I'm foolish enough to believe the people who've welcomed, fed, pampered, healed, sheltered, and clothed us aren't plotting something besides escorting us home and letting us go on our merry way?"

"Yes."

"I'm shocked you'd doubt me so." Kai patted Drew's cheek. "I haven't trusted a thing that's happened since Isla invited two strange men to follow her into the mountains. Now, let go of my arm. If I'm to spy on Beckham and hope he shows his hand, I don't have much time. For a fellow who likes to pretend he's in charge, he walks rather quickly."

Drew let go of Kai's arm and slid open the one window their bedroom offered. "One of these days, you'll get us both killed."

"Probably." Kai had one foot on the windowsill before he froze. "I'll do what I can to make sure that day is a long time from now. And if I can save you from sharing my fate, I will." He stepped back into the room and looked to Drew. "We can part ways as soon as we reach Ilara. I hear Wyrain has a fine fleet of ships."

Drew shook his head, looking through the window behind Kai's shoulder. "I've yet to find a force strong enough to make me abandon you." He pulled a worn silver token from under his pillow and tossed it to Kai. "You dragged me here to have me healed. I'd have died in the forest if you'd let me. Be careful. I don't want that chivving thing tossed back to me too soon."

Kai kissed the token and tucked it into his pocket. "We should find a better mark. Gold? Jewels? Saving each other's lives should be celebrated by more than passing a bit of silver back and forth."

"Go, you slitch." Drew sank onto his bed, digging his knuckles into his eyes.

Kai watched him for one more moment before pulling himself through the window and up onto the roof.

The warm night air surrounded him, offering a hint of a reward for traveling on a roof made of such brittle material. He closed his eyes, listening to the sounds of the bastion.

Children's voices came from the north, where a building almost as long as the village housed the sorcerer children who'd been newly rescued from Ilbrea.

The leaves stirred in the breeze, whispering as though telling secrets even Beckham didn't know.

Someone to the south chopped food with a heavy knife. To the west, the sound of a poorly concealed argument broke through the evening's quiet.

A rumble of conversation carried under it all, traveling to the east.

Kai grinned as he followed the voices, risking a run as he kept to the very peak of the thatched roof where the center beam could hold his weight.

Shadows shifted on the road in the distance as he reached the edge of the healer's home where he and Drew had been kept. The next roof over was only four feet away and had been built to the exact same height.

Kai made the leap without pause, following the shadows.

He ran along the peak of the next roof, trying not to think of the fright he might be giving to the people below his feet as he caught sight of Beckham's thistle-brown hair glistening in the moonlight.

Someone walked beside Beckham. A shorter person. A woman from the shape of the body, though the person did wear pants, unlike most of the women in the bastion.

Kai gritted his teeth as he leapt across another gap between houses.

Beckham nodded to something the person beside him said. Not with enthusiasm, more with resignation, as though accepting an unpleasant task.

They cut south, leaving Kai to tiptoe down the slope of one roof before leaping to the next.

The thatching crackled beneath his weight as he landed. He held his arms wide, pinwheeling them as he tried to find his balance.

A sharp shout sounded from inside the house. Kai sprinted up to the peak of the roof and down the other side, barely catching Beckham's shadow as he passed through a gate and into a garden behind a house a full story taller than the surrounding buildings.

"I don't mind a challenge." Kai leapt to the next house over, steadying himself before jumping across the road and onto the garden wall.

His heart shot into his throat as his boots skidded on top of the wall. He threw himself sideways, twisting as he fell. His ribs smacked against the stone, sending a jolt of pain into his spine as he gripped the wall.

He held on for two breaths, splayed on top of the wall like a helpless slitch, before pushing himself to his feet. The shock of the near-fall zinged through his muscles, but his limbs obeyed as he walked across the top of the stones to the building beside the garden.

After a little jump to catch hold of the beam at the bottom of the roof, he only had to pull himself up and swing his legs onto the thatching.

He lay on the roof, reaching higher, feeling between the rough layers of leaves for the nearest batten bracing the thatch.

"Are you the only one who's allowed to speak?"

Kai froze as someone shouted.

A low, steady voice, as though the speaker were trying to calm the shouter, came next.

Kai eased himself higher, centering his weight above the batten.

"You ask too much," the same voice shouted.

"You don't understand," a woman responded. "We cannot give in to selfish desires."

Kai inched forward, making his way toward the closest window.

"I'm going to Ilara," a girl said. Her voice lacked the formal tone of the others in the room. "I don't chivving well care what any of you have to say about it."

Isla. Kai smiled. *Welcome to our journey.*

"Going into Ilbrea is risky for anyone with magic in their blood," a woman said, "and far too dangerous for us to even consider sending you, in particular."

"No one is sending me anywhere," Isla said. "I am choosing to go."

"That isn't a decision you can make on your own," a man said. Beckham by the sound of it. "You have joined the Brien. You have obligations—"

"Are you going to kill me for leaving?" There was a twisted sort of laughter in Isla's voice. "Going to lock me up? Didn't end very well for the last people who tried that."

"Isla, I know you want to help. But sometimes, the best way to do that is by staying away from the fight." A new voice spoke, this one lower and calmer than the others had been.

"I am more than capable of taking care of myself," Isla said.

"You're valuable." The low voice spoke again. "Losing you to the Guilds—"

"I'd die before I'd let them touch me again," Isla said.

"That brings me no comfort," the low voice said.

"Your comfort is hardly my concern." Isla's tone was sharp with anger.

Kai inched toward the window. He'd only need a quick peek to know who was speaking with such authority.

Beckham had politely questioned Kai and Drew. Beckham had taken them on walks around the bastion, giving them well-planned glimpses of the safety the Brien sorcerers had built far away from Ilbrea before escorting them back to the healer's house to be tucked into their room. Beckham had offered aid in reaching Ilara. Beckham had seen them pampered with clothes, food, and ale. Beckham had said and done everything possible to make Kai and Drew want nothing more than to help the people who'd given them shelter in the scary southern mountains.

Beckham had made it clear to anyone but a chivving fool that Beckham wasn't the real power in the bastion.

Knowing what the Brien sorcerers really wanted, knowing who actually held the power in the bastion—those would be invaluable bits of information.

But having a face to go with the voice that tried to calm Isla was a start and too valuable a sliver of knowledge for Kai to dismiss without even trying for the prize.

"Isla, you're still young," the low voice said.

"*Now* I'm young." Isla laughed. "You didn't seem too concerned about my age when you asked me to kill for you."

Kai reached the edge of the roof and leaned his torso over the lip, gripping the beam beneath the thatching for support.

Beckham and a woman stood with their backs to the window. Isla and the fourth person weren't in view.

"I regret the blood on your hands." The low voice spoke from out of sight. "I regret ever having to give the order to kill. That is my burden to bear."

"I bear it, too," Isla said. "And I'm sure I will have plenty more blood on my hands before my work in Ilbrea is through."

Footsteps carried across the floor.

Kai rolled back onto the roof, pressing his arms to the thatching, freezing as he waited for someone to shout that they'd spotted him through the window.

"Following your heart may seem like a wise and noble choice now," the low voice said, "but that road is often filled with the worst pain."

"Pain and I are old friends. Did you forget?" Isla said.

More footsteps and the sound of a slamming door came from inside.

Kai shut his eyes.

"We should stop her," Beckham said. "We barely got her out of Ilbrea last time. If the Sorcerers Guild catches hold of her—"

"She'll die before she lets them lock her away," the low voice said. "You heard the girl. She wasn't lying. She'd choose death over service to the Guilds."

Having Isla on their journey to Ilara would be an asset. Though Kai had never been fond of sorcerers, Isla had already saved him and Drew once. If they ended up in another fight, they'd have a better chance of survival with her on their side.

"We should stop the whole party from going," the woman who'd gone silent for so long said. "We have no obligation to set the Ilbreans free, let alone help them."

"How high a cost are we willing to pay to—"

A sharp slap on Kai's mouth distracted him from the rest of Beckham's words.

Kai moved to sit up, but the thing that had struck his face kept him pinned down. He reached for his mouth with one hand while punching up with the other, trying to hit whoever had attacked him but finding only open air.

He tried to yank at the thing covering his mouth, but there didn't seem to be anything there. His weight shifted as something gripped his ankles, lifting him up and off the roof, dangling him upside down.

Fighting against the force, he looked up toward his feet. A vine-like branch had bound his ankles together. The vine continued to grow, winding its way up his legs as it carried him away from the roof and into the walled garden.

Kai stretched his hands toward the ground, keeping his arms as far from the vine as he could. He breathed in through his nose and gave as loud a scream as his muffled mouth allowed. His stifled shout sounded pathetic even to his own ears.

The vine lowered him closer to the ground, carrying him to a tree in the darkest corner of the garden.

A knife. A sword. A flame. All things that could help him. None of them things he had.

Kai tensed his legs and kicked them apart with all his might. Pain banged through his shins, but his bindings didn't give.

Chivving, cact of a chivving demon's spawn! Kai tried to shout the words but only managed a sad string of groans.

The vine that bound him creaked as it joined with the tree, solidifying into a branch that kept Kai dangling above the ground like a trussed-up pig.

A figure shifted in the darkness, walking toward Kai with a knife in hand.

Kai crossed his arms and glared at the figure, refusing to show fear even if he was about to be gutted like an animal.

"Give me one good reason I shouldn't kill you." Isla stepped out of the tree's shadow, the starlight's gleam offering just enough light to perfectly display the anger on her face. "Or better yet, drag you back up there and turn you in for spying."

Kai tapped his lips with his finger.

"Scream for help, and I'll pull your intestines out through your mouth." Isla waved a hand, and the pressure on Kai's mouth vanished.

"Coming from most people, I'd think that an entertaining threat. But from you, beautiful Isla, I take it very seriously."

"I will gladly kill you for spying on the people who've welcomed you into their home." Isla pointed her knife at Kai's groin. "Try to flirt your way out of this again, and I'll make sure your death is painful."

"I think you were kinder when you were refusing to speak to me."

"So, I shouldn't offer you a chance to explain?" Isla nodded to Kai's binding.

The vine tightened, giving his legs a painful squeeze.

"I don't trust Beckham. He's agreed to help us far too easily. Which makes me trust him even less than I did when he allowed two strangers to enter the safety built for the children rescued from Ilbrea." Kai paused, waiting for a response that didn't come. "Either he's a fool, which I don't think is true, he has some ulterior motive he wants to see carried out in Ilbrea, which is probable, or he's planning to kill Drew and me in our sleep before we even begin our journey, which I can't actually rule out as the most likely scenario. All things considered, a little spying seemed the most peaceful way to find out exactly why Brien sorcerers would be willing to help Ilbrean saelk."

Isla stepped toward Kai, leaning closer in a way that might have felt like she was going kiss him had she been anyone else the gods had ever created.

"Now that you've spied on us, what do you think of Beckham?"

"He's definitely planning something in Ilara he doesn't want Drew and me to know about. But if his aid will get us home, then I'll happily trot along in your wake and part ways at the city gates. If we find ourselves as enemies after that, at least we'll always have fond memories of the time we shared."

Isla stepped aside and flicked the vine binding Kai.

He pressed his hands toward the ground just in time as the vine unfurled, dropping him. He curled in on himself as his hands hit the grass then threw his weight backward, ignoring the jab of pain as his spine rolled over a root, and sprang to his feet.

"I suppose I should be impressed by that." Isla tucked her knife into the sheath on her belt.

"You did just dangle me upside down with magic. I had to show off at least a bit." Kai winked.

"You annoy me when you do things like that."

"Does it matter? If Beckham gets his way, I'll be leaving soon, and you'll be staying here. We'll never see each other again."

"Beckham's not getting his way." Isla paced in front of the tree. "I don't care if I have to tunnel out of here, I'm chivving well going to Ilara."

"I knew you'd grown attached to me."

Isla growled a laugh.

Kai sat beside the tree, watching her pace, her anger coming across as much more genuine than Beckham's mock worry had managed. "After all the days I spent staring at the back of your head, I trust you more than I trust Beckham, which is telling since you're the one who forced Drew and me to come here."

"I did nothing of the kind."

"You're right. We could have gone off on our own and died instead."

"Exactly."

"But, even though I trust you more than I trust Beckham, I can't believe you'd defy him to accompany Drew and me."

"Believe me, I'm not going for you." Wind stirred the grass at Isla's feet, lifting dirt to swirl around her ankles.

"Then why? If you managed to escape Ilbrea and the Sorcerers Guild—"

"Did I?"

"Sit." Kai patted the ground beside him.

"We're not friends."

"You're going to choke me with dirt if you keep pacing."

Isla looked down. The grass stopped twisting with the unnatural wind. "Sorry."

"I enjoy a little dirt after dinner. Now, come on. If I make you mad, you can just kill me." Kai patted the ground again. "The Sorcerers Guild has wounded us both. I'm sorry for whatever damage they did to you."

"I thought I'd escaped them. I was honestly that foolish." She sank down to sit beside him. "I'd done my bit, gotten out of Ilbrea, and I was going to live a peaceful life reveling in the beauty of all that magic can be."

"Sounds nice."

"It was. But I just"—she swallowed hard, like her own words were trying to choke her—"I can't forget everything they did to me. I got away. I escaped the Sorcerers Tower."

"I've never even heard rumor of anyone accomplishing such a feat."

"I should be free. But it's all still burned into me. I can't let it go." She gripped her forearm, right on the place where the Lady Sorcerer would have branded the Guilding mark into her flesh.

"That doesn't mean you have to go back." Kai held his breath as he dared to touch her shoulder.

"It does. I'm not the only one who couldn't move on. Someone I care about went back. They went because of me. It doesn't matter what lies Beckham tries to feed me. My heart is in Ilbrea, and I'm here. I should be there. I should be fighting. I need to fight."

"Can they not fight on their own? The one you love?"

"He can. He's got a fine skill with a blade. He's chivving fearless, too." Isla looked up to the stars. "But he'd be safer with me fighting beside him. I don't care what he wants. I don't care if I have to face the Lady Sorcerer herself. I can't just sit here while he's in Ilara. I can't lose him."

"He's lucky to have someone like you to worry over him." Kai lifted her hand away from her mark.

"Lucky to have a fool who's chasing him right into the hell she escaped?"

"That part is a bit foolish." He nudged her with his shoulder.

"But going after him, is it wrong?" Isla met Kai's gaze. Her eyes looked different. Younger. More afraid. "Am I a fool? Dooming myself just to chase after the man I love?"

"Depends. Are you going after him because you're afraid he won't want to come back to you or because you're afraid something will happen to him and he won't make it home alive?"

"He knows what they did to me, all of it." Tears glistened in Isla's eyes, sparkling in the starlight. "Every torment. Every scar. The Guilds hurt us both so badly. He wants to make them pay for all of it. He wants to destroy them. He'd proudly die to make it happen."

"Vengeance is a deadly pursuit." Kai squeezed her hand. "If you love him that much, you should go after him. Fight by his side, use your magic to defend him. Just make me one, easy promise."

"I don't like promises."

"If you get cornered by the purple Lady, take her out with you."

"It would be my pleasure."

"It was nice to finally meet you, Isla." Kai leaned back against the tree. "The you beneath the silence and anger, I mean."

"A moment of weakness. It won't happen again." She stood, brushing the dirt off her skirt. "You should get back to the healer's. If they find you out here, they'll suspect you've been spying."

"I take it that means you won't be turning me in." Kai winced at the pain in his shins as he got to his feet.

"We're going north to destroy the Sorcerers Guild. Everyone

who fights on our side is valuable. Even if all they offer is misplaced charm."

"My value runs far deeper than that." Kai bowed. "Don't worry. If Beckham doesn't kill me in my sleep, I promise I'll prove my worth."

NIKO

We're being herded.

For so long, I thought I was going mad. Now I'm sure reason has not abandoned me. There is a creature in the darkness, and it is forcing us along the path of its choosing.

We finally entered an open space after the days spent in that terrible tunnel. The cavern was large enough to swallow my light without letting us see the far side. We decided to circle the perimeter, hoping to finally have a choice in our path forward.

The cavern was as large as your father's palace and offered three exits leading to new paths. We stopped at the tunnel we'd come through, taking a moment to decide which way might finally lead us to the surface.

That's when we heard it. A scratching in the darkness, like knives grating against stone. The sound lasted only a minute before the thunder of falling rocks echoed through the cavern.

We ran up the tunnel we had already traveled, seeking shelter.

When the crashing of the rocks finally fell silent, we ventured back into the cavern. Two of the exits had collapsed. Great gashes sliced through the stone above the debris. The marks were parallel, like a beast's claws.

I have never heard of a monster with the ability to gut a mountain. Not even in legends.

The only route left open to us has forced us farther south. I don't know what lies in this direction. We have no choice but to follow the path the monster laid out for us and hope we find a way to survive whatever the beast is driving us toward.

For the first time, I'm truly afraid I won't be coming back to you.

Our only weapons are knives. If the monster's claws can slice through stone, I don't think we have a hope of defending ourselves.

If I die down here, you'll never know how many letters I scrawled onto the stone. You'll never know how hard I tried to come back to you.

If the mountain has any mercy, she'll set us free. If freedom is already lost to us, I'm glad you'll have our family to comfort you when you realize I'm not coming home.

I hope Mara tells you how much I loved you. And Adrial tells you I was going to return with a ring, ready to propose to the only woman who could ever capture my heart.

I am so sorry, Allora.

Please forgive me for leaving you. I never should have ridden away from Ilara.

"Are you done scrawling on the stone?" Amec rolled the criolas from hand to hand as he sat against the wall five feet away from Niko.

"Tired of keeping watch already?" Niko dipped his fingers into the tiny puddle he had drizzled onto the rock, using the water to finish his letter on the wall.

I will love you always,
   Niko

"I don't mind keeping watch," Amec said. "But if you're not going to sleep, I might as well curl up for a bit."

"I'm done writing." Niko dried his fingers on his pants. "I can take the first watch."

"No, no, you sleep now that you've finished writing that tome of a letter that will disappear as the water dries."

"At least I'll have written it." Niko lay down with his pack beneath his head. He didn't know how long he'd gone without a pillow or even a blanket for warmth. He'd have welcomed a nip of frie to banish the chill that had seeped into his bones if he could have found it.

"Do you think the beast will gut us tonight?" Amec asked.

"I doubt it." Niko closed his eyes. "If all it wanted was a meal, it could have killed us ages ago."

"I didn't think monsters could want things that take the sort of planning it's used to herd us for days on end."

"Generally speaking, they can't." Niko shoved his hands under his arms, trying to rid his fingers of the cold of the cavern.

"Then how can this one?" Amec's tone held a genuine enough question for Niko to actually bother opening his eyes.

"I've been thinking about that while we've been walking, and I've come up with three possibilities."

"Why haven't you told me what they are?"

"We both got tired of talking a few hundred miles ago."

"Well, I'm eager to hear what you have to say now."

Niko's back protested as he sat up.

"Come on, Niko. What great wisdom can the map maker offer?"

"I don't know if you'll find any of it comforting." Niko paused, offering Amec the chance to tell him to lie back down and keep quiet about what horrors might lurk in the darkness. "The most obvious possibility would be a ghost or spirit of some sort. The tale of the city of death tells of a place where specters roam through the darkness, claiming the lives of anyone who travels into their realm. We found a city in the darkness, and it was far from the realm of the living."

"Ghosts don't fit the animal claws. What's the next one?"

"It could be a sorcerer in possession of magic that can tear through stone. That would almost fit with the legends of the Black Bloods."

"The spirits of bandits who roam through the eastern mountains? Wouldn't they count as ghosts as well?"

"Some legends have the Black Bloods as ghosts." Niko leaned against the cavern wall. "But if you dig deeper than the scary stories told to keep children from straying too far into the woods along the edges of the mountain range, the Black Bloods begin to look a bit more like mortal men who sneak out of the woods to kidnap children. If you start to believe there's any truth to a group of men surviving in the eastern mountains and somehow escaping Ilara again and again, logic says there must be magic somewhere in the Black Bloods tale. They'd need it to stay alive."

"Facing a rogue sorcerer doesn't sound much more cheerful than being stalked by a ghost."

"I did warn you."

"Keep going then." Amec pulled his knife from its sheath and placed it by his side.

"There isn't a legend that goes with the third option. At least not one that relates to the eastern mountains. But I think a sorcerer's claimed beast makes the most sense."

"What's that now?"

"Using magic to bind an animal to your will. The creature must then follow the sorcerer's commands. The Sorcerers Guild banned any form of animal magic so long ago, the practice only exists in children's tales and histories now, but in the early days of the Guilds, manipulating animals was common."

"Why did they ban it? Seems like the sort of thing the sorcerers would love lording over normal folk."

"None of the books I've read mention why it became forbidden." Niko dragged his fingers through the length of his beard.

"Something terrible must have happened for the sorcerers to give up a power like that."

They sat in silence for a few moments.

"The possessed animal part makes sense," Amec said. "But I've still never heard of an animal that could tear through stone. Not even a bear could do a thing like that."

"I know."

"But?"

"There is an old legend from the southern mountains, where the range separates Ilbrea from Pamerane. Magically made animals, built by the will of their creator, and given life by a stone filled with the power of the sorcerer who formed them. If I were going to create a beast to roam through this endless chivving night, I'd give it eyes to see in the darkness as it stalked its prey and claws to tear through stone."

"I shouldn't have asked. There's no good in me knowing the ways the claws could have been created as they tear through my gut. Won't help me survive." Amec rolled the criolas to Niko. "You take first watch. All I'd see are ghosts and monsters coming out of every shadow. I'd be useless."

"You could never be useless." Niko pulled his own knife from its sheath. "I'd have lost my mind long ago without you."

"Thanks, Niko."

They drifted back into the comfortable silence of two people who had run out of things to say but weren't offended by the lack of conversation.

Niko wanted to get up. Wanted to keep walking until they could find a way out. But the darkness had long since taught him the value of rest. Their bodies needed time. If fatigue brought illness, they'd lose all hope of escape.

Really, they should have gotten ill long ago, trapped in the darkness with only moss and mushrooms for food. But something in the mountain kept them well. Something in the mountain made sure they always had enough food and water to keep going.

Niko shook away the thought, unwilling to let his mind travel to even darker legends than the tales of beasts with stone hearts.

He gripped the thickness of his beard. He'd never grown so much facial hair before. He'd always been careful to keep clean-shaven whenever possible, so he didn't have a gauge to measure time by the length of his beard. But the hair growing in so dense, and his legs' ability to carry him for miles day after day, made him sure he wasn't malnourished. Which didn't seem possible on a diet primarily of fungus.

You should be keeping watch, not pondering impossible questions.

It should be Mara and Tham here, not me.

He hated himself for even thinking it. He didn't want them to be trapped in this place—he cared for them too much. He wouldn't have switched places with them even if Dudia himself had given Niko the choice.

But Mara and Tham would have fared better in the darkness than he had.

Mara would have known something useful about eating food foraged in caves. Tham wouldn't have been afraid to march into the darkness to hunt the monster that lurked just out of sight. They would have had each other. Even in their worst moments, when hope began to fade, they would have had the person they loved most by their side.

But the person Niko loved most was far away, and the mountain seemed determined to never let him see her again.

Niko pictured his friends around him. The last time they'd all been together at Winter's End, on the balcony Allora had arranged. They were talking and laughing. Allora's hair glinted in the light from the candelabras.

The image shifted in his mind. Tham leaned forward, placing his hand on Niko's shoulder. *Walking through the dark won't bring you closer to the light. If you want a way out, fight for it.*

But that wasn't right. Tham hadn't said anything like that on Winter's End. Tham hadn't said much at all. He rarely did.

"That doesn't mean he's not right." Niko dragged his hands down his face. "Amec, I can't take this anymore."

"You're done watching? I haven't even fallen asleep."

"We can't keep stumbling through the dark, knowing there's a beast behind us."

"If we had another choice, I'd be happy to take it."

"I'm going after the monster." Niko rolled the light to Amec.

"You've finally lost your mind."

"Just stay here. Listen for me, and if I call for help, try and find me." Niko pushed himself to his feet.

"You can't just wander into the dark, Niko. Some of the caverns here are massive. If we separate, we may never find each other again."

"Which is why I'm leaving you with the light." Niko pulled on his pack and picked up his knife.

"Why under the stars do you want to go into the darkness?"

"To see if the monster kills me. Or if it comes closer. Or if it's only attracted to our light and stops following. To do something chivving different, because walking on and on hasn't gotten us anything but more wear on our boots and less sanity in our heads."

Amec tossed the criolas to Niko.

"You need to keep this," Niko said.

"Put it in your pouch to douse the light."

"This is my idea. I'm not going to ask you to stumble through the black with me."

"We're not separating." Amec stood and pulled on his pack. "The only thing worse than being stuck down here would be being stuck down here alone. And, even buried in the bowels of some godsforsaken mountain, I am a soldier assigned to protect the map makers of the eastern mountains journey. I'd be betraying my duty to the Guilds if I let you walk into the darkness alone."

"But that doesn't mean you have to stake your life on my horrible idea."

"I'd skip through the black naked singing pub tunes if I thought it might give us a chance to get out of this chivving place." Amec gripped his knife. "Douse the light, and let's see if we get our guts torn out."

"May Aximander watch over us poor lost slitches." Niko tucked his criolas into the pouch on his belt.

Darkness swallowed them.

Niko blinked at the blackness as his mind screamed that the total absence of light could not possibly be real. His heart raced, thumping in his ears as his body begged him to run.

"Should we walk?" Amec said. "We'll have to be careful not to tumble over a cliff, of course."

"We might as well cover some ground. Grab onto my pack."

Amec touched his shoulder before his fumbling grip found Niko's pack. "This is a chivving nightmare."

"It certainly is."

Niko took a small step. The ground stayed firm beneath him.

He held his hands in front of him as he slid his foot forward, moving another small step.

On and on, step after terrible step, they made their way through the darkness.

Time seemed to hold still. Or perhaps it had sped up, racing against his heartbeat.

Surely, they had walked the length of a city. Unless madness truly had seized Niko's mind and they were still standing in the exact same place.

Dudia, let us find an end to this darkness.

One more step. You're a chivving map maker, take another step.

A chill tensed Niko's shoulders as his hands found a wall of solid rock blocking their path.

"Left or right?" Niko pressed his palm to the proof that they'd actually traveled on their journey through the utter black.

"Right. It'll keep your knife hand free."

"Is that something they teach soldiers?"

"No, just a bit of common sense."

Niko allowed himself a tiny laugh, just enough to shake away a bit of the tension that had tightened around his lungs.

He trailed the fingers of his left hand along the wall as he crept forward, keeping the knife in his right hand in front of him to warn him of any walls.

Clack. Clack.

The sound came from up ahead.

Clack. Clack.

Not the sound of water dripping on rocks or the scratching of claws against stone.

Clack. Clack.

Niko headed toward the sound, moving as quickly as he dared in the dark.

Clack. Clack.

The sound didn't change rhythm or move away as they got closer.

Clack. Clack.

Not an animal. An animal wouldn't make a sound like that. Not that steadily. There would be no reason for it.

Amec shifted sideways, keeping a grip on Niko's shoulder as he walked beside him.

Clack. Clack.

The sound stopped.

Niko froze, holding his breath, waiting for something else to happen.

A minute ticked past.

Goosebumps grew on his arms as every instinct he had told him someone was watching him.

The air in front of him shifted, warming as though another breathing being were sharing his space.

Niko lifted his hand from the wall, sliding his fingers toward the pouch on his belt.

His hand trembled as he loosened the top and lifted out his criolas.

The sudden light dug into his eyes, blurring the scene in front of him, but not enough to disguise the tip of the sword aimed for his throat.

NIKO

"This may be the worst moment to say this," Niko said, "but I have never been so grateful to see a stranger in my life."

The woman holding the sword didn't speak as she moved her blade closer to Niko's throat.

A low growl came from Niko's right. He glanced down, careful not to move his head. A beast, whose eyes reflected the glow of Niko's criolas, bared its teeth as it sniffed the air. The animal looked like it should have been a massive cat, or perhaps *had* been several massive cats someone had pieced together. Black fur covered most of its head, but the body was a patchwork of white and honey-toned pelts.

"At this point, I'm even glad to see your animal friend," Niko said.

The cat gave another growl.

Niko flinched as the cold metal tip of the woman's sword pressed against his throat.

"Careful, Niko," Amec warned.

"Please lower your sword," Niko said. "We have no intention of fighting you. We have knives, you have a sword…and massive cat on your side. A cat who, if I'm not much mistaken, can tear through stone well enough to collapse tunnels. We've been trapped down here for a very long time. We are no threat to you. I beg you, if you have any mercy, please help us find a way out."

"Who are you?" The woman didn't lower her weapon.

"Nikolas Endur and Amec Finlay," Niko said.

"What clan?" the woman said.

"Clan?" Niko asked.

"Don't play with me or I'll slit your throats."

"We have no clan," Niko said. "We were a part of a map making journey—"

"Ilbreans." The woman spat the word like a curse.

"Yes," Niko said. "We're both members of the Guilds."

Niko gasped as the tip of the woman's sword pierced his skin.

"How did you get down here?" the woman asked.

"I'd be happy to tell you our whole tragic tale," Niko said, "just as soon as there's no longer a blade to my neck."

The cat rocked back on its haunches as though preparing to pounce on Amec.

"It's quite a thrilling tale, I promise. It even involves a bit of magic and an abandoned city," Niko said.

"Have you seen anyone else since you've been down here?" The woman still didn't move her blade.

"That depends," Niko said. "Is it your creature who's been following us?"

"I sent him to bring me anyone he could find below the mountains."

"Then no," Niko said. "The only hint of another living thing we've encountered is your cat."

The woman sheathed her blade. "Come with me."

"Will you lead us to the surface?" Amec said.

"The mercy of your freedom is beyond my power." The woman stepped around them, heading back the way they'd come.

The beast growled at them, as though warning of the pain it would inflict if they refused to obey.

"We're not arguing." Niko gave the creature a nod before turning to follow the woman.

"You're bleeding," Amec said.

"A small price to pay for meeting someone who might be able to help us." Niko pressed the heel of his hand to the wound on his neck, wishing he had a bandage, or even a clean cloth, to use instead.

"Don't fool yourselves. I don't care about helping you." The woman strode confidentially through the darkness, turning toward a tunnel that broke through the cavern wall before Niko's light had even reached the opening. "You may wish my croilach had never found you."

"Croilach. Is that the creature's name?" Niko glanced back to be sure Amec hadn't been eaten by the beast before following the woman into the narrow passage.

"Croilach don't have names," the woman said. "I created the creature to serve me. It's not a pet to be cherished."

"One of your guesses got pretty close then," Amec whispered.

"Even if the croilach doesn't have a name, surely you do," Niko said.

"Don't try to befriend me, Ilbrean," the woman said. "I care more for the beast than I do for your kind."

They walked in silence for a long while, the woman leading them from one passage to another without hesitation. They cut through a chamber where moss dripped from the walls and down a tunnel where Niko had to bend over to keep from smashing his head on the low ceiling.

That tunnel led them into another large cavern. There was nothing to mark which direction was which—no path, no wall to follow—but the woman never hesitated as she led them through the sea of black.

"How long have you been down here?" Niko asked. "Has this always been your home?"

"I used to live in the light. But I gave up everything to come down here. To help recover what my clan lost because of Ilbrea."

"What did you lose?" Amec asked.

The woman didn't answer.

The sound of rumbling water carried through the darkness.

Niko tipped his head toward the noise, trying to be sure he hadn't imagined it. A new moisture filled the air.

"Is that the outside?" Niko's heart pounded against his ribs.

The sound grew louder still, but the woman just kept leading them onward.

Mist had begun to touch Niko's skin before his light found a new opening in the stone wall. The opening didn't have the shape of a naturally formed tunnel. Someone had skillfully carved the archway that cut through the thick layer of stone and into the chamber beyond.

A sense of awe pushed past the disappointment and fatigue in Niko's chest as his light revealed the space.

A waterfall twenty feet high tumbled into a rushing river that cut the chamber in half. On one wall, four large niches, like stables, had been carved into the rock. On the opposite side, two empty doorways led to rooms Niko longed to explore. On the far side of the water, a bare floor and perfectly smooth wall led up to the arched ceiling. But there was no bridge and no hope of swimming across the river before being swept through the opening in the cavern wall and out of sight.

"What is this place?" Niko asked.

"Proof that Ilbreans should stay well away from the eastern mountains," the woman said.

"It's magnificent," Niko said.

"There are other places like this." The woman led them toward the stables. "Larger. More glorious. Made by the magic of our ancestors. People like you should never have dared to set foot here. Not in the eastern mountains, and not below. If you never see sunlight again, your blood will be on the hands of the Guilds. Not my people." She pointed to one of the stalls. "In. Both of you."

The croilach growled as Niko hesitated.

He held his light into the stall. The space was bare, without even a stray bit of rock on the smooth stone floor. He glanced to Amec before stepping into the stall. Amec looked like he was battling a strong urge to bolt into the black but followed without argument.

Penned in is no worse than eternally wandering through the darkness.

"You speak of your people?" Niko said. "Who are they?"

"The Black Bloods." The woman held her palm toward the ground. A faint glow radiated from the stone floor inside the stable's doorway. She raised her hand, as though trailing her fingers up the fabric of a finely made curtain.

Amec gripped Niko's arm as the glowing stone began to move, growing up, following the woman's hand toward the top of the doorway. The stone thickened as it grew, changing from shimmering filaments to rods as thick as Niko's fist.

The woman tapped her fingers against the top of the doorway, and the bars attached to the ceiling, locking Niko and Amec inside the stall as the shimmering blue stone darkened to pure black.

"I'll probably be back for you," the woman said. "Try not to die."

She turned and walked away, leaving her croilach behind.

"Niko." Amec's voice trembled. "Have you ever seen magic like that before?"

"I've never even heard of magic like that." Niko slid his pack off and set it at the far end of the stall.

"We've got to get out of here," Amec said.

The croilach growled.

"I don't know if that's possible." Niko sat against the wall. "And honestly, I'd rather stay."

"We've just been trapped by a mythical sorcerer and there's a magically made beast guarding us."

"Exactly." Niko tipped his head back and closed his eyes. "We can bargain with a sorcerer. We have nothing to offer the darkness but our bones."

ALLORA

Silence filled the palace. The guards didn't move as they lurked outside her door. There was no swishing of maids flitting through her sitting room, polishing everything while Allora was supposed to be sleeping.

Allora lay in bed for a long while, listening for any hint of someone hiding inside her walls, watching her.

You've gone mad. There is no one hiding.

She couldn't comfort herself with her own lie.

Surrounded. Trapped. Always watched.

The covers rustled as she pushed them back and slid her legs over the side of her bed. She paused for a moment, listening again.

She didn't need long. Just a few minutes without anyone watching her. A chance to make one final choice for herself.

The night stayed silent. She tiptoed to her writing desk.

But she couldn't write at the desk. Not so close to the window. Not if the sorcerers had found a way to read the imprint of the letters that had been written upon the wooden surface. Her hands shook as she picked up a pen, inkwell, and piece of parchment.

She held her breath as she opened the door in the corner of her room and slipped into the bathroom. The marble floor would be too hard to be indented by even the firmest writing. There were no windows in the room. No way for anyone to see her.

A chill washed over her as she sank to the floor. If someone were watching her now, they would know she was hiding on purpose. There could be no pretense. Did any of the bathroom's marble walls hide passages or places for Ciara's spies to lurk as they watched her? Would a flock of sorcerers burst through the stone to stop her?

I will never be safe again.

Her hand shook as she opened the inkwell. She stared at the parchment for a moment, pen in hand, knowing time was far too precious to be wasted but unable to form the necessary words. She let out a breath, stilled her nerves, and began to write.

I am sorry I cannot say these words in person, but I know now that I may never have the chance to speak freely again.

I am watched. Everywhere I go, every time we speak, they are watching me. Ciara Clery is not my guard. She is my jailer. I fear her.

I used to think the old Queen was shy or tired from grieving all the children she had lost, but I think I understand now. She was terrified of the sorcerers. They want the King to have an heir, no matter the cost. The Queen failed them.

They killed her. I'm almost certain of it. Whether it was poison or some more magical means of murder, I don't know. But Ciara has made it perfectly clear the sorcerers decided the old Queen was no longer fit and had to be removed.

They will do the same to me if I'm not pregnant quickly enough after the wedding.

I've always thought I would become a mother. I understand what is expected of a wife, even if she is not marrying her husband for love. I knew when I accepted the King that my children would be his heirs. I hate the girl I was for being too naïve to see the danger in being taken to the King's bed.

I am nothing but a breeding mare to the sorcerers. If they deem me unfit, I will be put down.

I can never say this to you in person. Ciara is now with me any time I am not alone in my room. I don't know what my punishment will be if she finds out I dared to write this down.

You and I have both long understood the damage the sorcerers do to Ilbrea as they snatch every bit of power they can scrape into their claws.

But you need to know the full extent of their greed.

The King is powerless. He does nothing without their consent. It is the sorcerers who rule Ilbrea, and I fear their grip on the Guilds is only getting stronger. Each time the commoners rebel, the sorcerers tighten their grasp on our beloved Ilbrea.

Now, I am caught within their trap.

I should never have accepted the King's proposal. I should have been wise enough to run from Ilara and not just from my father's house. I should have gone south where it is never winter. Or crossed the eastern mountains and made Wyrain my home.

I have put my father in danger by being here. They will use him against me. They will use you against me, too, if they think they can.

After you read this, you must not visit me anymore. Do not try to rescue me. Do not tell my father what I have written.

I have no hope of escape, and every hint I give of how much I cherish our friendship puts you in greater danger. The closer they think we are, the more they will use us against each other.

I do not write this letter in hopes of aid or pity. I only needed you to know why there must be distance between us.

You have suffered too much, and I couldn't bear the thought of you believing I no longer care for you.

Ciara has threatened to hurt you as a way to punish me. She means it. I cannot endanger you, or the family you will soon have.

Know that I am happy for you. You have accomplished so much. You will be the best of husbands and a remarkable father. It brings me so much comfort to know you will not be alone. Your life will be magnificent, my dearest friend.

I will always hold you in my heart, but for my sake, become a pleasant acquaintance and nothing more. I will be at your wedding, but I cannot greet you as the brother you know I consider you to be. I'm so sorry.

You must warn Mara and Tham to keep their distance when they arrive home from their journey. I will keep pressing the King to find Kai's ship. I have to. But when Kai comes home, tell him he must stay away from me as well. Tell him I always knew he would come back to us. I knew the sea would never hurt him.

I will miss our clan so much. You have brought more joy to my life than anyone has a right to wish for.

Please be careful. I will try to avoid her anger, but I don't know how long I can keep Ciara happy. Her wrath will come eventually, and I must make sure you are spared.

I am so proud of you, and I will love you forever,
Allora

Allora reread the letter, swiping the tears from her cheeks so they wouldn't fall and smudge the ink.

I have never been more alone.

She swallowed the sob that pounded against her throat.

I fled to this prison.

She blew on the parchment, making sure the ink was dry before folding the letter into a square that could fit in her palm.

Letting her tears fall freely, she picked up her ink and pen. She paused in the doorway, listening for any sound before creeping to her desk and putting everything back in its place.

She pulled out the long, silk stocking she'd hidden under her pillow before slipping off the shoulders of her shift. She tucked the letter inside the stocking and tied the silk around her ribs. She shrugged her arms back into her shift, concealing all hints of the letter hidden beneath.

41

NIKO

"We might starve." Amec leaned against the bars of their cage. "After all this time wandering through the chivving darkness, we might actually starve."

"Don't be ridiculous." Niko weighed the heavy leather pouch in his hand. "We'll die of dehydration first."

"I don't think the difference matters."

"Sure it does." Niko felt through the leather, trying to decide what, other than stones, Adrial and Allora could have hidden inside. "Dying of dehydration happens much faster."

"Do you think she'll feed our bodies to the beast?"

The croilach growled in response.

Niko wasn't sure if the growl meant the beast looked forward to making a meal of their corpses or was disgusted by the thought. Either way, he felt quite sure the croilach could at least tell when they were talking about it.

"Save your strength. Sit. Rest." Niko shook the pouch, listening to the sounds of its contents clacking together.

"Still not going to open it?"

"It's not time yet." Niko tucked the pouch into his pack.

"I'm not sure how many more chances you'll have."

"A dear friend told me to open the pouch if I got truly desperate." Niko leaned back against the wall.

"We could be dead and eaten soon."

"I don't want to tempt the gods to sharpen our torment by declaring this the depths of our despair. Besides, that woman will be back soon."

"I really doubt that."

"She will." Niko dragged his fingers through his beard. "She left us here, which means the decision to kill us won't be hers alone. She's also down here looking for someone or something, I'm really not too clear on which."

"We already told her we didn't see anyone else."

"We could have been lying. We could have found corpses and not thought to mention them. We could have found other traces of travelers trapped in the dark. She didn't do nearly a good enough job of questioning us to just let us die."

"Wonderful." Amec sat against the opposite wall. "I hope they ask us nicely. I think I've proven myself to be a man with a modicum of bravery, but I don't think I'd do well with torture."

"It would be a pity if they tortured us. We haven't a single decent thing to tell them other than I'm a chivving Ilbrean map maker who's been lost underground for months."

"Maybe this is their way of torturing us. Leaving us in here to slowly weaken. Grinding down our already shattered spirits. Keeps their hands clean while making me wonder if it wouldn't be better to beg the croilach to slice through the bars and eat us."

"We can't give up now." Niko closed his eyes. "We've spent too long trying to get home. Besides, evisceration would be a terrible way to go. Unless you know how to ask the beast to tear straight through our jugulars."

"It wouldn't work anyway." A man's voice came from the darkness.

"Let us out of here." Amec sprang to his feet and clutched their prison's bars.

"Even a croilach can't slice through stonework created by a trueborn," the man in the darkness said.

Niko eased his hand toward the hilt of his knife. "I might find that to be more interesting if I knew what a trueborn was."

"If you won't lead us out of this abominable darkness, then at least let us go where we can find food and water," Amec said.

"Food and water?" the man said. "Has the mountain provided you with such things?"

"Wouldn't have stayed alive for months down here without it," Niko said. "At least, I think it's been months. Is it midsummer yet?"

"No," the man said. "Not yet."

"That's nice." Niko pushed himself to his feet, still gripping the hilt of his knife. "I'd hate to have to tramp through the snow to get back to Ilara."

"Ilara," the man said. "You're from the Guild's capital city?"

"I was born along the mountain road." Niko peered into the darkness. He could see nothing but the croilach in the light of his criolas. "I made my way up to Ilara when I became an apprentice for the Map Makers Guild."

"If you grew up along the mountain road, you should have known better than to venture into the eastern mountains," the man said.

"If there were a reliable account of people living below the mountain, I would have stayed well away." Niko picked up his criolas and held it close to the bars of their cell. He still couldn't see any hint of the man he spoke to. "But *trueborn* and whatever clan you belong to, those I've never heard of."

"You've never heard of the Black Bloods?" the man asked.

"Only as a story to frighten children," Niko said.

"Have you ever heard of the Brien?" the man said.

"The Brien?" Niko thought for a moment, his mind racing back through all the books he'd read while sitting on the floor of a mausoleum. "No, I can't say that I have. Though, I'll admit to not being the most dedicated of scholars when it comes to my histories."

"I'm not concerned with history," the man said. "Have you heard of a trueborn Black Blood who recently ventured into Ilbrea?"

"I still don't know what a trueborn is," Niko said.

"I'm a trueborn," the woman who'd found them said.

The stone bars that kept Niko and Amec trapped shimmered a deep blue.

"I hold the mountain's magic in my veins," the trueborn said. "Stone magic is the power the mountain has granted me."

A buzz cut through the air as a small stone shot between the bars, whizzing past Niko's ear before lodging itself in the ceiling.

"Ah." Niko brushed the back of his hand against his ear to check for blood. "Thank you for that excellent demonstration."

"Can't you just melt away the bars and let us out?" Amec said.

"The lost trueborn Brien," the man said, ignoring Amec's plea, "have you heard of her?"

"Heard of a woman with the power to manipulate stone? That sort of magic is news to me." Niko pressed away the ache of despair gnawing at his chest. "If your plan is to lock us in here until we tell you about this woman, you might as well kill us now. As much as I'd like to save our lives, we haven't a chance of helping you."

"Why not?" The trueborn's tone held an edge of anger.

The croilach growled and stood to pace in front of their cage, clacking its claws against the ground.

"I don't think you understand the Guilds," Niko said. "I'm not a sorcerer, let alone a high ranking one within the Sorcerers Guild. There's no chivving possibility of them letting ordinary Ilbreans find out an unguilded person holds any hint of magic. Say nothing of a kind of magic I've never heard of someone from the Sorcerers Guild possessing. They'd do anything to cover that sort of thing up."

"Why?" the man asked.

"Power." Niko leaned against the bars. "Fear. The ability to continue manipulating everyone in Ilbrea. The thrill of bending the Guilds to their will."

"Niko," Amec warned.

"It's true," Niko said. "We allow the sorcerers dominance because we have no hope of fighting them. Any admission of magic beyond their control would prove they aren't all powerful and that the Lady Sorcerer can be defeated."

"You're not fond of the sorcerers?" the man asked.

"I have nothing against people with magic in their blood," Niko said. "But the Sorcerers Guild has done a great amount of harm to the Guilds and Ilbrea."

"You could be hanged for saying that." Amec tightened his grip on his knife as though the Lady Sorcerer herself waited in the darkness.

"This lost trueborn you're looking for," Niko said. "She went into Ilbrea?"

"We hope," the man said.

Niko closed his eyes. "I might be able to help you find out if she was ever spotted in Ilbrea, but only if you can get me back to Ilara."

"You're in no position to make bargains," the trueborn said.

A rock whizzed through the bars, nicking Niko's ear.

"I'm not trying to negotiate." Niko winced as he pressed the back of his hand to his bleeding ear. "I'm offering to help you, but I can only do it from Ilara."

"Do what?" Amec asked.

"Look for the sort of oddities the sorcerers usually forget to hide," Niko said. "They erase all hints of magic from the histories but let the legends remain. They wipe out all mention of magic in the wild but make the records appear as though an entire village was destroyed by a storm that couldn't possibly have reached so far inland. Was this lost trueborn of yours the type to fight against the Guilds?"

"Yes," the trueborn said.

"Then if I got back to Ilara, I could search through the Soldiers Guild's records, look for any cluster of casualties that doesn't match a reasonable fight," Niko said.

"You have access to those records?" the man asked.

"No." Niko pulled his hand away from his still-bleeding ear. "Not legally, at any rate. But I have enough connections to be able to find someone who does. The head scribe is as good as my brother, and I'll be proposing to the Lord Map Maker's daughter as soon as I get out of this dark hell and back home."

"How did you get down here to begin with?" the man asked.

"We found a—"

"No," Niko cut across Amec. "We've given them enough information for nothing."

"Does the croilach need to convince you to talk?" the trueborn said.

The beast lunged for the bars, gnashing its teeth. Niko hadn't noticed until that moment that the monster's fangs didn't fit with its head. The trueborn had given the croilach overly long teeth when she'd pieced it together.

"We need food, water, and to be let out of this chivving cell." Niko backed just far enough away from the bars to be out of reach of the beast's claws. "If you're just going to leave us in here to rot, then you'll be getting no more information from either of us."

"It would be fun for her to make them talk." A new female voice spoke from the darkness. "Bryana said she wants to see them."

"We can't risk our elder down here," the trueborn said. "And neither of them should set foot in the stronghold."

"They'll have to," the man said. "Bring them with us, and let the consequences be tomorrow's worry."

"As you say," the trueborn said.

Lights flickered to life beyond the reach of Niko's criolas.

Ten people stood outside the bars of the stall-made-cell. All of them armed, all of them looking as though they'd like nothing better than to let the croilach feast on Ilbrean flesh.

"This stronghold," Niko said, "how far away is it?"

"Would you rather stay inside your pen?" The trueborn stepped up beside the croilach.

"No," Niko said. "Just a question."

The trueborn touched the stone bars, which shimmered a pale blue as they melted away.

"I assume the stronghold is farther south." Niko sheathed his knife and pulled on his pack.

"Why do you say that?" a man with short black hair and a scar on his jaw asked.

Niko recognized the voice of the man he'd already been speaking to.

"The croilach had been herding us south," Niko said. "When we reach the stronghold, will we be beyond Ilbrea's southern border?"

"No," one of the women said.

The croilach stood, stretching its back like a normal cat before padding away toward the arch that led into the darkness.

"Don't try to fight us, and don't try to run. If you do either, the croilach will pounce out of the darkness and kill you." The trueborn stepped aside, allowing Niko and Amec to leave their prison.

"Ah, but if your beast kills us, you'll never be able to hear the thrilling tale of how we got trapped down here." Niko stretched his shoulders before stepping out into the open.

The trueborn glared at him.

"We won't run," Niko sighed. "As we've said before, we're well aware it would do us no chivving good."

"You should drink." The man held out a waterskin.

"Gladly." Niko took the skin, sniffing the water before taking a small sip. He swished the water around in his mouth. "A bit silty, but I don't taste any poison."

"Poisoning isn't my style," the man said.

"Let's be on our way, then." Niko took another drink before handing the waterskin to Amec. "I've spent quite enough time in this chamber."

"You may regret your haste when Bryana questions you." A woman led the group toward the archway.

"Who might Bryana be?" Niko asked.

"The Elder of the Brien Clan," the black-haired man said.

"Excellent. And who might you be?" Niko shivered as he stepped through the arch and back out into the vast black below the mountain.

"Paiman," the man said.

"It's a pleasure to meet you, Paiman," Niko said. "And the rest of you?"

"We're not in a pub, Niko." Amec passed the water back.

"No offense to you, Amec," Niko said, "but after so long with only your company, I want to make sure I haven't completely lost my social graces."

Their party headed south, keeping near enough to the cavern wall for their lights to touch the stone, as though their leader wasn't as confident in navigating the darkness as the trueborn who'd made the croilach.

"And you, madam." Niko looked to the trueborn. "What might your name be?"

"I don't have a name," the trueborn said. "I don't need one anymore. I promised myself to the darkness until we discover the fate of the one we lost. My croilach doesn't speak. Why should I have a name when there is no one to say it?"

42

ADRIAL

Adrial willed his heart to slow as he made his way across the courtyard to the stables. A hundred panicked voices screamed in his mind, shouting all the horrible things that could have happened to Ena.

Allora's letter had warned him. A simple piece of paper she'd slipped into his hand as they sat in the royal garden. If the sorcerers wanted to punish Allora by hurting Adrial, he could imagine no worse torment than Ena being taken from him.

He'd gone to check on Ena the night before, to ease his fears of the sorcerers stealing her away. She hadn't been in her shop or her room. He'd waited as long as he could, but she hadn't come home.

Ena's boots had been gone, and her knife.

If the sorcerers had taken her, at least she had a weapon to defend herself.

A blade can't fight against magic.

His fingers started to tingle as he reached the stables, as though all his nerves had caught fire and the flames were searching for a place to break out of his body. He gave the grooms a nod and tried to smile but couldn't make his face form the familiar expression.

The walk to the stairs seemed to take forever. He needed to reach her shop.

But, if he were going to find something horrible, he would rather walk forever than learn that everything he had ever wanted had been brutally destroyed by the sorcerers.

Ena, the child...if anything had happened to them, it would be his fault. In trying to save them, he'd doomed them. Their blood would be on his hands.

Adrial steadied himself against the walls as he climbed the stairs.

He'd seen her shop by the warehouses after it had been ransacked. Everything smashed. Ink everywhere. He'd thought there was blood on the floor. Her blood.

But the sorcerers wouldn't be so crude.

I may never see her again. I may never hold the baby.

Pain sliced through Adrial's chest, but he kept climbing. His hand shook as he reached toward the door.

Dudia, please protect her.

He knocked.

The sound of footsteps came from inside. "Who is it?"

"Ena?" Adrial opened the door and stumbled into the shop.

She stood by the table. Alive. Whole. A pestle in one hand, a sieve in the other.

"You're alive." Adrial didn't feel any pain in his hip as he walked toward her. It was as though he were floating in a blissful dream.

"Yes, I am." Ena set the pestle and sieve on the table.

Adrial caught her hand, holding it tight, needing to feel her palm against his. He touched her cheek, brushing her hair behind her ear, marveling at the warmth of her skin.

"What's happened?" Ena asked.

"I thought the sorcerers had taken you." Tears burned in Adrial's eyes. "I came here last night, and you were gone. I couldn't find you. What happened? Did they hurt you?"

Ena leaned forward, brushed her lips against his cheek, and whispered, "You worry too much, scribe. I can watch out for myself."

"I couldn't breathe, Ena. I thought something had happened to you."

"You can't race in here all in a panic, tell me the Lady Map Maker palmed you a note warning that the paun sorcerers are threatening you, and expect me to just pace in my shop." Ena pulled a bowl of dark berries from the side of the table and set them beside the sieve.

"What are those?" Adrial reached for the berries.

"Supplies." Ena swatted his hand aside.

"But those weren't on any of your lists. I never had anyone gather those for you."

"I know." Ena scooped berries into the sieve and used the pestle to press their juice into a metal pot. "That's why I went to get them for myself."

"You're not allowed to leave the library."

"I know that as well." Ena set the sieve down. "But I've told you before, if the scribes don't want anyone climbing over the library's walls, they shouldn't have made it so easy to do."

"Ena, that's too dangerous."

"Climbing is only dangerous if you fall." Ena winked.

Adrial followed her as she went to the other side of the workshop to collect a bundle of white flowers and a little wooden box.

"That's not what I mean." Adrial stepped in front of her, blocking her path back to the table. "If the Sorcerers Guild decides to hurt me, they will go after you. If anything were to happen to you or the baby, I would never forgive myself."

"None of that fault would fall on you." Ena stepped around him. "And you blaming yourself for the evil done by the chivving paun sorcerers wouldn't help anyone. It would be their fault. So many terrors are their fault."

"I know. The Sorcerers Guild has done unforgiveable things."

"And you don't even know what they've hidden out of sight of the scribes." Ena plucked the tiny white flowers from their stems and tossed them into the pot.

"But staying inside the library, where you aren't tempting Sorcerer Clery, is the best way to keep you safe."

Ena laughed.

"Please, Ena." He laid his hand on her arm.

"I'm not afraid of the sorcerers, scribe." Ena tossed the barren flower stems onto the table and rounded on Adrial. "They are not immortal. They are not gods. We do not have to cower before them."

"Ena—"

"A sorcerer who lives free of the Guilds can fight against the paun who hide in their stone tower. Get a sorcerer to use enough magic to burn out, and they're as helpless as a babe until they recover."

"Burn out?" Adrial glanced toward the door, making sure he'd shut it behind him.

"A sorcerer can only push so much magic through their body at once. If they go too far, it can take them weeks to recover."

"What?"

"Even a healthy sorcerer can be killed by a non-magical hand." She touched the stone pendant that hung around her neck. "A knife to the back will kill them as easily as it will you or me."

"Sorcerers are impossible to attack."

"Not if they don't see you coming." She took his face in her hands. "They are vulnerable. And I will not live in fear of them."

She went back to her work, stirring the tiny flowers into the pot.

Adrial watched the blooms sink into the dark liquid. As the pale petals disappeared, the color of the mixture changed, lightening from deep purple to pale gold. "Ena, how do you know sorcerers can be killed? And what do you mean by *burn out*?"

He reached toward the pot. There was something in the mixing, something beautiful and strange, not meant to be seen by innocent eyes.

Ena slid between him and the table, the curves of her body pressing against him as she tipped his chin so her lips were only a breath away from his.

"Don't ask questions you know I won't answer."

"But none of it makes sense." He swallowed, but the pressure in the front of his throat stayed. He backed away, creating a hateful space between them.

"Still afraid to touch me, scribe?" Ena took his hand and placed it on her hip.

"No, of course not." Heat flooded his cheeks.

"We are to be married." She placed his other hand on her hip. "Will ours be a proper marriage?"

"What—how do you mean?"

"I will have only you, and you will have only me?" She wrapped her arms around his neck.

"I don't—" Adrial looked over her shoulder, searching for salvation, though the last thing he wanted was to be saved. "I'm not marrying you because I expect anything from you. The last thing I would ever want is for you to feel some obligation to—"

She brushed her lips against his. "You'd better stop blushing every time you touch me, or people will be quite confused as to how we ended up with a baby." She kissed him again, teasing his lips with her tongue as she drew him nearer.

He wrapped his arms around her, holding her close. The exquisite feel of the curves of her body pressing against him drove every hope of reason from his mind. The taste of her made him forget anything else had ever existed.

She pulled her lips from his but didn't back away. "You are protecting me by marrying me. But do not forget that I will protect you. I will protect my husband. Do not doubt me, and do not question me. It's the only way I can keep you safe."

"As long as you're safe, that's all that matters."

"It's not." She gave him one more kiss before taking his hands and stepping away from their embrace. "Now go. Make pages for the Princess's vellum. I'm getting married soon, and I have a massive amount of work that still needs to be done."

"I'll stay. I'll help you."

"I don't need help." Ena added more berries to the strainer. "I only need a bit of peace to work."

"If you're sure." Adrial headed toward the door. "Just stay here, please. Stay safe."

"Out, scribe." Ena shooed him away with her pestle. "I'm very busy doing important work."

"Right. Thank you." He stepped out onto the stairs and closed the door behind him.

He stood on the top step for a long while, trying to make reason line up with the beautiful dream of holding Ena in his arms.

There were dark things—horrible, dark things—she would never tell him about her life before Ilara. But anyone knowing about the sorcerers' weaknesses seemed impossible. They could not be defeated. No one in Ilbrea had a hope of fighting them.

"Nothing is as impossible as Ena marrying me."

He shut his eyes, savoring her scent still clinging to his clothes. The scent of the woman he loved. The woman who would be his wife.

Shadows lurked around her, and she embraced the danger. She touched the darkness as though it were her home. Her fate-born companion.

The library was his home, his safety, his resource. If Ena knew how to fight a sorcerer, then somewhere someone must have made a record—an account of the sorcerers' vulnerabilities. If he wanted to protect her, all he had to do was find the right book.

NIKO

The annoying throbbing in Niko's wounded ear didn't bother him half so much as the terrible feeling of being lost.

The twisting tunnels the Brien traveled through were more labyrinth than passage, with branches splitting away so often, Niko couldn't help but wonder how many poor explorers had permanently lost their way before a useable route was discovered.

The question balanced on his tongue. Someone had been the first to reach the vast land of caverns below. Tales of their adventure should be the kind told around campfires, if the Brien did such things. But his days trotting through the darkness with the Brien had taught him not to expect satisfying answers.

"This isn't where she went when she left us locked up," Amec said, keeping his voice low, though the Brien were too close for him to hope they wouldn't hear. "She wasn't gone long enough to walk all this way and come back to get us."

"No, she wasn't," Niko said.

The passage turned again, sloping downward as it cut west.

"So where did she go?" Amec asked.

"*She* has ears," the trueborn said.

"So where did you go?" Amec said louder.

"It's not your concern," the trueborn said.

"Perfect," Amec said. "Glad I asked."

No one bothered speaking as the tunnel leveled out and turned east again.

Niko longed to be able to map their route, not just so he might have a chance of escaping should the need arise, but to feel the tingle of magic joining map to mind. But he'd run out of sorcerer-made scrolls ages ago.

It's for the best. Creating a map of this place would only encourage more fools to get lost in this hell.

"Douse your light," the trueborn said.

"What?" Niko shook himself back into the reality of trudging up the tunnel's slope.

"Douse your light, or I'll shatter it," the trueborn said.

"You'd be a fool to shatter it." Niko tucked his criolas back into the pouch on his belt. "If you break a criolas, the magic trapped within tends to cause a bit of an explosion."

"I know quite well how a lae stone works," the trueborn said. "And I'd shatter it in your hand to make sure you're the one who bleeds."

"A lae stone." Niko looked down to his pouch. "How strange that you have a different name for them."

"More like the Ilbreans got their name wrong," Paiman said. "That magic comes from the Black Bloods."

"Does it?" Niko scrubbed his fingers through his beard. "Fascinating."

"Why?" Paiman asked.

Niko thought for a moment as they cut around a corner that was angled like they were skirting the side of a building. "If the Sorcerers Guild did steal the idea of criolas from your lae stones, that means at one point, either the Sorcerers Guild knew of your people and learned from their magic, or some of your people went out into Ilbrea and joined the Sorcerers Guild. Or, several centuries ago, a group of Black Bloods became the sorcerers we now have in Ilbrea. I'm not sure which is most likely. Or most frightening."

"Why frightening?" Paiman asked.

"If they've managed to cover up knowing about an entire clan living in the eastern mountains, they've hidden even more from the people of Ilbrea than I suspected," Niko said.

"It's worse than that," the trueborn said. "There are five clans, and our history in the eastern mountains goes back to before the Guilds ever tainted the lands to the west."

"Five clans." Amec sounded as though he might faint. "But the road to Wyrain runs straight through the mountains, and—"

"And it's nigh on impossible to find a Black Blood who doesn't want to be found," Paiman said.

"Yet, you're searching for one," Niko said.

"And we'll keep searching until we bring the lost one home," the trueborn said.

"You certainly deserve credit for determination," Niko said.

The tunnel narrowed, leaving barely enough room for them to walk single file. Before the horrible feeling of being trapped managed to firmly dig into Niko's chest, the group stopped.

"Everything all right?" Niko rose up on his toes, trying to see over the people in front of him. It looked as though they'd reached a solid wall.

"We're here," Paiman said.

The light in the narrow tunnel dimmed as each of the Black Bloods tucked away their lae stones.

Paiman was the last to douse his light.

The complete black of the passage set a chill on Niko's neck, as though he could feel the croilach watching him again.

"Niko?" Amec whispered.

"I'm still here," Niko said.

A rumbling came from in front of them, seeming farther away than the wall they'd encountered should have allowed.

"Keep moving," Paiman said.

Niko reached forward as he walked, waiting to run into a solid wall or into the person in front of him. Or worse, for something to leap out of the dark and run into him.

He raised his hand to head height, trying to find the top of the wall they were walking toward to keep from cracking his head against the stone, but there was nothing. He took a deep breath, steadying his nerves.

The air smelled different. The tinge of stone wasn't as strong. The air seemed lighter, too. A bit warmer.

Please. Aximander, I swear I will be the most faithful of your servants if you lead us back into the sunlight.

The soft scuffling of footsteps came from Niko's left. He fought the instinct to recoil and reached toward the sound. His fingers didn't meet a stone wall as reason demanded they should.

A throaty laugh came from the darkness.

"Stop," Paiman said.

Niko froze in place, rocking forward as Amec knocked into his back.

"We've brought the two Ilbreans here on Bryana's orders," Paiman said. "Give us passage."

More footsteps came from the darkness, like a dozen people were creeping nearer, studying their party.

"Bryana won't take kindly to delays," Paiman said.

"The watcher goes back," someone whispered.

Niko's shoulders tensed. The voice seemed to have come from right beside him.

"She's the one who found them," Paiman said.

"The watcher goes back," the voice whispered again. "The watcher cannot cross the threshold."

"Tell Bryana to send for me," the trueborn said. "If she needs to speak to me, I will meet her in the darkness."

The soft sound of boots on stone retreated up the passage

toward the terrible labyrinth. No one spoke until the sound had disappeared.

"You could have let her through," Paiman said.

"She gave a vow," the voice said. "We gave a vow."

"Then keep your vow and let us through," Paiman said. "Or would you rather I tell Bryana we were delayed by you?"

"We will open the way," the voice said. "But don't assume you will always be granted such easy passage. We work at the will of the mountain."

"We all *live* by the will of the mountain," Paiman said.

A rumble and the grinding of stone on stone came from Niko's right. A dim beam of light carved shadows into the space around them. Niko searched the darkness for the one who had spoken but could see only the group he'd been traveling with.

Their party moved forward, toward the light. It didn't hold the blue tinge of the criolas or lae stones. The light held a golden glow, like a torch...

Or sunlight.

Niko clenched his fists, trying to ignore the thudding of his heart as he followed Paiman into the next chamber.

The light came through a crack in the stone wall, a slit barely wide enough for someone to sidle through.

Niko spun around as the rumbling and grinding started again.

The wall behind them shifted, closing off the pathway to the tunnels. Not sliding like a door, but growing back together, as though the mountain were healing a wound in its rock.

"Come on, then," Paiman said. "Bryana wants you brought straight to her. If you survive the meeting, we'll get you washed and fed. You may be eating in a cell, but we won't let you starve."

The woman at the front of their party took off her pack and slipped into the crack in the wall.

"This cell," Niko said, "does it have a window?"

"No." Paiman side-stepped into the gap.

Niko took off his pack and let out a long breath before sidling into the stone. The wall arced toward his face, as though it might collapse on him if he took one wrong step. He moved inch by inch, keeping to a slower pace than Paiman.

The light ahead grew stronger as the tunnel curved, giving him a view of the top of the chamber beyond.

The ceiling had been carved by a skilled hand, or perhaps even by magic. The etched swirls created an image of a mountain range, though Niko didn't recognize any of the peaks. Golden light filled the room, casting shadows on the massive work of art. The shadows didn't flicker as though they'd been cast by torchlight.

Paiman stepped aside, revealing a rank of armed guards in purple uniforms. But not the Sorcerers Guild's purple—the shade was wrong. And women stood among the pack, just as armed and deadly looking as the men beside them.

A flutter of anticipation filled Niko's chest. He allowed himself a smile as he stepped out into the chamber beyond.

There were no windows. No sunlight.

Golden lae stones had been set into the walls, casting a sun-like glow over the chamber.

Grief gouged a hollow wound where Niko's lungs had been. His limbs grew heavy, as though all the miles he had traveled had suddenly cracked through the foolish hope he had carried and would bury him alive in this unending tomb.

You're not allowed to give up. Allora is waiting for you.

Niko shoved aside his bitter disappointment, focusing instead on what the room did offer.

Thirty armed guards. Three proper doors leading out of the stone chamber. A tree-like design carved into the far wall.

If they've seen trees, they've seen sunlight.

Niko let the thought comfort him as he bowed to the guards.

"Are you quite done?" Paiman asked.

"My apologies," Niko said. "But I've found that whenever one is confronted with a mass of armed strangers, the best course of action is usually to be polite until it's proven that hostility would lead to a better chance of survival."

Amec stepped up beside Niko and bowed deeply. "You all have lovely swords."

"Enough." Paiman headed to the door farthest away from the carved trees.

One of the guards stepped out of their place, opening the door before Paiman could reach for the latch.

Niko's heart leapt into his throat as he peered into the corridor beyond. Blue lae stones had been set into the walls.

Paiman and his people walked in front of the group while the pack of guards followed close behind Niko and Amec. The amount of people surrounding him and the consistent light of the corridor were enough to set Niko's nerves on edge, telling him to run back to the darkness and solitude, even though his heart still screamed its longing for the open air.

Will I ever again feel at home on the crowded streets of Ilara?

Aximander, please let me live long enough to find out.

They walked up a flight of carved stairs and through a doorway into another lae stone-lit passage. Doors lined the corridor, and signs of life trickled into the hall.

Niko's mouth watered as the scent of baking bread drifted in from somewhere, melting his trepidation of being surrounded by people. The low rumble of a man's voice came through one door followed by a woman's sharp reply.

Niko wanted to throw open the doors and embrace the people who hid behind the wood. Any hint of life beyond pure survival felt like a miracle granted by Dudia himself.

Up another flight of stairs, and they began passing people. None of them wore uniforms, and most looked a little afraid of the strangers being escorted by a horde of guards.

A woman grabbed her son by the shoulders, yanking him out of Paiman's path and tucking the boy behind her back.

Niko gave the woman what he hoped would be accepted as a genuine and meek smile.

The woman averted her gaze.

"I gather you don't have many outsiders visiting your stronghold." Niko took a few quick steps to walk closer to Paiman.

A young girl darted through a door, slamming it shut behind her.

"The stronghold is only for the Brien," Paiman said. "As a rule, no one outside our clan is allowed to enter this haven."

"Then I am even more grateful for being brought here," Niko said.

"I don't think we know whether or not to be grateful yet," Amec said.

"But you aren't scaring people because you're outsiders." Paiman slowed his pace as he neared a polished wooden door flanked by guards.

One of the guards stepped forward and opened the door for their party.

"You've been underground for a long time," Paiman continued as he led their group into a wide corridor with an arched ceiling. "You look like beasts who've clawed their way out of a child's nightmare."

"You'd think Brien children would have hardier spirits if they grew up with croilach," Amec said.

"Those unnatural creatures are never allowed to enter our halls," Paiman said. "To bring a stone made monster into the stronghold would be a betrayal to the clan. The creator would be executed."

"That seems a very reasonable rule to me," Niko said.

The corridor ended at a wide set of stairs that twisted as it slowly cut up through the stone. Bannisters had been carved into the walls, and evenly spaced niches held stone statues.

A woman made of white marble clutched a baby to her chest. A man froze mid-step, his arms spread to his sides as though he were trying to take flight. A woman knelt as though begging for mercy.

"These statues are beautiful," Niko said.

"You should speak less when you meet Bryana," Paiman said.

"Do you think she'll be kinder to us if he's quiet?" Amec asked.

Three women pressed themselves against the wall to let Paiman's parade pass.

Paiman didn't speak again until the last of the guards had reached the women. "You'll find no kindness left in Bryana, but idle talk could stoke her rage. That is something you want to avoid."

"Duly noted," Niko said.

His legs had started to burn before they reached the top of the staircase.

Another door blocked the path forward, this one even better guarded than the last. Still, the guards opened the door for Paiman without argument, allowing them to enter the grandest chamber yet.

Chandeliers dripping with tiny lae stones hung from the ceiling. The gray of the stone walls had been inlayed with black, white, and green marble, creating an image of a mountain's slope. A woman stood on top of the mountain, clutching a baby to her chest, just like the statue along the stairway.

Benches and unlit fireplaces dotted the room. People in finely made clothes stood in clusters, as though Paiman had interrupted them while they'd been in the middle of very important gossip.

All of the finely dressed people in the chamber turned to face Paiman as he passed. They lowered their chins and gazes, as though in reverence.

"I hate to admit my ignorance," Niko said, "but who are you, Paiman?"

"A Brien," Paiman said.

The others who had traveled through the darkness with Paiman all seemed to tense in unison.

"You seem to be a very important Brien," Niko said. "Are you a war hero? A princeling?"

"I'm the second in line for Bryana's place as Elder of the Brien Clan." Paiman stopped in front of a set of intricately carved doors. "I am merely a humble servant of my clan."

"I'm not sure they understand that," Niko said.

"Tell Bryana we've brought the Ilbreans." Paiman looked to one of the guards.

The guard nodded to Paiman before stepping through the solid stone wall.

Niko's heart jolted into his throat as he blinked at the place the guard had been only a moment before.

"Oh, that was"—Amec took a few deep breaths as though he might be ill—"that was not natural."

"Have you never met a sorcerer?" Paiman said.

"I've met one," Amec said. "But they didn't walk through walls."

"The Sorcerers Guild likes to hide what their people are capable of," Niko said. "They only let us see their magic when they want to show off or terrify us."

The guard stepped back out of the wall. "Rather pointless to have magic if you're not allowed to use it."

"I've never questioned it," Niko said. "Asking that sort of thing could easily get a man killed in Ilbrea."

The guard held Niko's gaze for a moment before looking to Paiman. "She's ready for you."

With a flick of the guard's finger, the doors swung open.

Bright light filled the chamber beyond.

The room had been built of shimmering white stone. A woman wearing a purple gown sat on the white throne at the end of the room. Behind her, a wall of wide windows looked out over a valley surrounded by towering cliffs. The midday sun shone on the trees that blanketed the valley floor, making their leaves sparkle like a sea of emeralds.

Niko stepped into the throne room, holding his hands in front of him, reaching for the nearest ray of sunlight.

The warmth touched his skin.

A joyful relief crashed through his chest, stealing all his reason. He fell to his knees, caring nothing for dignity as the sunlight caressed his tear-stained face.

44

ADRIAL

"Sir, it's time." Taddy bounced from foot to foot as though incapable of stopping his momentum. "Lord and Lady Karron are here. And Sorcerer Clery. The Lord Scribe is ready, as well."

"I'll be out in a moment." Adrial shooed Taddy back into his sitting room.

"Yes, but sir—"

Adrial shut the door behind his apprentice, holding onto the doorknob for a moment, needing the firmness of the metal in his grip to assure himself he hadn't slipped into some sort of strange and wonderful dream.

"I'm getting married." Saying the words out loud sent Adrial's head spinning. "I'm getting married."

He hurried to his desk, carefully marking the book he'd been reading before taking it to his wardrobe. He hadn't found anything useful in the book, not really.

The text was an obscure account written by a soldier who'd fought alongside the sorcerers when the people of Pamerane had tried to come across the southern mountains to invade Ilbrea. Adrial had yet to read anything in the soldier's tale worth considering the book to be illicit. And he had found the volume among the library's collection, so the book had not been deemed heretical by the Scribes Guild at the time of its writing more than one hundred and fifty years ago.

None of that stopped Adrial from kneeling beside his wardrobe and reaching up under the lip of the wood to tuck the book into the carved crevice where not even the most fastidious of maids would find it.

He stood, straightening his robes before taking one last look around his room. The room he would soon share with his wife.

She'd insisted on it. Really, it was only practical if people were to believe they'd conceived a child so quickly.

He touched the extra blankets at the foot of the bed. He'd be comfortable sleeping on the couch beside her, just as Ena had when the sorcerers had kept him unconscious for so long. He felt sure she'd try to insist he take the bed instead, but he wouldn't allow it. She needed her sleep, and plenty of space to feel safe.

They couldn't share the bed, either.

He'd carefully considered the arrangement, and it would be better for them both if they slept separately. Never touching. Always maintaining the boundaries their friendship demanded.

But she'd still be close to him.

Her scent would fill their room. His head would swim with it every morning.

Joyful bliss filled his chest, making it seem utterly impossible he hadn't exploded from sheer ecstasy.

He'd keep her safe. He'd find a way to make her happy. He'd protect their child. If only he could—

"Sir, we really do need to go." Taddy pounded on the door.

"Coming." Adrial checked the front of his robes one more time before hurrying out into the sitting room.

Taddy still bounced from foot to foot. Sweat had begun to glisten on the poor boy's brow.

"Lead the way." Adrial bowed.

"Thank you, sir." Taddy trotted toward the door, nearly

ripping the doorknob off in his haste to get into the hall. "There are other Guild leaders here, too. Lady Green is here, and Lord Nevon."

"Really?" Adrial said. "I made sure they were invited, but I didn't think they'd come."

"I think everyone in the Guilds would be here if they could." Taddy walked down the corridor so quickly, he had to double back to keep from getting too far ahead of Adrial's carefully controlled stride. "After all the horrible things that have happened since Winter's End, this is a chance for a bit of joy. And Ena's going to be the Lady of the Scribes Guild someday, and the only people who really know her at all are the two of us."

"I suppose you're right."

"I'm the only apprentice who's being allowed to attend." Taddy puffed up his chest. "I must say, all the others were shriveling with envy."

"It would have been wrong for Ena and me to get married without you there." Adrial let his joy show on his face as they reached the wide staircase that led down to the scribes' offices, meal halls, and gallery.

Scribes, servants, and familial residents lingered in the corridor below—all those who hadn't been granted an invitation by the Lord Scribe but wanted to witness at least a bit of the festivities.

Adrial nodded to as many of them as he could.

It's not me they want to see, anyway.

Soldiers and scribes' guards stood outside the door to the gallery, all of them armed as though prepared to march straight into battle.

If the Demon's Torch comes, they'll be ready for him.

Ena had seemed so sure the man hadn't attacked the cathedral, as though she knew him well enough to predict his actions. Which must mean the legends of a man whose soul had been consumed by fire were true. Or at least true enough to warrant fear.

Not tonight. There will be no attack tonight. We're safe. I'm not important enough for my wedding to be a target.

But if the Demon's Torch knows Ena, will he try to save her from me?

His smiled flickered as he passed through the gauntlet of soldiers.

"Head Scribe." Allora greeted him just inside the gallery, giving him a courteous nod instead of the beaming smile and kiss on the cheek that should have been her greeting.

Adrial tucked his hands behind his back, offering Allora a reverent bow before meeting her gaze.

Thank you. I miss you. The others will come home and we'll find a way to help you. Adrial wished he could speak the words, but not here. Not now. Not with the lives of his bride and his child at stake.

You have not been abandoned, Allora.

"I was beginning to think poor Taddy had lost you." Allora shifted her gaze to the apprentice.

Taddy made a noise like a blissful whimper as his face turned scarlet.

"Just collecting myself," Adrial said.

"I wish you all the happiness in the world," Allora said. "Marriage will be a wonderful adventure for you."

"You'll soon follow him." Sorcerer Clery stepped close to Allora's shoulder.

"But not so soon for my wedding to be a distraction from another couple's bliss. Head Scribe, do find some time to visit me before the snow returns." Allora stepped away from Adrial, turning her attention back to the gathered crowd.

"Yes, Lady Karron." Adrial bowed to her, letting his joy smother his worry. "You are most gracious."

"Head Scribe." Tammin hurried from the front of the room,

stopping to bow to Sorcerer Clery and Allora before continuing. "Lord Gareth is ready."

"Right." Adrial forced his lungs to accept air as he followed Tammin toward the front of the gallery.

Lord Gareth stood beside Lord Karron.

The creases on Lord Karron's face had shifted from their usual placement, lifting slightly as though pride or joy had relieved a bit of his worry.

Lord Gareth beamed at Adrial, waving him up onto the dais at the very front of the room. "Are you ready, Adrial?"

"Yes, sir." Adrial stepped up onto the platform, his heart ricocheting against his ribs as he looked out over the sea of people staring up at him.

"May your marriage bring you as much joy and purpose as your place within the Scribes Guild," Lord Gareth whispered.

"Be happy, Adrial." Lord Karron gripped his shoulder before stepping off the dais to join the crowd.

Two scribes' guards opened a door in the side of the room.

Adrial held his breath as Ena stepped into the gallery.

No one walked with her. No one could have. The power and beauty that radiated from her had a palpable force, as though a magic beyond anything Adrial had ever known surrounded her.

The crowd parted as she stepped into the aisle that would lead her to Adrial's side.

She wore a white gown, but the color of Adrial's Guild was the only concession she'd given to being the head scribe's bride.

Her gown cut lower in the front and back than Guild custom allowed. She wore the black stone pendant around her neck, still on the same simple cord, refusing the jewelry the Scribes Guild had offered her. She'd added more colors to her hair, mixing in strands of every pigment Adrial could ever dream up. A delicate hint of silver weaved through the little twists that pulled her hair away from her face.

She was not the inker who scaled walls and dove into waterfalls. She was powerful and beautiful beyond all imagining. A queen from a fairy story who rode into battle, slaying all who stood against her.

Ena met Adrial's gaze as she stepped up onto the dais, giving him a hint of a smile that cracked through his panic. Fire burned in her eyes, but he did not fear the flames.

Maybe the legends were wrong.

Maybe the Demon's Torch was a woman whose soul had been consumed by the inferno of her wrath.

If he was to marry a queen of vengeance, then Adrial would let the blaze of her soul consume him. And even as he crumbled to ash, he would savor every moment by her side.

She reached for his hand as she took her place beside him.

"Our words and deeds create the stories that follow us through our lives." Lord Gareth looked to Adrial as he spoke for the crowd. "For the men who lead the Guilds, the tales of our lives shall continue to be told long after we are gone. May your legacy be one of justice, compassion, and truth that Ilbreans will tell with pride for generations to come."

Lord Gareth lifted Ena and Adrial's joined hands, raising them for all to see. He pulled a shimmering white rope from his pocket, pausing for a moment before winding the end around Adrial's wrist.

The thin cord seemed to hold a greater weight than logic deemed possible, as though Dudia himself wanted to be sure Adrial understood the importance of his vows.

Lord Gareth wrapped the rope around their joined hands before tying the end around Ena's wrist. He gave Adrial a nod.

"I shall honor you with truth of word, wisdom of deed, and strength of spirit as I cherish our union." Adrial pushed the words past the knot in his throat, willing the heat in his eyes not to betray him with tears.

Ena looked down at their joined hands. The light caught on the silver woven through her hair. A charm hung near her temple. A little silver bird like the one marked on her ribs. The gift Adrial had commissioned for her and had nearly been too cowardly to give her.

She tightened her grip on his hand. "I shall honor you with truth of word, wisdom of deed, and strength of spirit as I cherish our union."

Lord Gareth tapped the knot in the rope near Ena's wrist.

Light shone from the fibers as the magic the sorcerers had placed in the binding burst to life. The warmth of the spell sank into Adrial's skin, on the edge of burning scars into his flesh as though the stars themselves wanted to warn him of the pain that lurked in the shadows cast by his joy.

Ena stepped closer to him, ignoring the sparks and smoke of the dissolving rope.

"From the dirt we all have come. And to the dirt we all must go." She whispered the words of the common marriage vows in his ear.

"With the blessing of Dudia, and under the protection of Saint Alwyn, you are joined as one," Lord Gareth said.

Ena ignored him, laying her free hand on Adrial's cheek. "May our journey be sweeter for standing by each other's side."

The world spun as she kissed him with a hundred people cheering their union.

He didn't know the rope had vanished until she pulled her hand from his grip to place her palm above his heart.

"Come, husband. Ilbrea is waiting for us."

45

ENA

Musicians had been brought in to play. Their lively music filled the gallery, tempting the paun to dance. Tables, heavy with more food than a village could eat, had been set up to one side, and fancy bottles of chamb and frie were consumed by the dozens.

I let them look at me, the beautiful rotta who married her way to the top of the Guilds. I could see it in their eyes, the difference between those who pitied me for marrying a man with a limp and those who feared me for breaking through their ranks so easily.

Adrial beamed through it all. His joy radiating off him as though he'd swallowed a star.

I wished more of the guests would spend their time watching him than me, but I was a beautiful bird, an exotic creature to the paun.

I couldn't allow their gazes to keep me from doing my work.

Four vials, that was all I had prepared.

The first, I poured into a bottle of frie the soldiers who'd been invited as guests seemed so desperate to down. They probably wouldn't die, but they would all be ill enough to need a healer's care.

The second, I poured into Lady Green's cup. As the leader of the Healers Guild, she stood a chance of stopping my brew in time. But from how quickly she drank, I doubted she would feel the effects of the poison until she'd gone far beyond even the sorcerers' ability to heal.

The third, I poured into Scribe Tammin's cup after she congratulated me and told me she was happy Adrial had found someone who brought him such joy. I felt no guilt as I watched her down her tainted frie. Someone in the Scribes Guild had to drink my brew, and her loyalty to the head scribe made her the simplest choice. Tammin would have a horrible night, but when her fever broke, she would recover without lasting injury.

The fourth vial, I'd made to protect my family. My husband. The child. They were all I had left.

I've given too much.

I could not allow the paun to take the last little bit of life I had clung to.

"You look divine." Allora finally approached me, her sorcerer in tow, both with glasses of chamb in their hands that would have cost enough coin to buy food to last a common man weeks.

"I have you to thank for that." I smiled for the Lady Map Maker. "Your seamstresses are very talented."

"That's not what I meant," Allora said. "I'm very happy for you."

"Thank you, Lady Karron." I gave her a bow, slipping my fingers into the pocket of my dress where I'd hidden the last of my vials. "May your union be just as happy as mine."

Allora tensed.

"I'm sure it will be." The paun sorcerer stepped forward.

I glanced to Allora.

"I beg your pardon," Allora said. "Sorcerer Clery, please allow me to introduce Ena Ayres."

The foreign name sent a stab of shock through my heart. I had become a paun's wife. His place in the Guilds would blot out everything I had been.

"It's an honor, sorcerer." I bowed again, dragging the tiny cork from the vial with my thumb and letting it fall to the floor. "I've met so few from your Guild before."

"What a pity," the paun said.

"Truly." I glanced to Allora before stepping closer to the sorcerer, pretending to believe the Lady Map Maker wouldn't be able to hear my words. "I hope I will soon be familiar with more from your Guild. My husband has a deep respect for the power held within the Sorcerers Tower." I tipped the vial over her glass. "It is the duty of the strong to protect the weak, even if they are too naïve to understand the danger they are being rescued from."

"I must admit, I had my doubts about the head scribe marrying a common-born woman. But those strong enough to climb are strong enough to survive." The paun raised her glass to me. "To finding new allies."

I bowed to her and gave a nod to Allora as I walked away before the sorcerer had finished swallowing a sip from her glass.

I took the shortest path to Adrial's side, cutting through the dancers. I let the vial slip from my grip as I crossed through their weaving pattern. The thumping of their feet covered the sound of the glass hitting the stone floor. The boots of a black-haired scribe smashed the vial, destroying the last evidence of my crime.

They made it so simple. Even the revelers that stared at me only saw my beauty. None of the paun looked past the curve of my breasts and colors strewn through my hair to notice the hunter prowling through their midst.

Adrial had been surrounded by a pack of fawning scribes.

Tammin stood near him, sweat already blossoming on her brow. Taddy stared up at Adrial, the sweet boy basking in being the only apprentice invited to the festivities.

"We've much work to do," one of the women scribes said. "The world doesn't stop just because of a bit of tumult."

"It's a matter of protection," one of the men said. "The violence cannot be allowed to spread beyond the city. The southern scribes don't have walls to hide behind."

"Our duty to the people of Ilbrea must be considered first in all things," Adrial said.

"All things?" I slipped between the scribes to take his arm. "Even now, husband?"

Red crept up Adrial's cheeks. "Well, tonight is about celebration."

"Good." I kissed his cheek then smiled for the paun. "You'll have to excuse me, but I must demand my husband's attention."

The flock of scribes parted as I led him toward the dancers.

"Ena"—Adrial's fingers trembled as he laid his hand on mine—"I'm not one for dancing, but I'm sure I can find someone who'd be thrilled to take my—"

I kissed him, wiping away whatever horrible thought made him consider having another man twirl his wife around on his wedding night.

"I said nothing about dancing, scribe." I let my cheek touch his as I whispered over the music. "I'm tired of being surrounded by paun. Take me away from here."

"Of course. Absolutely." He led me toward the door.

I took his hand, wrapping his arm around my waist and nestling close to his side.

The stares of the guests followed us as we left our wedding long before the evening was due to be done. Their murmurs carried over the music, but the chatter didn't matter. A husband and wife running away to enjoy their wedding night would be lost in the chaos to come, and no one would question where the inker and the scribe had gone.

Adrial didn't speak as we walked up the wide stairs to the corridor where the scribes lived. He tried to keep his gait even on the steps, as though afraid if I felt his limp I'd run from our marriage.

I kept silent. After all he'd given to protect me, he deserved one night without my needling his pride.

"Did you have a moment to eat?" he asked as we neared the door to his...to our rooms.

"Not a bite."

"I can have something sent up."

"Have a servant scurry around fixing food for the wife of the head scribe?"

"I—they're well paid." Adrial turned to me. "And we don't have a way to fix food for ourselves here."

I kissed him, letting my lips linger on his. "I'm not hungry."

"Well, just be"—the scarlet of his cheeks crept up to his temples—"let me know if you change your mind."

He opened the door to our sitting room. Vases of flowers covered the tables, and candles had been lit on every surface capable of holding a light.

"I didn't ask them to do that." The color vanished from his face.

"They were being kind." I locked the door behind us. "You're better liked than you think, scribe."

"Everyone is excited for a bit of cheer." He stood frozen between two clusters of candles, as though trying to decide if blowing them out or leaving them lit would cause him less anguish.

"For fertility." I pointed to the bundle of purple night bloom flowers hanging over the door to the bedroom.

"By the Guilds." His hands shook as he went to the door, reaching up as though to tear the flowers down.

"Leave them." I took his hand, leading him into the bedroom. "Let the women think their flowers worked."

More candles and flowers decorated the bedroom. The scent of rich, summery oil carried over the scent of the blooms.

"I have extra blankets." He pulled away from me, brushing off the purple petals strewn across the bed. "The couch is very comfortable. I'll be quite happy there."

"On our wedding night?"

He grabbed his blankets, clutching them to his chest for safety. "Really, it'll be a nice change. Sleeping on the couch might renew my perspective and vigor."

"Will you at least help with my buttons?" I turned my back to him, pulling my hair aside. The dress barely had twenty buttons, all low enough I could've reached them if I'd been truly determined.

"Of course. Silly, I didn't think of it." He set his blankets down on the couch.

He was so careful not to touch my skin as he unfastened the buttons, racing through the task as though desperate to flee.

"We've shared a bed before. Is it so different now that I'm your wife?"

"No, of course not. Well, yes sort of. I just don't want to assume…" His words faded away as I turned toward him, letting my dress fall to the floor.

"You've also seen me naked before. Has that changed as well?"

"Nothing has changed. Our friendship is the most precious thing in the world to me." He kept his gaze fixed on my eyes. "But you are legally my wife."

"And you don't want me?" I stepped closer to him.

"I don't want any affection or intimacy born of obligation or pity. The last thing I would ever want is for you to feel as if you owed me anything. I don't think I could bear it."

"And if it's not an obligation." I placed my hands on his chest. "Would you reject me then?"

"I'm not rejecting anything."

"You are. I am your wife. You are my husband. This is the only wedding night we will ever have, scribe. Don't turn me away." I kissed him, slowly, carefully, giving him a moment to pull away before I began unfastening the neck of his robes. "I promise you this is what I want."

He reached up, his fingers grazing my sides, tracing the curve of my hips.

I backed away just enough to pull his robes over his head.

He finally looked at me, taking in the body I had just sworn to be his. He touched the scar on my ribs I'd gained saving his life. "I will never deserve you."

I pulled on the string that held up his underclothes, letting them fall away before kissing him again, pressing myself to him so not even the gods could come between us.

He twined his fingers through my hair as he tasted my lips, and the urgency of his wanting grew.

I drew him toward the bed, lying down on the petals some poor fool had scattered across the blankets to honor the head scribe's wedding.

He lay on top of me, his eyes lit with something I chivving well knew to be love. Deep, profound, soul-shaping love I could never hope to deserve.

He kissed my neck, my breasts, my stomach where the child grew, exploring every bit of me as though my body were his first taste of freedom.

I took his face in my hands, drawing him up so my lips could meet his. "Will it hurt you?" I touched the horrible wound a monster had left on his hip so long ago.

"I don't care if it does." The bliss in his eyes dulled as he shied away from me.

"I don't ever want to add to your pain." I wrapped my legs around him, not allowing him to leave me. "There are many ways of enjoying each other."

"All I know is how badly I want you." He pressed his forehead to mine, his lips hovering deliciously close to my own. "I don't care what the consequences are."

"Then we'll have to try it and see." I pulled him closer, locking our bodies together. "We have thousands of nights to look forward to. We've promised a lifetime to each other. You're mine now, scribe."

I kissed him until I forgot what pain was, and the fire in my soul changed from rage to wanting.

For a few blissful moments, the world wasn't a dark and horrible place.

Before I curled up to sleep in his arms, two among the Guilds had fallen from the poison made by my hand.

But no one dared to interrupt the newly married scribe.

I teased him awake with joy, and news of the murders still hadn't come.

The safety of my marriage bed protected me as anger and accusations spread among the Guilds, rooting out old feuds and rumors, separating those who had clung to their alliances for protection.

A crack in the dome, that was all I had managed. But the weight of the Guilds was meant to crumble, and cracks can destroy kingdoms if the damage spreads.

I stood at the center of the paun now, sparking hatred in their hearts instead of lobbing common blood at their gates. I would burn them from the inside out.

They would never see my hand in their ruin.

The Guilds of Ilbrea series continues with Viper and Steel.

Ena's story began long before she journeyed to Ilara. Turn the page for a glimpse into the Inker's past.

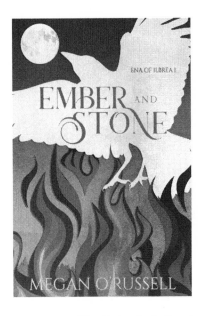

Uncover the mysterious past of Ena Bairn, including the true identity of the Demon's Torch, in the *Ena of Ilbrea* series. Turn the page for a sneak peek of book one, *Ember and Stone*.

1

The crack of the whip sent the birds scattering into the sky. They cawed their displeasure at the violence of the men below as they flew over the village and to the mountains beyond.

The whip cracked again.

Aaron did well. He didn't start to moan until the fourth lash. By the seventh, he screamed in earnest.

No one had given him a belt to bite down on. There hadn't been time when the soldiers hauled him from his house and tied him to the post in the square.

I clutched the little wooden box of salve hidden in my pocket, letting the corners bite deep into my palm.

The soldier passed forty lashes, not caring that Aaron's back had already turned to pulp.

I squeezed my way to the back of the crowd, unwilling to watch Aaron's blood stain the packed dirt.

Behind the rest of the villagers, children cowered in their mother's skirts, hiding from the horrors the Guilds' soldiers brought with them.

I didn't know how many strokes Aaron had been sentenced

to. I didn't want to know. I made myself stop counting how many times the whip sliced his back.

Bida, Aaron's wife, wept on the edge of the crowd. When his screams stopped, hers grew louder.

The women around Bida held her back, keeping her out of reach of the soldiers.

My stomach stung with the urge to offer comfort as she watched her husband being beaten by the men in black uniforms. But, with the salve tucked in my pocket, hiding in the back was safest.

I couldn't give Bida the box unless Aaron survived. Spring hadn't fully arrived, and the plants Lily needed to make more salves still hadn't bloomed. The tiny portion of the stuff hidden in my pocket was worth more than someone's life, especially if that person wasn't going to survive even with Lily's help.

Lily's orders had been clear—wait and see if Aaron made it through. Give Bida the salve if he did. If he didn't, come back home and hide the wooden box under the floorboards for the next poor soul who might need it.

Aaron fell to the ground. Blood leaked from a gash under his arm.

The soldier raised his whip again.

I sank farther into the shadows, trying to comfort myself with the beautiful lie that I could never be tied to the post in the village square, though I knew the salve clutched in my hand would see me whipped at the post as quickly as whatever offense the soldiers had decided Aaron had committed.

When my fingers had gone numb from gripping the box, the soldier stopped brandishing his whip and turned to face the crowd.

"We did not come here to torment you," the soldier said. "We came here to protect Ilbrea. We came here to protect the Guilds. We are here to provide peace to all the people of this great country.

This man committed a crime, and he has been punished. Do not think me cruel for upholding the law." He wrapped the bloody whip around his hand and led the other nine soldiers out of the square.

Ten soldiers. It had only taken ten of them to walk into our village and drag Aaron from his home. Ten men to tie him to the post and leave us all helpless as they beat a man who'd lived among us all his life.

The soldiers disappeared, and the crowd shifted in toward Aaron. I couldn't hear him crying or moaning over the angry mutters of the crowd.

His wife knelt by his side, wailing.

I wound my way forward, ignoring the stench of fear that surrounded the villagers.

Aaron lay on the ground, his hands still tied around the post. His back had been flayed open by the whip. His flesh looked more like something for a butcher to deal with than an illegal healer like me.

I knelt by his side, pressing my fingers to his neck to feel for a pulse.

Nothing.

I wiped my fingers on the cleanest part of Aaron's shirt I could find and weaved my way back out of the crowd, still clutching the box of salve in my hand.

Carrion birds gathered on the rooftops near the square, scenting the fresh blood in the air. They didn't know Aaron wouldn't be food for them. The villagers of Harane had yet to fall so low as to leave our own out as a feast for the birds.

There was no joy in the spring sun as I walked toward Lily's house on the eastern edge of the village.

I passed by the tavern, which had already filled with men who didn't mind we hadn't reached midday. I didn't blame them for hiding in there. If they could find somewhere away from the torment of the soldiers, better on them for seizing it. I only hoped there weren't any soldiers laughing inside the tavern's walls.

I followed the familiar path home. Along our one, wide dirt road, past the few shops Harane had to offer, to the edge of the village where only fields and pastures stood between us and the forest that reached up the eastern mountains' slopes.

It didn't take long to reach the worn wooden house with the one giant tree towering out front. It didn't take long to reach anywhere in the tiny village of Harane.

Part of me hated knowing every person who lived nearby. Part of me wished the village were smaller. Then maybe we'd fall off the Guilds' maps entirely.

As it was, the Guilds only came when they wanted to collect our taxes, to steal our men to fight their wars, or to find some other sick pleasure in inflicting agony on people who wanted nothing more than to survive. Or if their business brought them far enough south on the mountain road they had to pass through our home on their way to torment someone else.

I allowed myself a moment to breathe before facing Lily. I blinked away the images of Aaron covered in blood and shoved them into a dark corner with the rest of the wretched things it was better not to ponder.

Lily barely glanced up as I swung open the gate and stepped into the back garden. Dirt covered her hands and skirt. Her shoulders were hunched from the hours spent planting our summer garden. She never allowed me to help with the task. Everything had to be carefully planned, keeping the vegetables toward the outermost edges. Hiding the plants she could be hanged for in the center, where soldiers were less likely to spot the things she grew to protect the people of our village. The people the soldiers were so eager to hurt.

"Did he make it?" Lily stretched her shoulders back and brushed the dirt off her weathered hands.

I held the wooden box out as my response. Blood stained the

corners. It wasn't Aaron's blood. It was mine. Cuts marked my hand where I'd squeezed the box too tightly.

Lily glared at my palm. "You'd better go in and wrap your hand. If you let it get infected, I'll have to treat you with the salve, and you know we're running out."

I tucked the box back into my pocket and went inside, not bothering to argue that I could heal from a tiny cut. I didn't want to look into Lily's wrinkled face and see the glimmer of pity in her eyes.

The inside of the house smelled of herbs and dried flowers. Their familiar scent did nothing to drive the stench of blood and fear from my nose.

A pot hung over the stove, waiting with whatever Lily had made for breakfast.

My stomach churned at the thought of eating. I needed to get out. Out of the village, away from the soldiers.

I pulled up the loose floorboard by the stove and tucked the salve in between the other boxes, tins, and vials. I grabbed my bag off the long, wooden table and shoved a piece of bread and a waterskin into it for later. I didn't bother grabbing a coat or shawl. I didn't care about getting cold.

I have to get out.

I was back through the door and in the garden a minute later. Lily didn't even look up from her work. "If you're running into the forest, you had better come back with something good."

"I will," I said. "I'll bring you back all sorts of wonderful things. Just make sure you save some dinner for me."

I didn't need to ask her to save me food. In all the years I'd lived with her, Lily had never let me go hungry. But she was afraid I would run away into the forest and never return. Or maybe it was me that feared I might disappear into the trees and never come back. Either way, I felt myself relax as I stepped out of the garden and turned my feet toward the forest.

2

The mountains rose up beyond the edge of the trees, fierce towers I could never hope to climb. No one else from the village would ever even dream of trying such a thing.

The soldiers wouldn't enter the woods. The villagers rarely dared to go near them. The forest was where darkness and solitude lay. A quiet place where the violence of the village couldn't follow me.

I skirted farmers' fields and picked my way through the pastures. No one bothered me as I climbed over the fences they built to keep in their scarce amounts of sheep and cows.

No one kept much livestock. They couldn't afford it in the first place. And besides, if the soldiers saw that one farmer had too many animals, they would take the beasts as taxes. Safer to be poor. Better for your belly to go empty than for the soldiers to think you had something to give.

I moved faster as I got past the last of the farmhouses and beyond the reach of the stench of animal dung.

When I was a very little girl, my brother had told me that the woods were ruled by ghosts. That none of the villagers dared to cut down the trees or venture into their shelter for fear of being taken by the dead and given a worse fate than even the Guilds could provide.

I'd never been afraid of ghosts, and I'd wandered through the woods often enough to be certain that no spirits roamed the eastern mountains.

When I first started going into the forest, I convinced myself I was braver than everyone else in Harane. I was an adventurer, and they were cowards.

Maybe I just knew better. Maybe I knew that no matter what ghosts did, they could never match the horrors men inflict on each other. What I'd seen them do to each other.

By the time I was a hundred feet into the trees, I could no longer see the village behind me. I couldn't smell anything but the fresh scent of damp earth as the little plants fought for survival in the fertile spring ground. I knew my way through the woods well enough I didn't need to bother worrying about which direction to go. It was more a question of which direction I wanted to chase the gentle wind.

I could go and find fungi for Lily to make into something useful, or I could climb. If I went quickly, I would have time to climb and still be able to find something worth Lily getting herself hanged for.

Smiling to myself, I headed due east toward the steepest part of the mountains near our village. Dirt soon covered the hem of my skirt, and mud squelched beneath my shoes, creeping in through the cracked leather of the soles. I didn't mind so much. What the cold could do to me was nothing more than a refreshing chance to prove I was still alive. Life existed outside the village, and there was beauty beyond our battered walls.

Bits of green peeked through the brown of the trees as new buds forced their way out of the branches.

I stopped, staring up at the sky, marveling at the beauty hidden within our woods.

Birds chirped overhead. Not the angry cawing of birds of

death, but the beautiful songs of lovebirds who had nothing more to worry about than tipping their wings up toward the sky.

A gray and blue bird burst from a tree, carrying his song deeper into the forest.

A stream gurgled to one side of me. The snap of breaking branches came from the other. I didn't change my pace as the crackling came closer.

I headed south to a steeper slope where I had to use my hands to pull myself up the rocks.

I moved faster, outpacing the one who lumbered through the trees behind me. A rock face cut through the forest, blocking my path. I dug my fingers into the cracks in the stone, pulling myself up. Careful to keep my legs from being tangled in my skirt, I found purchase on the rock with the soft toes of my boots. In a few quick movements, I pushed myself up over the top of the ledge. I leapt to my feet and ran to the nearest tree, climbing up to the highest thick branch.

I sat silently on my perch, waiting to see what sounds would come from below.

A rustle came from the base of the rock, followed by a long string of inventive curses.

I bit my lips together, not allowing myself to call out.

The cursing came again.

"Of all the slitching, vile—" the voice from below growled.

I leaned back against the tree, closing my eyes, reveling in my last few moments of solitude. Those hints of freedom were what I loved most about being able to climb. Going up a tree, out of reach of the things that would catch me.

"Ena," the voice called. "Ena."

I didn't answer.

"Ena, are you going to leave me down here?"

My lips curved into a smile as I bit back my laughter. "I didn't ask you to follow me. You can just go back the way you came."

"I don't want to go back," he said. "Let me come up. At least show me how you did it."

"If you want to chase me, you'd better learn to climb."

I let him struggle for a few more minutes until he threatened to find a pick and crack through the rock wall. I glanced down to find him three feet off the ground, his face bright red as he tried to climb.

"Jump down," I said, not wanting him to fall and break something. I could have hauled him back to the village, but I didn't fancy the effort.

"Help me get up," he said.

"Go south a bit. You'll find an easier path."

I listened to the sounds of him stomping off through the trees, enjoying the bark against my skin as I waited for him to find the way up.

It only took him a few minutes to loop back around to stand under my perch.

Looking at Cal stole my will to flee. His blond hair glistened in the sun. He shaded his bright blue eyes as he gazed up at me.

"Are you happy now?" he said. "I'm covered in dirt."

"If you wanted to be clean, you shouldn't have come into the woods. I never ask you to follow me."

"It would have been wrong of me not to. You shouldn't be coming out here by yourself."

I didn't let it bother me that he thought it was too dangerous for me to be alone in the woods. It was nice to have someone worry about me. Even if he was worried about ghosts that didn't exist.

"What do you think you'd be able to do to help me anyway?" I said.

He stared up at me, hurt twisting his perfect brow.

Cal looked like a god, or something made at the will of the Guilds themselves. His chiseled jaw held an allure to it, the rough stubble on his cheeks luring my fingers to touch its texture.

I twisted around on my seat and dropped down to the ground, reveling in his gasp as I fell.

"You really need to get more used to the woods," I said. "It's a good place to hide."

"What would I have to hide from?" Cal's eyes twinkled, offering a hint of teasing that drew me toward him.

I touched the stubble on his chin, tracing the line of his jaw.

"There are plenty of things to hide from, fool." I turned to tramp farther into the woods.

"Ena," he called after me, "you shouldn't be going so far from home."

"Then don't follow me. Go back." I knew he would follow.

I had known when I passed by his window in the tavern on my way through the village. He always wanted to be near me. That was the beauty of Cal.

I veered closer to the stream.

Cal kept up, though he despised getting his boots muddy.

I always chose the more difficult path to make sure he knew I could outpace him. It was part of our game on those trips into the forest.

I leapt across the stream to a patch of fresh moss just beginning to take advantage of spring.

"Ena." Cal jumped the water and sank down onto the moss I had sought.

I shoved him off of the green and into the dirt.

He growled.

I didn't bother trying to hide my smile. I pulled out tufts of the green moss, tucking them into my bag for Lily.

"If you don't want me to follow you," Cal said, "you can tell me not to whenever you like."

"The forest doesn't belong to me, Cal. You can go where you choose."

He grabbed both my hands and tugged me toward him. I tipped onto him and he shifted, letting me fall onto my back. I caught a glimpse of the sun peering down through the new buds of emerald leaves, and then he was kissing me.

His taste of honey and something a bit deeper filled me. And I forgot about whips and Lily and men bleeding and soldiers coming to kill us.

There was nothing but Cal and me. And the day became beautiful.

Order your copy of Ember and Stone *to continue the story.*

THE GUILDS OF ILBREA SERIES RETURNS
WITH VIPER AND STEEL

Coming Summer 2022

ESCAPE INTO ADVENTURE

Thank you for reading *Myth and Storm*. If you enjoyed the book, please consider leaving a review to help other readers find this story.

Dive deeper into the world of the Guilds on MeganORussell. com/ilbrea, where you'll find exclusive Ilbrean content, a peek behind the scenes, and updates on new books.

As always, thanks for reading,

Megan O'Russell

Never miss a moment of the magic and romance.

Join the Megan O'Russell readers community to stay up to date on all the action by visiting https://www.meganorussell.com/ book-signup.

ABOUT THE AUTHOR

 Megan O'Russell is the author of several Young Adult series that invite readers to escape into worlds of adventure. From *Girl of Glass*, which blends dystopian darkness with the heart-pounding danger of vampires, to *Ena of Ilbrea*, which draws readers into an epic world of magic and assassins.

With the *Girl of Glass* series, *The Tethering* series, *The Chronicles of Maggie Trent*, *The Tale of Bryant Adams*, the *Ena of Ilbrea* series, and several more projects planned, there are always exciting new books on the horizon. To be the first to hear about new releases, free short stories, and giveaways, sign up for Megan's newsletter by visiting the following:

https://www.meganorussell.com/book-signup.

Originally from Upstate New York, Megan is a professional musical theatre performer whose work has taken her across North America. Her chronic wanderlust has led her from Alaska to Thailand and many places in between. Wanting to travel has fostered Megan's love of books that allow her to visit countless new worlds from her favorite reading nook. Megan is also a lyricist and playwright. Information on her theatrical works can be found at RussellCompositions.com.

She would be thrilled to chat with you on Facebook or

Twitter @MeganORussell, elated if you'd visit her website MeganORussell.com, and over the moon if you'd like the pictures of her adventures on Instagram @ORussellMegan.

ALSO BY MEGAN O'RUSSELL

The Girl of Glass Series
Girl of Glass
Boy of Blood
Night of Never
Son of Sun

The Tale of Bryant Adams
How I Magically Messed Up My Life in Four Freakin' Days
Seven Things Not to Do When Everyone's Trying to Kill You
Three Simple Steps to Wizarding Domination
Five Spellbinding Laws of International Larceny

The Tethering Series
The Tethering
The Siren's Realm
The Dragon Unbound
The Blood Heir

The Chronicles of Maggie Trent
The Girl Without Magic
The Girl Locked With Gold
The Girl Cloaked in Shadow

Ena of Ilbrea
Wrath and Wing
Ember and Stone

Mountain and Ash

Ice and Sky

Feather and Flame

<u>Guilds of Ilbrea</u>

Inker and Crown

Myth and Storm

Viper and Steel

<u>Heart of Smoke</u>

Heart of Smoke

Soul of Glass

Eye of Stone

Ash of Ages

Made in the USA
Middletown, DE
14 April 2022

64216533R00250